PIGTOWN

Also by William J. Caunitz

One Police Plaza
Suspects
Black Sand
Exceptional Clearance
Cleopatra Gold

WILLIAM J. CAUNITZ

PIGTOWN

CROWN PUBLISHERS INC., NEW YORK

Published by Crown Publishers Inc., 201 East 50th Street, New York, New York
10022. Member of the Crown Publishing Group.

Random House, Inc., New York, Toronto, London, Sydney, Auckland

CROWN is a trademark of Crown Publishers, Inc.

Manufactured in the U.S.A.

Design by Leonard Henderson

Library of Congress Cataloging-in-Publication Data
Caunitz, William J.
    Pigtown / William J. Caunitz.
        p.   cm.
    I. Title.
PS3553.A945P5   1995   94-44509
                                                                    CIP

ISBN 0-517-57497-7

10   9   8   7   6   5   4   3   2   1

First Edition

For my loving wife, Pat,
who showed me the road to happiness.

ACKNOWLEDGMENTS

I wish to thank the following people for their generous help in the writing of *Pigtown*:

Lieutenant Dan Flynn and Police Officer Dennis Kane, 71 Precinct, NYPD, for sharing with me their special knowledge of Pigtown; Ms. Mary Ann Ajemian, president of the Ambriola Corporation, for taking the time out of her busy schedule to introduce me to the cheese industry; Mr. William Henning, CEO, Swiss Rose International, for his informative talks on the dairy business; Mr. Marvin Haas, CEO, Chock Full o' Nuts, for teaching me about corporate finance, particularly the Green Bay Exchange; Dr. Keith Manning of Manhattan's East Side Animal Hospital for sharing his keen insight on rottweilers; Mr. Ray Maluchi for teaching me how to use the Cellmate to intercept cellular telephone calls; Richard Dienst of the law firm Dienst and Serrins, a friend and a terrific lawyer, for taking the time to explain how the NYPD's "Trial Room" really works; Mr. Chet Dalzitzki, director, NYPD's Photographic Unit, for teaching me how to use the department's photographic tracking system; Detective Joe Vincent, Jr., NYPD's Electronic Intelligence Section, for his insightful instructions on how to eavesdrop on a park bench; my buddy in Charlottesville for again sharing with me his bag of dirty tricks.

My grateful thanks to Sharon Nettles for using her computer wizardry on the manuscript. And to my good friends Drs. Steven Lamm and Barry Zide for sharing their medical knowledge with me.

My friend and editor, James O'Shea Wade, for again turning his magic pencil loose on the manuscript.

My agents, Knox Burger and Kitty Sprague, for going the extra mile to make the manuscript right and for always being there for me.

PIGTOWN

1

When Detective Joe Borrelli yanked open the door, he found Beansy Rutolo's body propped on the base of its spine inside an ancient white Westinghouse refrigerator. His legs were squeezed up against his chest, and his hands were stuffed under his ass. His left eye was closed; the right one was half open, exposing a sliver of white. Beansy's mouth was wide open, as though he had shouted a plea for life a second before he died. A jagged bullethole gaped above his left eyebrow. What was left of the back of his skull was glued into a mound of clotted blood against the wall of the box. Most of the rear part of Beansy's skull, along with a large chunk of his brain, was splattered across the living room.

"Beansy really pissed somebody off," Detective Calvin Jones said, bending for a closer look at the body.

Borrelli looked around. A mound of dirty dishes cluttered the sink. The contents of the refrigerator had been thrown on the floor: a head of iceberg lettuce, soda bottles, a broken baking dish full of lasagna. Leftover peas had spilled from their Tupperware container; an unopened carton of milk had ruptured.

A doorless archway connected the kitchen with the living room. "He was whacked in the living room and carried in here," Borrelli told his partner, padding his way around the mess on

1

the floor. Standing under the archway, looking back into the living room, Borrelli added, "He must have been standing a little in front of that pool of blood, near the sofa, when they shot him. The force of the bullet toppled him backward, and when he went down he dragged the end table and the lamp with him." Borrelli looked at his partner. "Beansy didn't live here, did he?"

"Nah. This is Andrea Russo's place," Jones said, brushing his palms across his gleaming black shaved head. The refrigerator light made his skin look almost purple.

Stepping back from the refrigerator, Jones scratched his heavy jaw and said to his partner, "And then the perps, hadda be at least two of them, dragged 'im in here and stuffed him into the box."

"Yeah," Borrelli agreed, shifting his brown eyes toward the living room. He carefully observed the trail of blood that stained the blue shag carpet in the living room a deep brown and continued in the kitchen, making a bizarre accent on the sunflower-patterned linoleum. "This is one messy hit. I don't think they planned on whacking him here."

"Beansy and the doers come here for a meet or something, they get into an argument over something, they do Beansy, and then panic because they don't know what to do with the body, so they put the sucker into the icebox," Jones said, bending to examine the heel print in the blood.

Borrelli nodded agreement and brushed his fingers through his wavy black hair. At thirty-six he had the haggard look of a man juggling too many girlfriends.

"The crime scene guys just pulled up," the uniformed sergeant called in from the living room door.

"Let's wait outside until the lab boys get done," Borrelli said, leading Jones through the front door.

The two detectives stood glumly on the worn gray boards of a broad front porch that once bore the weight of rockers and gliders and was now devoid of any furniture, in a neighborhood where a footstool wouldn't last the night. They watched as the crime scene detectives slid their battered black valises out of a dark green station wagon.

The patrol sergeant's radio motor patrol car was parked at the curb in front of the wagon. Leaves from a sickly looking maple tree in front of the crime scene on Brooklyn's Rutland Road were just starting to turn as September eased closer toward the fall.

Borrelli stepped off the porch and lit a cigarette. The massive concrete towers of Kings County Hospital and Brooklyn State Hospital loomed in the bright morning sunlight on Clarkson Avenue, a few blocks away. He turned and looked at the emergency service police officers who were stooping over and combing the weedy backyard, their eyes fixed on the ground as they searched for the murder weapon. "A made guy gets popped and it's treated like an accident case today. A few years ago, this place would have been crawling with headquarters brass and television cameras." Borrelli seemed almost wistful.

"There's so many of them being offed these days that one nickel-and-dime pinky-ring is no big deal," Jones said, looking at the three remaining one-story frame houses on the block, with their pitched roofs and porches with peeling paint, overgrown with yellow weeds. Large parcels of weed-choked land separated each house; old tires and the skeletons of stolen cars decorated each vacant lot. To the west, the Jackie Robinson Housing Projects stood on the stretch of land once ruled by Ebbets Field and the Brooklyn Dodgers. Modern apartment buildings a block away towered over the small houses. Looking east at the two-story brick Trump homes that were built in 1935 to replace many of the farmhouses, Jones found himself trying to imagine what the tiny valley of Pigtown had been like as farmland with wooden shacks, chicken coops, and pigsties. "It's hard to believe that there were pig farms in this section of Brooklyn up until the sixties."

"Pigtown used to be a big wiseguy hangout, now it's nothing but low rent," Borrelli said. He gazed off at the distant limestone Seven One Precinct police station that looked like some medieval manor house, perched six blocks away atop the steep rise of Empire Boulevard. "The ol' Seven One has seen a lotta changes over the years."

"Every precinct in this town has seen a lotta changes."

"Yeah, but not like the Seven One. C'mon, let's do the canvass and see if any of these drones saw anything."

"What about the boss?"

Borrelli looked at his watch. "It's ten to twelve. He finishes his piano lesson at noon. I'll call 'im then."

Lieutenant Matthew Stuart, the whip of the Seven One Detective Squad, sat at a Steinway parlor grand piano, his long fingers gliding effortlessly over the keyboard as he played Beethoven's Sonata in B-flat Major.

Stuart had loved music since he was a kid and always wanted to play the piano, but there had never been time to take lessons. Then, five years ago, his wife had walked and he'd found himself divorced, and suddenly there'd been a lot of time, more than he'd known what to do with. He had been determined that he was not going to spend his time sitting on the pity pot or drowning his loneliness in a vodka bottle the way a lot of divorced cops did; so a few years ago, for his fortieth birthday, he'd given himself a present of piano lessons and begun scheduling himself for a day duty every Tuesday and taking an eleven o'clock meal hour so he could go to his teacher's comfortable apartment on the ground floor of a turn-of-the-century brownstone on Brooklyn's Fenimore Street to take his lesson.

"That was good, Matt," said Denise Ritter, a handsome woman on the threshold of fifty, with lustrous black hair. She was sitting on a chair next to her pupil, watching his still awkward fingering with her limpid gray eyes that seemed to miss nothing. "You have to pay more attention to your fingering." She pointed to the sheet music. "In the second measure, what fingers of the right hand should play the G and B?"

"The second and fourth."

"That's right. But you did not use your second and fourth, and you ran out of fingers. Please play it again."

As he began to play, a serene expression settled over his face. He was a well-built man just under six feet, with high cheek-bones and a long, angular face that gave his handsome features a look of openness and vulnerability. He had deep green eyes and wavy brown hair that was thinning in front and was starting to streak gray and was layered over the tops of his ears in a fashion that suggested just a touch of vanity as well as a minor denial of middle age.

Matthew Cosgrove Stuart had been sworn into the NYPD on January 1, 1974. Six months later, when his class of six hundred rookies graduated from the Police Academy, he had been the only one assigned to the coveted detective division. All of his classmates had assumed that Matt Stuart had a "heavy wire," someone very influential, on the "Fourteenth Floor," as the police commissioner's office in One Police Plaza was referred to in the Job. But they were all wrong; the truth was that the Job owed Matt, and the department always paid its debts.

Stuart spent the next nine years working in the Tenth Detective Squad in Manhattan's Chelsea District. When he was promoted to sergeant in 1984, he was assigned as the second whip in the Seventeenth Homicide District in Queens. Three days before he was to be promoted to lieutenant, in December of 1987, he received a telephone message directing him to report "forthwith" to the chief of detectives office. C of D Al Steinman, a gruff man who did not believe in mincing words, was sitting behind mounds of case files when Stuart walked into his thirteenth-floor office. Steinman looked up at him, yanked the ragged cigar out of his mouth, and said, "You're getting made in three days, what squad do you want?"

"The Seven One," he said without a second's hesitation.

"That's what I thought you'd say," Steinman said, plunging the cigar back between his thick lips with a satisfied grunt.

Walking out of the chief's office, Stuart thought, The bastards will always owe me.

• • •

Denise Ritter watched her pupil's fingers moving back and forth across the keyboard. Unconsciously her eyes slid down to the Glock nine-millimeter automatic pistol hugging his right hip, and the handcuffs, and the cloth pouch containing an extra magazine. She wondered, not for the first time, how this gentle man with a love of music could be in such a deadly occupation. She had a deep curiosity about what he was like in his police world, that world he never talked about.

Stuart slowly raised his long fingers from the keyboard as he finished playing.

"For next time, work on your balance and your pedaling," the teacher instructed her student crisply.

Stuart smiled at her and said softly, "I'll promise to—" His beeper went off. He looked down at the window and asked, "May I use your phone?"

"Of course."

He walked over to the oval Victorian table and picked up the portable handset, punching in the number of the Seven One Squad. Sitting on the sofa that faced matching chairs upholstered in faded brocade, he glanced around the room at the music memorabilia, posters of long-ago concerts and operas, busts of Beethoven and Mozart, a large etching of the grand staff. He smiled at his teacher; she smiled back.

"Seven One Squad," Detective Jerry Jordon answered.

"What's up?"

"Beansy Rutolo got himself popped in Pigtown."

"Location?"

"Four-oh-one Rutland Road. Borrelli and Jones are over there now doing the canvass."

"Witnesses?"

"None so far."

He smiled again at his teacher, while keeping his tone businesslike and level. "Notifications?"

"The c of d, Operations, and the borough, along with the ME and the DA, have all been notified, and entries made in the telephone message book."

"Is the ME going to respond?"

"He said to bag 'im. He'll do him at the morgue."

"I'm on my way." Standing, Stuart punched the off button and returned the telephone to its cradle. He slid his blue blazer off the back of the chair and, swinging it around his shoulders, said to his teacher, "I'll see you next week."

The detectives were still standing on the porch, comparing their canvass notes, when Stuart drove up in the unmarked department car. "No murder weapon, so far," Borrelli said to the whip as he came up the steps.

"How did you find out about it?" Stuart asked, looking at the cops searching the deep yard for the murder weapon.

"An anonymous 911 call," Borrelli said. "I ordered a copy of the tape."

"Who was the first sector on the scene?" Stuart asked.

Borrelli replied, "Only the sergeant and his driver responded to the call."

Jones slipped a folded sheet of paper out of his suit jacket. "I had Records fax Beansy's rap sheet to the Squad."

Stuart took the dead man's criminal record. After reading it, he looked at his detectives and said, "Beansy was sixty-eight years old. He skated until he took his first fall in sixty-two for grand larceny auto. During a long, full life of crime, he took five collars and only did one stretch inside, seven and a half to fifteen for a manslaughter two that was knocked down from murder one."

"Beansy was a cautious man," Borrelli said, grinning.

"He certainly wasn't careful enough today," Stuart said, looking around the one-story bungalow. "Who owns this place?"

"Andrea Russo," Jones said.

"Daughter of Tony 'Two Chins.' Right?" Stuart asked.

"Yeah," Borrelli said. "After he got popped back in eighty-two, Andrea moved back in with her mother. The old lady died last year. Andrea lives here by herself now."

"Is she still on the shit?" Stuart asked.

"The word is she worked herself up to an eight-hundred-a-day habit, and then a year ago she checks herself into a rehab and cleans up her act. She's been on the straight and narrow ever since," Jones said.

"I hear she's even taking night courses in LaGuardia Community College," Borrelli added.

"That's real nice, but she's still tending bar at Holiday's," Stuart said with a nasty edge to his voice, and turned the knob of the front door, which was covered in peeling green oil-based paint.

He found himself in a tiny living room crowded with large black furniture of elaborately carved wood with gilt decorative detailing. At the far end sat a large golden lamp with a pleated off-white shade fringed in golden tassels. Time stopped in 1934 around here, he thought, nodding to the sergeant.

A detective from the crime scene unit was snapping pictures of what was left of Beansy; another was using a camera on a tripod to photograph a heel print impression in the blood on the floor. A ruler and identification labels lay beside several other impressions. White fingerprint powder smudged the wood and glass surfaces. Another detective was vacuuming the sofa and surrounding area. Two bored ambulance attendants were sitting on a gurney in the living room, waiting impatiently for the detectives to finish.

Stuart went over to the sergeant and signed the crime scene log with his name, rank, command, and time entering the crime scene. After doing that, he glanced over at the morgue attendant and asked, "Was he pronounced?"

"Yeah, he's officially dead," said one of the attendants, a fat, wheezing, pasty-faced man. Looking at the detectives inside the kitchen, he added, "Any chance of hurryin' 'em up? It's almost time to eat."

Stuart glanced with annoyance at the fat man and walked into the kitchen.

"I'll be done in a second, Lou," the photographer said, using the diminutive of "lieutenant" that was routine on the Job, as he snapped photographs of the broken eggs, scattered vegetables, spilled milk, and soda bottles. After the detective finished taking the official pictures, Stuart walked over to the refrigerator and bent in close to examine the body. He retched at the stench. Beansy's sphincter muscle had given way and his bowels had voided. Stuart pulled out his handkerchief and covered his mouth and nose with it. A ribbon of dried blood came out of the left ear. Sticking his head inside the box, he saw no powder burns around the puffy entrance wound on the forehead. He felt Beansy's neck: it was stiff from the downward constrictions of rigor mortis, while the shoulders and lower torso were limp. He unbuttoned the dead man's sportshirt and tugged it down over the shoulders. Lividity's plum-red skin discoloration had not yet started, but gravity would soon cause the blood to sink to the lowest parts of the body.

Jones and Borrelli stood behind the whip, watching.

"Whaddaya make it?" Borrelli asked.

" 'bout three hours," Stuart said.

"That would make the time of death around nine-thirty," Jones said.

"Give or take some, yeah," Stuart agreed, waving his hand at the ambulance attendants, beckoning them to remove the body.

They wheeled the gurney into the kitchen. The fat one worked his arms around the dead man's chest while his partner locked his arms around the legs. "Someone unzipper the bag," the attendant called out.

Jones went over to the gurney and pulled down the black body bag's zipper.

"Now," said the short, older attendant.

They struggled to get the body out. Beansy's head was yanked out of the bloody crust; a gory mass tumbled out of the shattered gaping rear of the skull and plopped on the bottom of the box, splattering the fat attendant's blue work uniform. They carried Beansy over to the gurney and tossed him on top of the body bag.

"He has to be searched," Stuart said, looking at the sergeant.

The uniformed cop came over and began carefully turning the dead man's trouser pockets inside out. A large wad of money and two sets of keys were in the right pocket. A handkerchief and a broken comb were in the back pocket. He took a watch with a heavy gold bracelet off the left wrist of the corpse and tried to get off the diamond pinky ring but couldn't. He tried twisting it off, and that didn't work. Stuart went over to the sink and turned on the faucet. He wet a bar of soap and, going over to the body, picked up Beansy's hand and lathered the pinky. He tugged off the ring and handed it to the cop.

The cop dumped the watch and the ring into a property envelope and, wiping his hands on the dead man's trousers, looked at the sergeant and said, "That's it, boss."

Stuart took both sets of keys and walked into the living room. He tried the first set on the front door; they didn't work. He tried the other set; they did. Back in the kitchen, he gave the policeman back the other set of keys, saying, "Let's count the money."

The policeman counted out the wad, stacking it on top of Beansy's blood-spattered chest. "Twenty-one hundred dollars," he said, stuffing the bills into the evidence envelope and sealing it.

Stuart looked down at the lifeless face: It's strange how life has a way of working itself out. I've owed you for a long time, Beansy, you prick, and now I'm finally getting the chance at payback. He looked over at Jones and Borrelli. "Let's go to Holiday's and talk to Andrea Russo. And while we're there, we'll pay our respects to retired Sergeant Scumbag."

2

Holiday's bar, located in a dingy one-story brick building near the corner of Lincoln Road and New York Avenue, had the word *Saloon* painted in peeling gold letters across its windows. The facade above was a mosaic of green and white tiles with an "R" of glazed orange tiles in the center. The "R" stood for Tony "the Ton" Russo, who built the place in 1894 and was shot to death inside on Christmas Eve 1897.

A long cherrywood bar, to the right of the entrance, stretched across the worn wooden floor, ending at a walk-in refrigerator sheathed in the same fine wood. Sitting on a specially built ledge behind the bar was a stiff felt hat with a dome-shaped crown and narrow brim. This was the derby that Tony "the Ton" was wearing the night his life ended.

Paddy Holiday had bought Russo's in 1976 while he was still working as a sergeant in the NYPD's Intelligence Division. He had registered the business in his sister-in-law's maiden name in order to get around state law and police department regulations prohibiting policemen from owning or having a financial interest in bars and cabarets. When he retired from the Job in 1982, he had the place transferred to his own name.

The blades of one of the five grease-blackened fans projecting from the stamped tin ceiling were turning slowly when Stuart and the detectives walked in shortly before one o'clock.

Paddy Holiday was sitting at a table in the corner, talking in hushed tones with two Rastafarians sporting dreadlocks and brightly colored, oversize caps with full flattops mashed down over the sides of their heads.

Andrea Russo, a tall, shapely woman with long black hair, was polishing the bar with a hunk of white cheesecloth.

Seeing the detectives walk in, Holiday pulled out of the huddle and said in a warning voice, "The Squad is here," using the term for "Detective Squad" that was routine in the department.

The Rastafarians quickly scraped back their chairs and got up, heading for the entrance. Borrelli and Jones ambled over to the bar. Stuart moved to the left of the door and, leaning up against the wall, watched the departing men.

"Good afternoon, gentlemen," he said as they brushed past.

Andrea Russo came over to the detectives and asked, "Want something to drink?"

"We're on duty," Jones said, smiling and brushing his hands over his gleaming head.

"No shit," she said, moving away, wiping the bar. Stuart took the chair across the round table from Holiday. Keeping his voice low so Andrea couldn't hear, he said, "I was surprised to see some of the Posse in here."

"Every Rastafarian you see ain't part of them drug-dealing Posses," Holiday snapped.

"Those two are," Stuart said, looking directly into Holiday's small blue eyes. "How are the mob guys treating you these days? As good as they did when you were still in the Job selling them information?"

"I'm just a retired cop trying to make a living," Holiday protested, his face taking on a flush of anger.

"Paddy, how you scooted out of the Job with your pension is still one of the great mysteries."

Holiday had a way of talking as if every word were being squeezed out of him. "I did my twenty and threw in my papers." He had a crooked nose, dirty blond hair, and manicured nails that looked like shiny talons at the ends of his bony fingers. And his hooded eyes had a sharklike deadness.

Stuart looked him straight in the eyes, trying to catch some expression or emotion in their blue emptiness. "The word I hear is that you were selling information to the pinky-rings. And just as IAD was about to drop the net over you, you jumped ship."

"Loo-ten-ent, you shouldn't believe the rumors you hear in the Job, they're bullshit." He pulled a filthy handkerchief out of his pocket and blew his nose vigorously.

Stuart looked around the bar. His eyes fell on a wall niche right behind Holiday, containing a French banjo clock encased in an African mahogany cabinet. The brass plate had the date *1840*. "Beansy been around today?"

"I ain't seen 'im in a couple of days. He probably went to AC to try his luck on the tables," Holiday said.

"He never made it to Atlantic City. Somebody clipped 'im this morning."

Holiday's eyes narrowed, making crow's-feet. "You sure?"

"Yeah, I'm sure. You gonna tell me you didn't hear anything?" Stuart made no effort to hide his contempt.

"Not a word." He gave Stuart an exaggerated surprised-innocence look and said, "Who'd wanna whack Beansy? He was practically retired."

"Bullshit." Stuart spat the word out and lowered his voice, so Holiday would listen carefully. "In the old days the mob guys gave social clubs to their big earners. Today it's video stores. Beansy had a string of them along Nostrand and Kingston Avenues. Where did he earn most of his money?"

"I don't know shit about those organized crime guys. With me, it's a polite 'Hello and how are ya?'"

Stuart pushed his chair away from the table and got up. At the bar, he smiled and said, "Hello, Andrea."

"Hi," she said, making a pretense at wiping a glass.

"I need to talk to you."

Her face went still, and she glanced fearfully at Holiday. "About what? I haven't done anything wrong."

"We can't talk here, Andrea. Get your pocketbook, we'll take a drive to the Squad." Looking at Holiday, he added, "I'm borrowing your bartender for a while."

Holiday shrugged, indicating his indifference, but his lifeless eyes followed them as they left.

The Seven One Squad was on the second floor of the lime- and sandstone fortress that sat atop the crest of a hill at Empire Boulevard and New York Avenue. There were two massive, ornate lanterns bracketed to the wall on both sides of the entrance. Borrelli and Jones escorted Andrea upstairs to the squad room while Stuart walked behind the high desk in the first floor's muster room. "We just brought in a woman for questioning in connection with the Rutolo homicide," he told the ruddy-faced desk sergeant as he wrote down the information on Andrea on the department scratch pad alongside the blotter.

The desk sergeant looked up at the wall clock, noting the official time, and began making his blotter entry that said at 1320 hours Lieutenant Matt Stuart was present and stated that one F/W/29, known to the department as Andrea Russo, was brought upstairs into the squad room for questioning in connection with a homicide carried under UF61 #15707. After doing that, the sergeant ruled off his entry, looked up at Stuart, and asked, "You gonna need a policewoman?"

"No. I have a female detective doing day duty."

The detective squad room took up half the second floor; the rest was used as a locker room and offices for community relations and the precinct's plainclothes anticrime and narcotics units. A row of metal desks was lined up against the windowed side of the squad room, and across from them was a large holding pen; next to it were the interrogation room and the records/office supplies room. Several corkboards crowded with composite sketches of wanted mutts and department orders were scattered over the walls, along with a tattered American flag. On the wall alongside Jones's desk hung a large Malcolm X poster.

When Stuart walked into the squad room, Detective Helen Kahn was at her desk typing reports, while her partner, Jerry Jordon, was on the telephone attempting to calm a mugging victim. Andrea Russo slumped dejectedly on a chair near the Squad's computer. Smasher, the Squad's hundred-pound black rottweiler mascot, with a head like a bowling ball, was stretched out at her feet. Stuart went directly over to the command log on top of the glass library cabinet and made an entry that Andrea Russo was present in the squad room along with Detective Helen Kahn. He ruled off his entry and, going over to Andrea, said gently, "Let's you and me have a talk." He motioned for her to follow him into the interrogation room.

Helen Kahn waited until Stuart and the witness entered the room before she went into the supply room and slid back a panel, exposing the blackened one-way mirror that gave her a clear view of the interrogation room.

Borrelli came into the supply room and stood beside her.

Jones, who was Smasher's handler and therefore excused from any of the Squad's housekeeping duties, filled Smasher's large bowl with dry dog food and went and stood with Borrelli and Kahn in the supply room.

"Why am I here?" Andrea asked as her eyes darted anxiously about the small room.

"I hear you're going to college," Stuart said, attempting to put her at ease.

"What the fuck is that your business?"

"I get off on seeing people better themselves. Cops are like that."

"In a pig's ass they are."

"This cop is. I remember two years ago when we handed you a collar of possession with intent to sell. I'm happy you made it back to the living."

Her eyes fell to the table, then rose defiantly to confront him. "My life ain't your business."

During his time on the Job, Stuart had met a lot of women whose personalities had been scarred and hardened by whoring and drugs; he had learned that the only way to break through their protective scab was to peel away the crust with tenderness, to show them that somebody really cared about them.

Watching her, he decided that hidden beneath the cheap makeup was a beautiful woman who had yellow ribbons dancing around inside her large black eyes. She was wearing jeans and a black bodysuit that betrayed the outline of nipples through the Lycra. "Your great-grandfather built the original Russo's bar, didn't he?"

"Yes, and my grandfather ran it until he died."

"You've lived in Pigtown all your life, haven't you?"

"All twenty-nine years. When I was a kid I used to play in the Laresca piggery on Hunterfly Road." A sad look clouded her face. "They're all gone now, the Larescas, the pigs, and the road."

"Ol' Man Time don't have friends," Stuart said, folding his hands on the table. "You must know Beansy Rutolo for a long time."

"Him and my dad were friends."

"Is that why you lent him the keys to your house?"

"I don't lend anyone my keys."

"Do you have a duplicate set?"

"Yeah, Mary Terrella, my neighbor across the street, keeps them for me. What the hell is all this about Beansy and my keys?"

"Did you see Beansy today?"

"No, I didn't. What the hell is going on? Why am I here?"

He looked directly into her eyes and said, "Somebody murdered Beansy and stuffed his body into your refrigerator."

She looked at him in stunned silence, then burst into tears, burying her face in her hands.

"Beansy had your house keys in his pocket."

"My keys are in my bag," she said, opening her pocketbook and pulling them out. Sniffling, she dangled them in front of him.

"How do you suppose he got the keys to your house?"

"How the hell do I know? You're the detective, you figure it out," she said, wiping her eyes with the back of her hand.

Inside the supply room, Jones nudged Kahn. "Do you think she's leveling?"

Kahn shrugged. "She looks for real to me."

Andrea looked at Stuart. "Who'd want to kill Beansy? He was such a nice old guy."

"Did you know he was going to your house this morning?"

"Of course not. I told you, nobody gets my house keys."

Stuart's eyes sent a message to the two-way mirror. "Mary Terrella your neighbor has your duplicate set."

"Yes."

Intercepting the whip's look, Jones said gently to his partner, "The boss wants us to go talk to Mary Terrella."

The detectives left the supply room, leaving Kahn behind to watch the interrogation. This was SOP whenever a male member of the force questioned a female witness. It protected the officer against vindictive accusations.

"Do you know of anyone who had it in for Beansy?"

Dabbing her eyes with a tissue she had fished out of her handbag, she shook her head. "Everyone liked Beansy. He was more interested in his family cheese business than in being a wiseguy." She pulled a fresh tissue out of the packet.

"What about his cheese business?"

"Bolonia cheese. I think his father started up the company before Beansy was born."

"Does the mob have a piece of it?"

"How the hell should I know that? You think those guys tell me anything?"

Looking at the tiny chunks of mascara clinging to her eyelashes, he said, "What are you studying in college?"

"I want to be a kindergarten teacher."

"I think you'll make a great teacher."

A tiny smile pinched one end of her mouth. "Thanks."

"Being a teacher means walking on the right side of the street, and that means assuming certain obligations."

"Like what?"

"Like helping us get the people who did Beansy."

"I don't know anything about that," she said, looking away from him.

He didn't believe her. "How do you get along with Holiday?"

"I do my job and he leaves me alone."

"Was Beansy in the bar this morning?"

"I already told you, no."

His smile bore a trace of impatience. She shifted nervously in her chair. "You don't believe me, do you?"

His lips shaped the word *no*.

Her face screwed itself up in anger as she retreated into a hostile silence.

"If you do know something, and Holiday knows that you know, he also knows that you had a drug problem, and he just might consider you a liability," Stuart said.

"I want a lawyer," she announced sullenly.

"You don't need one. You're not a suspect. You can leave any time you want."

Turning in her chair, she looked at the dull mirror. "I suppose there is someone behind that thing looking at us." She stuffed the pack of tissues back in her purse and gripped it firmly. "I'm out of here." She heaved herself out of the chair.

He called after her, his voice full of real sympathy, "Let me help you."

She paused, looked directly at him. He saw the fear in her eyes. She started to say something, changed her mind, and hurried out of the room. As she passed the closed door of the supply room, she kicked it and said, "You can come out now."

A lone police car was parked in front of the Rutland Road crime scene as Borrelli drew the unmarked car in to the opposite curb in front of an old frame house shaded by a great chestnut tree. A rooster crowed, and the late afternoon sun was peering through clouds.

Mary Terrella, a stocky woman in her late thirties, was inside the utility shed attached to the side of her house, taking clothes out of the washing machine, when she heard car doors slam.

Looking out the window, she saw the same detectives who had interviewed her earlier walking up the path. She cursed under her breath and quickly stepped outside to make sure that the dry well was hidden behind the browning hydrangea bushes. It was a constant fear of hers that the city would somehow discover her illegal drainage hole and make her fill it in with cement. She walked over to the house and was waiting as Jones stepped onto her porch. She greeted the detectives with, "I didn't see nothin', I didn't hear nothin', and I don't know shit."

"You're a real community-minded citizen," Jones said with heavy sarcasm.

"Nothing's changed since this morning," she said, adjusting one of the blue hair rollers on the side of her head.

Jones leaned against the porch railing, looking at the yellowing clematis clinging to the trellis. "Actually we came back to pick up Andrea Russo's house keys. She asked us to get them from you."

Her face wrinkled with distrust. "What keys?"

"Andrea wanted us to do her a favor and get them for her. We had to take her set as evidence," Borrelli said.

"Why didn't she come herself?" she asked.

"Because she has school tonight, and the charm boat she works for won't give her time off to come and get them herself," Borrelli said.

She eyed the detectives. "If you're lying . . ."

"We're not," Jones said with a weary edge.

"Wait here," she said, and walked inside the house.

After she had gone inside, Borrelli looked at his partner and asked, "What do you think?"

"I think she saw the people who came with Beansy and left without him."

"She ain't gonna be an easy one to break. We're going to have to find the right buttons to push," Borrelli said.

Mary Terrella came back and handed Jones the keys.

They thanked her and went across the street. Walking in front of the parked patrol car, Jones waved to the two bored cops inside who'd been assigned to the "fixer" outside the crime scene. Standing on the porch of Andrea Russo's house, Borrelli tried the keys in the two locks on the front door. They worked. As they were walking back to their car, Jones looked at his partner and asked, "How many ladies you dancing with these days?"

"Four," Borrelli said proudly.

"Doesn't it get complicated?"

"Yeah, it does. But the problem is, I love 'em all."

"What you gotta do is ask yourself which woman you want to spend the rest of your life cheating on."

Inspector Patrick Sarsfield Casey, the commanding officer of the Twelfth Detective District, which included the Seven One Squad, was the oldest member of the NYPD. Department regulations dictated mandatory retirement at age sixty-three. Casey was sixty-five and still working, because five days before his sixty-third birthday he'd filed an age discrimination suit in federal court, enjoining the department and the city from forcing him to retire. The case was currently winding its way through the overloaded court calendar.

Casey was a big man with a thick wavy mane, bushy white eyebrows, and a Roman nose that set off his handsome face. The inspector was always referred to in the Job by his full name, Patrick Sarsfield Casey, as a sign of respect.

"What ya got on the Rutolo homicide?" Casey asked, his large form filling the doorway.

Stuart looked up from the case folder. "We have people who should have seen the perps, but won't give them up, and some physical evidence, like heel prints."

Going over to peer out through the steel window grating, Casey asked, "Are you going to solve it or dump it into the dustbin?"

"We're going to make arrests."

Casey turned from the window and focused on a fight card that was framed in shiny black wood. It was on the wall next to the precinct boundary map. The top of the card advertised a middleweight contest between Al "Bummy" Davis and Rocky

Graziano on Friday, December 19, 1961, at Madison Square
Garden. Casey's eyes slid from the poster to Stuart's. Their stares
held a shared secret. "Beansy had a lot of friends, in and out of
the Job," Casey said.

"I know."

Casey gazed down into the tiny valley with the weed-covered
pigsties. "Pigtown is in its last throes."

"This whole command is in its last throes," Stuart said, waving
his hand across the precinct map. "The western part of this shithouse, along Nostrand and Flatbush Avenues, is black and poor.
North of Eastern Parkway is loaded with Hasidim, and in the
east, Rastafarians, and down here in the south, a few diehard
Italians clinging to the past by their fingertips. And none of
them like each other. This is September and we're carrying
twenty-six hundred more cases than we had for all of last year."

"It's the same all over the city, Matt, you know that. We're getting buried in homicides and dope."

"That's true. But the Seven One is the Crown Heights
Precinct, remember the riots? When they were burning and loot-
ing, and the top brass in this job took cover in temporary headquarters, refusing to let us do our job, waiting for the mayor to
give them the go-ahead?"

"The cops were finally turned loose," Casey said in admon-
ishment.

"Yeah, but only after Mattarazzo, the PBA trustee, stormed
into the headquarters van, shouting, 'They've been burnin' and
lootin' for two days, when are we going to take some fucking
police action?'"

Casey held his hands out wide, indicating helplessness. Then
he asked, "How long you going to give Beansy?"

"I can't take anybody off the chart to work the case, but I'm
going to give it as much time as it takes to break it."

Casey glanced at the fight card. "I know you figure you owe
Beansy for what happened years ago, but keep in mind that the
mayor hates the department. So you don't want to make waves.
He's looking to take it apart and parcel it out to his politically

correct scumbag friends in the so-called communities. They're looking to make one gigantic pork barrel out of this Job, the same way they did with the board of ed., Off-Track Betting, and the department of traffic."

"Boss, I figured that one out by myself a long time ago," Stuart said, wanting to change the subject. He didn't like talking about city politics or what the politicians had done to the city. "How's your court case going?"

"It takes time, but we're going to win." Casey's tone was combative. "It's unconstitutional to force a man to retire at sixty-three. I'm in my prime, for crissake." He looked back out the window and said quietly, "I hear Paddy Holiday is involved in the Rutolo homicide."

"The woman who owns the house where Beansy was popped is one of his barmaids." Stuart wondered how Casey had gotten the word so quickly.

"The Job owes Holiday a fall. He gave up a lot of our undercover operations when he was working Intelligence."

"If I ever get the chance to step on him, I will," Stuart said bluntly.

"I'm outta here," Casey said, looking up at the wall clock. "Get me your 'B' list."

Stuart walked outside into the squad room and over to the command log. He flipped back the hard cover and slid out a manila folder, then returned to his office to hand it to his boss.

Casey chucked it open and wrote a name and telephone number onto the mimeographed sheet. He looked up at Stuart. "Forty years ago, when I came on the Job, this was called the 'vulva file.' Then in the middle seventies, when women started to come into the Job, the name was changed to the 'significant other file.' Now it's the 'B' list."

"The Job's an adaptable organization, boss."

"I wish it wasn't so fucking adaptable," he said, slipping the folder onto Stuart's desk. "I signed out at the borough to here, so if my wife is looking for me, she'll call here. Tell her I'm at the Rutolo homicide. I'm going to be at the K of C, playing poker, drinking malt whiskey, and smoking cigars. What the hell's happened to this world? Martha gets on my case if I drink or smoke at home. It's not politically correct to smoke in any precinct or squad room because the pussies in the Job are afraid of getting cancer."

Stuart smiled broadly. "It's not that bad, Inspector."

"Bullshit it ain't. I bet if I looked inside the precinct icebox, I wouldn't find one six-pack. But I'd sure as hell find a lot of Perrier and rabbit food." At the door he turned and, looking at Stuart, asked, "Anyone in your life yet?"

"No."

"Shit-can the past and get yourself a life already."

"It's not that easy."

"That's because you can't get out of your own head." Reaching for the knob, Casey said, "You'll know you have it made with a woman when you find yourself making love to her and not her pussy."

The blowups of the heel prints found at the crime scene were pinned to the corkboard in Stuart's office. Black lines highlighted the points of identification: an embedded pebble, a chipped nail head, the manufacturer's "Anvil" trademark, a badly worn down right side.

Borrelli, Jones, Kahn, and Jerry Jordon were standing around in the whip's office, listening to their boss analyze the print.

Stuart, one arm draped over a five-drawer file cabinet, was studying the photographs of Beansy and the blood trail. "Whoever made that heel print was slew footed. See how the left heel is worn down only on the right side?" He went over to the board and looked at the enlargements of the photographs that had been taken of the scene, overhead views snapped by a detective from the right seat of one of the aviation unit's helicopters. That tiny valley, four or five blocks long, with the few remaining battered houses with peeling porches and empty pigpens, collapsed chicken coops, set against a background of today . . . modern apartment houses, supermarkets, garages, rows of cramped two-family brick houses, the past squeezed almost out of existence by the present.

The telephone on the whip's desk rang. Kahn snapped it up. "Kahn, Seven One Squad." She covered the mouthpiece, looked at Borrelli, and said, "It's Laura, she wants to know if you're here."

"Tell her I'm on patrol."

She tossed the receiver at him. "Tell her yourself. . . ."

Grabbing the phone and slipping his hand over the mouthpiece, Borrelli glared at Kahn and said, "Detective Kathy Career's feminism is showing."

"Fuck you, Lance Romance," she said to Borrelli, shaking her trademark brushed-gold bangles down to her wrist.

Borrelli cupped his hand around the receiver and whispered into the mouthpiece.

Jerry Jordon, a wiry guy with hazel eyes and a latticework of thin steel gray hair on the sides of his head, had nineteen years on the Job and liked to make love to his wife of twenty-two years, play with his four kids, and drive stock cars in his off-duty time. He spoke up for the first time in the meeting. "That Russo dame and her neighbor could give the whole thing up if they wanted to."

"Yeah," Stuart said, nodding his head in agreement. Looking at Borrelli, he added, "You and Jones dig into Terrella's background, see if there isn't something there we can use as a lever to pry her open."

"What about Russo?" Kahn asked.

"I'll check her out," Stuart said.

Borrelli looked over at the wall clock. "Want us to get right on it?"

Stuart checked the time; it was six-fifty. "The morning'll do."

The detectives walked slowly out of the office.

Stuart leaned back in his seat, listening to the flood of police calls coming over the Squad's radio. Ten-ten, man with a gun on Kingston and Union; ten-ten, man shot at Nostrand and Midwood; ten-ten, drug sales, Crown and Utica; ten-thirty, robbery in progress, Flatbush and Winthrop; ten-ten, screams for help, President and Troy.

Suddenly street sounds were overpowered by the wailing of police sirens as the Seven One's radio motor patrol cars responded to the emergency calls. Soon all twelve of the precinct's RMPs were out of service on jobs. The patrol lieutenant's crusty voice crackled over the radio, ordering the precinct's plainclothes anticrime and narcotics units to pick up jobs. Stuart looked at the speakers standing on top of the file cabinets and thought, Stereophonic misery.

3

A pale moon peeked out from behind the clouds as Matt Stuart walked into Junior's restaurant in downtown Brooklyn. He liked Junior's because it was one of the few eateries left that still put bowls of pickles and coleslaw on the tables along with a basket of rolls. He slid in behind a burgundy-colored banquette and looked up at the Tiffany lampshade look-alikes before his eyes surveyed the circular counter as he looked for the man he was supposed to meet. He hadn't showed yet.

Matt looked at the time; it was seven-thirty. He speared a sour pickled tomato onto the small plate and cut into it. Juice squirted out. He was gazing out the large plate-glass window, watching the comings and goings of LIU students across Flatbush Avenue, when the waiter, a skinny, maniacally cheerful guy from Bangladesh, came over to take his order: corned beef on onion rye, a salad, and a side of onion rings.

As the waiter walked off, scribbling the order on his soiled pad, Matt reached into the basket, broke off a piece of skinny pumpernickel, tossed it into his mouth, and resumed gazing out the window, his mind resurrecting that long-ago Sunday, a week before Christmas 1961, when he was eleven and his parents took him downtown to the Fox to see the movie *Pinocchio*. Afterward they went to Junior's for dinner. His dad left them right after dessert because he had to rush to the Seven One to do a four-to-twelve. Matt's life was never the same after that damn Sunday.

The waiter brought over his order. Stuart had just bitten into his sandwich when the stink of clinging cigarette smoke made him look up. The man standing by his table was wearing blue warm-ups with red piping and air-cushioned Nikes that looked like moon shoes. Stuart patted the empty space next to him on the banquette.

Detective Carmine Vuzzo sucked in his gut as he squeezed into the booth and picked up one of Stuart's onion rings. "So why the call?" he said, tossing the chunk into his mouth.

"How's Intelligence?" Stuart asked, licking a smear of mustard off his finger.

Vuzzo combed his fingers through his thick head of black hair and said, "Going downhill like the rest of the Job." More onion rings, a sly smile. "So? What's up?"

"Beansy got himself whacked this morning. My squad caught the case."

"I heard." He grabbed a pickle out of the bowl, snapped it in half, and tossed one end into his mouth. "How long's it been, three years since we talked? And now you call me when some wiseguy gets himself whacked."

"Yeah. Sorry, but this one is special for me."

Vuzzo still wasn't happy. "You could'a called once or twice to see how we're doin', Mary and the kids. Little Joey is your godson."

"Life is full of could'as, Carmine."

Vuzzo tossed in the other half of the pickle and said, "You were always good with the cards, though, birthdays, Christmas, anniversaries, I'll give ya that."

Matt leaned close and said, "After Beansy got hit, I figured I'd reach out to the Job's resident expert on the Gambino crime family for help."

A big smile creased Vuzzo's face. "I bet most people you've spoken to tell you what a terrific guy ol' Beansy was."

"Yeah, that's the song I've been hearing."

"It's all bullshit," Vuzzo said scornfully. "He was a killer like the rest of them. Only he got off on playing Mister Rogers." Another one of Stuart's onion rings went into his mouth before he folded his arms across the table, one on top of the other, and said, "Lemme tell you a story 'bout ol' Beansy. Neil Dellacroce, the Gambino underboss, dies, and Paulie Castellano bypasses John Gotti and makes Tommy Bilotti the new underboss." He plucked a pickle out of the bowl and bit it in half. "Big Paulie hates Gotti's guts and don't wanna see him, so he don't go to Neil's wake. That's a serious breach of wiseguy etiquette, and pissed a lotta people off at Paulie. Paulie, not being any fool, wants to make things right with Neil's son, Buddy, so he asks Beansy to set up a meet with Buddy so he can offer his personal condolences. Beansy sets it up at Sparks Steakhouse. So, as you know, when Paulie and Tommy B arrive at Sparks, Beansy is waiting outside, all smiles. Paulie and Tommy get out of the car, and Gotti's shooters run up to them and give 'em a lead tarantella. Beansy walks over to Paulie, his lifelong paisan, bends down and calmly feels for a pulse that ain't there, and walks off down the street. A really caring person."

Stuart ate the last of his sandwich and said, "Then Beansy had enemies."

"All those guys got enemies. Sometimes they harbor grudges for years before payback time."

"Whose 'get even' list was Beansy on?"

Vuzzo threw up his hands in frustration and said, "Who knows? Like most of them, the list is endless."

"What's the real story on that cheese business of his?"

"Around the turn of the century his grandfather finagled the license as sole importer of Bolonia cheese in this country. And that license is passed on from generation to generation. Beansy had big bucks coming in from that business. That's why he didn't give a shit about going higher in the crew."

Stuart casually changed the topic, asking, "What do you hear on Paddy Holiday these days?"

Vuzzo pulled a sour face that revealed a mouthful of badly

capped teeth and said, "His name keeps cropping up on wires. His latest scam is brokering junk deals between drug guys and Rastafarians."

"Why would anyone use him as go-between?"

"Because none of the drug crews trust niggers. They won't deal with them. So our distinguished retired sergeant brokers and cuts himself a taste."

"Ever hear of a couple of gals named Andrea Russo and Mary Terrella?"

"Not off the top of my head. I'll check the files and get back to you." Vuzzo was clearly not going to get any deeper into this; there was a note of finality in his voice.

Stuart's gaze fixed on the pickle bowl, to the green juice and little yellow seeds, and he asked softly, "How's Pat?"

"She's okay. She was dating some asshole lawyer who only knew from trusts and acquisitions. She gave him the ol' heave about a month ago." He looked Stuart in the eyes and said, "Why don't you give her a call?"

Stuart felt a tightness in his chest. "What for? When your sister walked, she walked for good."

"Why don't you get fucking real? You could still get her back."

He looked at his former brother-in-law and said, "That part of my life is dead."

LaGuardia Community College is housed in a group of gray, flat-roofed converted factory buildings clustered along Queens Boulevard at the foot of the upper ramp of the Queensboro Bridge. The main building on the campus used to be a chewing gum factory.

After leaving Junior's, Matt drove to the college and parked across the street from the school in the driveway of a bank, so that the front of his car was facing the college. Because he was the whip of a busy squad and was always on call, he was given a "category one" auto to take home with him. It was a dark blue Buick Regal that had a telephone and a department radio that received all the uniform and detective bands.

As he sat behind the wheel, watching students entering and leaving the buildings, he realized that most of them looked older than regular college kids; they weren't dressed in trendy baggy clothes but had on less stylish outfits. Many looked tired, as though they had put in a day's work before going to school. He had heard some Queens cops from the One Fourteen talking one day while waiting to testify in court, and they'd referred to LaGuardia College as Crayola U. But he also knew that the students who went there called it the Last Chance Saloon.

During the drive there he kept chiding himself for having asked Carmine about Pat. He hadn't planned on doing that; it had just popped out. He had thought he'd gotten over her. His hands tightened around the steering wheel.

Despite the bright street lighting, Matt almost didn't spot her walking out of the main campus building. She was wearing stonewashed jeans, white Keds, and a brown sweater stretched down almost to her knees. Her hair was pulled back in a ponytail, and she had an olive-green gas mask case, U.S. Army issue, slung over her left shoulder. He figured her books were inside. He got out of the car and called out her name. She froze in her tracks and did a slow about-face. When she spotted him across the street, waving, she seemed to wilt, suddenly looking older. She walked slowly across the street toward Stuart, watching the oncoming traffic.

Approaching him reluctantly, she cast a wary eye inside the car and asked, "What do you want?"

"I thought I'd offer you a ride home."

"The last charmer who made me that offer stuck a gun in my face and made me give 'im a blow job."

"See ya 'round, Andrea," he said, making a move to get back into the car.

"Wait a minute." She walked up to the open door and regarded him with curiosity. "No tricks?"

"No tricks. I promise."

She went around the front of the car, opened the passenger door, tossed her book bag inside, and got in.

A tape of Brahms's piano quintet was playing on the car stereo. They rode in silence until they were driving over the Pulaski Bridge connecting Queens and Brooklyn. She was watching the Manhattan skyline when she suddenly turned and looked at him and asked, "How did you know when I'd be leaving school?"

"I telephoned a friend on campus security. He got your class schedule from the registrar."

She nodded and returned her attention to the view of the city that seemed suddenly like a mirage under the moonlight.

He glanced at her and said with genuine warmth, "I'm really glad that you're making a life for yourself."

She glared at him and didn't respond. He pressed on, trying to establish a rapport. "It must have been hard for you, going back to school."

"Sorta."

"Was it hard getting back into the books?"

She relaxed, her expression less hostile and guarded. "I hadda teach myself a lot. But I got into the swing of it."

"You gotta know that you're never going to be really free until you get Holiday off your back."

She pointedly ignored him and looked out of the passenger side window.

"I could arrange a new life for you far away from here. You could start over with enough walking-around money to see you through school."

Her head whipped around; she spoke in a bitter, depressed voice. "And what do I have to do to get this new life? Tell you and the DA lies? Testify that I saw and heard things I didn't?"

"All you'd have to do is tell the truth."

She looked at him and asked scornfully, "Whose truth? Socrates's, Paddy Holiday's, Beansy's, or yours?"

"*The* truth."

She spread her legs wide apart, pointed angrily to her crotch, and snapped, "That's the only truth men know." Slamming her knees shut, she glared out at the gas station on McGuinness

Boulevard. Their silence lengthened, her anger seeming to fill the car.

As he was driving along the Brooklyn-Queens Expressway he saw the Williamsburg Savings Bank's pyramid touching the distant sky. The cold barrier between him and Andrea reminded him of how it had been with Pat at the end. He did not want to feel that kind of helplessness ever again, so he looked at Andrea and said, "I'm only trying to do my job and help you at the same time."

She lowered her eyes and said softly, "Thanks for nothing."

The police car that had been stationed outside Andrea's house had gone back on patrol when Matt pulled up to the curb and reached across the seat to chuck open the door. As she was getting out, he said, "If you ever need a friend, call me." He handed her his card with his unlisted office phone number.

A puzzled look came over her face. "Why are you being so nice to me?"

"Because I know what it's like to be alone."

She slammed the door, ran up onto her porch, and disappeared inside her darkened house.

Across the street, Mary Terrella released her grip on the parlor curtain and reached for the telephone.

4

The first subtle rays of the new day seeped into the frilly bedroom of Helen Kahn's Vesey Street co-op in Battery Park City on the southern tip of Manhattan Island. She looked across the queen-size bed at the clock radio, saw that it was 4:36 A.M., and turned her attention to the man balancing himself on one leg while he thrust the other into his trousers. She could feel his semen oozing out of her body and felt unclean, as if she had been defiled.

How did I ever allow myself to get involved with this guy? she thought. He's married and will never be anything more than a middle-of-the-night fuck. I wonder what he'll do if his wife wants to make love when he gets home? He'll probably tell her he's so strung out from the Job that he can't get it up.

He was buttoning his shirt, his mind obviously somewhere else, his thoughts far removed from Helen.

She hadn't even wanted to have an affair. It began so innocently. They met at the Holy Name's St. Patrick's Day dance. He was reasonably good-looking and wasn't wearing a wedding ring, so she agreed to a dance. It was a fox-trot, and he didn't hold her too close and didn't try any of that fancy dry humping. And she liked his shoes, she'd always been big on men's shoes. He was wearing soft leather wingtips with a thin decorative band halfway between the tip and the first eyelet, and his socks were blue high-risers with a gray diamond-shaped design. After the dance they went out for coffee; a week later, a movie. The Job gave them a lot in common to talk about, and he never once came on to her. He told her he was married after that first movie and talked openly about his children and his home.

What a fool, what a fool I am. The bastard conned me. He's good, I have to give him that. I'm thirty-one, my meter's running, and I'm in a no-win situation. I'm out of playing-around time.

Lieutenant Ken Kirby slid his holstered .38 S&W Chief off the dresser and stuck it into his waistband, clipping it onto his belt. He looked at her and came over, smiling. Lowering himself onto the edge of the bed, he brushed a forelock from her brow. He kissed her and began kneading her nipple through the sheet. "You have beautiful tits."

"Thanks a lot, sport." She crossed her legs, wishing he'd go.

"You're a world-class fuck, Helen."

"As world class as your wife?"

A bleak smile touched one corner of his mouth. "It's different when you're married."

You scumbag, she thought. "You'd better get going, you have a long drive out to the Island."

"Why don't we go away for a weekend?"

She looked surprised. "How can you do that?"

"I'll tell Dot that I have to go out of town on an extradition caper," he said smugly.

She looked deep in his eyes, searching for the warmth of his soul, but found only a cold emptiness. I'm really seeing him for the first time, she thought. His poor wife. He's a lowlife, and what does that make me? She dropped her eyes and asked, "Would your wife believe you?"

"Sure she would. Dot knows that IAD lieutenants are the purest of the pure."

Helen pulled the covers up to her neck and looked up at the ceiling. "I don't think I can right now, Ken. I'm carrying forty-two open cases, and we just caught another homicide. I'm really up to my neck."

Kirby made a dismissive gesture with his hand. "Beansy Rutolo is a five-and-dime hit. Solving gay and racially motivated hits are what make careers today, not wiseguys. Nobody gives a shit about them anymore—except your lieutenant, for some reason." He stood up, looked down at her, and said, "I'll be in touch."

She sat up, wrapping and firmly securing the sheet around her, and got out of bed. She didn't want him ever to see her naked again. They walked silently out of the bedroom and across the living room to the door. He pulled her into his arms and said, "You know a cop named Janet Clark, works steady midnights in the Sixth?"

"No."

"You might wanna whisper in her ear that somebody dropped a kite on her, alleging that she's eating on the arm in the Triangle Diner on Hudson Street and doing the owner of the diner on her meal hour, which is city time."

"She must be a fast eater."

Suddenly he slipped his hand between her legs, pushing up the sheet. "I've been assigned the investigation. See, we're not all bad guys in IAD."

She grabbed his wrist and pushed it away from her body.

"What's the matter?"

"I'm tired. You wore me out."

"We really get it on together, don't we?"

"Yeah, you're terrific, Ken," she said, reaching past him and opening the door, nudging him out.

After he was gone, she locked the door and, letting her makeshift sarong fall to the floor, ran into the bathroom. She stepped into the shower, turned on the hot water, and tried to clean away the awful feeling of self-disgust, thinking, The bastard always leaves me with some IAD tidbit like he's throwing a fish to a trained seal.

The Seven One Squad's detention pen was crowded with the late tour's dregs when Matt Stuart walked into the squad room early Wednesday morning. Six hours of sleep had given him a more cheerful outlook. Smasher, wearing his black, green, and orange bandanna, sat on his haunches outside the heavy wire mesh detention cage, staring in at the prisoners, emitting a steady, low growl. The Squad's six typewriters were being used by detectives and cops doing their arrest paperwork. The three wastebaskets overflowed with pizza boxes and stained Chinese food cartons. Two floor fans lazily stirred the faintly rancid air.

Stuart walked over to the command log and signed himself present for duty. As he was ruling off his entry, he felt someone's cold stare and looked up. One of the prisoners inside the cage, a big black man, with biceps bulging across his dirty T-shirt, was glaring out at him. He was sitting on the floor with his back up against the wall; his head was swathed in a bloodied gauze turban. Their eyes locked, and Stuart thought, That bro got a real bad attitude.

As Stuart walked across the squad room, heading for his office, Hector Colon, a forty-five-year-old swarthy detective with a weather-creased face and a full Pancho Villa mustache, got up from behind his desk and followed him inside. Tradition dictated that Colon, as the senior detective doing night duty, brief the whip on what went down during the tour.

Stuart looked down at the sixty sheet, a chronological record of all the cases that the Squad caught during the night. "You've been busy."

"The natives were restless," Colon said, flicking his thumb at the silent radio speakers. "A half hour ago this place was jumpin', and now, not a peep."

"Our clientele are probably all juiced up and calling it a night. Anything heavy go down that's not entered on the sixty sheet yet?"

"No, it's all there, chronologically, as per the *Detective Guide.*" He brushed the tips of his fingers across his full mustache. "Those 911 tapes on the Rutolo homicide arrived last night in the department mail. I stuck them in your top drawer." He began riffling through the wire "in" basket on the desk and yanked out a department bulletin. "This crap arrived in the mail."

Stuart read the bulletin. It announced that applications were now being accepted for the newly created civilian title Voucher Officer, whose duties would be to collect all evidence stored at patrol precincts, including firearms, money, narcotics, jewelry, and art, for delivery to the Borough Property Clerk. Felony arrests would not be a barrier to appointment. Starting salary, $30,000. Stuart gave an exasperated sigh, balled up the bulletin, and tossed it into the wastebasket. "The bastards are pork-barreling the Job to death."

"I got paper to do," Colon said, and walked outside.

Smasher lumbered in and crumpled by the side of the desk. Stuart scratched him behind the ears and slid open the middle drawer, took out the 911 tape cassette and a portable tape deck, then inserted the cassette into the machine. The woman's voice was obviously distorted. "Get the cops over to Four-oh-one Rutland Road. Somethin' bad's happened." He replayed the tape a second and third time.

"Recognize her?" Helen Kahn asked, walking inside. She wore a dark green skirt and a black blazer.

He glanced up at the clock. It was a little before eight. "What are you doing in so early?"

"Couldn't sleep. Can I hear it?" she asked, indicating the tape deck as she lowered herself into the chair at the side of his desk. As she crossed her legs, the hem of her skirt rode above her knees.

They listened to the tape. Kahn's perfume had the delicate scent of lilacs. "It sounds as though she tucked her tongue into the corner of her mouth as she made the call," she said.

Stuart switched off the machine. "She certainly didn't want us making her."

She regarded him with mild curiosity. "You think Russo was leveling with us about her keys?"

"No way. She's hiding something."

"Think maybe she could have been Beansy's squeeze?"

The barest hint of a smile crossed his face. "From the way I've heard Andrea Russo talk about men, I don't think she's into them anymore."

"I can relate to that," she said. She rose and went out into the squad room.

Stuart opened the Rutolo case folder. The autopsy protocol stated that the cause of death was a gunshot wound to the head. A photograph of the death bullet was pinned to the onionskin; it showed a deformed lead slug with some of its lands and grooves clearly visible. By examining the number and width of the grooves, and their direction of twist, along with the degree of twist of the spiral, the ballistic technician had determined that the bullet had been fired from a .38 Colt Special. His father's service revolver had been a .38 Colt Special. Because modern munitions contain lead compounds that are transferred from the barrel with the bullet, the ME had been able to determine that the shooter was standing about four feet away from Beansy when he fired. Stuart looked up at the corkboard, focusing on the crime scene photos of the living room.

Borrelli and Jones arrived within five minutes of each other. Jones was wearing a tan sports coat and a tricolor African cap.

One by one the late tour detectives finished their paperwork and drifted off into the locker room to wash off the night's crud and grab some z's before going to court to arraign their prisoners.

Jerry Jordon arrived, wearing a lightweight gray suit with an "I Love Stock Cars" button pinned to his lapel. As he walked in, the desk officer telephoned up to the squad room to say that the paddy wagon had arrived to transport the prisoners to court.

Jordon went into the supply closet and lifted a handcuff chain off the hook. Back outside, he slid his nine-millimeter out of his holster and handed it to Jones. He pulled the cotter pin out of the cage's locking bar and rammed the bar out of its sleeve. The other detectives gathered around the cage. Smasher's growl was louder now.

Jordon swung open the gate and motioned a bare-chested, stocky white guy outside. He spread-eagled the prisoner against the steel mesh and began running his hands slowly over the prisoner's legs. Cops learned to do their job from the fatal mistakes of other cops. The rule was, Never assume that a prisoner has been properly searched. Lots of cops were under tombstones because someone had missed a weapon on the initial search. Jordon carefully ran his hands up the inside of the prisoner's legs and under his crotch.

"Kiss me first," the prisoner growled.

Jordon squeezed his testicles. The prisoner howled. "That's a cop's kiss, scumbag," Jordon said.

After the prisoner had been searched, he was cuffed to the steel chain and another prisoner brought outside and stretched out over the cage. When all had been searched and cuffed, three uniformed cops convoyed them downstairs to the waiting paddy wagon.

The day duty detectives took plastic bottles of spray cleaner out of their drawers and began spraying their work spaces. Soon the stench of the late tour was smothered in evergreen and lemon.

Kahn watered the cactus plant on her desk and put the watering can back on the windowsill. She sat down and picked up the telephone, dialing an extension in Patrol Borough Manhattan South. A familiar woman's voice came over the line, "Sergeant Esposito."

"Hey, Miranda, how's it going?" Kahn exchanged a little gossip with her friend and then, in a casual tone, got to the point. "You know a gal in the Sixth named Janet Clark?"

"Yes."

Kahn shook her brushed-gold bangles down her wrist and said softly, "Whisper to her to stay away from the Triangle Diner, and to stop doing the owner on city time."

"Ten-four," Esposito said, using the radio code for acknowledgment.

Returning the receiver slowly, Kahn thought, Ken, you IAD lowlife.

Stuart came out of his office and went over to Kahn. "Let's go for a ride."

As she was reaching under her desk for her pocketbook, the

telephone rang and Stuart snapped it up. "Seven One Squad, Stuart." After listening to the voice at the other end, he slipped his hand over the mouthpiece, looked over at Jones, and said, "Calvin, it's Plaintiff."

Jones's face screwed up in anger. "Every Wednesday 'fore payday Plaintiff gotta call and break my balls. 'Don't forget my alimony check,'" he mimicked. Grabbing the receiver and holding the mouthpiece away from his mouth, he shouted, "Fuck you, Plaintiff," and slammed the receiver down.

Borrelli started singing "Love Is a Many-Splendored Thing."

Andrea would never forget the gruesome sight that greeted her on Tuesday night when Stuart dropped her off at home. She had entered the house apprehensively; dark shadows shimmered across the walls and ceilings. An eerie cone of light came from the kitchen. Leaning her back up against the door, she heard Stuart's car drive off. She felt desperately alone and exploited. As she stared at the light reaching into the living room from her kitchen, a chill prickled the hairs on the back of her neck, and she shivered.

Walking across her living room, she saw the upended table and lamp and the dark stains in her carpet. The refrigerator door had been left open. Her mouth opened in silent dismay when she saw the lasagna, and the broken eggs, and the gore inside the box. Her home had been violated, and she felt a deep sense of revulsion. She wrapped her arms around herself and began swaying side to side, tears streaming down her face. "That lasagna was supposeta last the week," she cried, wiping a thin strand of mucus from her nose.

Suddenly her sorrow was replaced by an overwhelming feeling of anger. She stormed into the kitchen and kicked the head of lettuce across the floor. She whirled, slamming the refrigerator door, cutting off the source of light. "Holiday, you prick."

She left the kitchen and went into her bedroom, where she got undressed and climbed into bed without showering. She'd deal with everything in the morning; right now she needed to close her eyes.

When morning came, a crowing rooster brought Andrea out of her sleep. Sunlight washed over her bedroom, etching irregular outlines of leaves on her bed and walls. She stretched, savoring the comforting warmth of her quilt. She sprung up, tossing off the covers. Had it been one of those dreams that seemed real? She leaped from her bed and ran into the kitchen. "Shit!" She took a broom, mop, and a pail with two big yellow sponges inside and began cleaning up the mess.

Two hours later she rested her chin on the mop handle and surveyed her work. Good job. She liked a neat, clean house; it made her feel good about herself and her life. She'd come a long way since the days she was peddling her ass to buy drugs. She looked up at the sunflower clock above the sink: 8:45 A.M. She was glad today was Wednesday, and that she had only one class tonight. She had to be behind the stick at the bar by ten-thirty to set up for the lunch crowd of truckers and taxi drivers who wolfed down Holiday's awful food and seemed to love every mouthful.

She wanted to shave her legs and take a nice, slow shower. She smiled when she realized that she was naked. She went into the bedroom and looked at herself in the closet mirror: flat stomach, firm breasts with large pink crowns. Her bush was sprouting wings. If she had still been into men, she'd have taken a run over to her electrolysis lady on Ocean Avenue for a tree trimming, but since she wasn't, she could live with all the hair. Sucking in her gut, she preened for herself.

"Just like every other guy I've met in my life, Stuart wants to help me," she said to her reflection. "I'm a barmaid ex-junkie with a rap sheet, and this guy wants to be my friend, and he won't come in my mouth, either. Gimme a fuckin' break," she said, and stepped into the shower.

That Wednesday morning, Franklin Gee and James Hollyman, the Rastafarians who were always talking their secret shit with Holiday, were huddled around a table near the kitchen when Andrea walked into the bar just after ten. When the door closed behind her, it cut off the bright sunlight, leaving her in a dark, dank place stinking of stale beer and cigarettes.

Paddy Holiday's cold eyes swept over her. She felt his chilling stare and hurried behind the bar, depositing her pocketbook in the drawer under the antique cash register. Except for Paddy and his friends, the place seemed empty. She wondered how long it took the Rastafarians to braid their dreadlocks. She figured it had to take hours.

She reached under the bar for a roll of paper towels and a bottle of spray cleaner and began wiping off the top of the bar and emptying ashtrays. She caught the faint aroma of simmering sauces wafting out of the kitchen. After cleaning the bar, she began setting paper placemats in front of each stool. She had just reached for the silverware tray under the bar when she looked up to see Paddy and the dreadlock twins standing at the bar. The Rastafarians were giving her that damn toothy Jamaican grin of theirs.

Hollyman leaned over the bar, his face inches from hers. "One day I'm goin' to catch you, woman, and we're goin' to have ourselves a party."

She slapped down a knife on the side of the placemat. "Even if you caught it, you couldn't ride it," she hissed, placing a spoon next to the knife.

"How are things going?" Paddy asked.

"Good," she said, setting another mat.

Paddy clutched the bar with his hands and began doing standing pushups. "Did Stuart break your balls yesterday?"

Her stomach went hollow. "He questioned me for a while, then I walked. No big deal. I came back here, but you'd already split for the day, so I went to school."

"You tell 'im anything?" Paddy asked, moving backward.

She tried to put on a convincing smile. "There was nothing for me to tell him, was there?" She started to move off. Holiday grabbed her wrist, pinning her to the bar. The dreadlock twins' grotesque smiles grew larger. Holiday moved his face close to hers. "How'dya like livin' the clean life?"

"I like it, Paddy."

"Think you'll ever forget how to give head?"

Fear crept up her back. "Are you kidding? It's like riding a bicycle. You never forget." She tried to break his grip on her wrist.

Holiday smiled at the two men. He looked back at Andrea. "Think you'll ever forget who your friends are?"

"No," she said weakly.

Holiday's fist caught her on the temple; she fell, sprawling onto the floor. Gee and Hollyman rushed behind the bar and dragged her out.

"In the storeroom," Holiday ordered, going and locking the front door.

They carried her through the swinging kitchen doors. The elderly man who cooked the mediocre lunches for Paddy looked down at the pots on the stove. He continued stirring his gravy as if it were perfectly normal to have women dragged through the kitchen every day. Gee opened the storeroom door. Cartons of liquor and tins of condiments were stacked against the wall, along with demijohns of cherry peppers. They tossed her into the crowded space. She cowered up against a case of single-malt whiskey.

"Why are you doing this?" she screamed at her tormentors.

Holiday filled the doorway. "You're fucking over your friends, kiddo."

"I am not!" she shouted.

Holiday moved his face closer. Little black hairs sprouted out of his nostrils. "You forgot to tell me that Stuart drove you home last night."

Mary, you bitch, you fucking spy. "There was nothing to tell, Paddy. He was waiting for me when I got out of school. He drove me home, said he wanted to help me. He didn't even ask me any questions about the case, I swear."

Holiday tossed her an impatient look. "I don't like being bullshitted."

"I'm not. I wouldn't lie to you."

Holiday's eyes narrowed, searching her face for the lie. He saw only her fear. He looked at Gee and Hollyman. Mimicking their Jamaican singsong, he said, "What you t'ink, man?"

"I t'ink maybe da woman got a sweet pussy for da policeman," Gee said.

Holiday kneaded her left nipple. She cringed at his touch. "You got the hots for Stuart?" he asked, squeezing hard.

"I don't have the hots for anybody," she said, slapping his hand away from her body.

"Does he have the hots for you?" Holiday asked.

"Maybe," she said.

"I want you to get close to that policeman. Give 'im head, fuck 'im, do whatever you gotta do. I wanna know whatever he knows about Beansy."

She brought her eyes up to Holiday's face, confused. "You know I don't do that stuff anymore."

Holiday slapped her, snapping her head against one of the stacked cartons. "You're goin' fuckin' do whatever I tell you to do." He reached under his shirt and slid a .38 Colt Detective Special out of his in-trouser holster. He grabbed her hair with his left hand, yanked her head back, and forced the revolver's barrel into her mouth. He cocked the hammer. "You don't do what I tell you, you're dead meat. Understand?"

Gagging, she managed to mumble, "Yes."

"Good." He uncocked the hammer and withdrew the revolver from her mouth. "My two friends here would like to find out if you can still ride that bicycle."

"Please, Paddy. Don't make me do that. I'll get close to Stuart, I promise."

Holiday adjusted his expression, smiled. "Oh, I guess everyone's entitled to one fuck-up. But, please, Andrea, work with me on this."

"I will, Paddy." At that moment she would have done anything to get out of the storeroom, just so that she could breathe and escape from the place where, she knew, she had touched death.

• • •

Daniel Lupo got up from behind his desk and walked out onto the terrace.

He was dressed in an immaculately tailored gray Armani suit, blue shirt, and dark blue tie. His suite of offices was on the twenty-sixth floor of the Chanin Building in Manhattan, across the street from the Grand Hyatt Hotel on Lexington Avenue and Forty-second Street.

He walked across the dark red tiles to his telescope and pressed his eye against its eyepiece, turning the focusing knob as he carefully scanned the windows of the hotel. The curtains in one of the bedrooms were split, a man and woman were in bed. The man was on top of her; her legs were wrapped around his hips, and she was gyrating wildly. Lupo's heart beat faster; he sharpened the focus. Finally tearing himself away from this free bit of entertainment, he muttered, "Back to work," and went back inside.

Frank "Frankie Bones" Marino sat on a leather sofa next to his nephew, Carmine, a thirty-eight-year-old MBA with manicured nails, dark wavy hair, and a dark business suit. An open attaché case lay on the sofa beside Carmine.

Lupo sat in his chair, still thinking of the couple across the street in the hotel. "What's on the agenda?"

A confident smile lit up Carmine's handsome face. "Those wires you ordered placed inside the law firms are beginning to pay off. Wiggham, Golden and Klein are working on the acquisition of the Lancaster Group by the Marcum Corporation."

"How far along are they?" Lupo asked, lacing his hands behind his head and leaning back.

"They're hoping to announce in about a month," Carmine said.

Lupo smiled out of one corner of his mouth. Installing wires in telephones, lamps, and chairs of the big law firms was one of his more brilliant ideas. He snapped forward, exchanging a satisfied smile with his great, thick-necked friend, whose forehead was pitted with acne scars. We've been together so long, we can hear each other's thoughts, he thought, picking up his eyeglasses from the desk and cleaning them with the bottom of his tie. "What did Lancaster open at today?"

"Thirty-four and five-eighths, down a quarter from yesterday," Carmine said.

"Has the stock been getting a lot of play?" Frankie Bones asked his nephew.

Carmine consulted his spreadsheet. "Nothing out of the ordinary."

Lupo put his glasses back on and said to Carmine, "I want you to start our offshore guys buying up Lancaster stock."

"How much do you want them to buy?" Carmine asked.

"As much as they can," Lupo said, noticing the gleam in the back of Carmine's dark eyes. "Any other deals ready to go?"

"There are a few things we should take a look at in a couple of months, but nothing right now," Carmine said, taking a stack of spreadsheets out of his attaché case. "Here are the profit statements on our video stores for August. Want me to go over them with you?"

"Put them on my desk, and then leave your uncle and me alone for a few minutes. We got some personal things to talk over."

"Of course," Carmine said. He placed the sheets on the desk and walked from the room.

When the door closed, Frankie Bones said, "I never trusted that kid."

"He's your brother's son, for crissake."

"That means blood, not trust."

Lupo's eyebrows rose quizzically, seeming to slide up his long, balding forehead. "What happened?"

Frankie Bones raised his stubby hands and let them fall onto his lap. "Holiday fucked up. He had two black guys drive Beansy to the meet. They go inside the house with him, one of them wised off, told Beansy no Italian was going to tell the Brothers how to spend their money. Beansy cold-cocks big-mouth, and the other nigger takes out a piece and shoots 'im. Afterward they realize they just whacked a made guy, they panic, and stuff 'im in the fuckin' icebox."

"You were supposed to be there to talk to Beansy when he got to the house."

"Danny, I got stuck in traffic on the damn bridge."

An exasperated sigh. "Do we know who these guys are?"

"Yeah, we know."

"Why are we still using Holiday? He ain't one of us, he's a cop."

"We use him to deal with the niggers, and he's got quality wires into the police department. Over the years his information has always been on the money. He saved us a lot of heartaches."

Lupo shook his head impatiently. "But we know his sources. They're all on our payroll."

"But they'll only deal through him."

"Do the cops have anything on Beansy?"

"No, they don't know shit. Holiday's on top of it, he'll keep us informed."

Lupo got up and prowled around the room, trying to see all the angles. "We've been washing dirty money into legit businesses for the past twenty years. I'd hate to see it blow up in our faces because of screw-ups in the street."

Frankie Bones responded confidently. "Ain't no way what happened in Pigtown is goin' to reach us here."

"It's already reached us here, Frankie Bones. You think we can afford to let a curly-headed nigger do one of our people and walk?"

"I guess we gotta do something."

"Yeah, and soon." Lupo sat down and played idly with a gold letter opener on his desk. "We're losing respect on the street. People we do business with are afraid, they don't know who can be trusted. Sammy Bull, the underboss, rolls over on John and testifies, he testifies against his boss. Unfucking heard of, I still can't believe it."

"I know, I know," Frankie Bones said, shaking his head in disbelief.

"We can steal more money with less risk by being legitimate, but we gotta maintain respect in the street."

"Whaddaya want me to do?"

Lupo had already come to a decision. "I want you to take both of them out, I want it done now, and I want it done messy."

"You want I should use our people?"

"I want you to coordinate the hit. Use our people to stalk them, but bring in a 'Dixie cup' to do the job, someone we can toss away in case there's a problem. That way we wouldn't have to take out one of our own."

"Done like a dinner."

Lupo reached into the humidor on his desk and took out a cigar. He lit it slowly, his eyes fixed on Frankie Bones. "How's the other thing going?"

"We're almost ready to move. I'm worried, Danny. Too many people know about this thing." Frankie's big, bald, oversize head retracted between his shoulders as he instinctively assumed a defensive posture. His shrewd, piglike eyes glittered with menace.

Lupo tried to reassure him. "I know, but we can handle it."

"Remember, we're talking serious money here. We were supposeta take part of the shit out of the Queens plant and hide it in the cheese factory. It's too risky leaving it all in one place. Now what are we gonna do without Beansy? He was the key to this whole thing."

"I've been thinkin' on that. I figure we're gonna have to deal with Beansy's niece, Angela."

Frankie's expression conveyed his doubts. "She's straight, and besides, she hates our guts."

"Ain't nobody that straight. I'll feed her a line of shit and offer her three or four grand a week. Our old friend greed will bring her around."

"It's worth a shot. Maybe she still got the hots for you?"

"That was a long time ago."

Frankie Bones lit a cigarette and tossed the match into the onyx ashtray. He looked at Lupo and said, "Sammy the Milkman called earlier."

Lupo's tongue fished a sliver of tobacco from between his front teeth. "How is our milk hijacker?" he asked.

"He grabbed a load of liquid milk off the turnpike last night and unloaded it at the bottler in Glendale. Like always, he drove the empty tanker to the docks, where it was supposeta be loaded onto one of Charlie Kee's ships. The Chinaman pays us sixty grand for the tanker and then sells it in China for two hundred and fifty K."

"Ain't capitalism wonderful," Lupo said, holding the cigar under his nose, savoring the aroma.

"The problem is that the ship that was supposeta take the tanker truck back to China broke down. She's carrying a bunch of boat-jumping Chinamen that gotta be unloaded somewhere along the East Coast, so by the time they're ready it'll be another week and a half. The cops and the milk company are searching high and low for the tanker truck. It ain't easy stashin' a big thing like that." He dragged on his cigarette and said, "The Milkman wants us to hide it until the ship gets here."

Lupo got up and walked over to the sliding doors that led out onto the terrace. He stared out at his telescope, lost in thought. "Tell me about those liquid tanker trucks."

"They're shiny oval tubes sitting on top of an eighteen-wheel flatbed. They got their own refrigeration unit and valves in the back that pump out the milk."

As his mind raced, Lupo said absentmindedly, "The guy in Glendale sells the milk to large discount food chains, right?"

"Yeah. All those big outfits got their own labels."

"How do they load the milk into the tanker?"

"Through a hatch on top of the tanker."

"How big is this hatch?"

"I don't know exactly, but it's big enough for a man to climb inside. Federal health regulations make them disinfect the inside after each load."

Lupo walked away from the sliding doors and crossed the room to the sofa. He sat down next to his friend. "I've been thinking that we oughta find another way to ship the shit to Camacho in Chicago. We've been using those moving vans too long. We could ship the stuff inside the tanker. In a week and a half we could make two, maybe three trips. That way if some-thing should happen, we'd only take a hit on one load."

"I like that idea, Danny," Frankie Bones said. "We'd need clean paper on the tanker, but that ain't no problem." He leaned over the arm of the sofa and crushed the cigarette in the ashtray. "How we gonna stop the stuff from sliding all over the inside of the tanker, maybe breakin' open?"

"We could wedge in some wood around the sides of the load, or build some kinda corral to hold the stuff in place, or we could just lay each wheel flat and wrap them up in bubbly plastic or something."

"Yeah. It should work. Let's do it." He turned sideways and looked at Lupo. "On that other thing, the dreadlock crew might get pissed when we ice their brothers. Could get messy, bad for business."

"If the hit creates a problem, we'll deal with it. But they gotta go. And the bottom line is we're all businessmen. So if there's a problem, we'll just negotiate. I want you to leave now and take care of it. And Frankie, make sure it's messy."

Frankie Bones got up off the sofa and waddled toward the door.

Lupo took off his glasses and called after his friend, "Send in that nephew of yours, I'm going to give him a fast course in longer living."

He leaned back and closed his eyes, gently rubbing the lids with his forefingers, his thoughts on the screwing couple across the street. As soon as he finished here he was going to call up Terry and tell her to get ready for him. He wanted to be lashed hands and feet to the bed. He wanted pain, a lot of it. He heard Carmine come in but continued massaging his eyelids as he patted the empty space next to him on the sofa. He opened his eyes, put on his glasses, and said, "When I told you to start buy-ing Lancaster I saw a bulb go on in your eyes, like maybe you fig-ured you'd pick up a few shares on the sly for yourself."

"I'd never do anything like that, Danny, you know that."

"I know nothing. You realize that the SEC checks all stock

transactions in the U.S., so if you did start buying up Lancaster before the deal was announced, some guys wearing black shoes with thick soles would be around to ask you where you got your information from."

"I swear, the thought never entered my mind."

Lupo dusted his palms together. "You like to go mountain climbing?"

Carmine's lip twitched. "Mountain climbing?"

"Yeah. Along the mid-Atlantic Range. Know where that is?"

He squirmed in his seat. "No."

"It's east of Miami, about two and a half miles down in the Atlantic. The last guy who had your job figured he'd go into business for himself in Grand Cayman using our information, so when he arrived back in Miami, we sent him and his family mountain climbing."

Carmine felt a piercing sensation of terror. Beads of sweat popped out at his hairline. "Swear to God, Danny, I don't even think about doing that kind of crazy stuff."

Lupo lifted a palm in his direction and said, "I'm glad we understand each other."

After Carmine fled the office, Lupo picked up his phone and dialed his girlfriend, Terry.

The facade of the flat-roofed building on Rangoon Street was stucco, and the two loading bays had curtains of thick translucent plastic slats, hung like venetian blinds, to cut down on the loss of refrigeration when trucks were being loaded and unloaded. The factory was in Jersey City, New Jersey, about one mile west of Liberty State Park and an hour's drive from the precinct. On a clear day, Manhattan's ragged skyline ringed the horizon.

Detective Helen Kahn had driven the whip there in one of the Squad's unmarked cars. They did not talk much during the fifty-minute ride from Pigtown. Both of them were lost in their own thoughts: she, thinking about Kirby and their nonrelationship; Stuart, lost in his own recriminations over his failed marriage.

Kahn drove the car into the parking lot on the side of the building. The sign stretching across the top of the loading bays read "The Albertoli Company." She parked the car; they walked around to the front of the building. Railroad tracks ran down the middle of the street.

Stuart looked at the barrel-vaulted facade of the Science Center off in the distance. The double-door entrance of the Albertoli Company led into a large office, where three women sat at desks with stacks of ledgers piled in front of them. A handsome woman in her late forties, with steel gray hair wrapped in a bun in the back, looked away from her computer.

"May I help you?" she asked the strangers.

"I'm Lieutenant Matt Stuart, and this is Detective Helen Kahn. We'd like to speak with whoever is in charge," Stuart said, holding up his shield and ID card.

She picked up the telephone and said calmly to the person who answered, "They're here." Returning the receiver, she looked at Stuart and said, "Someone'll be with you shortly."

We were expected, Stuart thought, looking around. The office was decorated tastefully with beige carpet and sofas of brown Italian leather. Oil paintings adorned the walls. Stuart walked over to admire a landscape.

Inside an office on the other side of the aisle from the bookkeepers, a woman applied fresh lipstick. She snapped her compact closed, left the office, and walked up behind the detectives.

"Hello, I'm Angela Albertoli," she said. "Please follow me."

She led them into her office. A large oil of a park with two white swans on a glistening pond was hung on the wall behind her desk. She waved toward the sofa and sat in the chair behind her desk. She shook a cigarette out of the pack and lit it with her gold Gucci lighter.

Stuart said, "We're here because—"

"I know damn well why you're here, Lieutenant," Angela said, blowing a stream of smoke into the air. "You're here because my name ends in a vowel."

"We're here because Beansy Rutolo was murdered, and we have information that he owned this company," Stuart said.

"Well, I'm here to tell you that you heard wrong, Lieutenant," Angela said, and dragged deeply on her cigarette. "Albertoli was founded by my grandfather at the turn of the century. When he died, my mother and her brother inherited the business. But my uncle, Anthony Rutolo, AKA Beansy to you people, wanted nothing to do with the running of the company. He preferred being a gangster. So he sold his rights in the business for a percentage of the profits to be paid out over his lifetime." Looking at them defiantly, she slowly stubbed out her cigarette in a large crystal ashtray. "My mother and father built Albertoli into what it is today. My uncle had nothing whatever to do with the operation of this company."

Kahn crossed and uncrossed her legs. "Did he ever come here?"

She shook her head. "He respected my parents' wishes and stayed away. He knew damn well all the trouble he caused us over the years."

"What trouble?" Stuart asked.

"My uncle was a soldier in the Gambino crime family," she said, bitterness creeping into her voice. "The FBI and the police were always trying to connect Albertoli to organized crime. For years the IRS audited our books each year. It got so bad that our lawyers and accountants wanted us to drop Albertoli for a generic name. My parents and I refused."

Stuart leaned forward in his seat. "We're not suggesting that your company is involved in anything illegal. We're trying to solve your uncle's murder, nothing more."

Angela's expression betrayed her mounting anger. "My uncle died like he lived, a gangster, a disgrace to his family. I'm not even closing the plant because of his death, and I'm not going to the wake. I'll go to his funeral only out of respect for my mother."

"Are your parents still active in the business?" Stuart asked.

"My parents are retired," Angela said. "My dad pops in every now and then."

Stuart asked, "Does the name Andrea Russo sound familiar?"

"No, it doesn't. My uncle wasn't the type of man to discuss his life with anyone." She looked at her wristwatch. "If there is nothing else, I have a business lunch and I don't want to be late."

"Sure, no problem. Thank you for your time," Stuart said, standing. "There is one thing," he said, looking at her sheepishly. "I'm a real cheese addict, but I don't know a thing about how it's made. Wonder if you would be kind enough to have one of your people show us around the plant?"

"Yeah, I'd like to see it, too," Kahn chimed in.

Angela looked at him, trying to decide what she was going to do. She opened her Bottega pocketbook, dropped in her cigarette lighter, closed the bag, pushed back her chair, and said, "I'll show you around." She led them back into the outer office and through a door that emptied into a cavernous warehouse, where the air was heavy with the earthy smell of cheese.

Stuart inhaled deeply, savoring the pungent aromas. "I love that smell," he said.

She smiled knowingly. "Yes, it does get to you after a while."

Stuart watched forklifts glide up and down the stacked skids of cheese forms, carrying the molds in which, Angela explained, the cheeses were made. Other men pushed hand jacks stacked with cartons of cheese.

Angela put her palms on her hips and said, "We have twenty thousand square feet, nine thousand of which is taken up by refrigeration. Each refrigerator has its own backup compressor. We can't afford breakdowns."

"I understood that Albertoli is the sole importer in this country for Bolonia cheese," Stuart said, looking around the plant.

"Yes indeed." Angela seemed pleased by his genuine interest. "Our family and the owners of Bolonia have been friends since our grandfathers were boys together."

They strolled among skids of cheese. Kahn walked over to a pile of cheese on the floor that appeared to have been dumped.

"That stuff goes to the undertakers," Angela said. She scooped up a package from the pile and held it up to them. The wedge had mold on it. "When we receive a shipment from Italy, we check each piece. Sometimes the cheese is bruised or molded. Everything that is shipped out of here has to be perfect, so we set the bruised stuff aside and sell it to the undertaker." She smiled at their puzzlement. "That's the name the trade has given to the people who buy damaged cheese."

"What do the undertakers do with it?" Stuart asked.

"They cut off the blemishes and bad mold, then sell it to large cheese companies who repack it and resell it as processed cheese to supermarkets around the country. Those cheese sticks, and thin slices you see in stores, come from undertakers," Angela said.

Stuart noticed how relaxed and confident she was when talking about her business. He wanted to keep her talking. "Cheese is big business, I guess."

The cheese queen smiled broadly. "Five million pounds of it is purchased by American consumers annually. I'd call that big."

"Me, too," Kahn agreed.

Angela said, "Most of the cheese production in the States is done by independents. Most of the big-name cheese companies do not produce cheese. They buy it all at the Green Bay Exchange."

"In Wisconsin?" Kahn asked.

"Yes. The Green Bay Exchange is where the independents sell their cheese to the industry," Angela said, plucking a package off a skid and handing it to Stuart, who, holding it in his palms, inhaled its strong aroma.

"That's pecorino Romano. It's very sharp," said the cheese queen. "Pecorino means sheep, and Romano means Roman style."

"So it's Roman-style cheese made from sheep milk," Kahn said, sliding her hand inside her blouse and adjusting the shoulder strap of her bra.

"How do they make cheese?" Stuart asked.

"I haven't the time to go into the fine details," Angela said, "but basically, the better cheeses are made from sheep milk that is boiled in large vats, separating the curd from the whey. The curd falls to the bottom of the vat, leaving the whey, which is drained off, leaving the curd. A starter is then added to the curd."

"A starter?" Stuart asked.

"A catalyst that turns the curd into different kinds of cheeses," Angela told him.

"What do they use?" Kahn asked.

Angela shrugged. "Depends on the kind of cheese they're making. It can be anything from the bacteria in a deer gut to potato skins. It's the enzymes of the catalyst that reproduce, creating the different kinds of cheeses. Manufacturers continue to regrow the bacteria in the enzymes from generation to generation. Some of them last for as long as five hundred years."

Stuart's brow furrowed. "Those starters must be closely guarded secrets."

"They are," she said. "It's the starters that make the tunnels in Swiss cheese and give our pecorino Romano its sharp, pungent taste."

"I guess there are a lot of people who'd pay big bucks to get their hands on the Bolonia starters," Stuart said.

"They're closely guarded in Italy," Angela said confidently. She looked at her wristwatch. "I really have to go to lunch now."

"Thank you for your time, and your help," Stuart said, walking beside her toward the door, pretending to watch the skids of cheese being driven out of one of the refrigerators.

Denny's Gym occupied the entire second floor above a group of boarded-up stores on President Street, on the easternmost tip of the Seven One Precinct. The gym's discolored green walls and peeling ceiling added to the shabbiness of the place. Four boxing rings dominating the center of the floor had sagging ropes and badly worn canvas floors. The speed bags were threadbare; old fight cards adorned the walls, along with glossy photographs of forgotten contenders. Generations of stale sweat filled the air. Despite the shabbiness, Denny's was still the threshold place for the neighborhood boys to come to, to try to realize their dreams of escaping the neighborhood and its poverty.

Manny Rodriguez shadowboxed in front of the faded wall mirror. Perspiration soiled his sweats and coursed down his face. Three left jabs, a right cross, all the time fantasizing he was a middleweight contender. Champion. One day he was going to be champion, he was going to have it all, money, fame, pussy. He was only nineteen, and he'd already had four professional wins with no losses. He bobbed, weaved, his curly black hair jouncing as he ducked under an imaginary right and countered with his left uppercut, his eyes all the time fixed on his own reflection.

Suddenly he caught sight of the Hippo watching him from across the room. His eyes narrowed as their eyes met. He wondered how long he'd been there watching him work out. Manny threw two fast jabs and followed with a straight right to the face, then stepped over to the rickety chair against the wall and snapped his towel off the back. Walking across the gym toward the locker room, wiping his face and neck, he wondered what kind of job the Hippo had for him this time. The last time he was paid five hundred bucks to do some collection work for a shylock. Collection had been expedited by a bat to the welsher's kneecap.

As he walked into the dingy locker room, he heard the Hippo's raspy voice call him from behind a row of lockers, "Back here, kid."

A short, muscular man with a thick neck, small gray eyes, and a flattened nose with enormous nostrils, the Hippo was leaning up against a locker when Manny walked into the aisle. "You looked like a real contender out there, kid," the Hippo said, throwing a right cross that Manny slipped easily and countered with a right-hand tap on the Hippo's thick chin.

"You got the speed, the reflexes, the power, and you got heart. You got it all, kid, including the most important thing, the right friends."

"All I need now are the right fights."

The Hippo pretended to have hurt feelings. "Hey, ain't we moving you along? Didn't we fix you up with four easy ones?"

"Yeah, and I'm really grateful, but I wanna make a big payday."

The Hippo moved closer, whispered, "We got a little job for you that'll earn you big."

Manny picked up one end of the towel that he had slung around his neck and wiped his face. "What kinda job?"

"We want you to whack a couple of niggers."

"Who are they?"

"'It's not important. What's important is that it's gotta be done now."

"You mean like right away?"

"Yeah, kid, right away—like now. It's in the neighborhood." The Hippo slid a slip of yellow paper out of his pants pocket and opened it, spreading the crudely drawn map across a locker door. "De're gonna be in a nigger joint named Dreamland, on Nostrand Avenue, between Union and President. We're gonna have blocking cars here on Union, and here on President." He moved his stubby forefinger over the blocking locations. "We got people stalking 'em now." He looked at his heavy gold watch. "Dey should be in Dreamland in about forty minutes. We got someone across the street who'll give you the high sign dat de're inside the joint. You do a drive-by, when you get the go-ahead, drive around the block, we got someone who'll dial 911 and say a cop's in a gunfight at the other end of the precinct. Dat'll make all the cop cars go barrel-assin' to the other end of the precinct, leaving you plenty of time to go in and do what ya gotta do."

Manny's cool, professional eyes studied the map. The sounds of speed bags echoed off the metal lockers. "Equipment?"

"Everything ya gonna need is in a bag under the seat of the old Buick parked across the street in front of the bodega."

Manny looked the Hippo straight in the eye. "Revolvers, right?"

"Of course. Pros never use automatics. The fuckin' things always jam when you need 'em most."

"Who's the wheelman?"

"Don't worry about who, just know he's the best. We got a time problem here, dat's what you gotta worry about. Dese two guys are gonna be alone for about twenty minutes before the rest of their nigger friends show up. You gotta get in, do the job, and be outta there before the others show."

"How much time do we have?"

The Hippo looked at his watch. "It's two now. They get to Dreamland about two twenty-five each day."

"Who are these *pescados*?" Manny asked, using the Spanish word for dead fish.

The Hippo slid his hand into his jogging suit and pulled out an envelope, which he passed to the contender.

Manny opened the flap and took out two police department mug shots of Hollyman and Gee. "Official cop pictures; I'm impressed." He looked up at the Hippo. "What are ya payin'?"

"Three big ones." The Hippo lowered his voice to a hoarse near whisper. "Our people don't want them to look nice. You got two pieces in the bag under the seat. They're both loaded with exploding rounds. *Make 'em messy corpses.*"

Manny looked at the mug shots. "They musta pissed some-body off big time."

"Yeah, kid, big time."

The wheelman was another "Dixie cup" about the same age as Manny. His black sideburns had been razor cut above his ears, and he was wearing an expensive black leather coat. As soon as the contender slid into the car, the wheelman drove out of the space. The early afternoon traffic was light. The two men didn't say a word to each other. The driver kept his eyes on the road while Manny pulled the bag out from under the seat and opened it: two Colt .38s and a brown baseball cap.

"There's a empty pizza box on the backseat," the driver said, "in case you wanna use a prop."

Most of the abandoned buildings they drove past were cinder-blocked shut. Junkies congregated around crack houses while lookouts searched out strangers. When the driver turned into Rutland Road, it was as if they had passed into a different country, with tree-shaded streets and large, well-tended houses set way back from the curb, surrounded by lush, manicured lawns. Women wearing designer clothes and ritual wigs pushed baby carriages and sat on porches, drinking tea. This part of the Seven One was where the Hasidim lived.

Three blocks later they were driving through the Hispanic section, where men in undershirts played curbside checkers and Latin music blared from tenement windows. Manny spotted a burrito joint.

"I wanna get something to eat; pull over and stop. It'll only take me a minute." The driver did as he was told. Manny opened the door and hurried into the restaurant. He came walking out a short time later, eating a burrito wrapped in aluminum foil and holding two more in his free hand.

Dreamland was in the middle of a rundown block on Nostrand Avenue, shoehorned between a minisupermarket and a travel agency. The club's facade was black marble, with one small window fringed in tiny green blinking bulbs. As they drove past, the wheelman lifted his chin toward a man sitting on a stoop across the street from Dreamland.

"There's our lookout."

Manny bit into his second burrito and glanced at the man on the stoop. He was young and, unlike Manny and the driver, black. Sporting spiked pigtails, he fit perfectly into the neighborhood scene. A Walkman was plugged into his ears, and he was holding it in his hand, swaying to the rap. Manny tried to spot the blocking cars but couldn't. The wheelman drove around the block; he took a walkie-talkie out from under his seat and, pressing the transmit button, said, "Yo, ma man, talk to me."

Swaying to the rap music, the man with the spiked pigtail said into his Walkman, "They're inside, and alone. When you hear the sirens, go. But make it quick, 'fore the rest of the brothers get there."

The wheelman drove around the corner to New York Avenue and parked, with the motor running.

Manny bit into his burrito. He was always surprised when he did a job for the Hippo that he never got nervous or excited the way he did whenever he climbed into the ring. My heart don't even beat fast, he thought, listening to the rising crescendo of police sirens. The *whoosh* of sirens rose from parallel streets and then slowly died away as the patrol cars sped to the radio code ten-thirteen, assist patrolman. Manny pulled the bag out from under the seat, looked at the wheelman, and said, "Drive around the corner and double-park a few doors down from the bar," lifting the bottom of his T-shirt and tucking one .38 into the waistband of his jeans. He put on the baseball cap with the sun visor in front and reached behind to take the pizza box off the backseat. He raised the cover and put the second revolver in the empty box, taking care that the grip was facing him.

The wheelman double-parked a few doors down from Dreamland. Manny took a final look at the police mug shot of Hollyman and Gee. He got out of the car, palming the pizza box in his left hand, holding the last burrito in his right. Stepping into the doorway, he took a fast bite and tossed away the remainder.

Hollyman and Gee were sitting alone at the bar. The place smelled of cleaning disinfectant. The sudden rush of sunlight caused the two men at the bar to look over their shoulders at the stranger. "What the fuck you doin' here, white boy?" Hollyman snarled.

"Somebody called, ordered a pizza *con mucho* chiz," Manny said, affecting a Spenglish accent and moving closer to his victims.

"Hold it right there, ma man," Gee said, sliding off his stool. "Nobody here ordered no pizza."

Manny slid his right hand into the box, curled his fingers around the checkered grip, and fired, hitting Gee in the chest and hurling him backward against the bar, where he crumpled to the floor. Hollyman made a desperate attempt to dive behind the bar. The shooter's second round caught him in midair, splaying him across the top. Manny yanked the revolver from the box, ran up to them, and fired two rounds behind Hollyman's ear, exploding his face. Gee's eyes were open, his body thrashing on the dirty floor as his life's blood emptied from his mouth. Leaning down, Manny held the .38 a few inches from Gee's right eye and fired two rounds. When the head blew open, brains splattered over Manny's legs. He scraped the gore off with the box, tucked the .38 into his waistband next to the one he had not had to use, and hurried from the bar, anxious to get back to the gym.

5

During the drive back from Jersey City through the Holland Tunnel, Kahn glanced at the whip and asked, "What's the story with that fight poster in your office? Did you know any of those fighters?"

"Al 'Bummy' Davis was a friend of my dad's." He did not tell her that the nickname "Bummy" stood for Bum, or that Bummy Davis had been paid to take a dive in the Graziano fight but instead got pissed off at Graziano in the third round and knocked out the contender with a straight to the jaw.

The Sunday that Matt's father left his family in Junior's restaurant to go to work was the day that the wiseguys caught up with Bummy. Matt's dad had finished his tour and was driving home when he came down with diarrhea. He shouldn't have gorged on Junior's pickles. He looked across the street, saw Russo's, and decided to double-park, run in, and use the toilet. Bummy Davis was at the bar, bragging about his knockout, when a man wearing dark glasses entered and shot Bummy twice in the back of the head.

Patrolman Stuart came running out of the toilet just in time to see the shooter running out of the bar. He got outside and looked down the street, only to see the getaway car speeding off. He ran to his car, jumped in, and tried to give chase, but his engine wouldn't turn over, so he leaped out and ran after the getaway car on foot. He stopped after a fruitless block and returned to the bar.

The Palace Guard was furious that Patrolman Joe Stuart had been inside a known gamblers' hangout a week before Christmas. To the schemers and plotters of the Job, the only reason for a cop being in a joint like Russo's at that time of the year was to pick up a holiday gift for himself.

Russo's Christmas money had always been picked up by the captain's bagman and, after being lumped together with the rest of the holiday money, distributed up the chain of command. Anyone who tried to make a score on his own was considered a renegade and a troublemaker.

The schemers and plotters did a round-robin and consulted the "F File" on Joe Stuart. The word came back loud and clear: He was an honest cop who did not eat or shop on the arm or participate in the Job's Christmas tradition. The Palace Guard decided that even if he was honest, he shouldn't have been inside Russo's, so they decided to take a piece out of Joe Stuart and served him with charges and specifications charging him with cowardice.

No other cop in the history of the NYPD had ever been so charged. Matt's father was suspended from duty. The newspapers picked up on the story and turned it into a headline. "Stuart's father is a coward," Matt's classmates taunted him, goading him into fight after fight.

The department trial was held in the Seven Eight Precinct's ornate trial room. The Palace Guard offered a plea bargain: cop out to failure to take proper police action and be restored to duty with the loss of fifteen days' vacation. Joe Stuart told them to shove it.

On the third day of the department trial the defense called a surprise witness, one Beansy Rutolo. He testified that he saw Patrolman Stuart give chase, try to start his car, then leap out and run after the speeding vehicle. Joe Stuart was acquitted. But the damage had been done. For the remainder of his time in the

Job, other cops would look funny at him and walk stiff-legged around him, wondering if he really had taken police action. The scandal stuck to Matt, too, all through high school and followed him onto the Job.

Beansy had not only saved his dad's job, he also had prevented the family from breaking up the way most dismissed cops' families did. What none of the detectives in his squad would ever know was that Stuart owed Beansy big time. Now was his chance to repay the debt in full measure.

Kahn had just driven past the Prospect Park Zoo when Borrelli's curt voice crackled over the radio. "Lou."

Stuart keyed the mike. "Yeah?"

"Location?"

"The zoo."

"Eighty-five at N and U."

"On the way." Stuart cradled the receiver, wondering what they were going to find at Nostrand Avenue and Union Street.

A radio motor patrol car, its flashing bar light painting the street with red and yellow hues, was parked in the middle of the intersection, its two-man crew on foot, detouring traffic. A stretch of yellow crime scene tape formed a restrictive cordon around Dreamland's entrance. A black patrol sergeant and three policemen manned the police line, calming the angry crowd of Rastafarians.

Kahn pulled up next to the crime scene station wagon. As Stuart was getting out of the car, he spotted Jones talking to a group of Rastafarians. The detective was wearing his customary African hat and scarf, his face a mask of calm that was at odds with his tense body language.

The bodies inside Dreamland had no faces; only jagged shards of bone and clotted gore remained. A photographer was snapping pictures. Stuart bent to examine the body next to the bar. Borrelli walked out from behind the bar and came over to the whip.

Stuart glanced up at him. "Do we know who they are?"

"We found no ID on them, but we think they're Paddy Holiday's friends, Hollyman and Gee."

"Any witnesses?"

Borrelli scratched his head and replied, "We got three people who were coming out of the market, next door. They saw a white guy, maybe Hispanic, wearing a brown cap and holding a pizza box, get out of a car and walk in here. None of them can agree on his age, height, or weight. Only that he was young and had an olive complexion. I had them driven to the Squad to work on a composite with the department artist."

"Anything on the car or the driver?" Stuart asked, standing up and stretching, his hands pressing into the small of his back to relieve his tension.

"An old Buick or Chevy, blue, black, New York plates. The driver was a young white male with razor-cut sideburns."

"There's some dental work left on this one," Kahn said, examining the body splayed across the bar.

Stuart watched the crime scene detective dusting the bar for prints. "Who's doing the canvass?"

"The borough flew in six detectives to help out. EMS pronounced, and the ME is not going to respond," Borrelli said.

The same two morgue attendants who had responded to Beansy's homicide were standing at the far end of the bar, waiting.

Borrelli said, "Just before this thing went down, a phony thirteen was phoned in to 911."

"A cop in trouble at the other end of the precinct, right?" Stuart said with a cynical edge.

"Yeah. This was no nickel-and-dime hit," Borrelli said angrily, watching Jones walk into Dreamland to join them.

The big detective came over to the whip, looked down at the headless corpse, and said, "According to my Rastafarian brothers, these faceless decedents were Hollyman and Gee. Whoever washed them knew their schedules, because they came here every day to talk business, and were only alone here for a short period of time."

"Does any of the Posse know who did it and why?" Stuart asked.

"They be knowing, but they ain't tellin'," Jones said. "Some of the Rasties told me that they saw some wiseguy types parked in cars at Union and President and Nostrand. I figure they were the crash cars to protect the shooter's getaway."

Stuart nodded and strolled off, examining the crime scene. As he walked outside into the small entryway, a glint of something on the ground caught his eye: a half-eaten burrito in an aluminum sleeve. He bent down beside the sandwich. It looked fresh, so he poked at it gingerly to make sure.

He looked out at the crowd gathered behind the police line, for the most part black and poor, and thought, There ain't nobody in this part of town throwing away a half-eaten burrito; most of 'em don't know where their next meal is coming from, and there are no burrito joints in this part of the Seven One. I bet this belonged to the shooter; he was in a hurry because he had to do them before any of the Posse showed up, so he took a fast bite and tossed the rest before he went inside. Stuart called inside to the photographer, "Take some shots of this burrito."

A crime scene unit detective came over with a plastic evidence bag and tweezed the burrito into it. Borrelli entered the newly found evidence into the crime scene evidence log. Watching him do this, Stuart suddenly felt almost sure that this hit was payback for Beansy.

Jerry Jordon walked into Dreamland, came over to the whip, and said, "The witnesses are driving the artist nuts. They can't even agree on the shape of the shooter's head."

"So much for eyewitnesses," Stuart said in disgust.

Jordon said in a low, confidential tone, "Lou, while I was back in the squad room Patrick Sarsfield Casey phoned. He wants you to call him back in the borough."

Stuart motioned his detectives into a huddle. "I want you to stay here and do another canvass. Try and find some people who can ID the guy who got out of that car and came in here. I got a feeling on this one. If we work fast, we just might get lucky. I'm going to take the burrito to the Latent Squad and see if they can lift any prints off that aluminum." He looked at Kahn. "Helen, I want you to bang out the 'Unusual,' and when you fax it up the chain, include Beansy's 'Unusual.'"

"You want we should drag Paddy Holiday in for a heart-to-heart?" Jordon asked.

"That would be a waste of time," Stuart said. "He's only going to talk when we have his balls in a vise."

Stuart went over to the crime scene log and signed out the burrito: name, rank, time, description of property, destination, reason for taking evidence. He took a manila property clerk envelope out of the portable clerical case and put the burrito inside.

A sudden rain shower drummed on the windshield as Stuart inched his unmarked car through the traffic crawling over the Brooklyn Bridge into Manhattan. He unhooked the cellular telephone from the car's console and scrolled through the speed-dial memory bank until he came to Detective Borough Command Brooklyn South. He pressed the send button. A gruff voice answered, "Brooklyn South Detectives."

"Patrick Sarsfield Casey, please." He smiled to himself, thinking, The Job won't be the same without Casey in it.

The inspector's booming voice came onto the line.

"Matt Stuart, Inspector."

"Those homicides you're catching are tossing my clearances into the toilet. You gonna break any of them?"

"I got a feeling we're going to hit a home run on both homicides. It figures that Hollyman and Gee were payback for Beansy. There's a possibility we might have come up with the perp's prints on some aluminum we found at the scene. If we grab the shooter fast, we have a good shot at getting the paymaster."

"Good, that's the kind of shit I like to hear from my squad

bosses." Casey's voice lowered to a conspiratorial whisper. "The c of d wants a favor."

"What?"

"He'd like you to pick up a detective from Pickpocket and Confidence. The guy's name is Paul Whitehouser."

Stuart clamped his jaw. The chief of detectives was dumping a detective from one of the Detective Division's most sought-after plums into a shithouse. "What's the problem?"

"He can't keep his dick in his pants."

"Boss, I run a busy shop, I don't need any more headaches," Stuart said.

"Hey, Matt, get with the program. This is a command performance. The c of d is only going through the motions of asking."

"Where's Whitehouser's weight?"

"He's the c of d's nephew."

"That's just great," Matt said, and pressed the off button, wondering what the real story was on Whitehouser. He was glad the Latent Squad was in One Police Plaza. He'd pay a visit to the Ice Maiden and get the real lowdown on the newest member of his squad. He reached across the seat for the property clerk envelope.

Lieutenant Bill Manning, a tweedy guy with an affection for bow ties and briar pipes, was the whip of the Latent Squad, the unit responsible for matching up fingerprints developed at crime scenes with the prints of the mutts who left them. He was standing inside his corner cubicle, puffing furiously on his pipe, when Stuart walked in. "Matt, how are you?" he asked, extending his hand. "What brings you to the Big Building?"

"I hear you fingerprint wizards have developed a way of lifting latents off aluminum foil."

"Yeah," Manning said proudly. "We got something real new. Why?"

Stuart showed him the evidence bag containing the burrito. "This is from a warm homicide."

"How come you're playing errand boy and not one of your

detectives?" he asked, watching Stuart through the swirl of pipe smoke.

"Because every one of my people is in the field working cases."

Manning bit down on his stem, nodded, and said, "Let's go."

He led Stuart outside and down a wide aisle lined on both sides with computer terminals manned by technicians conducting split-screen fingerprint comparisons. He opened a steel fire door halfway down the aisle and motioned Stuart inside. It was a large room, with counters bracketed to the walls. The space in the center of the room was empty. The walls and ceiling were blanketed in buff-colored firebricks, and a metallurgical oven was embedded in the wall to the right of the entrance. Four large black dials ran down the oven's right side, and a thick glass window allowed technicians to look inside the oven. Atomizers and Bunsen burners were on the counters. Five gray metal supply lockers stood against the wall opposite the oven. A window air conditioner hummed softly.

A beautiful black woman in her early thirties, wearing an open lab coat over a pleated beige skirt and black sweater, was sitting at one of the counters examining a fingerprint through a linen tester. A gold ankh cross hung around her neck.

"Della, this is Lieutenant Matt Stuart from the Seven One Squad," Manning said. "Matt, this is Detective Della Johnston, our resident expert on lifting prints off aluminum."

She smiled at Stuart. "Hi, Lou."

Manning handed her the evidence bag. "Do me a favor and see if you can lift anything off the foil."

She slid off the stool and signed the evidence into the property log. After concluding the official entry, she took the bag containing the burrito out of the envelope and placed it on the counter. Using a slender probe with scissor grips and a flat clamp end, she tweezed the burrito out of the plastic Ziploc bag. She placed it down on a big piece of filter paper on the counter and, using toothpicks, gingerly moved the tapered slivers of wood along the foil's folds, unwrapping the sleeve just enough to be able to slide out the sandwich. With exaggerated delicacy, she pinched the end of the burrito with the probe and slid it out of its aluminum sleeve. Then she took the forceps and placed the remainder of the burrito on another piece of paper.

Stuart glanced out the window. The Horace Greeley monument in front of the surrogate court was white with bird droppings. The afternoon sun softened the edges of City Hall and the Woolworth Building in a warm golden haze.

Della went over to the row of supply lockers, opened the one second from the left, and came back with a handful of green-and-white capsules containing tubes of Krazy Glue. She unscrewed a capsule and shook out the tube and the green-crowned piercing needle. After unscrewing the cap, she pierced the tube's seal and squeezed the glue into a beaker. After doing that to the remaining tubes, she slid the beaker onto one of the Bunsen burners.

Stuart watched as the hot blue flame melted the clear glue into liquid. Della tugged on a baking mitt, took the beaker off the Bunsen burner, and poured the liquid into an atomizer. Next she picked up a ruler off the counter and inserted it inside the foil sleeve. Holding the ruler out in front of her, she carefully sprayed the liquid glue over the aluminum sheet.

Leaning in close to Matt Stuart, Manning confided, "We discovered that liquid Krazy Glue sticks to fingerprint oil."

After spraying the sheet, Della brought the foil over to the metallurgical oven and opened the hatch. She stuck her hand inside the oven and inserted the sleeve of aluminum onto a porcelain rod protruding up from the oven's floor. She closed the hatch and turned two dials.

After about five minutes, she turned off the oven and opened the hatch. The liquid glue had oxidized into gray ash adhering to the friction ridges of three fingers—two whorls and one loop.

"Now what?" Stuart asked Manning.

Manning said, "Now we use enhanced imagery to develop a photograph of the fingerprints, and then we go visit my friend AFIS to find out who those prints belong to."

"How long is that going to take?" Stuart asked, watching Della carry over a tripod-mounted camera with a long, bulbous lens.

"About thirty minutes to develop a photograph," Della said.

"I have to go to Personnel. I'll be back in a half hour," Stuart said.

One of the responsibilities charged by the NYPD's *Organizational Guide* to the commanding officer, Personnel Bureau is to establish and maintain standards of performance, accountability, and productivity for operational and supervisory personnel. In order to fulfill this duty, CO Personnel maintains the "Fucked File," or "F File," as it is sometimes referred to. These folders contain unsubstantiated allegations of misconduct, gossip, rumors, and hearsay against members of the service. Before any member is transferred or promoted, an official round-robin is made through the various Internal Affairs and Intelligence units within the Job, searching out any derogatory information against the member concerned. The F File is always consulted unofficially and in person by an authorized member above the rank of sergeant. Only the CO Personnel has the authority to add to or excise information from the F File, and this access makes CO Personnel a feared and powerful member of the Palace Guard elite.

Stuart stepped off the elevator on the twelfth floor, wondering what kind of reception he was going to get from the Ice Maiden: would he be "Matt" or "Lieutenant"?

The Personnel Bureau had many rows of desks, each of which had a civilian sitting in front of a computer terminal. Stuart stopped at one desk at the end of the wide aisle and said to the secretary, "I'm Lieutenant Matt Stuart from the Seven One Squad. I'd like to see Inspector Albrecht."

Without looking up at him, the fat lady asked, in the chiding tone of a civilian used to working for a powerhouse, "Do you have an appointment to see the inspector?"

"No, I don't. But I'd suggest you get on the horn and tell

your boss I'm waiting. I don't have the time to play mind games with you."

She looked up at him, chastened, dialed her boss, spoke softly, and then, slipping the receiver back, said, "Go right in, Lieutenant."

Inspector Suzanne Albrecht's name had never appeared in the F File because she had gone to great lengths during her twenty-three-year career to keep her personal life personal. At forty-three she had never married, never received personal phone calls at work, never gone to department social functions, never joined any of the Job's religious or fraternal organizations, had gotten her promotions based solely on merit and hard work, and had never, as far as anyone in the Job knew, gone to bed with anyone in the department. The opinion in the Big Building was evenly split as to whether she was asexual or gay. Her nickname, the Ice Maiden, had come about because of her officious school-marm exterior, her anonymous, if existent, sex life—and because, by not revealing herself, Suzanne Albrecht had made men wonder what she had locked up inside.

Stuart knocked and walked into the glass cubicle that was her office. She was standing by her desk, reading a report. She wore a pin-striped business suit and a strand of pearls. Her high-necked blouse was buttoned to the top and had a lace collar and cuffs. Watching her reading through ugly oversize eyeglasses that marred her beautiful face, noticing she wore no makeup, and how her long auburn hair was severely swept back across her head and gathered into an unflattering bun in the back, he thought, Uh-oh, I get the icy version.

She looked up at him and said with impersonal courtesy, "What can I do for you, Lieutenant?"

'At's my Ice Maiden, he thought. Aloud: "I'd like to run a detective through the F File."

"Why?" She looked back down at the report.

"He's being dumped into my squad from Pickpocket and Confidence, and I'd like to know how big of a problem I'm inheriting."

She continued reading as if she hadn't heard him.

Stuart stewed in silence; he looked pointedly at his wristwatch.

"Am I keeping you, Lieutenant?"

"There are a lot of things going on in the Squad, Inspector. I really do have to get back there soon."

Still reading, she said, "There are a lot of things going on here, too, Lieutenant." She closed the folder, put it on her desk, and moved around behind it, sitting in her high-backed executive chair. Swiveling around to her computer terminal, she asked, "What else brings you to the Big Building?"

"A homicide investigation," he said with an air of detachment as he looked around her stark, impersonal office.

She logged on to the computer and input the secret access code that admitted her into the F File databank. "What is your detective's name?"

"Paul Whitehouser."

As she typed in the name, she asked offhandedly, "You doing a day duty?"

"Yes."

"Here we are," she said as Whitehouser's name scrolled onto the screen. "Your detective doesn't think women should be on the Job. He thinks their activities should be confined to the bedroom. He's had six sexual harassment complaints filed against him in the past four years, all of which were squashed by promoting the women concerned and transferring them to the assignment of their choice. He's also a married philanderer who envisions himself as Dirty Harry."

Stuart muttered a curse under his breath. "The Palace Guard will keep protecting him until he gets himself jammed real good, and then look to hang his current boss for failure to supervise, lead, train, and prevent."

"That is the usual drill, Lieutenant. Are you going to try and kill the transfer?"

"I'm going to do what I have to do."

A momentary smile softened her businesslike demeanor.

"You'll think of something, Matt, you always do." She exited the databank and plucked another report out of her basket.

When Matt Stuart returned to the fifth floor, he found Bill Manning looking over the shoulder of the fingerprint examiner and smoking his briar with great determination as he watched the examiner studying the fingerprints on the split-screen terminal. On the left side of the split screen shone an arrest fingerprint of a whorl, its unbroken friction ridges clear and distinct, spiraling around its core and flowing out past its deltas. On the screen's right was a latent of a whorl that had been lifted off the aluminum foil. Its broken friction ridges were not distinct, one of its deltas was missing, and its core was smudged.

"We just fed your latents into AFIS," Manning told Stuart.

Matt looked at the screen. "How does AFIS work?"

"The automated fingerprint identification system is the good guys' secret weapon. We're knocking the balls off the mutts." He took his pipe out of his mouth and, using it as a pointer, said, "Before AFIS, whenever latents were lifted at a crime scene, the examiner would have to work out the permutations of every possible filing formula and then manually search through thousands of fingerprints, searching out one particular one. An impossible job, could take years to search out one print. With AFIS, the latents are scanned into a computer using a special magnifying camera. The examiner marks the print's identifying characteristics and the computer translates them into a digital code, which the computer then compares with the codes on file."

"How fast does this thing work?"

"Eighteen hundred prints a second," Manning said. "AFIS picks out the top twenty possibilities and displays them one at a time on the split screen next to the latent lifted at the scene, so that the examiner can conduct a side-by-side comparison." He was as proud of his system as a kid with a brand-new bike.

"What about a rap sheet?"

"Once we get a hit, the laser printer churns out the perp's criminal record and latest mug shot."

Stuart checked the time. "While AFIS is running my latents, I'd like to phone the Squad."

"Use the one in my office," Manning said, putting his pipe back in his mouth.

"What's happening?" Stuart asked Jones when he answered the Squad's phone.

Jones sounded tired and more than a little discouraged. "We did two more canvasses and came up dry. All the paper is done, and Helen faxed the 'Unusual' to the Palace Guard."

"Any problem with the Rasties?"

"Not so far."

"I'll be back in a little while," Stuart said. He hung up and dialed Carmine Vuzzo at Intelligence Division, catching him just as he was about to leave for the day. "I spoke to Angela Albertoli, and she swore Beansy had no connection with the company."

"Bullshit. Beansy inherited half of the company when the old man died. You ever hear of a pinky-ring walking away from a money-making machine? Because that's what Albertoli is."

"She admitted he shared the profits, but she insisted that he had nothing to do with the day-to-day operations of the company."

"Maybe she's telling the truth, Matt. We could never come up with any hard intelligence that he was involved in the running of the company. But like I told you, those guys don't walk away from a score."

When Stuart returned to AFIS, the fingerprint technician was comparing side-by-sides. The technician's ass overflowed the edges of the chair he was sitting on. Using a felt pen, he circled points of comparison on the latent prints. Stuart's adrenaline surged when he saw the points of comparison reach twelve. The technician's double chin shook when he lifted his head to Manning and said, "We got a hit."

He typed something into the keyboard and then propelled his swivel chair to the laser printer on the right side of the split-screen computer. The printer hummed and began churning out Manny Rodriguez's rap sheet. When Stuart saw the top of

Rodriguez's head flow out of the machine, he said, "C'mon, c'mon, lemme see that pretty face of yours."

Spray-painted white graffiti defaced the stoop and first story of the three-story Romanesque Revival mansion. The handsome residence, located on Brooklyn's once exclusive Parkside Avenue on the southern fringe of the Seven One, had been purchased twenty-three years ago by a Jamaican dope dealer, who had turned its rich mahogany-paneled interior into furnished rooms. Manny Rodriguez's room was on the second floor, front.

Stuart and Jones were parked on the corner of Parkside and New York Avenues, watching Helen Kahn walking toward the mansion. Before leaving the squad room, Kahn had gone into the female locker room and opened the disguise locker. She'd taken off her bracelets, curled her hair up in blue rollers, and wrapped her head in a chartreuse scarf. She'd put on oversize triangle-shaped nugget earrings, taken off her black skirt and blouse, and tugged on kelly green stretch pants and a cotton sweater.

Before leaving, Borrelli had gotten Manny's unlisted number from telephone security. He'd dialed it several times without getting an answer.

Stuart had distributed Rodriguez's photo and rap sheet to his detectives. He did not want to hit the flat until he was sure Rodriguez was there, because he knew that if they went storming into the room and he wasn't there, the word would spread quickly on the street, and Manny Rodriguez would become one of the permanently missing.

Kahn walked down the street, aware of the tug of her nine-millimeter under her sweater. A woman approached her, wheeling a baby carriage decorated with blue fringe. Kahn stopped to admire the newborn. The mother tensed as the garishly dressed stranger bent over and cooed to her baby.

Watching Kahn looking at the baby triggered a sudden and unbearable memory for Stuart. A spasm of pain contorted his face as he thought of his son. He turned his head away, focusing his teary eyes across the street on the apartment house.

"Helen's into her maternal mode," Jones said. "I'd bet she'd be a good mother."

"I'm sure she would, too," Stuart said, brushing his eyes.

Kahn's eyes went to the windows on the second floor. She saw no activity. She gave the baby a final coo and strolled down the cracked walkway through the patchy, untended lawn into the mansion's vestibule. The name slots of each bell were crowded with different surnames. She spied a slot with a Manny del Rio and M. Rodriguez. He's getting cute with his names, she thought. Probably getting his welfare check under Manny del Rio. She rang the bell several times; no answer.

"He ain't in." She was short and fat and stuffed into a garish orange pants suit and was carrying a bag of groceries. "I just saw Manny on Nostrand Avenue. He was all dolled up, a man ready to party."

"He told me he was in training," Kahn protested.

"Humph. Men don't need no trainin' for what he's looking for, darlin'."

"Please don't tell that bastard you saw me, I don't want him to know I was here."

"I won't say a word, honey. I've been in that boat many times myself."

The night duty team was filtering into the squad room when Stuart returned. He briefed them on the Hollyman and Gee homicide and told them to scoop up Rodriguez if they spotted him during their tour, but not to ask around for him. "He'll run if he knows we're looking for him."

"You want us to stake out his flat?" Hector Colon asked the whip.

"No, I wanna keep it loose. We'll hit his flat in the A.M."

The detectives moseyed out of the whip's office. The night duty detectives got out the spray cleaners and began emptying wastebaskets. Plaintiff phoned Jones to complain that her car needed a new transmission. He slammed down the phone, looked across at Borrelli, and asked, "Wanna stop for a taste?"

"Can't, ma man. I got a woman in need of my bionic tongue."

"Stop for a few with me," Jones said.

"Ma man, booze screws up my sex life. After two drinks, getting laid is like trying to stick a clam into a slot machine."

Jones shrugged and phoned a lady friend who worked in the Fifth Squad. Outside, the darkness held the first real chill of autumn, and a wind suddenly swirled trash and leaves over the steps of the Seven One.

6

The two-story Colonial-style house on Harbor View Terrace was on a knoll overlooking the upper New York bay. The wide driveway leading to the two-car garage was lined on both sides with autumn mums. Stuart drove his car into the garage and walked into the kitchen. Matt's grandfather had had the house built during the Great Depression. His family had always lived in Bay Ridge, or the Ridge, as it was called by the people who lived in that small section of Brooklyn locked inside the cement tentacles of the intertwined Gowanus Expressway and the Leif Ericson Drive.

His great-grandmother's cuckoo clock was chirping nine when Matt walked into the large living room. Upstairs in the bedroom, he took off his jacket and tie, then unclipped his nine-millimeter and stuck it in a drawer in the bedside table along with his handcuffs and ammo pouch.

After, he went downstairs into the kitchen, opened the refrigerator, liberated a can of Miller from its plastic noose, and popped the top. Swigging beer, he walked out into the living room and over to the bay window. He looked out at the large container ships lying at anchor, their lights bright sparkles against the night. Off to his left, the Verrazano Narrows Bridge spanned the river majestically, its slivered cables aglow with lights; and in the far-off distance, where the black night sky met the ocean, a faint white light shimmered on the horizon.

He took another swig and listened. Only the ticking of the clock broke the silence of the empty house. He turned from the window, sat wearily on the sofa, and looked across the room at his grandfather's Steinway, its top covered with family photographs. His grandfather was posing in one of the many bars and grills he had owned in the Ridge and Flatbush. Rumor had it that he also owned whorehouses in Red Hook and Park Slope. A photo of his dad and his aunt Elizabeth, a Carmelite nun. They were posing in front of Saint Patrick's Cathedral. He looked at the photograph of his dad, outfitted in the Job's outmoded dark blue uniform, standing beside one of the old green-and-white radio cars. His beautiful mother and dad on Easter Sunday, posing in the Botanical Gardens. A family at Christmas.

He got up and walked over to the piano, sat on the bench, and began playing a Chopin nocturne, his eyes focusing on the photograph of him and Pat and David. The music carried his thoughts back to the wonderful years when he had a loving wife and a wonderful, bright son and the Job. On David's sixth birthday, a Sunday in June, three o'clock on a beautiful day, Matt had been in the backyard, barbecuing chicken and ribs, the trees full of smoke from his grill. Pat was busy in the kitchen, making her famous potato salad. They had just exchanged a loving look through the kitchen window when the phone call came. He had watched her answer it, and when he saw the frown come over her face, he knew that the Job would, once again, screw up another important moment in the lives of his family.

Two detectives from the Eight One Squad had been shot dead attempting to execute an arrest warrant that had been endorsed by the courts for Sunday service. He had dressed quickly, kissed his family good-bye, and been walking through the kitchen toward the garage door when he'd realized that he was going after a cop killer and had better take along an extra gun. So he'd gone back into the bedroom and taken down his .38 S&W Chief from the top of the closet.

He had rushed out to the car, which was parked in the driveway. David was standing there, waving good-bye to his dad. Matt looked out the rear window as he moved the transmission out of park. Only it had not gone into reverse—he had accidentally jammed it into drive. For the rest of his life, a brief and unspeakably horrible tape would play over and over again in his mind: David's body crushed between the front bumper and the splintered garage door. The sound track was the one awful crunch—David had not even had time to scream. It was his wife who had screamed, a keening that seemed to go on for a long, long time.

That Sunday his wonderful life had ended.

He banged his hands down over the keys of the piano, got up, and rushed upstairs to the bedroom. He stripped down to his briefs, took his jump rope out of the top drawer of the dresser, and began springing over the twirling rope.

Dr. Lamm, who had treated him after the tragedy, had helped him see that it was an accident and not his fault. The doctor had suggested that whenever the pain got to be too much for him, he should engage in some strenuous exercise like rope jumping to relieve the tension. But the pain and the guilt were always there, lurking just below the surface.

Pat was hospitalized for clinical depression for almost three months after the accident. When she came home, their life together was over. Matt immersed himself in the Job, unable to heal the gaping wound in the marriage. What he didn't grasp was the simple fact that Pat hated the Job. One day she just moved out. She didn't say anything or leave a note. She didn't have to. He understood. So now all he had in his life *was* the Job and the big empty house that his grandfather had built.

Helen Kahn had finished washing her undies and was hanging her bra on the drying wire stretched across the top of her tub when her phone started ringing. She darted into the bedroom and stopped short, staring down at the telephone on her night-stand, deciding if she was going to answer it. She was afraid that Ken was on the other end. She'd been avoiding him, trying to gather her strength for what she expected would be high drama when she ended it with him.

"The hell with it," she said, and grabbed the receiver. "Hello."

"Hi, gorgeous."

Her shoulders sagged. "Where are you, Ken?"

"I'm just leaving the office. Me and my raging hard-on can be there in fifteen minutes." His tone was one of smug assurance.

She sucked in a deep breath and said, "No, Ken. It's not going to work with us anymore. I can't see you."

His cold silence filled the line. "Helen, I'll come over, we'll talk."

"No, Ken, please. I need to get on with my life, and being involved with a married man isn't my idea of going forward."

"I love you. How could you do this to me?" His voice was trembling with barely suppressed anger.

She held the phone out in front of her, staring at the mouth-piece. He's rolling out his heavy guns, she thought, that bastard. "Ken, I've made up my mind."

"I'll get a divorce, we'll get married."

A cynical smile crossed her face. Sure you will, you lying prick, she thought. "Ken, let's say our good-byes now, and stay friends."

"Is there anyone else?"

"Yes, your wife."

His tone took on a threatening edge. "I could do you a lot of favors, Helen. On the other hand . . ."

"I don't need any favors, Ken." She did not want this conversation. "Ken, I'm very tired. We're making collars on a double homicide in the A.M., and I have to be up real early. I need my sleep. Good-bye."

"Just give me five minutes, fa' crissake."

She hung up and slowly curled up on the bed, staring at the silent phone. She lay there, her heart pounding, expecting him to ring her back. After five long minutes, when the telephone did not come to life, she rolled on her back and sighed in relief; she was free, she thought. But why didn't she *feel* free?

Stuart shook himself awake; he had fallen asleep after his exercise and a shower. It took him several moments to shake off his dream and realize that the phone was ringing.

"I've been thinking about sucking your cock all day," the sultry voice said when he picked up the phone.

Smiling as he stretched out on the bed, he said, "I hoped I'd be hearing from you tonight."

"Would you like me to come over?"

"I'd like that very much."

"A half hour."

Matt Stuart lay naked across his bed, watching the Ice Maiden slip out of her jacket and toss it aside. She stepped out of her skirt and began unbuttoning her blouse. A flush came to her cheeks as she took it off. She stood before him clad in skimpy black underpants, a lacy black bra, and black thigh-highs.

Matt's heart pounded as he watched her unfasten her bra and work down her underpants. She stood perfectly still, allowing his eyes to feast on her body, her full breasts with erect pink nipples, her sculptured mound of auburn ringlets, the tops of her thigh-highs set against her smooth, creamy skin. Her large green eyes, set well apart, were watching him stroke his erection.

He was always surprised at the ease with which they could slip into familiarity once she had taken off her clothes. She had the ability to effortlessly erase her Ice Maiden persona and assume the role of a sexually demanding woman.

Inspector Suzanne Albrecht had decided a long time ago that she was going to become the first woman police commissioner of the NYPD. A woman with that kind of agenda needed to pick her playmates carefully.

They had met by accident eight months ago in the Waldbaum's shopping center on Ocean Avenue. She had been carrying a bag of groceries to her car when the bag broke. He had rushed to help her pick up her food. It turned out that she lived a mile and a half away from him, in one of those grand prewar apartment buildings on Bay Ridge Avenue. After a short edgy period, their pure sexual hunger overpowered their Job-related paranoia. Their secret affair offered them both what they wanted at this stage in their lives: sex, release, excitement—all without commitment.

She came up to the bed and planted one foot on the mattress. "I'll keep on my stockings," she said, and began massaging her clit with her three middle fingers. "Do you like watching me play with myself?"

"Yes." He reached up and kneaded her nipple, his other hand stroking his hardness.

She moaned and slipped two fingers inside her body, moving them in and out rapidly. She removed her fingers and gave them to him. "Lick my pussy juice," she demanded.

He did.

Afterward they lay in each other's arms, allowing their silence to engulf them. He toyed with her hair lazily, breathing in the faint scent of her perfume. The cuckoo clock chirped in the distance. She turned her head and looked at him. "What are you going to do about Paul Whitehouser?"

"I'm not sure. It's not so easy to derail a chief of detective's contract." He turned his head, looked into her wide eyes, and asked, "How old is the c of d?"

"Sixty-two. He has to get out in eight months."

"Unless Patrick Sarsfield Casey wins his age discrimination suit."

"The word in the Big Building is that the fourteenth floor expects a decision on that in a couple of weeks."

His brows came together as he adopted a serious expression. "Suzanne . . ." He paused, choosing his words carefully. "How long are the personnel folders kept after a cop retires?"

"They're kept in my office for two years and then shipped to a warehouse in Queens, where they're stored for fifteen years before they're destroyed."

"Why fifteen years?"

"Because that's the average number of years a retiree lives after he gets out."

"What about the F File?"

She began rubbing her fingers across the film of sweat on his chest.

He watched the small lights playing in her eyes as she pondered his question. We just screwed our brains out and she has to think about giving me an answer, he thought; as easy as she can slip into her sex mode, she can slip back into her Ice Maiden mode. Giving her an encouraging smile, he said, "C'mon, Suzanne. It's important."

"It depends," she said.

"On what?"

"The nature of the allegations in the file, if there's a possibility that the retiree might bring discredit to the Job because of some real or imagined wrong."

"What about an ex-member who went to work for the bad guys?"

"How would the Job know?"

"Humor me. Assume we did know."

"Then we'd probably keep his F File."

Stuart was silent for a moment, debating how much to tell Suzanne, then said, "Retired sergeant Patrick Holiday, AKA Paddy, was assigned to the Intelligence Division. As a sideline he sold confidential information to the wiseguys. IAD was about to throw a net over him, but somehow he escaped with his pension."

"How'd he manage that?"

" 'At's what I'd like to know," Matt said, brushing a strand of hair from her eyes. "Holiday's up to his ass in my two latest homicides."

"How long is he out of the Job?"

"Six years."

"And you want me to resurrect his personnel folder and his F File, and give them to you." She ran her fingertips over his mouth. "I love the way you smile, Matthew, and I'm wild for your body, but you gotta know that if I do this for you, one day there'll be payback."

"Naturally." He moved his mouth next to her ear and glided his tongue around the rim. "Do you think it would be a violation of the *Patrol Guide* for a subordinate to ask a ranking officer to go down on him?" he whispered.

"Absolutely not," she said, and leaning over, she kissed him.

7

At six o'clock Thursday morning a white streak of lightning slashed through towering dark clouds as Detective Calvin Jones walked Smasher past Manny Rodriguez's house. The hundred-pound rottweiler tugged Jones over to the rusting fire hydrant and began sniffing. The animal raised its leg and added its contribution to the rust. Jones's gaze swept over the second floor of the defaced mansion. No lights shone behind any of the windows, nor did he see any human shadows moving about. He gave the all-clear signal by patting his African scarf with his left hand.

Stuart turned to Borrelli, who was behind the wheel of the unmarked car parked at the corner. "Let's go, quietly."

Borrelli drove the car up Parkside Avenue and double-parked in front of the apartment house next to Rodriguez's home so that the car was not visible from any of Rodriguez's windows. Stuart, Borrelli, and Kahn got out and closed the doors, careful not to make noise.

The detectives hurried along the pathway into the mansion's vestibule. Jones sat on the stoop with Smasher reclining on his paws beside him. If Rodriguez attempted to escape by taking a header out the window, they'd be there to meet him. The door leading into the hallway was locked.

Borrelli removed a thin strip of plastic from his wallet and inserted it between the door and the jamb, about an inch and a half above the lock, and began working it down. The lock snapped open; the stench of decaying garbage greeted them as they stepped quickly into the hallway. A mahogany staircase wound up to the second level; several of its vase-shaped balusters were missing. Three bulbs hung down from black ceiling wires. Their guns drawn, the detectives tiptoed up the staircase. They did not want to announce their presence, so they tried to take the steps quietly, but the treads were old and warped, and they squeaked.

When they reached the second-floor landing, Kahn swept the corridor with her nine while Stuart and Borrelli silently took up positions against the wall on opposite sides of the door leading into the front apartment.

His back flush with the wall, Stuart reached out with his right hand and curled his fingers around the doorknob, turning the brass knob slowly. His eyebrows came together in surprise when the knob moved all the way. Rodriguez probably came home with his load on and didn't lock his door, he reasoned, looking across at Borrelli and mouthing, "On three."

Borrelli nodded.

Kahn continued to check the hallway behind them.

Stuart mouthed, "One, two, three," and threw open the door. He darted inside in a crouch and moved to the left of the threshold in a combat stance, bending with both hands locked around his nine as it swept the flat.

"Shit," Stuart said, standing straight.

Manny Rodriguez was sprawled on his bed. He was fully clothed, save for one shoe that lay on the floor beside the bed. He was lying on his left side, his mouth open, eyes wide and empty. Blood had coursed from his ears and mouth, pooling on the bedsheet.

Stuart figured a head shot and ran his hand through the dead man's hair, searching for the entrance wound. He found it in the hairline about two centimeters behind the left ear, a small hole with smooth edges. Powder tattooing peppered the hair around the wound. He bent down, trying to find an exit wound. There was none.

He'd been a detective long enough to read the signs. The shooter had used a twenty-two, the hitman's magic wand: it propelled a shell not powerful enough to pass through the skull, so it ricocheted around, tearing up everything inside.

The weight of the body wrinkled the sheets around the corpse. The headboard of the bed was up against the wall, about a foot to the right of a window that looked out over Parkside Avenue. The pillow next to the window had an indentation, as though someone had been sitting on it. A chest of drawers with edges stained black by cigarette burns lined the wall opposite the bed. Above it hung a velvet portrait of Christ with blood seeping out of his crown of thorns.

A framed photograph of Rodriguez, posing with his boxing gloves held high at what must have been a fight he won, sat on the top of the dresser, along with a set of keys, a wad of bills, some change mixed with subway tokens, and an edition of the *New York Post* with a glaring headline that read 12 SLAIN IN 8 HOURS IN NYC.

Stuart examined the scene, his mind racing ahead. The shooter breaks into the apartment and sits on the pillow, waiting and looking out the window for Manny, he reasoned; when he sees him coming, he rushes over and plants himself behind the door. Manny comes in, doesn't bother to turn on the lights, and walks over to his dresser and empties his pockets. He moves over to the bed to get undressed; the killer steps up behind him and puts out his lights for good.

Stuart struggled his hand inside the dead man's shirt and felt his armpit. It was still warm. He ran his hand over the neck; it was soft. The downward spread of rigor mortis had not yet begun. He tugged up the blue shirt with the flowery design and bent down, looking at the stomach, and saw the slight purple discoloration of lividity. The blood was starting to fall to the body's lowest point.

"How long you figure?" Kahn asked.

" 'Bout an hour and a half, maybe two," Stuart said, bitterness creeping into his voice at the thought that someone was several steps ahead of him.

Borrelli counted out the wad of money and announced, "Twenty-seven hundred dollars."

"Payment for Gee and Hollyman," Stuart said.

"If they paid 'im, why whack 'im?" Borrelli asked.

"I can come up with several reasons real quick," Stuart said. "First, he might have been popped for something not connected with the Rastafarians. Maybe he was doing some guy's wife or girlfriend, or maybe he was into the shys big time, and they felt they had to turn him into a learning experience for other deadbeats." He tugged at his right earlobe. "Or, after they paid him for the hit, he might have said or done something that made them afraid he might roll over on them. Or . . ." He looked down at the body, his unspoken thoughts hanging heavily in the room.

Borrelli began to search the closet. Stuart took the chest of drawers.

Kahn plucked a pair of jeans off the rickety chair beside the dresser and pulled a folded envelope out of the back pocket. She lifted the flap and peered inside. Suddenly her beautiful face was frozen in shock. "Oh, my," she said, recovering her composure and passing the envelope to the whip.

Stuart muttered, "Oh, shit!" when he slid out the mug shots of Gee and Hollyman.

"Looks as though Rodriguez had some inside help in IDing the Rasties," Kahn said.

Stuart slipped the mug shots into his sports jacket's inside pocket, looked at his detectives, and said, "Forget you saw those mug shots."

The second platoon, 0800–1600, was filing out of the Seven One when Jones drove the unmarked car into the Squad commander's parking space in front of the precinct. Matt, Jones, and Smasher got out. Smasher pulled Jones over to several of his policemen friends, who petted him and fed him leftover late-tour pizza.

Walking inside the station house, Stuart waved to the desk sergeant, then passed through the muster room and climbed the steps up to the squad room. He had left Kahn and Borrelli back at the homicide scene to ensure that things were done properly. He had stressed the importance of making sure that the crime scene technicians vacuumed the bed, the pillow, and the floor around the pillow on the chance of picking up some trace evidence.

Jones followed his boss into the squad room and went directly into the storage room to fill up Smasher's bowl with dry dog food.

Stuart read the latest entries in the telephone message book and then went into his office to ponder what he was going to do about those mug shots. Every damn "do and don't" in the *Patrol Guide, Detective Guide,* and *Administrative Guide* required an immediate notification to IAD whenever a member unearthed the slightest hint of corruption. Providing a shooter with official NYPD mug shots of his pigeons fitted that bill very nicely.

Stuart took out the mug shots and looked again at the color photographs of Hollyman's and Gee's dour faces, their NYSID numbers emblazoned across their chests. The New York State Identification Division's number had been given the diminutive "Nisid number" within the Job. As he looked at the two mug shots, Stuart thought about what steps any cop had to take to obtain mug shots from the files.

Detectives forwarded a form called a "ninety" through department mail to the Photographic Unit. The ninety required the name, shield number, and command of the ordering officer and the NYSID number of the individual. The latest mug shots taken at the prisoner's last arrest were developed and forwarded through department mail. Where time was important, a detective could go to the Photo Unit and wait for "wet" copies to be developed.

Stuart slid the mug shots back into his jacket pocket. He was going to have to pay a visit to the Photo Unit. A dirty cop was lurking somewhere in the Job, and experience had taught him that stealth was the best way to bring him to ground. His time in the Job had also taught him that the best way to screw up an investigation was to bring in IAD incompetents. Most of the people assigned to that unit volunteered to escape the street they were too scared to work.

He reached into the side drawer of his desk and took out a blank "Unusual" form. An "Unusual Occurrence Report" was used to notify the Palace Guard of any newsworthy incident. Homicides used to be considered newsworthy, but with more than two thousand people a year being slaughtered in New York City, homicide "Unusuals" had become nothing more than busy-work for the Palace Guard. Old habits were hard to break.

He swiveled to the IBM Selectric II on a typing table next to his desk and filled out the who, what, where, when, and how of Rodriguez's death on the mimeographed form, omitting any mention of the mug shots. After doing that, he walked out from behind his desk into the squad room and faxed the report up the chain of command.

That done, he went back into his office and phoned Patrick Sarsfield Casey at Detective Borough, Brooklyn South. Although the inspector was the first in the chain to receive his fax, tradition demanded that he make a personal call to his boss and brief him on the case and its dangers.

Casey immediately asked Stuart, "Was there anything racially motivated about those Rastafarian hits?"

"Nothing racial, Inspector, just mutts blowing away other mutts."

"Your four open homicides are screwing up the district's clearances. Some people in the Big Building might get it into their heads that I'm too old to cut the mustard."

"Not to worry, Inspector. When we make our collars your clearances will soar, and it'll be because of your outstanding leadership."

"Cut the shit and tell me what you got on the Rodriguez hit."

"I think that the Rasties took Beansy out. And as we both know, in certain circles it's considered crass for a black guy to take out a pinky-ring. So they used Rodriguez for their payback."

"Your 'Unusual' states that you found twenty-seven hundred dollars in Rodriguez's apartment. That indicates to me that they paid him for the hit. Why'd they whack 'im, then?"

Matt let his silence speak for itself. Finally he brought the phone closer to his mouth and said, "When we tossed his flat, we came up with mug shots of Gee and Hollyman."

Casey's tone betrayed real concern. "I didn't see any mention of them in your 'Unusual.'"

"I know."

"Did you notify IAD?"

"No."

"You think someone in the Job tipped them off you were on to Rodriguez?"

"That's possible."

"How many of your people know about those mug shots?"

"None of them. I found them and I slipped them into my pocket without any of them seeing."

Casey chuckled and said, "I hope you eat pussy better than you lie. I guess you're going to Lone Ranger it, keep your people out of the investigation, do it all yourself, so that if the Palace Guard finds out, you're the only one who'll be offered up as sacrifice."

"I don't like bad cops."

"All right, play it your way for now, but keep me informed. And, Matt, we never had this conversation."

Stuart hung up and sat, staring thoughtfully at the phone, when suddenly his other confidential phone began to ring. He pulled out the bottom right-hand drawer of his desk and snapped up the red receiver. "Hello."

"Did you really mean it when you said you wanted to help me?"

• • •

Stuart parked the unmarked car on North Portland Avenue, a short street that cut between the low-income Walt Whitman Houses and Cumberland Family Care Center. Fort Greene Park was a block away.

The walls of the housing project at ground level had been turned into memorials to the murdered. Elaborate murals bearing the names and likenesses of the fallen had been spray-painted onto the walls. Memorial walls had sprung up through-out the city, honoring the victims of the urban bloodbath. They were the poor's final benediction to their dead. Someone had turned the wall on Stuart's right into a shrine by placing flowers in milk containers and candles in little glass cups on the ground.

"First they kill each other, and then the families and friends make these pitiful gestures. We respect the people we kill, man," he grumbled to himself just as he spotted Andrea Russo walking out of the park toward his car. She had a white kerchief around her head, with the folds pulled forward around her cheeks. Her kerchief momentarily reminded him of a nun.

Reaching across the seat, he opened the passenger door. She jumped in, slamming the door behind her. He quickly pulled away from the curb, heading down DeKalb Avenue, across South Elliot Place, and on to Flatbush Avenue. Then, during their four-minute ride on Flatbush Avenue, they drove past eight spray-painted crosses on stoops and sidewalks that marked the spots where people had been murdered.

"Do you think you were followed?" Stuart asked her.

"No. I took a cab from Pigtown to Fort Greene Park and sat on a bench for half an hour before coming to meet you."

They rode in silence. She kept turning and looking out the rear window. The Soldiers and Sailors Memorial Arch, the huge Civil War memorial, loomed ahead of them. Driving around the arch in Grand Army Plaza, Stuart saw two more memorial crosses.

He drove the unmarked car into Prospect Park. The big trees that shaded the great lawns were barren now, their leaves rotting in rain-drenched piles. He drove around the park's winding lake.

The boathouse was locked up and stacked-up canoes were chained to the dock.

He drove into the amphitheater's parking lot and kept the engine running. After checking that the doors were locked, he looked around the lot. One car was parked under the giant oak at the other end of the lot. A man and a woman were in the front seat.

He checked out the scene for human predators lurking behind trees and bushes. He saw none and then realized that it was only nine-twenty in the morning. Those mutts don't haul their asses out of bed until one, he thought, turning to look at Andrea and for the first time seeing the fear in her eyes.

"What happened?" he asked her.

Her voice trembling, she told him what Paddy Holiday had done to her.

Stuart felt both angry and responsible. "How did he know I drove you home?"

"Mary Terrella, my neighbor, told him. She must have seen you drop me off that night."

He gave her a puzzled look. He'd never met Mary Terrella. And his category-one car, like all the other category ones in the Job, was registered to a civilian front corporation. Even if this Terrella woman had taken down the license number, it would have taken someone with access to intelligence files to have made him as the driver of the car.

She sensed how worried Stuart was and asked meekly, "What'sa matter?"

"What's Terrella's connection to Paddy?"

"She's Frank Marino's girlfriend."

"'Frankie Bones' Marino?"

"Yeah." She shifted nervously in her seat. "Paddy wants me to get *close* to you. He's worried that you might come up with somethin' that could hurt him."

"Like what?"

"Dunno." She looked down at her hands. "They'd kill me if they ever found out I talked to you."

"Do you know that much about them?"

"No, not really. Beansy liked me, and I liked him. He was close to my dad and knew my mom real well. He sorta felt an obligation to look after me. When he died, my protection died, too."

"Why don't you pack your bags and leave?"

"I told you before, I got nobody to go to and nothing to do when I get there."

"What made you phone me, Andrea?" he asked quietly.

"I really thought Paddy was going to kill me yesterday. I was so scared. And I . . . I realized that you were right. I'll never be really free until I get them off my back. I'm trying so hard to make it in the world, I don't need them to bring me back down."

They sat in wary silence for a long minute before he asked, "What happened with Beansy?"

She drew a deep breath and said, "Beansy didn't drive a car, so Paddy had Hollyman and Gee drive him to my place for a meet with Frankie Bones. Something happened after they got there, and one of the Rastafarians killed Beansy."

"What was the meet about?"

"Dunno. Beansy'd use my place every now and then, but I never knew what went on when he did. He'd always slip me a hundred for my trouble."

Stuart played a sudden hunch. "Was there ever anything between you and Beansy?"

"Not really. Once a few years ago I threw him a mercy fuck, but only that one time."

"Did Beansy have his own set of keys to your place, or did he have to come and see you to get your extra set?"

Her eyes fell to the floor. "He always came and got my extra set. I'm sorry I lied to you about my keys."

" 'At's okay. But level with me now. Did Holiday order the hits on Gee and Hollyman?"

"Paddy don't give orders for hits. The smart money guys use him as a go-between with the Rastafarians, and because of his connections in your department. He'll always be a 'my friend' guy."

He knew she was referring to the way wiseguys made introductions. This is "*my* friend so and so" meant that the person being introduced was not a member of any crew, so everyone was careful what they said. This is "*our* friend" meant that the person was part of a crew and could be trusted.

He asked, "What kind of connections is Paddy supposed to have in the NYPD?"

"Big time, I hear."

"What kind of business did Paddy do with the Rastafarians?"

She spent several moments thinking before she answered, "I'm not sure. Every morning Gee and Hollyman would show up at the bar with shopping bags full of money. They'd leave it with Paddy."

"How'd you know the bags contained money?"

"Because one morning a bag toppled and money spilled onto the floor. I looked away; I didn't want to know, so I pretended not to see."

"Did you ever overhear any of their conversations?"

"Naw. They always kept it real quiet when they talked about business."

Stuart decided to try another possible angle. Somehow, somewhere, this all had to fit together. "Did you ever hear of a guy named Manny Rodriguez?"

"No."

"What was the connection between Beansy and Frankie Bones?"

"You never know with those guys. Lately they've been meeting a lot at the bar. Paddy never took part in their sit-downs. He'd always make himself busy in the kitchen."

"Any idea what they discussed?"

"No."

"What impressions did you have when you saw them?"

"I dunno."

"You must have thought something was going down when you saw them."

Her brow came down, causing wrinkles to form around the borders of her eyes. "They always greeted each other with that kissin' bullshit of theirs, but I got the feeling that Frankie Bones was the head guy."

"What made you think that?"

"Frankie Bones never came alone. He always hadda couple of gorillas along with him who'd come into the bar first to check it out."

"Did they ever use your house for a meet?"

"A couple of times, I think. Frankie Bones loves Bolonia cheese, so whenever Beansy showed up at the bar looking for my keys and he had a bag full of Bolonia wedges, I figured he was going to a meet with Frankie Bones."

Stuart pounced on this connection. "What do you know about the Albertoli cheese business?"

"Only that it's owned by Beansy Rutolo's family."

"Do you know his niece, Angela?"

"I knew her from the neighborhood when I was a kid. She's high rent these days, never comes around."

"Wasn't she always high rent?"

"Yeah, but when I was a kid she used to come around to dish with the older girls. She had the hots for Danny Lupo back then."

"That's a blast from the past. Whatever happened to him?"

"He married some Jewish dame from Sands Point, and Daddy set him up in his investment firm. Last I heard he'd gone legit."

Stuart's instincts told him that he was getting very close to where it all made sense. "What happened with him and Angela?"

"Nothing as far as I know. But when Danny L got married, Angela stopped coming around the neighborhood."

"Beansy wasn't a runaround, was he?"

"You never saw him with a woman, and he never talked about one."

"I believe Beansy had a long-term squeeze stashed somewhere. And I need to talk to her."

She looked at him. "Are you circumcised?"

"What?"

"Paddy's gonna ask me if I'm doing you, and I'm gonna have to tell 'im I am, and he just might ask me if you are."

"Tell him I am. Now what about Beansy's squeeze?"

"I'll ask around."

8

Matt Stuart returned directly to the squad room after his meet with Andrea Russo. As he was signing himself present in the command log, he heard a crash that seemed to come from the interview room. He ruled off his entry and walked into the storage room to find Jones and Kahn standing in front of the darkened glass, staring into the interview room as Borrelli and Jordon picked up a prisoner off the floor and planted him in a chair. Smasher was stretched out at Jones's feet.

Jones glanced at the whip and said, "That's the mutt who blew away the owner of the bodega on Kingston and Prospect Place."

"The one across the street from Brower Park?" Stuart asked, peering in at the thin boy slouching in the chair, one sneaker crossed over the other.

"That's the one," Kahn said. "After the owner forked over the lousy forty bucks in the register, the mutt made him kneel and put one into the back of his head. A passing scooter cop heard the shot and grabbed him exiting the store sticking a nine into his waistband. We also have three witnesses who were in the store at the time."

"How old is he?" Stuart asked wearily.

"Fourteen," Jones replied. "His name is Dion Foster, he's got a long juvenile sheet."

"He'll be tried as an adult on this caper," Stuart said.

In the interview room, Jordon picked up another wooden chair and turned it around with the back facing the prisoner. He sat down, folded his arms on the top of the chair's back, and asked, "What made you decide to stick up that bodega?"

"It be on my way to school. I didn't have no motherfuckin' money, so I went and get me some."

"Do you always take a gun to school with you?" Borrelli asked.

"Man, everyone be havin' a gun," Dion said.

Staring at the prisoner, Jordon said, "Just between you and me, Dion, after he gave you the money, why'd ya shoot 'im?"

"I felt like it," Dion said with the casualness of someone ordering ice cream.

Stuart searched out Dion's eyes for a spark of remorse, but all he saw was the cold indifference of a remorseless killer, a child born unwanted and thrown onto the streets to survive. Shaking his head at the senselessness of it all, Stuart left the viewing room and went into his office.

He had just made it around his desk when Kahn came in behind him and closed the door. She walked over to the chair at the side of his desk and sat, crossing her legs. Stuart opened the folder containing the intelligence reports on Russo and Mary Terrella and said, "What's on your mind?"

She shook down her brushed-gold bracelets and said, "I've been elected the spokesperson for the Squad. We'd all prefer it if you didn't do what you're doing."

He saw the concern in her face. "What am I doing?"

"You're going it alone, trying to protect us from the bad guys. I found those mug shots in Rodriguez's apartment. It's my responsibility to make the IAD notification."

Stuart held up his hand to cut her off. "Helen, I hold the bag for everything that goes down in this squad. There is no reason for all of us to put our heads on the block."

"Why don't you just make the damn notification?"

"You ever hear of IAD or Intelligence arresting one of their own?"

"No."

"That's because those units want their secrets kept, so they slap their bad cops on their wrists and let them slide with their pensions."

"Like they did with Paddy Holiday?"

"Maybe." He became aware of rockabilly music coming from the radio on Jerry Jordon's desk.

Kahn looked up at the precinct map and said, "Even the real Lone Ranger needed Tonto. I'm single, with nothing on my plate except watching *NYPD Blue* on Tuesday nights."

He regarded the way her black hair touched her shoulders, accentuating her bronze skin and long graceful neck. Her eyes gave a clear indication of her keen intelligence. She was a resourceful detective who kept her cool in tight situations. Her help would move the case along a lot faster. He needed her.

He picked up the intelligence report on Andrea Russo and handed it to her. "Read this." He started reading the other file on Terrella.

Mary Terrella had no arrest record but was suspected of dealing in stolen property and being a numbers runner for the Gambino crime family. She was known to be Frankie Bones Marino's girlfriend. The report went on to state that Marino, who lived in Whitestone, Queens, with his wife, Carmela, and their five daughters, never spent the entire night with Terrella.

They exchanged files and continued reading.

Andrea Russo's report listed her arrest record and stated that her father was a captain in the Lucchese crime family.

After Kahn finished, she put the file back on his desk, saying, "They're both clearly on the fringes of organized crime."

Stuart placed the reports side by side, his eyes flicking back and forth to the file numbers on the upper right-hand corners. "Some of the file numbers are the same."

She got up and stood beside him, placing her palms on the desk and bending to look at the numbers. Her ample breasts filled her blouse. "Those numbers without Russo's or Terrella's initials means they're cross-referenced from other surveillances," he said.

"Tech Services laid a camera on Frankie Bones and came up with Terrella, too," she said.

He handed her both intelligence reports. "I'd like you to get me copies of all those cross-referenced surveillance reports."

"You got it, Lou."

She took the reports and left, and a few minutes later Stuart walked out into the squad room. Smasher lumbered over to him and rubbed up against his leg. Stuart scratched the dog behind its ear and walked into the property room, where he took out the evidence bag containing Beansy Rutolo's personal effects.

The house at 112 Fenimore Street was situated in the center of a line of late-nineteenth-century yellow brick row cottages. A small square of dirt with a barren tree planted in the middle decorated the curb in front of each house. One Twelve had a green aluminum awning over its entrance. Stuart took out Beansy's keys and let himself into the vestibule, where he unlocked the heavy wooden inner door.

The musty smell of disuse filled the air. Mahogany sliding doors lined both sides of the high-ceilinged foyer. The door on the right led into a parlor; the one on the left, the living room. Ahead and slightly to the right rose a stately staircase, its treads carpeted in a blue-and-gold fleur-de-lis design.

Stuart walked into the parlor, looked around, and left, crossing the foyer to the living room. He was struck by the absolute silence inside the house. A black-and-white-striped sofa with two matching armchairs were grouped around a teakwood coffee table. He looked up at the rococo molding and spotted a spiderweb in the corner. He ran his finger across the film of dust on the coffee table and walked into the connecting dining room.

A large, ornate white dining room set filled the room. Cherubs decorated the edges of the china closet. He noted the blanket of dust on the table and walked into the kitchen. The long, narrow room had a window over the sink that looked out over a small backyard covered in weeds. The refrigerator was unplugged. He opened the door; a warm smell of old rubber and stale food leaped out at him. The box was empty.

Lining the walls on both sides of the sink were cupboards filled with plates and glasses. He looked into the pantry; the shelves were empty save for one lone can of tomato soup.

Under the sink he found a green wastebasket with a newspaper rolled up inside. He took out the can and unrolled the paper. His eyes widened. Beansy Rutolo reading *The Wall Street Journal*? The date on the masthead was Wednesday, August 18, 1993. He opened the newspaper and saw that an article on page three had been cut out. He put the paper back and returned the can to its place under the sink.

The king-size bed in the second-floor bedroom had a beige quilt and matching pillow shams. He lifted one edge of the quilt and saw a mattress cover, no sheets. He crossed the room to the closet. It contained white, blue, and brown summer shirts on wire hangers. Each of the five drawers of the standing chest was lined with paper. All of them were empty. He looked around the bedroom, wondering where Beansy Rutolo had really lived.

Two flower cars were parked at the curb in front of St. Thomas Church. The Renaissance-style church, once the center of one of Brooklyn's most affluent Catholic communities, had long since exchanged its upper-middle-class parishioners for the poor underclass. The once pristine neighborhood of two-family homes and apartment houses had deteriorated into a graffiti-covered slum of junkies, muggers, and dope pushers who preyed on the decent, hardworking people sentenced by poverty to live there.

Stuart parked his car across the street from the church. He did not toss his vehicle identification plate on the dashboard because he knew that if the mutts made the car as a police vehicle, they'd steal it. He got out and locked the car, then fished a quarter from his trouser pocket. But when he went to insert the money into the parking meter, he saw that the coin box had been ripped out. It was the same with all the meters on the block.

The hearse and the cortege had not yet arrived. The funeral mass was scheduled for twelve o'clock. He darted across Nostrand Avenue and entered the church. Once inside, he walked off to his right and went halfway down the side aisle, where he opened the door to the confessional and snuck into the priest's compartment, which gave him an unobstructed view of the church.

An altar boy walked from the vestry to the altar and lit the candles. The air inside was heavy with the accumulated years of incense. The few remaining Pigtown mourners began arriving, women bent with age, wearing widows' black clothing. They struggled through half a genuflection and sat in the pews. A well-dressed woman who looked to be somewhere in her late forties, a black alligator pocketbook hanging off her right shoulder, walked a quarter of the way down the center aisle and slid into a left-side pew without genuflecting. Her eyes were glazed and she was sobbing.

A clanging sound caused Stuart to look around at the entrance. The coffin was being wheeled inside atop a gurney. The mourners began wailing. The woman with the expensive pocketbook began crying uncontrollably. The pallbearers pushed the coffin down the center aisle, positioned it at the foot of the altar, and drifted off into the side aisles.

The cortege began filing into the church. Angela Albertoli came in, accompanied by an older couple. Stuart assumed they were her parents. Danny Lupo and Frankie Bones walked behind the Albertolis. Andrea Russo was also in the procession, along with Mary Terrella, whom Stuart recognized from surveillance photos.

Danny Lupo angled off to his left and gave the crying woman with the expensive pocketbook a quick squeeze of condolence on her shoulder. Stuart hadn't seen Danny L in over eight years, and he wondered just how legit Danny L had become.

The priest walked out to the altar.

Forty minutes later, when the mass ended and the priest had walked away from the altar, the mourners in the first pew began filing out into the aisle. The others waited until the immediate family had passed before stepping out and falling in behind them. Angela and her mother and father stopped to offer condolences to the crying woman, hovering over her and obscuring Stuart's view. Frankie Bones also went over to her and paid his respects.

Stuart waited for her to get up and leave.

She continued to sit in her pew, staring up at the crucifix above the altar long after the church was empty. Finally she got up and quickly left the church.

Matt waited until she got outside before he hurried after her. The cortege had left. A black Lincoln Town Car was parked at the curb. As the woman started down the steps, a chauffeur hurried out from behind the wheel and rushed around the front of the car to open the door for her.

Stuart walked across the street to his car and unlocked the door just as the town car drove away from the curb. When the black car had gone a block, Stuart drove out of his space and began tailing it. He lifted the arm of the console between the seats and punched in his personal access code for the computer set into the console behind the cellular phone. When the lime-green screen glowed, he punched in the license plate number of the black Lincoln.

The 1990 model was registered to Madeline Fine, F/W/50, of 2311 Bedford Avenue, Brooklyn, New York. He typed in the access code for a criminal record check on Madeline Fine. Four predicate names scrolled onto the screen, none of which had the correct age or address.

The Lincoln drove west on Winthrop Street and then turned south on Bedford Avenue, a wide street that began at Brooklyn's northern tip at McCarren Park and snaked through the entire borough, ending at Sheepshead Bay. They passed through neighborhoods of decaying apartment houses and through the Satmar Hasidic community, where men walking the streets wore long frock coats and skullcaps and had beards and uncut side-locks, and the women's shaved heads were wigged or covered with kerchiefs. As he drove past Erasmus Hall High School,

Stuart lowered the window to get some air and heard people calling to one another in Haitian Creole, a polyglot of French and various West African languages.

Stuart maintained his distance behind the town car, careful to stay in sync with the timing of the traffic lights. He kept wondering about the woman inside the Lincoln. She certainly didn't look the pinky-ring type. But that was something a cop could never be sure of. There were more than a few socially prominent women who got off on going to bed with wiseguys.

The town car continued driving south, past the part of Bedford Avenue that sliced the Brooklyn College campus in half. Once on the other side of the college, it was like entering a time warp. Mansions, their manicured lawns set way back from the street, lined both sides of the avenue. Some of the houses were well-preserved classical revival homes. Some had second-floor balconies behind their main colonnade.

The Lincoln turned into the circular driveway of a mansion that looked like one of the antebellum plantation houses Stuart had seen in movies. The woman got out of the car. So did the chauffeur.

Stuart pulled into a parking space half a block away and watched them talking. The chauffeur nodded to the woman and walked out of the driveway to a late-model Ford parked at the curb. He got in and drove off.

The woman walked up the steps of the plantation house lookalike, touched something fastened to the doorjamb, and let herself into the house.

I'll give her a few minutes, Stuart told himself. She might not be Beansy's squeeze, he mused, but whoever she is, she sure as hell got their attention back at the church.

The woman answered the door and looked with mild surprise at the shield and identification card in Stuart's hand. Then her black eyes flashed up to his placid face, where they remained for a second before she said, "Please come in, Lieutenant."

She led him through a foyer with a crystal chandelier into a living room furnished in tasteful opulence, where she motioned him to a Chippendale armchair. She lowered herself into a beige sofa with oversize pillows and cushions. "How may I help you?" she asked.

"You're Madeline Fine?"

"I am."

"Did you know Anthony Rutolo?" He saw the anguish fill her eyes and added, "I'm sorry. I need to ask you some questions. I'm investigating his death. I saw you at the church, and—"

She waved a silencing hand and said softly, "I understand." She pulled a linen handkerchief out of the sleeve of her smartly tailored black dress and began dabbing her tears. "In all the years Anthony and I were together, his world never collided with mine. And now that he's gone, a policeman comes to my home."

He sat there watching in silence as she cried. He felt sorry for her and wished he could say something to ease her sorrow, but he couldn't, so he just sat there. He felt uncomfortable, so he picked out a spot on the wall behind her and fixed his eyes there. She began taking deep breaths in an attempt to regain her composure.

"Can I get you a glass of water?" he asked.

"Please. The kitchen is back there." She pointed past the dining room.

He got up, went into the kitchen, took a glass out of the cupboard, and filled it with water. Back in the living room, he handed it to her and sat down. She clutched the glass with both her hands and drank.

"Thank you," she said, placing the glass on the side table.

"Would you prefer if I came back another time?"

She gave him a haggard smile. "I'd prefer to get this over with as quickly as possible." She sucked in a deep breath and added, "Ask me your questions."

"What was your relationship with Anthony?"

She lifted her chin and said proudly, "Anthony Rutolo was the love of my life. We had been together twenty-one years, eight months, and twenty-seven days."

"Were you his wife?"

"No. I'm not Catholic, and Anthony would never marry outside his religion."

"So you lived together."

"Yes." She saw his curious look and added, "You're asking yourself how a woman like me could be with a man like Anthony."

"Anthony wasn't exactly in the *Social Register.*"

"And neither am I, Lieutenant. I can tell you that Anthony was the kindest, most loving man I've ever known. He never discussed his business with me, and I never asked him questions."

"Certainly you were aware of what his business was?"

"Yes, I knew. But that didn't matter to me."

"In all the years you were together, he never once discussed his business with you?"

She shook her head emphatically. "Never. Anthony went to great lengths to keep me away from all that."

Stuart's eyes roamed the room. "Did he live here with you?"

"Of course."

"This is a long way from where he worked. He didn't drive, so how did he get back and forth?"

"Taxis and car service. Sometimes I would get a driver for my car and send him to pick Anthony up."

"You don't drive?"

"I do. But I hate driving."

"Everyone at the church appeared to know you."

He watched her expression carefully to see if she was telling him the whole truth.

"Anthony was a sentimental man. Every Christmas we would have his three closest friends over for dinner. And Christmas Eve we would visit his friends in a bar on Fourth Avenue. From the outside it looked like an ordinary bar and grill, but the inside was decorated like a winter wonderland, with ornaments from all over the world."

He started to ask the names of Anthony's friends but decided to play a different card. "Is that where you met Frank Marino and Danny Lupo?"

"Yes." She didn't seem at all surprised by the question.

"Do you know what they do for a living?"

"No, I don't."

"Was the name of the bar the Kings Inn?"

"Yes. How did you know that?"

"It's a major wiseguy hangout. You do know what a wiseguy is?"

"Of course I do."

"And do you also know that they murder people?"

Her eyes fell to her hands. "Yes. But Anthony never did any of that."

"Are you sure of that?" Stuart had a hard time buying this rosy version of the life and works of Beansy Rutolo.

"I am. The man I loved could never take another human being's life." She balled up her handkerchief, leaned forward, and said, "I'm going to tell you something that I've never told anyone, not even Anthony. I'm the child of Holocaust survivors. After the war my parents went to Italy to await their visas to come to the United States. While they were there, my mother fell in love with an Italian doctor. He was the real love of her life. When my parents' visas came through, my mother had to make a decision. She did the correct thing and came with my father to this country. Thirty years later, when my father was on his deathbed, he looked up at my mother and said, 'Now you can go back to Italy.' I swore that I would never make the same mistake my mother made. Anthony was my love, and I don't regret one moment of our life together." She sucked in a breath and said, "I'm very tired. Please leave now."

"Of course." He got up.

She walked with him to the door. In the foyer he turned to her and asked, "Did Anthony ever introduce you to any policemen?"

She smiled. "Hardly."

Outside on the porch, Stuart looked at the mezuza fixed to the doorpost, its presence bespeaking a Jewish household, and thought. A made guy from Pigtown living in the Little House on the Prairie with a high-maintenance dame who knows from nothing. I don't buy it. He touched the mezuza in mute tribute to the scroll housed within its case and hurried down the steps.

Madeline Fine stood at her living room window, looking out from behind parted drapes. When Stuart's car squealed into a U-turn and drove off, she walked over to her sofa and picked up the portable phone on an Adam side table.

"I just had an interesting visit from a policeman," she told the man at the other end.

Danny Lupo folded his cellular phone carefully and spun around in his chair, taking in the silver spire of the Chrysler Building. He took off his glasses, began massaging his eyes, and said, "Madeline Fine just had a visit from Stuart at her home."

Frankie Bones said, "So what? There's no connection with us. She shouldn't have gone to the church if she wanted to stay in the fucking closet."

Danny L spun around to face his old friend. He put his glasses back on and said, "I remember Stuart from years back. He was an honest cop, and there's nothing that can cause you more trouble than an honest cop with a hard-on for you."

"Look, Danny, if he gets in our way, we'll take 'im out."

Danny L frowned in disapproval at his friend. "We don't kill honest cops, you know that." He leaned back, regarding the ceiling. "Does Holiday have a cellular?"

"Like you wanted, everybody's gone wireless. Danny, I'm not so sure this cellular thing is smart. The cops can still lay a wire on a cellular phone."

"It ain't that easy. They gotta be close to do it, and they still need a court order."

"C'mon, Danny. We both know that they don't always get court orders. They lay a wire on your phone, get a lot of incriminating shit, and then make up fairy tales about how they got it."

"Cellular gives us an edge. I want you to phone Holiday now and see if the years have made Stuart reasonable."

Lupo kept staring up at the ceiling, remembering the ecstatic hours he had spent with Terry; he paid little attention to Frankie's conversation with Holiday. If he left the office early, he calculated, he could spend a few hours with his girlfriend before he had to go home. His wife had invited her loud-mouth sister and her chintzy husband to dinner. That's one guy I'd like to have whacked, he thought, watching Frankie Bones fold up his phone. "What did he say?"

"He said Stuart's still a hard-ass cop."

"If he's looking to take us out, we'll cut his legs out from under him."

Stuart drove the unmarked car along the long stretch of Flatbush Avenue that began at Empire Boulevard and ended at Grand Army Plaza, separating Prospect Park from the Brooklyn Botanic Garden.

He had just driven past the zoo's entrance when the question that had obsessed him for years began gnawing at his guts: Why did Beansy Rutolo step up to the plate to save his dad's ass? Pinky-rings simply didn't do that without an ulterior motive. He knew deep down that the question was better left unanswered; but on another level he also knew he had to know the answer.

He wondered if Madeline Fine knew why Beansy had saved his dad. People in love shared their secrets as much as they shared their dreams and their hopes. He didn't for one second believe that Beansy and his squeeze could be together for "twenty-one years, eight months, and twenty-seven days" without Beansy confiding things to her. He planned to pay Madeline Fine another unannounced visit—soon.

On his left he saw people riding horses along the park's bridle path. For some reason the sight of the horses made him remember his ex-brother-in-law, Carmine, telling him in Junior's that Pat had just ended it with a lawyer.

He used to get nuts whenever he thought of his ex in bed with another man, doing the things they used to do together. But now he had trouble even remembering what they used to do. Maybe that was a good sign.

His reverie turned to the Ice Maiden and how, wearing only her black thigh-highs, she would slink up to the side of his bed, stamp one foot up on the mattress, cast her sultry eyes on his, and, using both hands, open and reveal her sex. His ex would never have done things like that. Yet there was a tenderness of lovemaking with Pat, and a warmth of sharing domestic life together, that he had never experienced with another woman—and he doubted that he could ever find that kind of love again.

As he approached Grand Army Plaza, he eased the car out from behind a truck and drove up the curb cut of the winding driveway that emptied into the delivery entrance of the main branch of the Brooklyn Public Library. He rolled the car to a stop in front of the steel gate crowned with razor wire. He hitched over onto his left buttock and fished out his shield case. Holding it open, he pressed the shield and identification card against the windshield so that the guard peering from the other side of the gate could see them. The barrier swung open, and he drove inside.

The library's spacious first floor was crowded. A group of schoolchildren was being taught how to use the computerized catalog system.

As Stuart crossed the great space, heading for the reference section, he passed by the library's famous Egyptian collection and paused to examine funeral stelae and parts of ancient temples with friezes lauding great warrior kings in battle. He examined an obelisk covered with hieroglyphs that offered prayers to the gods Serapis and Isis. Finally, after admiring gold statuary of lions and ibexes, he walked over to the reference desk.

The librarian behind the counter had African locks—neat, tightly matted tendrils of hair. A small gold ring pierced her right nostril.

"I love your hair," he said.

She gave him a broad smile. "Thanks. It cost me a week's pay."

"It was worth it." He leaned his arms on the counter and added, "I'd like to see *The Wall Street Journal* for August 18, 1993."

"May I see your library card?"

He pulled out his shield case. When she looked at his lieutenant's shield, she smiled. "Where do you work, Lou?"

Her use of "Lou" for lieutenant told him that she came from a cop family. "Seven One Squad."

"My dad is a retired captain, and I have one brother a detective in the Seventh and another a sergeant in the Three Two."

"What's your name?"

"Brown."

"Is your dad Marcus Brown?"

"Yes."

"A lot of years ago your dad and me worked together in the ol' First Squad. Next time you speak to him, tell him Matt Stuart sends regards."

"I will, Lou," she said, and walked behind a gray partition, disappearing into the microfilm room. When she came back a minute and a half later, she was holding a box of spooled film. The bold-faced label on the box read "Wall Street Journal, July–December 1993."

She came out from behind the counter and led him to the room on the right that contained the viewing machines. She asked him if he knew how to use them, and when he assured her that he did, she handed him the box.

Five rows of tables filled the cramped room. Each table held six machines, square, boxlike things with grayish white screens. He walked over to the first table near the door and sat in front of the machine at the end.

He shook out two spools from the box, took the one marked "July, August, September," and slid it onto the spindle on the left side of the machine. After unraveling the film, he slid it under the retractable glass plate on the bottom, taking care that the notches on the film's edges were properly inserted into the pawls. He slid the unraveled end under the glass and threaded it into the rewind spindle.

He switched on the machine. The screen glowed eggshell white. He began turning the handle on the side of the machine, scrolling the microfilm across the screen. Columns of newsprint sped past the glass as he rushed through the days and weeks of July, slowing when he got to August 15. When he reached the eighteenth, he slowly moved the film to page three and began reading the article that had been cut out of Beansy's newspaper.

The story was written by Dick Goldberg and bore the headline CME APPROVES TRADES OF CHEESE FUTURES. The paper told its readers that the Chicago Mercantile Exchange had given its approval for the sale and trade of cheese futures on the commodities exchange.

The story explained that commodities futures were sophisticated financial instruments used by businessmen as a hedge against unforeseen future price increases or price decreases. Trading in the new futures had not been brisk, leading some commodities traders to speculate that there was no market for them. Stuart couldn't make any sense of it at all—if Beansy Rutolo wasn't involved in the actual operation of the family company, why would he care about the subtleties of cheese commodities? Or could this have no connection at all? Another visit to Angela seemed to be in order.

9

N ext morning, dressed to kill in a blue blazer and Sea Breeze shirt, lightweight gray slacks, and yellow tie patterned with blue monkeys, Stuart stood at his large living room window, sipping coffee from an oversize mug and watching the sun's rays dancing across the upper bay. Patches of fog still hovered over the waters.

He savored the strong French roast coffee as he watched an oil tanker lying at anchor. She was apparently carrying a full load, because she rode very low in the water. He turned and glanced into the entrance foyer, to his grandfather's carved mahogany commode. A maroon accordion folder lay on top; inside were Paddy Holiday's personnel folder and F File.

The Ice Maiden had delivered them last night. It had been after ten when she'd stepped into the foyer, slid the envelope on top of the commode, and cheerfully announced that she was going to fuck his brains out. He smiled as he thought about the high points of their night together. His left shoulder and inner thighs were black and blue from her rapacious love bites.

He was anxious to get to the office and digest Holiday's records. Whoever was feeding Holiday information might well have worked with him at one time. Also, Paul Whitehouser, nephew of the chief of detectives, was scheduled to report at nine. He wanted to be there to greet him.

The cuckoo popped out of its nest eight times.

Stuart took a final sip from the mug and walked over to the piano. He picked up David's picture. His son was astride a brown-and-white Coney Island pony. The roller-coaster ride loomed in the background. David's tiny feet barely reached the stirrups. The picture opened the dam holding back those memories. They had gone to Nathan's for franks, fries, and corn on the cob. Pat had worn a yellow sundress and—

He switched off the painful memory. Dr. Lamm had told him not to dwell on the past as he moved forward with his new life. He kissed his son's picture and returned it to its place on the top of the Steinway.

Some night duty detectives were still at their typewriters when Stuart arrived. He went over to the command log and signed himself present for duty at 0840 hours. He looked into the detention cage; sullen eyes stared back. Stuart went into his office and looked over the sixty sheet.

Hector Colon came in after him, stroking his luxurious, wide mustache and looking exhausted. He filled the whip in on the night's mayhem and then went back to his typewriter, eager to clean up and be gone.

Stuart untied the accordion folder and took out the personnel record first. It was inside an eleven-by-fourteen folder with Holiday's name, shield number, and tax registry number inscribed at the top from left to right. He opened it and unbuckled the metal paper fastener on top, then slid clumps of forms off the shiny holding arms. Because department records were filed chronologically, he began to read through the forms from back to front. He wanted to begin at the beginning.

Holiday had no military record. He was appointed patrolman on June 1, 1961. After six months in the Police Academy, he was transferred to the Nineteenth in midtown Manhattan. After his six months' probation was up, instead of being transferred out of his training command into a permanent command, he remained in the Nineteenth.

For many years it had been policy to transfer rookies into permanent precincts as soon as probation ended. Stuart pulled over the yellow pad and made a note: "Paddy remained in Nineteenth. Why?"

Holiday had received above average semiannual evaluations. He was awarded an excellent police duty for the apprehension of an armed robber. A sudden chilly breeze swirled through the open window and fluttered the papers on his desk. Stuart turned to the next form. A Change of Residence or Social Condition notified the Job that Paddy Holiday had married Maureen Quinn July 4, 1963.

Stuart flipped to a set of "green sheets," cop argot for departmental charges and specifications. Paddy Holiday and his radio car partner had been charged by IAD with accepting free meals, both on and off duty, at some of the city's best hotels and restaurants. At the department trial, all the restaurateurs and hotel workers swore that Holiday and his partner had only eaten there off duty and had always paid their bills. The two cops were acquitted.

Stuart leaned back in his chair. Why had IAD bothered to bring charges? They must have interviewed the restaurant and hotel people and gotten enough corroboration to substantiate the allegations, or else they never would have filed green sheets. Paddy got a helluva lot of people to change their testimony, he thought. This guy was a mover and shaker early on and certainly smart enough not to try to suborn witnesses himself. You don't have to be in the Job long to figure out how easy it is for wiseguys to reach out to people in the hotel and restaurant business. He picked up his pen and jotted on the pad, "Pinky-rings probably had their hooks into Paddy early on. How come nobody picked up on that?"

Holiday was promoted to detective and transferred into the Intelligence Division on July 13, 1964. Stuart flipped to the personnel data card to see if Holiday had any language or electronic specialties that would have qualified a guy with so little time on the Job for such a sensitive assignment. He didn't find anything to justify this career move. Did the wiseguy have enough weight to plant a mole even inside Intelligence? he wondered.

Holiday continued to receive above average semiannual evaluations while in Intelligence. On December 21, 1968, he was promoted to sergeant and remained in Intelligence. His continued assignment there after his promotion was another divergence from department policy. Stuart made a note of that. As he went through the file, he wrote down the name of any cop or detective associated with Holiday in any significant way.

When he finished going through the folder, he restored the forms to their chronological order and fastened them back in the folder. He picked up the F File, which was made up of single-spaced sentences typed on teleprint paper and fastened together at the top by a shiny bar. The date the unsubstantiated allegations or rumors came to the attention of the department was typed in the left margin.

Holiday's F File consisted of two sheets of paper. There were several allegations of adulterous relationships with civilians and policewomen. Five anonymous letters alleged Holiday's secret ownership in Russo's bar. Six unsigned letters told of Holiday's lavish lifestyle. But the real payoff was a narcotics detective's confidential informer who snitched that Holiday was peddling information to the wiseguys.

Stuart could find no record of any department follow-up to any of the allegations. He shook his head, appalled at the Job's inaction in the face of so many accusations, especially the last.

He unpinned an official communication from the CO Intelligence to the CO IAD that was attached to the last page of the F File. Holiday's boss at the time reported that six confidential investigations into organized crime's hold on the construction and carting industries had been blown. After each investigation was exposed, CO Intelligence "walked the cat back" over the cases, trying to determine what had gone wrong. He determined that Holiday was the common denominator in all of the foiled investigations; he had worked each one of them.

After the construction and carting fiascoes, CO Intelligence reassigned everyone connected to the cases. Holiday was put in charge of monitoring ethnic radio and television programs. CO Intelligence had requested an immediate IAD investigation.

If the F File contained only rumors and unsubstantiated allegations, how had an official communication gotten into it? Stuart reasoned that the boss of Intelligence must have smelled a rat in the woodwork and wanted to plant a record of his suspicions somewhere in the Job, so he'd sent a copy of his request to the untouchable F File.

Stuart quickly opened the personnel folder again and found that Holiday had filed for service retirement six days after CO Intelligence had forwarded his urgent request for an investigation. Department regulations required a member of the Job to file for retirement thirty days before his retirement. This was done in order to prevent a cop under investigation from escaping with his pension.

All kinds of bells and whistles should have gone off in IAD the moment they were notified of Holiday's impending retirement. Either someone inside IAD had stonewalled the investigation of Holiday until the thirty-day clock ran out or they had taken a look at Holiday's work in Intelligence and been unable to come up with anything solid to substantiate the suspicions of CO Intelligence.

Stuart began rubbing the sides of his nose. Ain't nobody in the Job who lives *that* much of a charmed life, he thought. Somebody shit-canned that case long enough for Paddy to escape. I need a wire into IAD. He heard a rustle and looked up to see Kahn coming through the doorway.

"Morning, Lou," she said, walking around the side of his desk. Luminous pearl earrings complemented the large pearl buttons on her black-and-white wool suit. She sat down and crossed her legs. From a large department multiuse envelope, she took out a handful of reports and photographs, saying, "Here are copies of the surveillance reports that were cross-referenced to Russo and Terrella."

He took them. Each report contained an abstract of a surveillance on other subjects that somehow related to Russo or Terrella. One was a synopsis of a phone tap on Terrella's home number that yielded up a conversation between Frankie Bones Marino and a Lucchese soldier named Tommy Esposito. The Lucchese crime figure wanted Marino to find out if the NYPD was conducting an undercover investigation into carting in the High Bridge area of the Bronx.

"And how am I supposeta do dat?" Marino asked.

"Ask Paddy Irish to find out."

Stuart looked at Kahn. "You read this stuff?"

"Last night."

Stuart picked up a handful of surveillance photos of Daniel Lupo's wedding. It had been held in the Arches, a posh catering hall in Great Neck. The intelligence pictures showed people arriving and leaving the wedding. He looked through them and then put them down.

Next he took up a batch of photographs of the wedding feast inside the Arches. They were table shots of the guests. A sly smile touched his lips when he realized that they had gotten hold of the official wedding pictures. He admired the ingenuity of the guys in Intelligence.

At each table half of the guests remained seated while the other half gathered behind them, standing and smiling, posing for the camera. A number in red ink was written above the head of each guest. Labels were pasted on the backs of each photograph, identifying the guests. Andrea Russo, Beansy Rutolo, and Madeline Fine were at table eleven. Four people at that table were unidentified on the label, Fine one of them. Andrea had told him she didn't know the name of Beansy's squeeze. So why the lie? And how much of what she said could be relied on?

Kahn handed him a sheet of paper. "I copied whatever Intelligence had on Mrs. Lupo and her family."

He read. Jacob and Sylvia Epstein had no criminal records or connection to OC. Jacob had founded the Franklin Investment Trust Corporation in 1949, then sold it to his son-in-law, Daniel, in March of 1978. Both Jacob and Sylvia were deceased. Their only child, Bonnie Epstein Lupo, had no criminal record or prior association to OC.

"We're going to have to take a look at this Franklin Investment Trust," he said, watching the line of chained prisoners shuffling out of the squad room. He scratched his chin thoughtfully. "Do we know how the Epsteins died?"

"No. But I'll find out."

Outside in the squad room, Jerry Jordon snapped up the ringing phone and called out, "Calvin, it's Plaintiff."

Jones grabbed the receiver and slammed it down.

Borrelli stuck his head into the office. "Whitehouser's here, Lou."

Stuart looked up at the wall clock: 0915. He said to Kahn, "Give me a few minutes and send Whitehouser in."

Kahn got up to leave. He noticed the strands of hair curling down alongside her ear.

He dialed Andrea Russo at home. When she answered, he leaped right at her. "I need to see you, now."

"I'm working on my term paper, and then I have to go to work."

"This won't take long. Five, ten minutes at the most." He waited for her answer; when it didn't come, he said, "It's important."

"Awright, awright. I'll meet you in half an hour behind the Downstate Medical Center."

He hung up just as Paul Whitehouser filled the doorway. Stuart pointed to the chair. Whitehouser lumbered over and sat, glancing up at the precinct map. "You're fifteen minutes late," Stuart said.

"I got stuck in traffic," he said with an air of indifference. His pumped-up biceps and pecs strained the fabric of his flashy jacket. His hair was slicked back with no part.

This guy's a real dickhead, Stuart thought. He's been coddled so long, he's forgotten why squad bosses are called "whips." Aloud: "Next time you're late, it's going to cost you a vacation day."

Whitehouser's moon face flushed, and anger made the veins in his neck stand out.

I'll let this guy stew in his juices, Stuart told himself as he reached for Whitehouser's personnel folder; it had arrived in the department mail the day before. As he flipped through the folder, he occasionally hurled a disapproving glance at the detective. Whenever he said something he made sure his voice had a disheartening edge.

He turned a page, said, "You've been dumped out of a lotta shops. You only lasted eight months in Pickpocket and Confidence." He continued reading. He could see sweat glistening in the detective's hairline. Either I bring him around or else I'm going to have to flop him back into the bag. "The word is you got an attitude problem with women."

"They don't belong in the Job."

"They're here, and they're not going away. And this is my shop, and I'm not about to let you fuck it up."

Whitehouser started to say something; Stuart held up his palm. "I don't want to hear it. Your uncle flopped you into this shithouse as a warning." He leaned over his desk and glared at the detective, saying softly, "This is the last stop, Paul. You got no place to go from here except back into uniform or out of the Job. Your uncle is history in a year, and when he goes your protection goes. Don't you think it's time to consider your wife and your children?"

He saw genuine fear in Whitehouser's eyes and softened his tone. "Paul, you're a good detective when you want to be. It's up to you. I'll work with you any way I can, but you gotta pull your weight."

Whitehouser gnawed his lower lip. "You'll get no grief from me, Lou."

Andrea Russo jumped into the passenger seat and slammed the door. Stuart drove off, heading east on Lenox Road.

"Why did you lie to me about not knowing Beansy's squeeze?"

She stared at him defiantly. "S'pose I did know? I wasn't about to give her up so you could bad-mouth Beansy to her. Those two were a real love story."

"I think Madeline knows a lot about Beansy's business."

"So what? You think she's gonna give up anything he might have told her? That'd be a betrayal of her man, and whatever he was or wasn't, he was her man, first, last, and always."

"Does Madeline have any business connections with Danny L?"

"Madeline's not connected to them in any way. She's legit."

Stuart was getting impatient with Andrea. "So how come she was at Lupo's wedding?"

"She was there because she's the bride's aunt. Sylvia Epstein and Madeline were sisters. Beansy met her at the wedding."

"Do you know if Madeline inherited any of the family business when her sister died?"

She looked at him incredulously. "You think any of those people talk any of that inheritance shit with me?"

"You could have picked up the word on the street or in the bar."

"Well, I didn't. Besides, I don't run with any of them."

He braked for the red light. "What do you hear about Danny Lupo these days?"

"The word is he's been legit for a lotta years."

"You believe that?"

She smiled and shook her head. "Those guys only get honest when they get dead." After a long silence, she looked at him and said, "Paddy asked me if I was doing you."

"Whatcha tell him?"

She smiled again. "That you give great head."

He turned right onto Remsen Avenue. Two white memorial crosses were painted on the trunk of a maple tree.

Andrea began brushing her fingertips over a small area of the dashboard, a thoughtful expression clouding her face. She reminded him of a desperate person attempting to summon up a genie to whisk her off to a better life in a better place.

"I want to be free, Lieutenant," she said. "Free of them and free of you." She wrapped herself in her arms. "I'm scared."

Gino's does not accept credit cards. The landmark Italian restaurant on the west side of Manhattan's Lexington Avenue, between Sixtieth and Sixty-first Streets, had for many years been a favorite haunt of the city's high and mighty.

The small bar in front of the entrance was crowded with lunchtime drinkers when Daniel Lupo walked in. He was greeted warmly by the host, a big bald-headed man with a five-hundred-watt smile and a firm handshake, who quickly showed the investment banker to a small table against the wall. Lupo noticed Dustin Hoffman and his wife sitting at a table in the rear. Two black men, one wearing a turban and the other an African cap, were speaking French across the checked table-cloth. As soon as he sat down, Lupo looked around the restau-rant, making sure that there were no faces that didn't fit in with the crowd. Lately he'd been getting the uneasy feeling that bad blood from the old days was slowly walking its way toward him. As always, he sat facing the entrance.

The host asked, "Can I get you somethin' to drink, Mr. Lupo?"

Lupo ordered a bottle of Antinori Chianti Classico.

As the host walked off, Lupo stared for a moment at the restaurant's trademark burnt sienna wallpaper patterned with tiny black-and-white zebras, then nervously shifted his attention to the bar. Where the hell was she?

A waiter came over and offered him the bottle of wine for approval. After glancing at the label, Lupo nodded. The waiter was drawing the cork from the bottle just as Angela Albertoli walked in. She stood at the entrance, looking around. When Lupo waved to her, she nodded and came over. As she approached his table, he stood. She pulled back her chair, and they sat together. She draped her lizard shoulder bag over the back of her chair and looked at him.

They sat staring at each other, the distant years a barrier. Fin-ally he broke the awkward silence. "Would you like a drink?"

She looked at the bottle of wine. "That would be fine."

He poured her wine and then lifted his glass in a silent toast. Her eyes moved slowly around the restaurant and then flashed back to him. "You've come a long way from Pigtown, Daniel."

"So have you, Angela."

She rotated the stem of her wineglass slowly. "Why did you ask me to have lunch with you?"

"When I saw you in church yesterday, I realized how much I've missed you over the years."

Her scornful laugh turned several heads. She leaned across the table, glaring at him. "You were the one who dumped me for that rich Jew from Sands Point. Remember!"

"That was business, you knew that."

"What's your problem, Daniel? You bored with your wife and your mistress, and looking for something else on the side?"

"The simple truth is I've missed you."

"You missed me so much that it took you over twenty years to pick up the phone."

He looked down at the table, trying to find the right response. She wouldn't be here if she didn't still have the hots for me, he thought. Then he blurted out, "I didn't feel I had the right to call you."

She avoided his eyes. He sipped wine, staring at her over the rim. She wasn't the gangly tomboy he'd known as a young man. But as hard as he searched, he was unable to find the fire that used to light up her eyes. She had the hard edge of a scorned woman in charge of her own life. He felt confident that he'd be able to rekindle that flame. Slowly, tentatively, he moved his hand across the table until their fingertips touched. She allowed them to connect only for a moment before she pulled her hand back. "You've changed, Angela."

She picked up a breadstick and pointed it at him, then declared, "There are several things I don't do anymore, Daniel. I don't eat butter or salt, and I don't suck uncircumcised cocks."

The woman at the next table looked around at her and smiled approvingly.

Lupo covered his dismay by signaling the waiter to come over. When the waiter came they both ordered salads and pasta. He wanted linguine with red clam sauce; she wanted angelhair pasta with lobster sauce. When the waiter walked away, she asked, "What do you really want from me?"

"I'd like to see what it would be like for us to be together again."

"And your wife?"

He flicked one hand dismissively. "Bonnie and I have an arrangement."

"Ah, an arrangement. A lot of men have them. They lie to their wives, and the wives pretend to believe them. But *this* woman won't be part of any such arrangement."

At that, the waiter brought their salads. Lupo was grateful for the distraction. This wasn't going the way he'd planned.

He attacked his salad and finished it quickly. The waiter silently put their main courses on the table and vanished.

"How's business?" Lupo asked her, brushing his napkin across his lips.

Wrapping pasta around her fork, Andrea said, "Very good. We're having an excellent third quarter."

"I'm wondering if you would be interested in a business proposition?"

She put down her fork and spoon, looked at him, and said, "And I thought you were only interested in my brains." She went back to wrapping her pasta around her fork. "I don't deal in your kind of business. You should know that by now."

"I'm a legitimate businessman with a legitimate deal," he snapped, his cheeks flushed.

She glanced across the table at him and inclined her head to one side. "I'm listening."

"One of my companies is looking for a place to store milk and cheese on a short-term basis."

"I don't have milk storage tanks."

"You don't need them. The milk will be in a refrigerated tanker truck. All we need is a large, secure space to park it in."

"Why me?"

"Because your late uncle told me that you had a large unused space behind your factory in New Jersey. And your plant would give us fast access to the city. But the main reason is that I trust you. You would never sell us out to hijackers. Liquid milk and cheese are cash commodities, as you well know. You can rip 'em off for big bucks."

"Why don't you build your own storage tanks?"

He gestured impatiently. "We're not in the milk business. For a limited time we're going to be able to pick up some liquid milk at a bargain price. We'll sell it for a quick profit to the large food discount chains, who'll put it in their own containers."

She seemed to find the explanation acceptable but asked, "And the cheese?"

"From an undertaker who's into the shys for some big bucks. We're taking a load off his hands for forty cents on the dollar and selling them to a wholesaler in Chicago."

"Sounds like robbery to me."

He grinned at her. "It's a cruel world."

She picked up her wineglass. "What are you paying?"

"Three thousand a week, cash."

"What about insurance?"

"We'll take care of that and security."

"I'll have to sleep on it, Daniel."

Lupo sensed that she would play, but didn't want to be pushed farther right now. "While you're deciding, I'd like to take a drive out and look around your plant to make sure that there's enough room."

"I'm going back after lunch."

"I have several meetings scheduled this afternoon. Suppose I drive out around five."

She pushed her plate to one side. "Make it around five-thirty."

Kahn parked the unmarked car in the official parking lot on the Avenue of the Finest behind police headquarters. She and

Stuart crossed Madison Street and walked up the wide orange brick staircase leading into One Police Plaza. People moved about the plaza, savoring the afternoon sun and the ethnic food stands.

Stuart and Kahn walked into headquarters and were immediately funneled into the security line marked out by blue webbing supported by metal stanchions. Stuart looked at the fifteen-foot bronze memorial statue that seemed to fill the huge lobby. It depicted a proud policeman wearing the old high-collar uniform and cap with a comforting arm around the shoulders of a young boy. Eric LaGuardia, son of the late, great mayor Fiorello LaGuardia, had served as the model for the boy, the son of slain patrolman Martin J. Gillen, Jr. Attilio Piccirilli had finished the statue in 1939.

The people moving through the cordon made their way up to eight turnstiles. Six policemen manned the consoles on the other side. As the cops came up to the gate, they inserted their identification cards in a slot on the turnstile. If the card was valid, a duplicate copy of it scrolled onto one side of the split screen. If the face on the ID matched the face waiting on the other side of the gate, a green light lit up and the cop pushed his way through the barrier.

As Stuart and Kahn moved up the line, Stuart read some of the memorial tablets that lined the lobby's walls. James Cahill was the first NYC cop killed in the line of duty: September 29, 1854. The last was Sean McDonald: March 15, 1994. There had been others since, but their tablets had yet to be cast and hung.

At last, Stuart and Kahn pushed through the turnstile. They moved to the right and walked down the wide staircase to C level. The corridor was lined with wooden pallets of teleprinter paper and computer spreadsheets. Old desks and file cabinets were stacked on their sides, and the ceiling was a jumble of pipes from which hung fluorescent light fixtures.

They made their way to room A-79. Detectives stood around, shooting the breeze in the corridor to the left of room A-79, in front of a four-by-four sliding glass pass-through window cut into the cinder-block wall of the corridor. They would speak through the window to duty clericals in the Photographic Unit. This was where detectives came to order "wet" mug shots and then waited for the photographs to be developed.

Stuart and Kahn went through a door next to the window and walked inside. The walls were covered with enlargements of color prints that had been taken by photographers assigned to the Photographic Unit: an armada of tall sailing ships coming up the Hudson River, Stormin' Norman Schwarzkopf's ticker tape parade up Broadway, the now famous July 4 fireworks display over the Statue of Liberty.

A large sign on the wall stated the grim fact that of all the cops killed in 1993, seven had killed themselves.

An orange leatherette sofa stood against the cinder-block wall to the left of the entrance; next to it, two hardy and seldom watered plants stuck up out of shiny metal containers. A waist-high wooden barrier with a single gate ran the width of the room. A young woman wearing pyramid-shaped nugget earrings sat on the other side of the gate, manning a telephone. She looked up at the visitors.

"May I help you?"

Stuart badged her and said, "I'd like to see the director."

Chet Soren, the civilian director of the Photographic Unit, came out from behind his desk as Stuart and Kahn walked into his glass-fronted office. "What can I do for you, Lou?" he asked as they shook hands.

"I'm doing graduate work at John Jay, and I'm thinking of writing a paper on photographic security in the Job," Stuart lied.

Soren's cherubic face beamed. "I set up the security system. What would you like to know?"

Stuart said, "When the Photo Unit receives a 'ninety' requesting mug shots, you develop the negative and send the pictures through department mail to the command of the member requesting them."

"That's correct," Soren agreed.

"What happens to the 'ninety'?" Stuart asked.

"It's entered into the computer tracking system and then destroyed," Soren said.

"How does the tracking system work?" Kahn asked.

"Every time mug shots are ordered, the name, shield number, and command of the requesting officer are entered into the tracking system. We're able to enter a mutt's Nisid number into the computer and pull up a list of every member of the service who ever ordered mug shots on that individual."

An idea suddenly came to Stuart, and he asked, "How long has the tracking system been in place?"

"Since eighty-one," the director replied.

Stuart jerked his thumb at the sliding glass window. "What about detectives who show up out there and order 'wet' copies?"

"Same procedure," Soren said.

Stuart scratched the back of his ear. "When a detective waits for a 'wet' one, does anybody check to see that the name on the 'ninety' he submits is the same as the name on his ID card?"

Soren's face took on a slightly worried expression. "No. We automatically assume that he's legit because he's been passed through building security."

Stuart glanced at Kahn. She got his message, opened her pocketbook, and took out a handful of mug shots. She handed them to the whip. Stuart began randomly shifting through the stack and pulled out Hollyman's and Gee's mug shots. He passed them to Soren. "Would you mind showing me how the system works?"

Chet Soren led the detectives out of his office and along an aisle of green clothing lockers that had plants hanging down over their sides. Row after row of sliding file drawers held the negatives of every person arrested by the NYPD. They walked by a huge Noritsa photo printer and over to the tracking system's computer. The civilian technician sitting in front of the screen wore jeans and a gray Gap sweatshirt. Soren handed the man the mug shots of Gee and Hollyman and said, "Print out their sheet."

The operator took the mug shots and typed in Gee's Nisid number. The tracking data with the names of all previous requestors scrolled onto the screen. The operator pressed another key, and the laser printer on the side of the console whirred to life.

At that moment Stuart's beeper went off. He opened his jacket and looked at the LED display. He turned to Kahn and said, "Call the Squad and see what's up."

Kahn walked away, looking for a phone.

Soren tore off Hollyman's and Gee's tracking sheet and handed them to Stuart. On Wednesday, September 21, the day Hollyman and Gee were whacked, a Sergeant Brown from IAD had ordered mug shots on the two men.

This was an emergency job, Stuart thought: he would have had to come here and wait for a "wet" set to be developed, which meant that building security probably had his ID card on the file tape for that day. And as a general rule, department tapes were kept for sixty days before being erased and reused.

Sergeant Brown from IAD, he mused. The name might be a phony, but the command wasn't. Whenever criminals em-ployed aliases they almost always used their real first name, and whenever cops tried to get cute, they might use a phony first and last name, but they almost always unthinkingly used their own command.

He slipped the printout into his jacket pocket and was thank-ing Soren for all his help when he heard the metallic jangle of Kahn's bracelets. When he saw her tense expression, his chest tightened. "What is it?"

"We caught a double homicide in Banjo High."

George W. Wingate High School at 600 Kingston Avenue was built in the shape of a banjo, with the main building a three-story-high circle resembling the drum and a long arcade of class-rooms looking like the fretted neck of the musical instrument.

When Stuart and Kahn arrived at Banjo High they found a lone RMP parked inside the schoolyard. A pool of blood had congealed on the ground under the tattered net of a basketball hoop, along with the chalked outlines of two bodies.

Stuart told Kahn to wait in the car. He got out, went inside the wire-fenced yard, and walked over to the radio motor patrol car.

The heavyset cop behind the wheel saw him approaching and stuck his head out the window. "The Squad brought it all into the house, Lou."

Standing next to the blue-and-white, Stuart leaned down and asked, "What went down?"

"A bunch of, you should pardon the expression, schoolchildren were playing spongeball. They got into an argument over some bullshit and got into a pushin' and shovin' match. One of 'em, a fifteen-year-old boy named Pablo Asante, runs home and comes back ten minutes later with a MAC-11 and proceeds to spray the schoolyard with nine-millimeter slugs. Two boys, one fourteen and the other fifteen, DOA on the ground."

"And the shooter?"

"Can you believe it? He hung around the schoolyard struttin' his macho bullshit until the first RMP responded and collared his ass."

Stuart looked up at the school windows. Students inside the building crowded around them, looking out at the police, making obscene gestures. One girl who looked about thirteen was sucking on three of her fingers, sign language for an oral sex act. Stuart looked at the chalked outlines on the ground, shaking his head with disgust at the incredible casualness of murder. When he'd come on the Job only twenty years ago, a homicide was high priority. Today no one gave a damn unless it was a high-profile killing. We respond to the scene, he thought, gather whatever physical evidence there is, canvass for witnesses, and go back into the house to do our paper. Then we just wait for the next homicide to come along tomorrow.

"Whitehouser asked us to stay here until you came, Lou. You need us anymore?" asked the RMP's operator.

"No. Thanks for waiting."

The radio motor patrol car slowly rolled out of the schoolyard, leaving Stuart staring down at the chalked outlines.

The squad room was crowded with witnesses. The detectives had spread them out around the room so they could not talk to one another, compare notes, change impressions. As the whip and Kahn entered the squad room, Whitehouser came over to them and said to Stuart, "The DA is using your office to take statements."

Stuart looked into the empty detention cage. "Where's the shooter?"

"Handcuffed to a chair in the interview room," Whitehouser said. "We had him inside the cage, but he kept wising off to the witnesses."

"Who's taking the collar?" Stuart asked.

"The uniform cops who grabbed him."

"Good."

Court proceedings ate a lot of man-hours, so Stuart was glad that the uniforms got the credit but would have to spend the time in court. Kahn went over and started to help Borrelli and Jones with the paper. Stuart walked into his office and nodded to the DA and the woman working the stenotype machine. The DA was questioning a witness who looked to be no older than thirteen.

Stuart walked over to a desk and picked up the phone and dialed. When he got the Ice Maiden's answering machine on her home phone, he waited for the beep, then said, "It's Matthew. Please call me at home tonight, it's important." He hung up, irritated by her rule outlawing personal calls to her when she was in the office. His next call was to IAD. When the cop on duty at the other end answered, he said, "Sergeant Brown, please."

"He died three years ago."

"Thanks." Replacing the receiver slowly, he thought: So Sergeant Brown bought the farm. So who's ordering mug shots, his ghost?

Frankie Bones Marino walked out onto the terrace of Danny Lupo's office. Lupo was glued to the eyepiece of his telescope. Frankie Bones could tell by the way he was stroking the tripod with his left hand that he was watching a woman. Danny L heard him approach and said, "Frankie, come look. I got this dame naked on a bed jerking off with a dildo."

"Not interested." He walked over to the parapet and looked down at the late afternoon congestion. The traffic was worse than usual. Frankie's squat body dwindled into insignificance against the background of the surrounding tall buildings. He lit a cigarette and tossed the match over the edge, watching it drift down until he lost sight of it. Then he turned and looked disapprovingly at Danny L, who was still playing at being a Peeping Tom. If he wasn't such a big earner, he'd be dangerous with that kinky shit of his, Frankie thought. "My lady friend just phoned me," he called out.

"And how is our dear Mary?"

"Concerned for us."

Lupo's hand froze on the tripod. He stepped back from the telescope, staring at Frankie. "And why is that?"

"Today is Friday. She cooks for me every Friday night. She hadda go out this morning to buy sausages and tomato paste for the gravy. As she was driving by Downstate Medical Center she spotted Andrea Russo getting into that police lieutenant's car."

Lupo's calm expression vanished. "What does Russo know about us?"

Frankie Bones's pudgy hands waved in the air. "Dunno for sure. I don't see how she can hurt us."

"She can hurt us with the past, Frankie. She's from the neighborhood. She knows things. Maybe she's working with this cop."

Frankie Bones dragged deeply on his cigarette and blew the smoke up at the water towers of the Chanin Building. "I phoned Holiday after I spoke to Mary. He told me that he ordered Andrea to get close to the cop in order to find out what he knew about Beansy's hit. He said that the cop is doing Andrea, and he figures that this morning was nothing more than a matinee."

"Holiday's an asshole," Lupo snapped.

He went inside and plopped down on the high-backed chair behind his desk. He took a cigar out of the humidor and, balancing it between his fingers, began rolling the Cuban beside his ear, listening to the crackle of tightly packed tobacco.

"Do you really believe Stuart is doing her?"

"I don't see him hopping into bed with a dried-up junkie."

"Me either."

Frankie Bones took a final pull on his cigarette and, crushing it out in the ashtray, asked, "What do you wanna do?"

Lupo's cold eyes sent out an unspoken but clear message.

Frankie Bones nodded. "Who ya wanna use?"

Lupo tapped his thumbnail against his upper tooth, thinking. "Give it to the Hippo."

"And the cop?"

"Get him off our backs." His tone was deceptively mild.

"Done like a dinner."

Lupo checked the time. "I gotta run over to Jersey and see Angela."

"Think she's gonna play?"

"I think it's goin' to be okay with her," Lupo replied, speaking more confidently than he felt.

Patterns of golden autumnal sunlight dappled the ground under the canopy of trees covering the hill behind Albertoli's parking field. In the west, twilight crowded the horizon, yielding to the darkness.

Angela and Danny Lupo stood outside, looking around the asphalt parking field.

"How come you never use it?" Danny L asked.

"We don't need to. Everything comes and goes through the bays on the side of the building."

"We could put four tankers in here if we had to."

"How are you going to ship your cheese?"

"Inside the tanker truck. It'll unload the milk at the bottler and refill with cheese for the return trip to Chicago. We'll save on transportation costs."

A sudden thought made Angela frown. "When you refill, the milk will taste like pecorino Romano."

"We'll flush out the tanks real good before we fill 'em up again."

He looked her in the eyes, and she turned her head, refusing to meet his stare. His confident grin annoyed her.

Lupo asked, "Can I look around inside the plant?"

She turned away quickly and walked toward the gray steel door at the rear of the building. She unlocked it. After striding past her, he gallantly held open the door. She brushed by him into the factory and its rich aromas of cheese.

He went over to one refrigeration unit and pushed aside the curtain of thick plastic vertical slats. "Could you make room for my pallets in here?"

"Your cheese is hard; it doesn't need refrigeration."

"Yeah, but this way we avoid mix-ups."

"Okay, if I agree to your deal."

Uncertainty crept into his voice. "It's a good deal, Angela. It costs you nothing, and you pick up some tax-free walking-around money."

She looked at him with a suspicious expression. "I find your sudden generosity out of character."

"It's good business, nothing more. You got the right space and location, and I trust you. This is a one-shot deal."

"I'm still not convinced you're being honest with me."

"Why are women so goddamn suspicious?"

"Because we know men."

"This is a legit deal," he said irritably.

"Is it, Daniel?"

"I'd never do anything to hurt you. You're from the neighborhood, f'crissake."

"You hurt me once. Bad."

Shaking his head in angry frustration, Lupo turned his back on her and stormed across the factory floor.

She tilted her head, watching him. "Where the hell are you going?"

"Home. In the morning I'll start looking for another place."

"I haven't said no."

He turned around; a smile flickered across his face. "You ain't said yes, either." Lupo stood there, waiting for her move.

She came toward him, the clap of her heels echoing off the concrete. She walked past him and gestured for him to follow her into the empty business office. Piles of hard-covered accounting ledgers covered the tops of three desks; the computers slept.

She switched on the lights in the conference room behind her own office. A long, oval-shaped table presided over the room. High-backed chairs embroidered with orange-and-black floral designs stood around the table. She moved to the chair at the head and sat down, pivoting her legs under the ledge.

"Do you remember this room?" she asked him.

He sat on the chair beside her. "Yes. We used to drive out here at night and make love on top of this table. We were too broke for motels."

"And do you remember the things we used to do?"

"Yes." He leaned over and tried to kiss her.

She turned her face away and got up from the chair.

"Do we have a deal?" he demanded.

She switched off the light and stepped out of the room. "Yes, Daniel. We have a deal. But only on the trucks."

10

Stuart opened his eyes and stared up at the sunlight creeping into his bedroom. Suzanne was in bed next to him. She was lying on her side with her back to him, legs spread wide under the sheets. She had phoned him late the night before in response to the message he had left on her answering machine. He'd told her he needed to talk to her. She'd come over and spent the night.

He stretched out his hand and began caressing her leg, slowly moving up her thigh to the warm, moist mound in the middle. For a sweet minute his hand lingered there, massaging her. She lay perfectly still, moaning with her eyes half closed. "Go for it, Matthew." He gently nudged her onto her stomach and mounted her, penetrating her from the rear.

When they were spent, they crowded into each other's arms, breathing rapidly. Suddenly she broke away and pushed herself up onto one elbow. Looking down at his face, she said, "More and more I find myself wanting to be with you. That's a bad sign for a woman with my agenda."

"I'm sure you'll manage to cope."

"Do I detect an edge?"

"No, not really. I've got a lot on my mind."

She kissed him lightly on his mouth. "It's eight, and I have a ten o'clock step class at the gym."

"I'll make us some coffee." He dragged himself out of bed and went downstairs into the kitchen. When he returned, Suzanne was in the shower. He went into the bathroom, pushed aside the curtain, and stepped into the tub. They lathered each other's body slowly, kissing under the cascading water.

A robin was hopping around the flower box on the kitchen window when they finally went in to make breakfast. They sat at the round table, drinking coffee and picking at the blueberry muffins that he had taken out of the freezer and nuked in the microwave. Holding her mug up to her mouth, Suzanne said, "It seems that we spend most of our time together in bed."

"I know." He put down his mug and said, "I need to ask you for a couple more favors."

"You're beginning to run up a big tab."

He smiled reassuringly. "I've never walked away from a marker."

"I know. I read your F File."

Their eyes joined briefly. "I need a copy of the Big Building's security tapes for September 20 and 21."

"What's the other favor?"

"IAD had an open case on Paddy Holiday before he got out. I need to see that case folder."

She ran her fingers over the bud vase in the center of the table. "I'm a one-way street, Matthew. I've never made a secret of that." She sighed. "I don't think I'm going to allow myself to get entangled in your little mystery."

"I'm asking a friend for help, Suzanne."

"I can't." She pulled his old white terry-cloth robe around herself more tightly.

"You got me Holiday's personnel folder and his F File. What's the big deal with this?"

"Do you really have to ask that? Holiday's ancient history as far as the Job is concerned. But Big Building security, and IAD case folders, old or current, are a whole different matter." She got up and went over to the sink. Staring out into the garden, she said, "I've dreaded you most of my adult life."

"Me?"

"Yes, you. I come from a cop family, too. My mother was a policewoman. She used to tell me stories about what it was like for women in the Job during the fifties and sixties. How every boss expected head on demand, how women weren't allowed on patrol, weren't allowed to sit for the sergeant's test, how in order to make detective they had to sleep with every asshole muck-a-muck in the Job."

"What the hell has that got to do with me, with us?"

"Everything." She whirled around to face him. "When I decided that I was going to be the first woman PC in the Job, I was willing to give up marriage and a family to accomplish what I wanted. But I always knew that lurking somewhere was a man capable of derailing me from the fast track to the fourteenth floor. I . . . I knew that one day I'd meet a kind, decent man." She looked away. "It gets lonely being the Ice Maiden."

When he saw the tears filling her eyes, long dormant feelings of tenderness and caring broke through the protective crust he had erected for himself. He went to her, taking her into his arms, pressing her face to his chest. "I'm sorry, Suzanne. Forget that I ever asked. I'm a resourceful SOB, I'll manage."

"Do you understand why I can't get involved?" She turned away from him. "Involved. Yeah, with you, too. It's not going anywhere, Matthew."

Stuart could feel the tenderness draining out of him. "I don't know if it can. There's too much of me that's still missing."

She took him by the hand and led him into the living room, over to the white sofa in the bay window with its view of the upper bay. She sat down and pulled him next to her.

The cuckoo popped out of the clock nine times.

"I've read *your* F File. Now I know that Beansy Rutolo saved the Job for your dad, so I can understand why you want to get the people who did him. But there's more to it than that, isn't there?"

Stuart looked away from her, trying to deal with his confused thoughts and emotions. "I don't like the current crop of schemers and plotters. They'll eat any honest cop alive who gets in their way." He looked her in the eye and added, "They're the descendants of Knight's Roundtable."

"Knight's Roundtable," she echoed. "That's one of those vague legends in the Job that everyone's heard of but nobody seems to know much about."

"You're the keeper of the F File. You're not going to tell me that you don't have the lowdown on the Roundtable?"

"I know what everyone else knows. That in the late fifties drug money began to flood the city, and the Palace Guard didn't know what to do about the enormous sums the cartels were willing to pay to get their drugs onto the street. So the current chief inspector at the time, Arthur Knight, called a secret meeting of all uniform and detective borough commanders." She frowned in concentration, trying to remember what she had read and heard. "They met on Thursday, October 2, 1963, at the Hotel Jefferson on East Fifty-sixth. They sat around a round table in a private dining room and decided the future direction of corruption within the Job. You know what their decision was? 'Good money' won."

"That's right," he said. "And good money won for the same reasons that the Five Families voted not to get involved in the drug trade. They all knew that the money was so big, they would lose control of their people. The men sitting around that round table decided that in order to control corruption, they were going to put their people in every sensitive assignment in the Job."

"It was all a big waste of time. Bad money won out anyway."

"Narcotics was the wave of the future," Stuart said.

"It's sad, isn't it?" She walked over to the piano and picked up a picture. "I've never noticed this one before. Your family?"

"Yes."

"Do you ever hear from your ex?"

"We have no reason to stay in touch."

She returned the frame, picked up another one. "I like this one of your dad and the nun."

"My aunt Elizabeth. My father's sister."

She put the picture back on the piano and began wandering around the room, looking at his things. She strolled over to the mahogany bookcase and ran her fingers over the spines of books.

She reached into the bookcase and slid out a glass-encased teakwood plaque with an old .32-caliber Colt revolver with a four-inch barrel. The metal plate on the bottom was inscribed "Patrolman William J. Stuart, NYPD. Appointed January 1, 1887. Retired July 2, 1927." She held it out to him. "Your grandfather?"

"Yes. His class was the first on the Job to be armed on duty."

"And today we're packing nines with fourteen-round magazines." She went over to the piano and sat on the stool.

"What about taking a drive to City Island later for some lobster?" Stuart asked.

"I'd love it." She looked up at him. He kissed the top of her head.

The weather-bleached wood of Rafter's restaurant was mirrored in the waters of Eastchester Bay. The City Island restaurant sat atop pilings on the water's edge of Belden Point, the island's southernmost tip.

Stuart and the Ice Maiden sat at a table with a great view of the bay. She had changed into khaki slacks and a white long-sleeved shirt. The sleeves of a yellow sweater were tied casually around her neck. She wore white Dock-Sides with brown leather laces and no socks.

They had both ordered two-pound lobsters, steamed and opened. He had ordered a bottle of Pouilly-Fuissé wine. Looking out across the bay at Big Tom Island, she said, "Rumor has it that Patrick Sarsfield Casey lost his suit. The decision should be coming down next week."

"Too bad. He was a good boss to work for."

She ran her finger over the stem of her wineglass. "Do you really believe that Knight's Roundtable yarn?"

"Absolutely."

"And do you also believe that there is a cabal of dirty cops who protect the bad guys?"

He sipped his wine, watching her. "I believe that there are people in this Job who have sold their shields."

They fell silent, both suddenly aware of the clatter of glasses and the buzz of conversations around them. They had been so preoccupied that they hadn't noticed the restaurant filling up with other diners.

He made idle circles on the table with his glass, watching her attack a lobster claw. This afternoon she was fully into the role of a beautiful woman sharing a long lunch with her part-time lover. He liked her sexual honesty. She was a woman who knew what she enjoyed and made no bones about it. He had had a brief affair once with a woman who would make love only in the dark, covered by a sheet, and who thought oral sex was a town in Oregon. Suzanne was an exciting, sexually confident, and assertive woman without inhibitions.

She looked up from the claw and caught him staring at her. "What are you thinking about, Matthew?"

"About the many faces of Suzanne Albrecht."

"And which one do you like the most?"

"This one, and the one I made love to last night and this morning."

She laid her hand on top of his. "Me, too."

An awkward silence came between them. They listened to the rhythmic lapping of the water against the pilings. After a while she said, "Most of the people I've met on the Job are honest and dedicated."

"But a few scumbags in the right places can do a whole lot of damage. One of the biggest problems in the Job is the 'Sweep it under the rug, I don't wanna know about it' phobia of the Palace Guard. They're so terrified of bad press that they would rather see bad guys walk than do anything that might jeopardize their lousy careers."

"You sound like a one-man IAD crusade."

"I'm one pissed-off cop."

She looked out at the boats sailing the open bay. "Your righteous anger makes me ashamed. You're trying to do your job, and I'm more interested in my career path than in being a good cop."

"When you're the PC you'll end the reign of Knight's Roundtable and his jolly band of thieves."

They picked up their glasses and made a silent toast. After they finished lunch they wandered the beach hand in hand, not talking, enjoying the glorious day and each other's company.

Afterward when he drove her home, she slid across the seat and kissed him tenderly. "Thank you for a wonderful lunch, a wonderful day."

"You're welcome."

She took his hand in hers and began tracing his veins. "I like the time we spend together, Matthew."

"I do, too."

She watched her finger moving over the blue network on the back of his hand. "Have you ever thought of marrying again?"

"Something broke inside of me when I lost David and Pat. There isn't a whole lot left to commit."

Suzanne's voice took on an impatient edge. "You're probably better off staying single. And me, too." She opened the door and got out. As he watched her disappear inside the lobby of her apartment building, an overwhelming feeling of loneliness and despair almost paralyzed him. He sat for a while, staring through the windshield, trying to decide what to do with the rest of his day. His piano lesson was on Tuesday, and he hadn't practiced a whole lot. There was a new Clint Eastwood cop movie he wanted to see. But in the end he decided to drive to the Squad, reread the case folders, and listen to cop chatter bubbling over the radio.

• • •

Andrea Russo arrived home a few minutes after seven Saturday night. She was bone tired and hurting from unusually bad monthly cramps. She planned to take a long hot bath to relax. After that she was going to watch a video of *Shadowlands,* with Anthony Hopkins. She'd heard that it was a real tearjerker. She loved tearjerkers. And after the movie she was going to crawl between the clean sheets and savor the comforting cool smoothness of the cotton as it turned into a cocoon of relaxing warmth. She did not have to work tomorrow, so she planned on sleeping late, reading the Sunday papers in bed, working on one of her term papers, and watching another tearjerker.

She walked into the bedroom, kicking off her sneakers. She unbuckled her belt and wriggled out of her jeans. She removed her blouse and bra and fell across the bed, staring up at the thin crack that zigzagged the ceiling. I must get around to plastering that damn thing, she thought.

As she reviewed the events of that day, she was puzzled by Holiday's unusual kindness. He'd even noticed she wasn't feeling well and sent her home early. He must have gotten laid last night, Andrea concluded. She lifted her pelvis and worked off her underpants, then tossed them on the bed. She sighed as a cool breeze slipped through the open window and caressed her body. She heaved herself off the bed and walked into the bathroom.

Joey "the Hippo" Montie drove the stolen car to Rutland Road and stopped in the darker shadows of a tree. He killed the lights and the engine. The .32 S&W tucked inside his white-and-blue designer warm-up suit was cold against his massive belly. His eyes strained as his gaze zeroed in on her house. Her rusted Plymouth Valiant was parked in front. The house was in darkness save for the reflection of the bedroom light. She's in the bedroom, he thought, checking out the rest of the street. Mary Terrella's place was in total darkness. No lovers parked anywhere; deserted street. He snapped on a pair of latex gloves and heaved his short, heavy body out of the car.

He kept to the darkest pools of shadows. When he reached
the Terrella house he stepped onto the porch and lifted up the
right front edge of the doormat. The key was there, just the way
it was supposed to be. He picked it up and walked across the
street.

Andrea stood in front of her bathroom mirror, rubbing
cream over her body. This was pamper time. As she rubbed the
lotion across her breasts, she thought of feeling a man on top
of her and began to feel her nipples getting hard. She moaned
as her fingers kneaded her tits. Her lethal weapon number
one, a two-headed vibrator, was plugged in and waiting under
the bed.

She walked back into the bedroom and was reaching under
the bed when she heard a scraping sound behind her. She
whirled around and gasped when she saw the almost grotesque
figure blocking the doorway. Fear gripped her body; her legs
began shaking, and she started to rock from side to side.

Hippo smiled as he looked straight at her with pitiless eyes.

When she saw the black hole pointing at her face, she
squeezed her eyes shut, clamped her hands over her face, and
begged, "Please don't."

The slug ripped between the ring and middle fingers of her
left hand, plowing into her skull a centimeter above her eyebrow.
The force of the impact threw her body on top of the bed, its
sheets soaked with her blood.

The Hippo tucked the .32 back inside his warm-up suit
and walked over to the bed to see what she had been reaching
for. When he saw the vibrator he let out a raucous laugh. He
always wanted to use one of them with Rose Marie but had
been too embarrassed to walk into one of those sex stores and
buy one. He unplugged the machine, stuffed it into his pocket,
and left.

Outside on the porch, he locked the door. Looking up and
down the block, he saw nobody, so he stepped back and
rammed his stubby foot into the door above the lock. The door

splintered open. He went back across the street and replaced the key under the Terrella doormat. His excitement mounted at the thought of watching his girlfriend use the vibrator. He hurried to the car.

11

W ho's catching?"
"I'll check," Whitehouser said, and walked over to the
sixty sheet on top of the library cabinet. This was the
second time in three hours that the same guy had called, wanting to know who was catching the new cases coming into the
Squad. Scanning the sheet, he saw that Borrelli had caught the
first two hours. Kahn was up now; Jones would cover the end of
the tour.

He went back to his desk and picked up the phone. "Who is
this, anyway?"

"Goldstein in Missing Persons. We got a missing seventy-year-
old male who resides in your precinct. His daughter reported
directly to us. I'll do all the paper on it and send whoever's up a
copy of the 'thirteen.'"

"Helen Kahn is up."

"Thanks," Goldstein said, and hung up.

Whitehouser replaced the receiver and looked across the
squad room at Kahn, who was bending over an open file
drawer, tucking in case folders. Great ass, he thought, getting
up and going over to her. "Goldstein in Missing Persons is
gonna be sending you a missing persons report on a seventy-
year-old male."

"Thanks," she said as she pushed in a case folder.

He moved closer so that his leg pressed against her. "You married or otherwise involved?"

"Something like that," she said, edging away from him.

"Too bad." As he walked away, he fumbled at her crotch.

She froze, unwilling to believe what had just happened. When she recovered from the shock, she wheeled and saw him leering at her. She walked calmly over to him and slapped him in the face with the full force of her outrage.

Borrelli and Jones looked up from their typewriters, stunned.

Whitehouser leaped up. "Who the fuck . . . !"

"What the hell is going down there?" Stuart barked from the doorway.

"Nothing," Whitehouser growled, slinking back to his desk.

Kahn walked back to the open file drawer. Stuart stormed through the squad room, passing her, saying, "In my office. Now."

She banged the drawer shut and followed him inside.

"What happened?" he demanded.

"Nothing, Lou. Just a misunderstanding."

"Helen, I'm not about to let some asshole screw up this squad. Now you tell me exactly what went down out there."

She avoided his glare. "Nothing, Lou."

His temples throbbed as his anger rose. "Outside, and send him in here." Helen's a stand-up gal, he thought. I'm going to have to act on my gut instincts.

She left the office, motioned for Whitehouser to go inside, and ran crying out of the squad room.

Borrelli and Jones ran out after her.

She ran down the hall to the female bathroom and darted inside, slamming the door behind her.

"You're out of here," Stuart barked at Whitehouser.

"For what?"

"Assholery in the first fucking degree, that's what." He snapped up the phone and dialed the chief of detectives' office.

The detective division's XO answered, "Inspector Gebheart."

"Inspector, this is Stuart from the Seven One Squad, I need to speak with the boss."

"It's Saturday, he's not around. What's up?"

"I've got a serious personnel problem. I'm either going to suspend or lock up the newest member of this command. But before I do, I'd like a little guidance from the c of d."

Stuart heard a stifled groan over the phone. "Whitehouser?"

"You got it, Inspector."

"Don't do anything until I get back to you."

"Ten-four." He hung up and glared at Whitehouser. "Wait outside."

"Lou, lemme explain, f'crissake," Whitehouser pleaded.

"You dealt this hand, not me."

Stuart went outside and looked around for Kahn. Not seeing her, he asked Borrelli, "Where's Helen?"

"She ran into the head, crying," Borrelli said.

Stuart hurried out of the squad room.

Borrelli glared at Whitehouser and said, "You're a lowlife prick."

Going along the corridor that connected the detective squad with the precinct's anticrime unit, Stuart saw her coming out of the bathroom. He went over to her. "You okay?"

"I'm fine, Lou. Thanks." She had repaired her makeup and regained her composure.

Jones came running out of the squad room. "Lou," he called out, "the desk officer just phoned up. We got a homicide at Four-oh-one Rutland Road."

Andrea Russo's body was spread-eagled across her bed. Her mouth was agape. Blood had coursed out of her mouth and ears and pooled around her head. Her chalky body was beginning to fill with rigor mortis contractions. Reddish purple lividity stains soiled the bottom half of her torso. Stuart's mouth closed in a narrow tight line as anger swelled in his chest. This was all his fault. He should have prevented this.

Why the hell her? Why? She was a harmless woman trying to drag herself up out of the slime she'd been born into. He bent down and closed her eyes forever.

"Take a look at her left hand," Kahn said.

Stuart examined the fingers. "The bullet passed between the ring and middle fingers," he said. "She must have seen the shooter and covered her face with her hands."

"The bedroom window is partially open," Borrelli said.

Stuart saw the sheen spread over her body, bent down, and rubbed his fingers over the cold chest. He raised his fingers to his nose, smelling the oils and creams of her toilette. He looked at her underpants on the bed and her discarded clothes. He stuck his head into the bathroom. Two used bath towels lay crumpled on the floor. Jars and bottles of body lotions and creams stood on the sink. "She gets undressed, takes a bath, does her thing before going to bed, walks out of the bathroom, and finds the shooter waiting for her. She throws her hands across her face, and bang, the lights go out forever," Stuart said.

"The front door was kicked in," Kahn pointed out. "She hadda hear the crash in the bathroom. She could have made a run for the window or something."

"That door was kicked in for our benefit," Stuart said. "I've never heard of a shooter crashing through a door to get to a mark. They're not about to give their victim a chance to go for a piece and blow them away. That lock was either picked, the door forced, or the perp had the key." He looked at Kahn. "When the crime scene boys get here, have them take that lock out and check it."

She made a note in her scratch pad. Borrelli, Jones, and Whitehouser came in. Kahn withered Whitehouser with a glare. Borrelli said to the whip, "Nobody home in the Terrella house."

Jones brushed his hands across his shiny head and said, "And we came up dry on the canvass. There's nobody around here. It's like a fuckin' ghost town."

Whitehouser came over to the whip and said, "Lou, the desk

officer received a call from an anonymous male who stated that a homicide had gone down at this address."

Stuart's eyes widened. "He said a homicide?"

"Yeah. I picked up on that, too, so I double-checked with the desk sergeant," Whitehouser said.

"'Homicide' sounds like a cop talking," Stuart said. "Nine out of ten civilians would have said, Somebody's been murdered, or shot, or killed."

Whitehouser picked up the phone in his gloved hand and dialed Missing Persons. When the detective at the other end answered, he said, "Lemme talk to Goldstein."

"Ain't no Goldstein assigned here, pal."

"Thanks." Whitehouser carefully returned the receiver. He looked at Kahn pensively and asked, "You catch this?"

"Yeah, why?" she said, concern just below the surface.

Whitehouser told them of the phone calls he had received asking who was "catching." "The caller no sooner finds out that she's up than the desk officer gets the call."

With concern written over his face, Stuart looked at Kahn and said, "It looks like someone wanted to make sure you caught this caper."

She bit her lower lip anxiously but didn't respond.

Stuart walked outside by himself and stood on the porch, staring out into the gathering darkness. Suzanne and City Island seemed like light-years ago. He wondered why anyone would want to make sure that Kahn caught this case. He had a creepy feeling that something weird was happening, and that Holiday was somehow involved. He kicked the post. Why is it that the scumbags always seem to win? he asked himself. No matter how hard we try, the body count keeps growing.

He heard the crunch of tires and looked up to see the familiar crime scene unit's station wagon rolling to a stop in front of the house. He watched as the detectives got out of the station wagon, walked back to the tailgate, and opened it up. As they were pulling out their black leather cases, he stepped off the porch and went over to them. "Got a piece of chalk?" he asked the younger one.

"Sure, Lou," the detective said. He snapped open the valise and handed him a piece.

"Thanks," Stuart said, and walked back onto the porch. He raised the chalk to the faded wood shingles to the right of the door and etched in a memorial cross.

Herta Renard's three-story house was a stone's throw away from the Triborough Bridge. This evening the second floor of the house was filled with the cries and moans of their lovemaking. They lay on her canopy bed. Patrick Sarsfield Casey, her married lover of twenty-eight years, was on top of her. She closed her eyes and bit his earlobe, allowing herself to be swept away by the rhythm of his violent thrusts. As their passion grew, their sweaty bodies came together and parted faster and faster until at last their shrill cries of pleasure choked in their throats.

He collapsed on top of her, gnawing her bare shoulder.

"I love you, Patrick," she said, arching her hips into him and scissoring him between her legs.

"Me too."

At fifty-five Herta Renard had the tight body of a thirty-year-old woman. Wisps of gray colored her short black hair. Over the years they had made a life together, seeing each other two times a week during the day and two nights a week for twenty-eight years. He rolled off her and glided his hand over her breast. "If I'm forced to retire, I won't be as flexible with my time," he said.

"We'll manage; we always have." She looked at him with questioning eyes. "Has Martha ever given you any indication that she knows about us?"

"No, never."

"All these years together and she—" She stopped midsentence upon hearing the phone inside the bedside commode ring. Years ago he had had the unlisted "phantom" phone installed on a separate line. They never used it; only the Job had the number. Whenever he visited Herta, the sergeant manning the borough's operation desk knew where to reach him if Martha was looking for him or the Job needed him.

"I'm sorry," he said. Leaning across her body, he opened the commode's door and pulled out the offending instrument. "Yeah?"

"The c of d just gave you a forthwith."

"Where?"

"Aperitivo."

Aperitivo restaurant on Manhattan's West Fifty-sixth Street was rumored to have the best spaghetti carbonara in the world. Plush burgundy banquettes lined the walls, and paintings of Italian villages with narrow stone streets hung from the rococo molding.

Chief of Detectives Kevin Hartman, a big man with deep blue eyes and thick jowls, was seated by himself on a banquette in the rear of the restaurant facing the entrance.

Louie, the dapper owner of the restaurant, greeted Casey as he walked in. "Good to see you," Louie said, shaking hands. "The man is waiting in the back for you," he said, leading Casey by the long bar into the dining area in the rear.

As Casey slid in next to the c of d, Louie asked, "What can I bring you from the bar?"

"A double Glenfiddich on the rocks."

"Better make it a fuckin' triple, Louie, he's gonna need it," Hartman said, adding, "And bring me another Absolut with a splash of Black Label." As Louie walked off, Hartman looked at Casey and asked, "How's Herta?"

"Good."

Hartman steepled his hands in front of his face as his cautious eyes swept the restaurant. Patrick Sarsfield Casey did the same thing, inching closer to the chief of detectives. Hartman whispered, "Stuart is looking to hurt my nephew. Isn't that guy a team player?"

"He's solid people, Kevin."

They fell silent when Louie came over with their drinks.

They touched glasses. Casey guzzled his Scotch, then said, "Maybe your nephew really stepped on his cock this time and did something that can't be swept under the rug."

"Bullshit. Short of a fuckin' homicide, anything can be covered over, you know that."

"Times have changed, Kevin. There are a lotta people out there looking over our shoulders, trying to turn us into a headline."

"How good do you know Stuart?"

"We go back a lotta years. I knew his ol' man."

Hartman nodded and drank, lowered his glass, and then raised it back up to his mouth and finished off the drink. He held the empty glass up to Louie, who nodded and walked back into the bar. "You and me are fast coming to the end of the road, Patrick Sarsfield Casey. Soon we're gonna have nothing but time on our hands."

"I could win my suit."

Louie walked over with their drinks; they fell silent as he served them. When he left, Hartman raised his glass to his mouth and said, "The rumor going around the Big Building is you lost. The decision is supposeta be coming down next week."

The color drained from Casey's face. "Win some, lose some," he said in a husky voice.

"You have forty-three years on the Job, so you'll be getting out with full pay," Hartman said.

"Yeah," Casey agreed glumly.

Hartman rolled his glass between his palms, his eyes on the ice cubes. "Your salary is eighty-five large. Not a bad pension. 'Course, taxes is gonna eat up a lot of that eighty-five." His eyes slowly roamed the crowded restaurant. He raised his glass and held it in front of his mouth, then said, "I can delay the decision long enough for you to file for three-quarters. A tax-free disability pension is a pretty nice cushion to have."

"I really appreciate that, Kevin. But we both know that White-houser has a problem, and that if it isn't Stuart who steps into him, it'll be some other boss. These guys have busy shops to run.

They can't allow some guy with a perpetual hard-on to run around their squads grabbing a handful of pussy whenever the mood hits them."

"Why the hell do you think I put him in the Seven One?"

Patrick Sarsfield Casey took his time considering the question. He took a slow pull at his drink and then said, "Busy shops mean grade money for the detectives who work there. Most of the detectives in the Seven One are second and first grade. And Stuart has commander's money. I figure you're going to see that Sonny Boy gets promoted, and then you'll wangle him three-quarters on some bullshit disability."

"You gonna do the right thing with Stuart for me?"

Patrick Sarsfield Casey pursed his lips, moving them in and out, mulling over the question. He finished off his drink and held up the empty glass to Louie. "I'd have to go before the medical board. What's my disability?"

"Heart. A guy your age is guaranteed to have something wrong with his ticker. I'll take care of everything."

A waitress came over to take their order. She had a heavy brogue.

Patrick Sarsfield Casey smiled at her and affected a brogue. "Where you from, darlin'?"

"Limerick. And you?"

"The Bronx."

Paddy Holiday left the bar and strolled over to the curb, where he lit a cigarette and tossed the match into the gutter. He wore a troubled expression and kept looking up and down the street as though he were expecting company.

"The bastard can't figure why we haven't scooped him up for questioning," Stuart said to Sergeant Warren Edmonds, whip of the Seven One's anticrime unit. Stuart had radioed him from the latest crime scene.

Every fiber of his cop instinct told him that Holiday had a hand in Andrea's murder. He wanted to take a look at the bar to see if Holiday and any of his friends were around.

Stuart and three anticrime cops were huddled inside the Seven One's lend-lease surveillance vehicle, a battered gray van decorated with a whirling mass of black graffiti. The blackened one-way observation ports were concealed by the black swirls. They had parked the van on Lincoln Road, two blocks east of the bar. The NYPD's Motor Transport Division rotated undercover vehicles on a biweekly basis among precinct anticrime units. This was done so that the vehicles did not become known to the precinct's resident scumbags.

"Do you think he did the Russo homicide, Lou?" Edmonds asked.

"He's no shooter," Stuart said, watching Holiday through the porthole. "But he sure as hell is involved."

"Are you going to bring him into the house for questioning?" Edmonds asked.

"Waste of time," Stuart responded. "He'd only ask for his lawyer. He's not going to tell us anything until we have him by the short hairs. Look at 'im out there, pacing up and down, expecting us to squeal to a stop, leap out of the car, and drag his ass into the house. Well, I'm going to let him stew. Let his concern grow into fear. Then I'll have my long-overdue talk with him."

Holiday walked to the corner and rested his shoe on the rim of the street lamppost. He bent over and tied his shoelace. Straightening, he tossed his cigarette away and cut diagonally across the street to the other corner, where he checked out the cars parked along the curb.

"What's he up to?" Edmonds said.

"Dunno," Stuart said, watching through the porthole.

Holiday reached into his yellow windbreaker and drew out a cellular phone. He opened it up and punched in a number. "Whaddaya doin'?" he asked the man who answered at the other end.

"We barbecued in the backyard. We're cleaning up now. I figured it's gonna be cold in a few weeks, so might as well take advantage of the good weather."

"You always were the outdoor type," Holiday said, tucking the phone between his chin and shoulder as he lit another cigarette.

The man lowered his voice. "How'd everything go?"

"Like it was supposeta."

"Good."

"I still don't know why you wanted to get that other person involved."

"That was personal, Paddy."

"I just hope it don't cause problems."

"It won't."

Holiday could hear the tumult of children playing in the background. "You sure you didn't leave any paper trails around the Big Building?"

"Hey, Paddy, gimme a break. I've been doing this shit for a whole lot of years."

Holiday sucked in a mouthful of smoke and blew it out his nose and mouth. "When's our friend's life gonna become a nightmare?"

"In a couple of days. I've already set the thing in motion."

"My people want this done right."

"It will be."

"I'm surprised that our friend hasn't been around to see me. After that thing happened today, I figured he'd be around to haul my ass into the Squad."

"He knows the first words outta your mouth would be 'I wanna call my lawyer.' So he probably figures why waste time goin' through the motions."

"Stay in touch." Holiday punched off.

In the tree-lined backyard of 11 Cherry Oak Lane, Syosset, New York, off-duty police lieutenant and devoted husband Ken Kirby folded up his phone and tucked it into the pocket of his shorts. Deep in thought, he walked over to the glass-topped picnic table and picked up his half-full can of Miller Lite. As he guzzled beer, his gaze wandered over to his third wife, who was dishing macaroni salad out of a large blue bowl into plastic storage containers.

In the four years I've been married to this one she's put on
four sides of beef, he thought. Lowering the can, he wiped his
mouth with the back of his hand and belched. Why do I let these
women suck me into marriage? He was fantasizing about a young
policewoman he'd just hooked. He looked at his watch; she was
working a four-to-twelve in the Tenth. Plenty of time to change,
give her a call, and drive in. This new one was a world-class blow
job. His thoughts turned to his last girlfriend. He was glad he'd
thrown Kahn into the snakepit with Stuart. Who the hell did she
think she was, dumping on me? She knew I was married from
the get-go, and now she gives me that "You're a married man"
bullshit. I'm gonna fix her ass real good.

He drained the can and walked up behind his wife, slipping
his arms around her waist. "How's it going, honey?"

"Who was that on the phone?"

"My one and only mistress," he said, nuzzling her earlobe.

She stiffened, her voice taking on a sarcastic edge. "It seems
that your police department is calling you in a lot lately. I never
realized just how important you were."

"Honey, when the Job calls, I gotta go."

Stuart watched Holiday walk back inside the bar.

"He always walks outside to make his phone calls," Edmonds
said.

"He's a cautious prick," Stuart said. "You guys maintain any
kind of a regular surveillance on Holiday and the bar?"

"Not really, Lou," Edmonds said. "We check 'im out during our
travels around the precinct. But like you know, we're mainly concerned with jump collars. I got ten people assigned to the unit,
and each one of 'em gotta get on the sheet with two felonies a
month, so we don't have a whole lot of time to play detective. But,
Paddy, we give 'im a look-see each tour."

"Do me a favor, keep looking in on the retiree. I'm particularly
interested in any visitors he might have."

"My pleasure, Lou."

The sergeant's portable radio crackled, "Lou, you on the air?"

Stuart recognized Borrelli's voice. Edmonds handed him the radio. Stuart keyed the transmit button. "Yeah?"

"You have a visitor, you'd better get back," Borrelli transmitted.

Stuart looked at the sergeant. "Let's head back to the barn."

12

Patrick Sarsfield Casey sat with his feet up on the pull-out leaf on the side of Stuart's desk, sipping Glenfiddich from his flask and staring out at the buzz of activity in the squad room.

The Saturday night mayhem had begun around six-thirty. The detention cage was filled with prisoners, and the overflow was stretched around the squad room, manacled to chairs and pipes. The detectives were occupied with the phones and their paper while uniform cops prepared their arrest reports.

Whenever the squad was this busy, Jones put Smasher on guard duty by feeding him his special "killer" diet, which consisted of two cans of wet dog food mixed with a liberal dash of hydrogen peroxide. This caused the rottweiler to foam at the mouth.

Smasher played his part well, sauntering around the room with a frothy mass of bubbles oozing from his mouth, emitting a low-grade growl, pausing long enough in front of each manacled prisoner to give off a bloodcurdling growl that drained the color from the prisoner's face. Occasionally he'd stop in front of the detention cage and shake his head violently, spraying the white spittle on the prisoners inside.

The prisoners sat perfectly still, terrified.

A burst of gunfire shattered the distant night. Patrick Sarsfield

Casey's ears pricked up; he decided that the rounds were probably coming from one of the ugly guns, a TEC-9 or a Cobray M-11. When he returned his attention to the squad room, he could not help but notice the unspoken hostility between Kahn and the newest member of the squad. They avoided each other's eyes, and whenever they walked around the room they gave each other a wide berth.

When Stuart came into the squad room, Patrick Sarsfield Casey swung his feet off the desk and walked to the window. "Close the door, Matt," he said when the whip walked inside. He took another swig from his flask, gazed out over Pigtown, and said, "I was getting laid this afternoon when I got a 'forthwith' from the chief of detectives. In all your time on the Job, haven't you heard of the chain of command? Squad bosses don't go over the heads of their district commanders with personnel problems. What the hell were you thinking about?"

Stuart didn't flinch under the onslaught. "The c of d dumped his problem on me, and I want it out of here. I've got no time to deal with an asshole like Whitehouser."

"Your problem is you've got open homicides piling up all over the place. Every whip in the Job has disciplinary problems. Exercise some leadership and deal with it, 'cause Whitehouser ain't gonna go away."

"That's the word from the c of d?"

"That's the gospel according to Hartman." He took another swig, passed the flask to Stuart. "The good news is that he's not going to be here that long."

Stuart wiped the spout with his hand and took a long pull of the single-malt Scotch, his mind racing: He just dumped him into this squad, so he's not about to transfer 'im out. And he don't have his twenty in. So? He handed the flask back, saying, "Hartman's going to get him three-quarters?"

"You just keep the lid on things here."

Stuart thought, Patrick Sarsfield Casey only goes to the flask after he's had a few, which means that he probably met Hartman at some restaurant, where they broke bread over a jug and made a deal. I wonder what his price was to save Whitehouser's butt? Since it's quid pro quo time in the Job, I might as well join in on the festivities.

"Get him down!" someone screamed from the squad room.

Smasher's front paws were up on a prisoner's lap. The rottweiler was baring his awesome teeth and growling into the terrified man's face.

"Smasher, leave the nice man alone," Jones said without looking up from his typewriter.

Smasher leaped off the prisoner and continued his patrol.

"You got Smasher trained real good," Patrick Sarsfield Casey said.

"That's Jones's job, he's really into dog training."

"Plaintiff still breaking his balls?"

Stuart smiled. "With great regularity." He looked at his boss and said, "I'll try my best to sit on this thing, but I can't make any guarantees."

"Kahn's your problem. Deal with it."

"I might not be able to deal with it."

"What the hell did he do to her?"

"He fondled her breast and groped her crotch," Stuart said. Though he didn't know exactly what went down, he went with his gut instinct.

"This guy don't belong on the Job. But we both know that sometimes we're forced to do things we don't want to do. Can you talk to her?"

Stuart was beginning to enjoy this game. "You know how these feminists are. She's liable to make a complaint to the DA or one of those antidiscrimination agencies alleging sexual harassment. Allegations like that would send the press and feminist groups into a feeding frenzy."

Casey rubbed his jaw uneasily. "Shit. Can you think of anything that might calm her down?"

"I gotta tell ya, she's a great detective. She's really into high-tech stuff. You probably know she caught the Russo homicide. In fact, a short while ago she was begging me to get her a piece of equipment to help her break the case. You know, I think if she got that toy, and I gave her her head on this investigation, she might just work off her anger. I think that might be the way to go."

A shadow crossed Patrick Sarsfield Casey's eyes. "And what might this toy be, Matthew?"

"A Cellmate," he answered, drumming his fingers lightly on the desk.

Casey glowered at Stuart. "You're putting the arm on me."

"Like hell I am. I'm telling you what I think it will take to get her mind off Whitehouser."

"That toy you want for her costs eight thousand dollars apiece. We only have a few of them in Narcotics and Intelligence. If you ever lost one, there'd be all sorts of hell to pay."

"We're not going to lose anything."

"Awright. I'll see what I can do. Whaddaya got on the Russo homicide?"

"Nothing."

"Well, you better get something or both our asses will be in slings." He screwed the cap back on his flask and slid it into his inside breast pocket. He looked at Stuart with a strange expression. "This is your RDO and you're here playing cops and robbers. Get a life already, Matt."

"I'm working on it."

"Glad to hear it."

He pawed the door open and left. As he walked out into the squad room, he made for Whitehouser's desk. Resting his palms on top of the typewriter, he bent down and whispered into Whitehouser's ear, "If there's a next time, I'm gonna personally put you out of the Job."

Walking from the squad room, he stopped to pet Smasher and said in a loud voice, "Kill! Kill! Kill!"

13

The tanker truck that parked outside Albertoli's factory on Rangoon Street Monday morning had a catwalk running around its sides wide enough for a man to navigate to the ladder leading up its oval side to the loading hatch on the roof of the tanker.

Lupo and Frankie Bones Marino were on hand early to check out the inside of the shiny tank that had held the liquid milk. Lupo took off his Armani suit jacket and draped it over the sideview mirror protruding out of the left side of the driver's cabin. He untied his silk tie and slapped it over his jacket. Frankie Bones hung his jacket over his friend's. He handed Lupo a pair of gray work gloves. Lupo tugged them on and climbed up the small ladder, on the back side of the driver's cabin, that led to the catwalk. Frankie Bones slipped on his gloves and followed him.

Lupo walked along the catwalk until he reached the ladder in the center of the tubelike trailer that led up to the loading hatch. Gripping the sides, he climbed up to the top and threw open the hatch cover. A stainless-steel ladder led down into the interior of the tank. Lupo started to climb down. His feet slipped on the damp treads; he cursed.

Lupo pulled a flashlight from his waistband and played the beam over the tank.

A white scum coated the sides of the tube, and puddles of milk were scattered over the floor. The air was heavy with the odor of sour milk.

Frankie Bones stepped off the ladder. "You can't breathe in this shit."

"Whaddaya think?"

"I think it's gonna work," Frankie Bones said.

"What we have the crew do is mop up the floor and carpet it with thick plastic. We then pack one layer of wheels across the entire floor. We pack the stuff tight in bubble wrap so there ain't a chance of it moving around." Lupo looked at his friend, a hint of concern in his eyes, and said, "The vans already brought the stuff here, right?"

"Yeah, it's stored in the refrigerator." Smiling, Frankie Bones nodded jerkily, and said, "I really like it, Danny. No cop is gonna think of looking inside a load of milk."

"We do the whole thing and then stash the tanker back here until Charlie Kee's ship makes port."

"What about Angela? Will she go along with that?"

"Leave her to me. Let's get outta here. I feel like I'm gonna pass out."

They climbed back up the ladder. Frankie Bones closed the hatch. Lupo sucked in a mouthful of clean air and looked up at the crystal blue sky. "Nice day."

"Yeah. It's the kinda day that makes ya glad to be alive," Frankie Bones said, walking across the plant's parking lot with his friend.

"Any problem with that thing over the weekend?"

"Naw. Hippo's a good man."

"What about that other thorn in my side?"

"This week." He flicked the ash of his cigarette into the crisp air, fixed his gaze on Lupo's face, and said, "The guy that Paddy Irish is usin' to set Stuart up tossed somebody else into the pot with him."

A quick movement tightened Lupo's eyes. "What do you mean, somebody else?"

"It seems this cop was banging one of Stuart's detectives, and she dumped him. And this idiot's been walking around with a hard-on over bein' tossed into the Dumpster, so he figures this is a good time for payback."

"Don't this moron think she just might figure it out and blow the whistle?"

Frankie Bones shrugged his shoulders.

Anger made the veins in Lupo's neck stand out. He stalked off, shaking his head and cursing. Then he whirled around, came back, and stuck a finger in Frankie Bones's chest. "I want you to personally deliver a message to Paddy Irish. Tell that guy that if anything goes wrong, I'm going to have him and his cop friend fitted with cement shoes."

"Done like a dinner, Danny."

Lupo raised his chin at the truck. "I want the molds packed inside, and I want them heading for Chicago by this afternoon."

"I'll take care of it."

Lupo lightly slapped Frankie Bones on the cheek. "Good." He turned away from his friend and walked inside the plant.

Angela was talking on the phone to a customer. When she saw Lupo in the doorway of her office, she waved him into one of the leather chairs in front of her desk.

As he sat down, he reached inside his blue suit and slid out a white envelope, which he placed on the desk in front of him.

Angela fixed her eyes on it as she talked. When she finished her conversation and hung up, he pushed the envelope across the desk to her. She opened the unsealed lid and peeked inside. "Do I need to count it?" she asked coyly.

"No." The grin she had found so irresistible so many years ago spread across his face. He rested his palms on the arms of the chair, looked directly at her, and said, "Will you have dinner with me tonight?"

She shifted uncomfortably. "I don't think so, Daniel."

"What about lunch?"

She pivoted around to her computer and said, "Call me later this morning."

• • •

Back in Brooklyn two and a half hours later, a black Buick sedan drove from Midwood Street into New York Avenue and parked across the street from Miami Court, a one-block cul-de-sac of attached brick bungalows. Frankie Bones sat in the passenger seat. A musclebound geek, wearing a white-and-silver warm-up suit and a heavy gold rope chain where his neck was supposed to be, sat behind the wheel. The name on his rap sheet was Joseph Ranaldi; his street name was Joey Hershey Bar.

"We'll wait here for a while and keep an eye on the bar," Frankie Bones said. "I wanna make sure there ain't no cops around."

"I never liked or trusted dat guy. He was a cop once and he'll always be a cop," he said, sliding a chocolate bar out of its wrapper.

Frankie Bones looked at the five balled-up candy wrappers on the floor. "Don't you ever get tired of eating that stuff?"

"No. It tastes good."

A battered gray van covered with swirls of black graffiti drove into New York Avenue, past Miami Court. "Check it out, man," barked Paul Siracusa, a portly anticrime cop in threadbare clothes.

Jack Nagel, a bald cop with a beard, peered through the porthole at the occupants of the Buick. "I wonder what they're doing parked there?"

"Drive around the corner," Sergeant Arlene Christopher, the day duty anticrime supervisor, called out to the driver of the van.

The surveillance vehicle was driven into Maple Street; at the corner it turned into Nostrand Avenue and made a left-hand turn into Hawthorne Street. A fire hydrant at the crosswalk of New York Avenue gave the anticrime cops a perfect place to park. They could watch the bar and the Buick from the inside of the van. The skinny driver steered the van into the curb in front of the fire hydrant and slid the transmission into park. Then he slouched down in the seat and pretended to be asleep.

A partition separated the cockpit from the van's interior. A corkboard was hooked onto the inside wall; it was crowded with mug shots and composite sketches of mutts wanted for crimes within the Seven One and adjoining precincts. A floor-to-ceiling wire mesh cage in the corner, up against the partition, contained the unit's theatrical props, including phony leg and arm casts, beards, mustaches, Hasidic frock coats, fur hats, a baby carriage, and a collapsible wheelchair with an attached portable oxygen tank.

Sergeant Christopher, a shapely brunette in her late twenties, wearing jeans and a white bodysuit under a black cotton blazer, reached inside her jacket for the portable radio hooked to her belt. She turned the volume knob to off, then put on a pair of tinted sunglasses.

Nagel slid the cotter pin out of the hole and swung open the prop cage. He reached inside and took out the baby carriage. Bracing it between his legs, he pulled out the two side latches and snapped the carriage open.

Siracusa took out a doll and put it into the carriage. He then took a pink cotton baby blanket and tucked it around the doll. He took out a clear plastic baby bottle full of milk and put it inside the carriage.

Christopher climbed out of the van. Nagel and Siracusa passed the carriage down to her. She took it from them and walked toward the corner.

The viewing portholes on the sides of the van did not allow the cops inside to maintain surveillance of vehicles ahead of them, so for this purpose Motor Transport had installed a periscope inside one of the van's air vents; the periscope also permitted the cops in the van to direct the driver so he could keep his attention fixed on traffic.

Nagel pulled down the periscope and watched Christopher pushing the carriage across New York Avenue. They were parked far enough into the crosswalk so that he could see up past Miami Court.

Christopher walked slowly toward the Buick, her catlike eyes looking sideways behind the dark shades of her glasses at the two men inside the car. When she reached the front of the car, she stopped and reached into the carriage, pretending to adjust the baby's blanket. She crept her hand over to the milk bottle and tossed it out over the top of the carriage.

Frankie Bones watched as she scrambled for the bottle.

She tossed the bottle back into the carriage, reached into the bag attached to the handle, took out another bottle, and, bending, pretended to put the bottle back into her baby's mouth. She pushed the carriage to the corner and crossed the avenue. Five minutes later she handed the carriage up to Nagel and climbed back into the van. "Whaddaya got, Sarge?" Siracusa asked.

"They're just sitting there watching Holiday's bar," she said. "We'll hang around for a while and see what goes down."

Inside the black Buick sedan, Frankie Bones looked at the driver and said, "Let's go see Paddy Irish."

"Want I should go in with you?"

"No. Wait in the car."

The Buick pulled up at the curb in front of the bar. Frankie Bones opened the door, reached up and grabbed hold of the roof, and hoisted himself out of the car. He strolled casually to the bar's entrance, threw open the door, and waved Holiday outside.

"What's up?" Holiday said, a nervous quaver in his voice.

Frankie Bones slid his arm around Holiday's shoulder and steered him down the block. "My people don't like that your friend tossed in the lady detective with Stuart. Getting personal is dangerous. We pay you money to do things for us, not to let your cop friends do whatever the fuck they want to do. You were told to get Stuart off our backs, and you let one of your cop friends get stupid."

"Frankie, this guy been doin' good things for us for a lotta years. He's one of our main connections in the NYPD. This is the first time he has ever gone personal. Trust me, there ain't gonna be a problem."

Frankie Bones's powerful hand clamped on Holiday's shoulder, pulling him close so their faces were almost touching. Holiday winced. " 'At's good. Because if there is a problem, you two are gonna be history."

A shocked look came over Holiday's face. "You guys wouldn't whack a cop."

"Dat's right, we wouldn't. But your friend ain't a cop, he's a fucking thief like us." He turned Holiday around, heading back toward the bar. "The niggers with the braids haven't been laundering as much as they usually do. Any ideas why?"

"Who knows? Maybe they made another connection, one that charges them less points. Maybe business ain't been that good. And maybe they're pissed off because of Gee and Hollyman."

Frankie Bones leaned his head alongside Holiday's and said, "You wouldna gone into business for yourself, wouldya?"

"No. I swear."

"I love when guys swear." He stopped, faced Paddy, stuck a finger under his nose, and said, "No fuck-ups, and no excuses."

Inside the surveillance van, Nagel said, "Holiday's going back into the bar." He looked at the sergeant. "S'pose we throw a tail on Frankie Bones, see what he's into these days."

"And whadda we do if he leaves the precinct or the borough?" Siracusa asked.

"We stay on 'em," Nagel said.

They looked at the sergeant. She peered out the periscope at Frankie Bones squeezing back into the car and said, "I say we do it."

The drone of the late morning traffic came from Empire Boulevard as Joe Borrelli drove the unmarked police car into Rutland Road. As soon as he spotted the black sedan parked at the curb in front of Mary Terrella's house, he slammed on the brakes.

"There's anticrime," Stuart said, gesturing to the gray van parked on the other side of the street a block and a half away. "Get us out of here."

Borrelli shoved the transmission into reverse and shot the car backward across Schenectady Avenue, backing into a no parking zone with a squeal of brakes.

Kahn, who was sitting behind the driver, patted Borrelli on the shoulder. "Nice driving, Joe."

Stuart snatched the handset out of its cradle and keyed the button. "Anticrime, whaddaya got?"

"Frankie Bones and the Hershey Bar are inside," Christopher radioed over the detective band. "We picked them up visiting the retiree. After they left him, they came directly here. We're gonna give 'em a tail when they leave."

"Thanks," Stuart radioed, and hooked the handset back into its niche.

They waited in silence for almost thirty minutes. Then the front door opened and Joey Hershey Bar stepped onto the Terrella porch. He stood beside the vine-covered trellis with his eyes fixed up on the police station straddling Empire Boulevard. Three minutes later Frankie Bones emerged from inside the house. He turned and kissed Mary Terrella good-bye, then the men walked along the stone pathway to their car.

Only after the black sedan had driven into Troy Avenue did the surveillance van pull slowly away from the curb.

"Let's wait a few minutes," Stuart said. "I wouldn't want her to think we saw her boyfriend leaving."

"You think Terrella had a hand in the Russo homicide?" Borrelli asked the whip.

Stuart's eyes swiveled to the memorial cross he had chalked onto Andrea's house. His answer came in a low, rough voice. "Yes, I do. I just don't buy that smashed-in-door bit."

Kahn said, "Crime scene took that lock apart. Their report states that it wasn't picked or raked open. Which indicates that the shooter gained entry with a key."

"Let's go visit Mary," Stuart said.

Borrelli waited behind the wheel as Stuart and Kahn stepped up onto the sagging porch. Kahn rang the doorbell. They heard the approaching footsteps from inside. "Yeah?" a woman barked.

"Police," Kahn said, sliding her shield case out of her blazer's vent pocket.

The door flew open. Terrella saw Stuart. Her eyes grew wide.

She clasped her hands to her face and stumbled a few paces back into the house, as though she'd been punched in the chest. Then, without warning, she hurled herself at them, her arms flailing, pushed past them, and ran out into the roadway, screaming, "Help! Help! Help!"

Borrelli leaped from the car and ran over to her, attempting to calm her. She darted behind the detective, using him as a shield, jabbing an accusatory finger at Stuart.

"Keep him away from me," she pleaded.

"He's a police lieutenant," Kahn said.

"No. No. He's not," Terrella shouted, and broke from Borrelli's protection and ran back inside the house, where she slammed and locked the door.

The detectives stood in the roadway, exchanging baffled looks. "What the hell do you make of that?" Borrelli asked.

Stuart said, "You see those eyes of hers? There was no fear there. We've just been had."

"You want to take down the door and drag her ass into the squad room?" Kahn asked.

Stuart spread his hands palms upward in a gesture of frustration. "That would not be a smart move. Let's go back to the squad."

Sergeant Arlene Christopher sat on the ribbed floor of the gray van, tugging off her jeans. She tossed them aside and plunged her legs into a beige skirt, which she pulled up over her body and zipped. Nagel handed her a black wig that she fitted on over her own brown hair. She thrust her hand into her bodysuit and worked up the receiver wire, which she plugged into her left ear. She lifted her hand and spoke into the sleeve mike. "Testing, one, two, three." Her voice came over the surveillance network loud and clear.

The anticrime team had trailed the Buick along Flatbush Avenue and over the Manhattan Bridge into Chinatown. It continued to head uptown.

The van was crawling along Third Avenue, lost inside a jumble of buses and trucks. The Buick was inching along eleven cars ahead and to the left of the van. The surveillance vehicle containing the cops crept into the intersection of Thirty-ninth Street and stopped, gridlocking the street in a mass of traffic, instantly bringing a cacophony of horns and profanity down on them.

Siracusa peered through the periscope. He called out, "They're trying to get all the way over to the left."

One by one, the cars and trucks untangled and drove up the avenue.

As the Buick turned west into Forty-second Street, Frankie Bones said, "Lemme out across the street from the office."

"You want I should wait?"

"I'm gonna be a while, so why don't you put the car away?"

"Okay."

When the Buick drew into the curb in front of the Hyatt Hotel, a city bus pulled in behind it, trapping it in the hotel's taxi queue. The van was stopped at the light across the Lexington Avenue intersection. Nagel shoved open the rear door and jumped down. Christopher followed. Nagel made his way through the stalled traffic to the north side of the street. Christopher crossed to the south side. Nagel rubbed the side of his nose and said into the sleeve mike, "Frankie is crossing to the south side of Four Two."

"I see 'im," Christopher radioed.

When Frankie Bones walked into the vaulted lobby of the Chanin Building and saw his nephew Carmine approaching him, he stepped off to his right, waiting in front of the lobby flower shop.

Christopher pushed her way through the revolving doors and walked past them over to the black glass building directory set into the marble wall.

"Where ya goin'?" Frankie Bones asked his nephew.

"I have to go pick up the law firm tapes."

Frankie Bones saw concern in his nephew's eyes and asked, "What's the matter?"

"Danny wants to start investing in discos, pizza parlors, and restaurants in Eastern Europe. I don't know if that's such a good idea."

"Danny L hasn't been wrong so far. Everything he puts money into earns big. We'll talk about it later."

Christopher ran her finger over the directory, pretending to search for a name. She muttered into her sleeve mike, "Jack, glue on to the guy with the black hair and briefcase pushing through now."

"Got 'im," Nagel radioed as Carmine Marino pushed through the door.

When Stuart returned to the Squad he found Patrick Sarsfield Casey installed behind his desk, drinking the bitter remains of the morning coffee. A black briefcase stood on his desk. The inspector rose and picked up the briefcase. "Here's your Cellmate. You can have it for seven days, then it's gotta go back to Narcotics. There's a phone number inside. Call the unit when you're finished."

"Thanks, Inspector." Stuart took the case and put it under his desk.

"Where's Kahn? I wanted to talk to her about what happened."

"I sent her and Borrelli to surrogate court and the Department of Health to check out a few things." He gazed out the window at Pigtown. "A strange thing happened this morning. We went to question Mary Terrella on the Russo homicide and she went ballistic on us. Ran screaming out into the street, then back inside her house and bolted the door."

"Any idea why?"

"It was an act." Stuart's expression was grim. "I have a feeling that I'm being set up."

Casey watched him speculatively for a long moment before he made an impatient gesture, saying, "Matt, don't go paranoid on me, hmmm? People don't frame cops."

"Yeah, you're probably right." But he didn't sound convinced.

Glancing sharply at Stuart, Casey said, "I know Whitehouser's a problem, but hang in there with him awhile longer. He's not long for the Job."

What do you get for saving his ass? Stuart wanted to ask, but he didn't. Instead he said, "I'll do what I can. But we both know that guys like that are their own worst enemies. And the hardest part is that when they take their inevitable fall, they always take somebody else along with them, usually their boss or partner who tried to cover for them."

"I know." His tone was placatory. He took a deep breath and said, "I might be retiring."

Stuart nodded. "The Job'll miss you. You're one of the legends."

"There are no legends in the fuckin' Job. Only assholes who think they're legends."

Detective Calvin Jones logged the telephone message at 1315 hours. It directed Lieutenant Matthew Stuart, Seventy-first Detective Squad, to report in civilian clothes to the Internal Affairs Bureau, 315 Hudson Street, Room 16, on Thursday, September 29, 1994, at 0900. "GO 15 applies."

The second message was logged at 1320 hours and directed Detective Helen Kahn to report at the same time. "GO 15 applies."

When Stuart stood in the squad room, reading the message for the first time, a jolt of anxiety punched his chest. Every cop's nightmare was to be snagged in the web of the Job's internal system of justice. The ominous "GO 15 applies" meant that he and Kahn might be subject to criminal charges or dismissal from the department. Had the scumbags at IAD found out about the mug shots they'd discovered at the Manny Rodriguez crime scene?

Stuart's mind raced through a litany of possibilities before he overcame his paranoia. He reached down into the library cabinet and took out the heavy looseleaf binder with the blue cover and the department seal. He opened it and thumbed rapidly through its pages until he reached the provisions of General Order 15, which had been incorporated into the *Patrol Guide* under the provisions of 118-9, titled "Interrogation of Members of the Service."

Jones walked over to him and asked, "What does it say?"

"That you can have a lawyer with you during interrogation, that you can invoke your constitutional privileges against self-incrimination, but if you do, you're fired. It goes on to say that they can only ask you questions specifically directed and narrowly related to your official duties, and any admissions of a criminal nature can't be used against you in any criminal proceeding."

"Bullshit."

"Exactly," Stuart said, and slapped the book closed. As he turned to go back to his office, he caught the worried glances of his detectives.

"Any idea what it's about, Lou?" Jordon asked.

"Not a clue," Stuart said.

The law firm of Richard J. Danzer represented the Lieutenants Benevolent Association and its members. When Stuart telephoned, he was immediately put through to Danzer. The lawyer's booming voice filled the line. "Matt, how are you?"

"I've been summoned to the snakepit on Thursday morning. GO Fifteen applies, and they want me there at oh nine hundred."

Danzer's tone became cool and professional. "Anyone else from the Squad summoned with you?"

"Helen Kahn, one of my detectives."

"I'll meet you at eight in the Mayfair restaurant. It's across the street from the snakepit."

Kahn walked a few paces ahead of Borrelli as they came off the steps of Manhattan Surrogate Court. The cloudless sky was a deep blue. As she walked, the sun lit her skirt, revealing the shifting ribbon of light coming through it. He saw the shadow at the apex of her thighs and felt the pull of excitement deep within him. He had often wondered what it would be like to be in bed with her. There had even been times when he had worked up his nerve to ask her for a date, but whenever he saw her, his resolve faded.

He took a deep breath and, walking up to her, gently placed a tentative hand on her shoulder. She turned, a questioning look in her eyes. He tried to sound light and confident, but the fear of rejection was knotting his stomach. "Whaddaya say we cut across the plaza and grab some lunch? My treat."

She saw the awkwardness behind his warm smile and said, "That would be nice, Joe."

They dashed across Centre Street and entered the wide plaza that led to police headquarters. The stone wall of the Municipal Building bordered the plaza's south side, while Saint Andrew's Church and the Federal Detention Facility lined the north side. Ethnic food stands and picnic tables with large umbrellas filled the space between.

They walked among the stands, deciding on their lunch, and in the end ordered sausage-and-peppers heros, French fries, and two large diet sodas. Borrelli ordered his soda without ice. They looked around the plaza for a table, but all were filled, so they went over to the long alley between the detention center and Saint Andrew's Church and sat on the church's side stoop. Kahn spread out one of her napkins on the stoop and sat. Federal marshals armed with shotguns and Uzi submachine guns patrolled the alley, guarding the prisoners' entrance to the Federal Detention Facility.

Ignoring the marshals' wary looks, they began to eat their lunch. From a stilted beginning, their conversation became more relaxed as they talked about the Job. She had always wanted to be a detective and had taken her undergraduate degree in criminal justice at John Jay College and her master's in behavioral science. Joe had done four years in the navy after high school. When he got out he drew a job hauling furniture across the country. One morning when he was back home in Brooklyn, he went down to the candy store to get the morning paper and noticed the banner headline of *The Chief,* a civil service newspaper. As he read the lead article, the idea of becoming a cop suddenly seemed right to him. He hated the thought of working in a factory or an office and was tired of driving eighteen-wheelers across the country. He liked the idea of rotating shifts and working outdoors, and the twenty-year half-pay pension was a big plus.

Dabbing the tip of a French fry into a dollop of ketchup, she asked, "How come you never married?" and immediately regretted her question.

"I used to think I was married to the Job." He grimaced. "But that's not the reason. I guess I just never got around to it." He looked at her. "And what about you, how come you never took the plunge?" When he saw sadness in her eyes, he felt remorse for having asked.

A wan smile settled across her mouth. "I've come close a few times."

"Hey, I'd better call in," he said, and slid the empty paper plate off his knees.

Watching him cross the plaza toward the bank of telephones, she thought angrily to herself, I've come close a few times. I wonder what he'd say if he knew every damn one of them was either married or an emotional cripple.

"The boss wants us back in the Squad," Borrelli said, coming over to her.

Picking up his plate, she said, "Thanks for lunch, Joe."

"Maybe we'll have dinner one night. You like Peking duck?"

"I love it."

14

S on of a bitch," Kahn hissed as she read the telephone message directing her to report to IAD. She went over to her desk and telephoned the offices of the Detectives' Endowment Association and made arrangements for an attorney to meet her Thursday morning at the snakepit. After she hung up, she picked up her watering can from the windowsill beside her desk and watered her plant. She returned the can to the sill and walked through the open door into the whip's office, looking both worried and angry.

Stuart was behind his desk, reading through the Russo case folder, while Jones, Borrelli, and Whitehouser stood in front of the corkboard, examining the photos of the various crime scenes. As Kahn walked inside, she was met with curious stares from the other detectives.

Stuart looked down at the yellow pad on which he had jotted "mug shots, who's catching? no Goldstein at Missing Persons, and you got a 'homicide.'" He looked up from the pad at Kahn and asked, "You got any enemies on the Job?"

She smiled at Borrelli. "A couple of ex-lovers, but none of them are sore losers."

"You ever mention those—" He caught himself, glanced over at Whitehouser, and let the rest of the question on the mug shots hang.

"No, not a soul," she said, understanding him.

"I have the feeling that someone is pissed off at us."

Her face brightened up; in a feisty tone she said, "Well, who-ever it is is just going to have to learn to chill out."

"You got that right," Stuart said. "Now. Tell me what you and Joe came up with."

She took her memo pad out of the side pocket of her blazer, flipped it open, and read, "Jacob Epstein, Lupo's father-in-law, went out of the picture on January 10, 1981, cause of death, cardiac arrest, secondary ventricular fibrillation due to coronary artery disease. His wife, Sylvia, bought the farm on July 15, 1989, cause of death, metastatic breast cancer."

Stuart leaned back, rocking. "Okay, so they died of natural causes. What about the Franklin Investment Trust? When did Lupo get his hands on the company?"

"He didn't," she said. "Old man Epstein sold him twenty-five percent of the stock in 1978. Epstein's will was probated in March of eighty-one. Excluding a few gifts to relatives and servants, he left his entire estate to his wife." She looked up from her notes. "Here comes the good part. When Sylvia died, she split the remaining seventy-five percent of the stock between her daughter and her own sister, Madeline Fine, who was Beansy Rutolo's girlfriend."

Stuart picked up a pencil and began tapping it on the edge of his desk. "So, Danny L doesn't own Franklin Investment."

"According to Sylvia Epstein's will, he doesn't," Kahn said.

"Franklin is a privately owned corporation," Borrelli said. "Lupo might have somehow forced his wife and her aunt to sign those stock certificates over to him."

"I met Madeline Fine," Stuart said, "and she didn't strike me as the kind of woman who does anything she doesn't want to do." He heard the shuffling of feet and looked out into the squad room to see Anticrime walking inside.

Sergeant Christopher walked into his office, followed by Nagel and Siracusa. She nodded hello to Kahn and proceeded to tell Stuart about tailing Frankie Bones to the Chanin Building and seeing him talking to a man in the lobby. "I sicced Nagel on him."

Nagel picked up the story. "I jumped back into the van and followed this guy to the garage around the corner of Forty-first. I tailed him to Lexington and Twenty-third, where some guy is waiting on the corner. This guy walked over to the van, tosses a package the size of a cake box inside, and walked off down Lexington. While we were following him, we did a record check. The car came back registered to a Carmine Marino of 15-42 Bayshore Drive in Whitestone. We checked; he had no rap sheet."

Stuart wrote the name and address on his yellow pad.

Siracusa added, "We tailed this guy back into Brooklyn. He drives back here, into the Seven One, and pays a visit to Dreamland, the Rastafarian club on Nostrand Avenue. We didn't wanna park because they'd probably make us white boys, so we did a couple of drive-bys and see this guy in a heavy-duty conversation with Isaac Ham, the dreadlocks' bossman."

At the mention of Isaac Ham, Stuart and Jones exchanged knowing smiles.

Siracusa was saying, "We parked four blocks away. Thirty-five minutes later this guy leaves the club and drives along Nostrand Avenue, making stops at travel agencies, jewelry stores, and check-cashing joints."

"Every one of those joints is a front for money laundering," Stuart said.

"After this guy does his Nostrand Avenue tour, he drives back to the Chanin Building and parks back in the garage," Nagel said.

Stuart asked Christopher, "How'd you like to help us play 'catch-up'?"

"Sounds good to me, Lou," she replied.

By two-fifteen the lunchtime crowd at Holiday's bar had thinned, but several burly drivers still sat at the bar, eating spaghetti and lasagna from large white plates. One of the men at the bar was gorging himself on a hero sandwich of meatballs and tomato sauce. Straw baskets filled with sliced Italian bread and cellophane-wrapped crackers and breadsticks were scattered along the bar. Unlit candles in red glass globes decorated the tables. A new barmaid worked the stick, a short, shapely woman in her late thirties with brightly painted lips, a heavy dose of mascara, and black lacquered hair. She wore a pair of jeans with the legs cut off just below her crotch and a crimson sweater that showed off her ample breasts.

A country-western song about truckin' and cheatin' on women blared from the old-style jukebox.

Paddy Holiday shouldered his way from the back through the swinging doors, carrying a tray of food. He went over to the table nearest the doors and set down the plates in front of three big men. Then he walked behind the bar to draw a pitcher of beer and spotted Jones standing at the end, wearing his African cap and scarf. Their eyes met briefly. Holiday turned away and brought the pitcher over to the table. He lingered there long enough to tell a dirty joke, then walked the length of the bar to where Jones was standing. "How's the Job treating you these days, Calvin?"

"The Job never changes, Paddy, you should know that. You got your good days, and you got your bad days."

"Plaintiff still breaking your balls?"

"Big time. She wants me to buy her a car."

"And whaddaya tell her?"

"I tell her nothing. I hang up as soon as I hear her whining voice."

Holiday leaned close to confide, "You know what sexual harassment is? It's paying alimony for pussy you're no longer fucking."

Jones lifted his mug in a mock toast. "I'll drink to that."

Holiday gestured to the barmaid to bring him another beer. She drew the beer and set it down on the bar in front of him. Holiday told her, "My friend's money is no good here."

She smiled at the detective and walked away. "Ever see tits like that?" Holiday asked Jones.

"She is one healthy woman." He looked at Paddy. "You sure replaced Andrea real fast."

Holiday either ignored or didn't pick up on Jones's sarcasm. "Rosa used to fill in for Andrea. Speakin' of Andrea, I sure hope you guys get the bastard who whacked her."

"This one we're going to clear fast. The shooter dropped something that's going to put him inside for life."

"No shit. What?"

"Paddy, I can't talk about that."

"Yeah, I understand. What brings you around here, alone?"

"I hadda drop something off at the Big Building and figured I'd stop in for a taste on my way back to the Squad." As he raised the mug to his mouth, his eyes swept once again over the barmaid's voluptuous body.

Holiday caught the look and said, "Would ya like me to introduce ya?"

Jones looked at him. "You pimping nowadays, Paddy?"

"Hey, I'm not into that. I just figured if you wanna get close to her, I'd put in a word for ya, one cop to the other."

"I'm not into white chicks."

"Whatever."

Jones chugalugged the remainder of his beer. "I gotta get back to the Squad." He reached into his trouser pocket and pulled out a thin wad of money. He fanned the wad between his thumb and forefinger, exposing a ten, two fives, and seven singles. He stripped two singles off the wad, placed them on the bar, and tucked the remainder back into his trousers, complaining, "That biweekly check don't go too far these days."

"I got some friends who could use an off-duty detective to chauffeur them around the city." Holiday added hastily, "Totally legit."

"No thanks. I spend all my off-duty time in the pursuit of pussy."

"Hey, my kinda guy."

Paddy walked over to the window and watched Jones get in the unmarked car and drive off. He stood there for a few minutes, casting his suspicious eyes up and down the street. A woman with a baby carriage was standing to the right of the bar's entrance, gabbing with another woman. A truck and two taxis were double-parked in front of the bar, and another truck was double-parked across the street from the bar.

Paddy walked out into the street. Ignoring the chitchatting women, he carefully eyeballed the trucks and taxis, then looked up and down the street. He walked to the corner, checking out the cars parked at the curbs on both sides of the street. He crossed the street and sat on the stoop next to the El Caribe bodega. He lit a cigarette and continued to observe everything going on. Satisfied that no cops were snooping him, he shifted his weight to his left buttock and withdrew the cellular phone from his right trouser pocket.

Across the street, Kahn, who had donned a brunette wig, big hoop earrings, and a black long-sleeved blouse pulled down over lavender stretch pants, reached into the carriage and slid back the blanket. She quickly opened the briefcase-shaped Cellmate and lifted up the rubberized short antenna. She snapped the toggle switch, and the LED screen glowed green. The battery-operated Cellmate targeted automatically and locked on to radio-beam transmissions generated by cellular phones that operated over the licensed eight and nine hundred frequencies. The device had an effective range of two city blocks and contained an automatic tape deck that recorded both sides of the conversation.

Christopher leaned over the carriage, pretending to play with the baby, and whispered to Kahn, "He's still dialing."

Kahn slowly turned the black scanning dial, attempting to lock on to Holiday's phone. The rapid electronic pulses of Holiday's dialing came out of the Cellmate at a very low volume. Kahn turned the volume knob to zero, looked to see that the recording indicator needle was fluttering, and, seeing that it was, slid the blanket over the Cellmate with the tip of its antenna protruding slightly over the edge of the blanket. Then she resumed her conversation with Christopher.

• • •

"Yeah, what is it?" Frankie Bones said into the mouthpiece of his phone.

"Somebody who works with that friend of ours just told me that they found something at the scene that will put your friend inside for life."

"'At's bullshit."

"S'pose it ain't?"

A thoughtful silence, then Frankie asked, "Can you check it out with one of your friends?"

"I'll get back t'ya," Holiday said, and punched off. He got off the stoop and crossed back across the street. The women were still talking in front of the bar. He leaned up against the lamp-post and dialed another number.

"Lieutenant Kirby."

"It's me."

"What's up?"

"That thing that went down in Pigtown over the weekend. I hear our friend found something at the scene. Can you nose around?"

"I'll look into it."

Detectives Jordon and Whitehouser were at their battered desks in the squad room, working the busy telephones, while Kahn, Christopher, Borrelli, and Jones gathered in Stuart's office, watching him snap open the Cellmate. Stuart pushed the play button; Holiday's conversation with Frankie Bones flowed from the machine. The detectives listened intently to the play-back. Next came the mechanical pings of the second number being dialed. Stuart placed his elbows on his desk, rested his forehead in his palms, and closed his eyes in concentration.

When Kahn heard her ex-lover's name and voice, the color drained from her face. Her eyes fell to the Cellmate's black face-plate, and her heart thundered inside her chest. Only her iron will prevented her from leaping to her feet, screaming, "You motherfucker!"

When that conversation ended, Stuart switched off the machine. He looked at each one of the detectives gathered around his desk, his face solemn. "I'm going to have a friend in Electronic Intelligence decipher those pings into a telephone number, and then I'm going after Kirby. Anyone got a problem with that?"

"Bury the bum, Lou," Borrelli said.

"We intercepted those transmissions without an eavesdropping warrant," Christopher said. "They can't be introduced in court against this Kirby guy."

"We'll invent some exigent circumstances," Jones said.

"Don't worry about that now," Stuart said. "The important thing is to see this guy gets exactly what's due him."

One by one the detectives filed out of the office and went back to their paper and telephones. Two uniform cops dragged a screaming prisoner into the squad room and threw him into the detention cage.

"I got my rights!" the prisoner shrieked, shaking the door of the cage.

"You got the right to remain silent. So shut the fuck up," the older of the two cops shot back.

Kahn rose slowly and walked over to the window, where she hooked her fingers through the latticework of the window grate. She bowed her head and stood motionless, remembering intimate moments she had spent with Kirby. Silent tears streamed down her face, dripping from her chin.

Stuart hurriedly yanked the bottom side drawer of his desk and grabbed a roll of toilet paper. He tore off an arm's length as he walked over to her and asked gently, "What's the matter?" handing her the paper.

She took the "cop handkerchief" and blew her nose, then dried her face.

"Want to talk about it?"

"Kirby and I were lovers," she blurted, and began crying again. "He's a lieutenant in IAD, and he's married with a bunch of kids." She bit down on the knuckle of her forefinger. "His poor wife and children."

"Who ended it, and when?"

"I did, a week ago. I guess I bruised his macho image of himself. I'm sure he's behind that IAD notification."

"You're probably right."

She began to sob again. He took her carefully into his arms and said, "We all make mistakes, Helen. Don't beat yourself up over it."

She filled her lungs with air and regained her self-control. "I'm all right, Lou. Thanks."

"Ken Kirby," he said almost to himself, and fell silent. He left her and went over to his desk and began rummaging through the case folders until he found what he was looking for. He yanked Holiday's personnel folder from under the pile and, standing, leafed through the pages, skimming them until he reached the section he was looking for.

Patrolmen Patrick Holiday and Kenneth Kirby had been served with charges and specifications alleging "eating on the arm" in restaurants and hotels within their command. When Stuart had first read the entry, he had assumed Holiday had the connections to reach outside the Job and "turn" the witnesses around. He looked at Kahn, who was tearing off another length of cop handkerchief. "Did Kirby ever talk to you about himself?"

"Ken lived a charmed life in the Job. Except for a short stint on patrol as a rookie, he's spent his entire career in IAD." She opened her pocketbook and took out her makeup compact. She opened it and looked at herself in the small mirror embedded in the lid. "I look like shit," she said.

"You'll wash up, put on some fresh warpaint, and you'll be as great as ever."

She snapped the compact closed, dropped it back into her bag, and said, "Thanks, Lou."

"It's been department policy for a long time to transfer people with every promotion, yet Kirby stayed in IAD. Any idea where his 'weight' is?"

"His father was Chief Thomas Kirby, who ran Narcotics back in the early sixties. He seldom talked about him, but whenever he did it was apparent he hated his guts."

"Why?"

"I got the impression the old man was an autocratic bastard who used to beat him whenever he got the urge."

Stuart threw open his office door and motioned the detectives inside, all except Whitehouser, whom he told to stay in the squad room and man the phones. The mutt inside the cage was singing "Onward, Christian Soldiers." As the detectives filed into his office, Stuart walked out into the squad room and over to the uniform cops. He looked down at the bloody meat cleaver on the desk. "Whaddaya got 'im for?"

The younger of the two said, "He chopped his girlfriend's arm off at the shoulder because she wouldn't give him money for another bottle of gin."

Stuart looked at the man inside the cage, grimaced in disgust, and walked back inside his office. "I wanna 'sit' on Paddy Holiday, which means picking him up in the morning and putting him to bed at night. I can't authorize overtime, but I'll try to make it up to you in straight time. I want whoever is on him to take the Cellmate and record every call he makes on his cellular. Any questions?"

The detectives looked at one another. Jones made an impatient little gesture and said, "We got no questions, Lou."

"One more thing," Stuart said. "I don't want Whitehouser to know what we're doing."

Thursday broke with the ominous threat of thunderstorms darkening the sky. As Stuart drove his category one car into Hudson Street, he glanced up at the gathering clouds and thought, Perfect weather for a visit to the snakepit.

He parked the car in the garage on Charlton Street just west of Hudson and walked to the restaurant. As he walked along Hudson Street, he suddenly realized that he had forgotten all about his piano lesson earlier in the week. He'd have to call

Denise and apologize. I'll tell her I was tied up at work, he thought, which was the truth. He'd reschedule for next Tuesday.

The Mayfair was similar to many of the city's fast-food eateries. A vertical revolving glass display case filled with oversize and overstuffed cream pies and cakes stood just inside the entrance. Silver-colored stools with red leatherette seats fronted a long counter running down the right side of the restaurant. The display case behind the counter held trays of Jell-O, rice pudding, and fruit salad. The open-front kitchen was at the end of the aisle that separated the counter from the back-to-back booths that crammed the center of the restaurant and lined its left wall.

What distinguished the Mayfair from other restaurants was its remarkable quiet. From the time of its opening every day at six in the morning until four in the afternoon, when the Internal Affairs Bureau ceased interviewing suspects and witnesses, the Mayfair's clientele was exclusively cops, their lawyers, and representatives of the various police line organizations. They conferred in whispered tones and gave their orders to taciturn waitresses, who, as they approached, made polite little sounds that temporarily halted the conversation at the table. All the cops and lawyers overtipped to ensure that whatever snippets of conversation the waitresses might have overheard there stayed there.

As Stuart entered, he was immediately struck by the humongous lemon meringue pie rotating inside the display case. One slice was missing. That's gotta be five million calories, he thought. Looking around the restaurant, he spotted Dick Danzer in a booth in the back. As he walked down the aisle toward his lawyer, he saw a grossly overweight cop ravenously shoveling the missing piece of lemon meringue into his mouth.

Sliding into the booth, Stuart said, "Morning, Dick."

"You're lookin' good, Matt. You must be in love."

"I'm always in love." He allowed himself a little bravado.

"In that case, allow me to pass on to you the sage advice of my father that has guided me through my four failed marriages.

'Any man who marries a woman who does not give phenomenal head needs his examined.'"

"If your wives were that great, why did you divorce them?"

"Alas, they divorced me. My problem is that I'm a romantic in search of the perfect woman."

A slight cough turned their heads. She was typical of many of Manhattan's waitresses—young, attractive, and obviously aspiring to an acting career.

"Have you eaten?" Danzer asked Matt.

"Only coffee."

"It might be a long day. I suggest a big breakfast."

They ordered pancakes, eggs, sausages, coffee, and dry toast. As soon as the waitress walked off, they folded their arms across the table and leaned their torsos forward until their faces almost met in the center of the table. Danzer whispered, "What's this all about, Matt?"

"Detective Helen Kahn and I are being set up by an IAD lieutenant named Ken Kirby."

"'Honest' Ken Kirby, scumbag extraordinaire."

"I gather you know him."

"Yeah, I do," Danzer said scornfully. "He likes to investigate allegations of misconduct against female members of the force. And if he gets them good, where they could lose the Job, he plays Let's Fuck a Deal. I represented a female sergeant in the Three Two who succumbed to his charms in order to save her job."

"How does a guy like that survive?"

A mocking grin wrinkled Danzer's face. "He survives for several reasons. He has 'weight,' he's an excellent investigator who's not afraid to work the streets, he's tenacious, and most important, he knows where all the skeletons are buried."

A slight cough dropped a curtain of silence over the table. Danzer took off his gold-rimmed glasses and cleaned them carefully with the fat end of his silk tie as the waitress set down their food and small plastic tubs of butter and maple syrup. "Look at all that cholesterol, and we order dry toast," Danzer said as he put his glasses back on, taking care that his silver-gray hair over-lapped the earpieces. Stuart noticed the slight puffiness under his deep blue eyes and wondered if he'd been out late last night seeking out his perfect woman.

When the waitress left, they again assumed the position. Danzer whispered, "Why do you think he's setting you up?"

"Some pinky-rings want me off their case."

"And Detective Kahn?"

He told him of her affair with Kirby.

Danzer leaned even closer to ask, "Are you and Kahn doing each other?"

"No."

"Allow me to rephrase, have you and Detective Kahn ever done each other?"

"No."

Danzer sat back, pleased. "Good, that simplifies things. Now all we can do is wait until we see what they have up their sleeve before we decide how to proceed."

"They can't get away with setting up a cop, can they?"

"It's done every day, Matt. The police department cultivates the illusion that there's real justice for cops, but it doesn't exist. The police commissioner brings charges against a member, his trial commissioner hears the case and hands down the verdict. The PC passes sentence, and any appeals are made to the PC. During the trial they can admit hearsay, they can put anything into evidence against a cop. And there's no presumption of innocence. You're guilty until you prove differently. You call that justice?"

"No, I don't," he said, cutting into his stack of pancakes. "Do you think Kirby will be involved in the interrogation?"

"Absolutely not. The Chinese wall is supposed to protect a cop who has been given testimonial immunity."

"What's that?"

"I really shouldn't use that term because it's not politically correct. Nowadays it's considered an ethnic slur. But, anyway, once GO Fifteen is given to a cop, it theoretically creates a wall like the Great Wall of China that separated and isolated the country from the outside world. Under testimonial immunity, a wall is created that separates the interrogation of a member from the investigation. Whatever a cop says during his interrogation is supposed to be privileged and kept secret from IAD's investigative arm."

A cynical smile pulled at Stuart's face. "How do they get around the wall?"

"You cops are too goddamn suspicious," Danzer said, a twinkle in his eyes. "They get around it by doing a synopsis of the transcript of the interrogation, which gets put on a worksheet that is then inserted into the case folder. Anyone assigned to IAD has access to that case folder, including detectives from the DA's office. They're always illegally obtaining evidence by breaching the wall."

Stuart shook his head and said, "It's ironic, really. We do that kind of shit all the time in the street."

"Do you understand your rights as I've just explained them to you, Lieutenant?"

"Yes, I do."

"Let the record show that Lieutenant Stuart is represented by Richard J. Danzer, who is present. I am Captain Timothy Mansfield, assigned to the Internal Affairs Bureau, and I will be conducting the interview." Mansfield had a long, angular face on a head that looked too big for his skinny body. His sharp green eyes were almost hidden under his overhanging brow, and his small ears were set very close to his head.

They were inside Interview Room 16, a sterile space with four low-back chairs arranged around a cheap conference table made of pressed wood. A microphone stood in the center of the table. No plaques or pictures adorned the walls, and the only decorating concession was the burnt orange vertical blinds on the windows.

Mansfield looked at Danzer. "Ready, Counselor?"

"Yes."

"Lieutenant Stuart, please speak into the microphone. Whatever is said in this room will be recorded, and the tapes locked up in our property safe to ensure their confidentiality."

"How reassuring," Danzer said.

Mansfield shot him a dirty look. "Lieutenant Stuart, did you know a woman named Andrea Russo?"

"Yes."

"Please tell us how you knew her."

"She was a witness in the homicide of Anthony Rutolo."

"What was your relationship with her?"

"Professional."

"Did you ever see her socially?"

"No."

"Did you ever see her during your off-duty hours?"

"Once." He did not mention his meetings with her at Prospect Park or behind the Downstate Medical Center; he had been on duty during those encounters.

"Tell us the circumstances of that meeting."

"I knew from interviewing her that she attended night classes at LaGuardia Community College. I waited for her one night and attempted to convince her to cooperate with us in the investigation."

"And what happened?"

"I met her and offered to drive her home. She said okay, and during the drive I was able to convince her to help us out with the investigation."

"Did she know you were going to be waiting for her after school?" Mansfield leaned forward. An involuntary twitch had developed in his left eye.

"No."

"When was this meeting, Lieutenant?"

"Tuesday, September 20."

"I see. When you drove her home, did she invite you inside?"

"No, she didn't." Stuart stole a look at Danzer, who was frowning.

"You said your relationship with Miss Russo was professional. Do you wish to stand by that answer?"

"Yes."

"Did you ever have sexual intercourse with Miss Russo?"

"No."

"Subsequent to your driving Miss Russo home, she has become the subject of a homicide that your squad is investigating. Is that true?"

"Yes."

He reached into the accordion folder resting against a table leg and took out a single sheet of paper. He placed it on the desk in front of him and said, "I have a copy of Russo's autopsy protocol. It states Miss Russo was killed by a thirty-two-caliber Smith and Wesson. Do you own such a gun, Lieutenant?"

Stuart put the brakes on his rising anger and said, "No."

"Are you in possession of any unregistered firearms, Lieutenant?"

"No."

"Is Detective Helen Kahn assigned to your command?"

"Yes."

"Did you ever have sexual relations with Detective Kahn?"

"No."

"Did you ever have sexual relations with Detective Kahn and Miss Russo together?"

"No."

"To your knowledge, did Detective Kahn ever force Miss Russo to have sex with her?"

"No."

Danzer sliced his forefinger across his throat.

Mansfield said, "Let the record show that the tape of this interview is being turned off at ten seventeen hours at the request of Mr. Danzer." He switched off the microphone.

"Where the hell are you going with this?" Danzer demanded.

Mansfield looked at the lawyer. "We have a complainant who alleges that Lieutenant Stuart had a sexual relationship with Miss Russo."

"Your complainant, Captain, is Mary Terrella, the girlfriend of an organized crime guy I'm investigating in connection with the Rutolo homicide," Stuart said.

"She's a pretty persuasive witness," Mansfield said. Looking at Danzer, he asked, "May we begin?"

"Yes."

Mansfield switched on the microphone.

Danzer leaned forward in his seat and said, "Captain, for the record I want to know if Lieutenant Kenneth Kirby is part of this investigation."

Mansfield's jaw muscles pulsed. "It's not our policy to tell the subjects of an investigation who the investigators are."

"I have reason to believe that Lieutenant Kirby is illegally involved in this investigation, and I am advising you and the department that any activities that violate my client's rights will result in a substantial lawsuit against the city, the department, and any individual members of the department connected to the case."

The twitch in Mansfield's eye was more pronounced.

Danzer continued, "I insist that no transcription of this interview be made onto any of the worksheets in the case folder."

"Your objection is duly noted, Counselor."

15

Stuart stood outside 315 Hudson Street, watching the parade of cops entering and leaving the building. They had been directed to report in civilian clothes because the Palace Guard considered it unseemly for the civilians working in the neighborhood to see just how many of New York's Finest were under investigation at one time.

Danzer had told him to wait outside while he had a private chat with Captain Mansfield. Stuart was anxious because it was during these in-house conferences that the Job laid its cards on the table and let the victim know what the game rules were.

The weather had cleared, and crisp stratus clouds were gathering in the eastern sky. An October chill tinged the air. Topcoat temperatures were around the corner. Kahn walked out of IAD headquarters shaking her head in disbelief. She went over to Stuart and, in a throaty voice, asked, "Was it as good for you as it was for me?"

"Better."

"Can you imagine those bastards," Kahn hissed. "I only wish I got off as many times as they said I did." She smiled disdainfully. "And with Andrea Russo, yet. She was definitely not my type."

"Mine either."

"Although I must confess I was intrigued by our wild sex life."

She held his eyes for an awkward moment before adding hastily, "But that's something better left to fantasizing about."

"Did they give you a real hard time?" he asked, wanting to change the tenor of the conversation.

"I was questioned by a female lieutenant who suffered from crotch rot. A prune-faced bitch who got off talking dirty. Who the hell thought up all that crap about us?"

"Kirby."

She nodded once and asked sadly, "Are you going right back to the Squad?"

"I have to wait for my lawyer. There's something I want you to do." He took hold of her elbow and led her away from the building. After he told her what he wanted, she smiled and walked away. He admired her self-assured gait as she walked off.

"Let's walk," Dick Danzer said a few minutes later as he left the snakepit.

At the corner of West Houston Street they stopped at a frankfurter stand and ordered two dogs with the works. Just before biting into his napkin-wrapped sandwich, Danzer said, "Mansfield spent twenty minutes trying to convince me that he's not really a bad guy. Even told me he worked in the Two Four and the Two Eight."

"All those guys try to convince themselves that they're not scumbags, but they know, just like we know. When you check their records you find that some of them did work busy houses, but always inside, never on the street."

Chewing his food slowly, Danzer looked at Stuart. "Mansfield seemed impressed with your record."

Stuart's face openly conveyed his disgust. "Why don't you cut to the bottom line, Dick."

Danzer licked a glob of mustard off his thumb and said, "Here's the deal they're offering. You and Kahn will be served green sheets charging improper fraternization with a witness in a homicide investigation. You both cop a plea, and you'll be fined thirty vacation days and Kahn fifteen. Their sweetener is you'll both keep your current assignments."

"And if we don't play?"

"Then you will both be charged with having sex with a witness, and you specifically will be charged with failure to supervise, failure to report misconduct by a subordinate, failure to take proper police action, and failure to do whatever else they can think of, in addition to the ever-loving charge of 'conduct unbecoming.'"

Danzer tossed the remainder of his sandwich into his mouth, worked a strand of sauerkraut out from between his front teeth, and continued, "Mary Terrella will testify that Andrea Russo told her all that bullshit, and you and Kahn will be convicted. You'll both be flopped back into uniform. Kahn will be suspended for three months without pay, and you'll be given a year's suspension in addition to losing your commander's money."

"Why not just throw us off the Job?" Stuart asked with an ugly edge.

"Because then you would fight in the courts to get your jobs back. And the NYPD frowns on the courts scrutinizing their quaint method of administering justice."

Stuart balled up his napkin and tossed it into the cardboard box at the end of the stand. "I think Kirby is nothing more than a messenger boy. He set things up inside the Job for the wiseguys, but there is just no way he'd pull a stunt like this without the okay from someone higher in the Job." He looked closely at his lawyer. "How long you been defending cops, Dick?"

"Twenty-seven years. And you know, Matt, there have been actual times during those years that I thought I'd figured out all the tricks that the Palace Guard had up their sleeves. And it's taken me all these years to learn that nobody who is not in the Job, no matter how close he might be to the Job, can ever really fathom what makes the damn thing work."

"Welcome to the club." Stuart watched an eighteen-wheeler struggle with the turn into West Houston. "You ever hear of Knight's Roundtable?"

"Of course. But all those guys are retired or dead."

"Suppose before one of them retired from the Job his slot was filled by an equally crooked cop, and the same thing happened when any of them died?"

"Then the descendants of Knight would still control corruption within the Job."

"And now 'good money' doesn't exist anymore," Stuart said, his hands clenching into fists. "There's no more precinct and division pads of nine hundred dollars a month for plainclothesmen to protect gambling operations. Today it's millions in payoffs to protect the free flow of narcotics throughout the city. And, Dick, you don't need a whole lot of people to do that, just a few people in the right assignments. The guys at the top get the real cream."

They walked west. Eastbound traffic was stalled. Looking straight ahead, Danzer said, "Did you know that the Five Families met six days earlier than Knight's Roundtable, on Saturday, September 27, 1963?"

"I knew they met before Knight's people had their meeting, but I didn't know when."

"And did you know that the wiseguys sent a representative to Knight's Roundtable to help straighten out any kinks in their sweet deal to keep 'good money' flowing to buy off the rest of the crooked cops?"

"No, I didn't."

The two men walked on, each thinking about what all this was leading to. Suddenly Stuart halted and turned to his lawyer. "Can you buy me some time, Dick?"

"I can get you a week, maybe a little more. What do you have in mind?"

"I'm going to fuck them before they fuck me!"

Ater saying good-bye to Danzer, Stuart walked back to the garage and slid his ticket under the change slot of the bulletproof partition. He paid the fifteen-dollar fee for the three and a half hours, which included the city's eighteen and a half percent parking tax, and drifted off to the side to wait for an attendant to bring down his car.

The garage's first floor was filled with very expensive cars whose owners had slipped the attendants five dollars to park there in order to protect their investments from the attendants' kamikaze driving. The squeal of brakes echoing off the ramp made him look up. He saw his car come to a screeching stop. He palmed a dollar into the attendant's hand and slid in behind the wheel.

He had just braked the car at the curb to check the oncoming traffic on Charlton Street when a signal blast of a car's horn whisked his attention across the street to the woman in the driver's seat of a late-model black sedan. Their eyes locked, and understanding flashed between them.

The sedan drew away from the curb, and Stuart maneuvered his car behind the other one. They drove north on the West Side Highway, along the extreme outer edge of lower and midtown Manhattan. Fifteen minutes later the World War II permanently moored aircraft carrier USS *Intrepid* appeared in the distance, her flight deck crowded with warplanes.

At Forty-eighth Street, both cars made sharp, left, hairpin turns and drove south a few blocks, pulling off through a break in the concrete dividers bordering the western edge of the highway. At the entrance to the Intrepid Air-Space Museum, both drivers tossed their vehicle identification plate onto the dashboard and got out. Stuart walked over and tinned one of the five uniform policemen assigned to the museum, told him they weren't going to be parked there long, and asked him to keep an eye on the cars.

"We'll take good care of it, Lou," the young cop said.

They paid the entrance fee and walked out onto the pier. The *Intrepid* loomed above them majestically, her guns long removed, her boilers long cold. Patches of orange rust and peeling battleship gray paint marred her proud hull.

Standing on the dock next to the USS *Growler,* a decommissioned submarine, Stuart asked, "How did you know where to find me?" He was suddenly aware of the immense sadness in Suzanne's eyes.

"I knew you wouldn't park in the street, and that was the nearest garage. I figured you would be inside talking with lawyers and IAD for a couple of hours, so I just drove up and waited. I threw in a twenty-eight and banged out the rest of the tour," Suzanne said.

He smiled at her use of cop lingo to tell him she took the rest of the day off. "And how did you know I'd been summoned to the snakepit? I don't recall telling you."

"A squad commander being given a GO Fifteen really turns on the Big Building's gossip mill."

He looked out over the guardrail at the *Growler*'s conning tower and the guided missile resting on the launch pad rising up out of the submarine's deck. "Why all the secrecy, Suzanne?"

She handed him two large manila envelopes. "I brought you a farewell present."

His mouth set hard. "Farewell?"

Avoiding his eyes, she said, "Yes. I've decided I can't go on like this, Matthew."

"Suzanne . . ."

She rushed a silencing finger across his mouth. "Please, no lies, not between us." She placed her hand on the envelopes. "One contains Paddy Holiday's IAD case folder; the other has a list of all the people who attended Knight's Roundtable, and their replacements up until December of ninety-three. I couldn't get my hands on the building's security tapes, but I know that they're stored in room six on the C level." Her eyes filled with tears. "I couldn't stand by and allow them to hurt you, I just couldn't." She scrutinized his face as though committing him to a special place in her memory. "It's going to take me a long, long time to get over you, Matthew Stuart."

"Suzanne, please, give us some more time."

"I can't, my darling. I'm not willing to give up on my career dreams for a man who's just not able to feel about me as deeply as I feel about him. The word, I'm afraid, is *love*."

That was the first time either one of us has used the word, Matt realized. "*Love?*" he echoed.

"What did you think I was talking about Saturday morning in your house and later that day in City Island?"

"I guess I never put it together. Sometimes I'm a little thick in the head." He was suddenly and fully aware of how much she meant to him. "Stay with me, please."

"I can't, not like this, Matthew. Sooner or later somebody from the Job will see us together and turn us into the Big Building's wet dream. I've built my entire career on an anonymous private life. I'm only willing to come out of the closet for a man who loves me and can commit."

"I'm still numb from the loss of my son, my family. I need time." She puckered her lips and blew him a kiss, then turned and walked away quickly, disappearing into the crowd of tourists.

He had the irrevocable sense that the only real connection, the only real warmth in his life, was walking away from him. Am I meant to be alone? he wondered. Do I love her? How can I open up enough to any woman to ever really *know?*"

He pushed the questions aside and looked at the envelopes she had given him. Like most cops caught up in the Job's intrigue, he had been swept along by events over which he had little control. He had been confused and uncertain. It scared him when he thought that what had happened to his father so many years ago was now happening to him. He had felt helpless at first, but now, as his grip tightened around the envelopes, he felt the strength of resolve surging through his body. Now he was armed; Suzanne had given him the weapon.

Anger had begun to seethe in him. He wanted to deal out some old-time retribution, to cause pain, to make them suffer. He wondered how many good cops had been hurt over the years by the descendants of the Roundtable.

After Kahn left Stuart, she telephoned IAD and asked for Lieutenant Kirby. When he answered, she hung up. She then phoned Borrelli at the Squad and told him what the whip wanted them to do.

Kahn was sitting by herself in a booth when Borrelli walked into the Mayfair restaurant forty minutes later. He slid in beside her. "I brought what we need," he whispered. "Is Kirby working today?"

"Yeah. I called and hung up when he answered."

"I IDed his car through DMV."

"Then let's do it," she said.

She paid her bill, and they left the restaurant. He crossed the street, while she headed for the telephone on the far corner. She redialed IAD and asked for Kirby. This time when he got on the line, she said, "How are you doing, Ken?" and gestured to Borrelli that she had him on the line.

Borrelli walked down Charlton Street and entered a parking garage. IAD had rented the garage around the corner from 315 Hudson Street for its investigators. Borrelli walked along the first level, to the left of a pole barrier, moving deeper into the garage, looking for Kirby's car. Not finding it, he walked up the ramp leading to the second level. The screech of straining wheels echoed throughout the garage. Borrelli kept searching for the car, at the same time keeping a lookout for any attendants who might ask him what he was doing there.

He finally located Kirby's cream-colored Ford parked on the second level. Borrelli looked around but saw nobody. He opened the shopping bag he had brought with him and took out a "slim Jim," a two-foot-long pliable metal strip about an inch wide and a quarter of an inch thick, with prongs extending at a right angle at one end. He worked the device over the top of the closed window and pushed the rod down along the inside. When the prongs reached the door-lock button, he slid it under the button's top and lifted it up, unlocking the car's door. He slipped inside.

He reached back into the bag, brought out a jar of white fingerprint powder and a brush, and spread the powder over the steering wheel. Soon latent fingerprint impressions began to develop on the wheel. Closing the jar, he pulled out white lifting tape from the bag, rolled it over the latent impressions, and then lifted up the prints by peeling off the tape. After gingerly placing each lifted impression inside a white envelope, Borrelli reached back into the shopping bag, took out a hand towel, and cleaned away all traces of the white powder. Gathering up his tools, he locked the car, and left.

Kahn was still talking on the phone with Kirby when she saw Borrelli turn the corner. Kirby had pretended he knew nothing of her visit to the snakepit. He even told her he wanted to see her again. His sheer nerve made her hate him more. "This is too painful, Ken. I shouldn't have called you." She hung up.

Stuart walked slowly through the corridor of sublevel C of police headquarters. He had passed through the lobby's security cordon six minutes ago. It was lunchtime, and the Palace Guard was hunkering into its favorite watering holes for its two-hour power lunches. The cluttered corridors were deserted.

He passed stacks of old desks and swivel chairs and came to room C-6. No combination pad was attached to the door, nor were any alarm wires visible. He looked up and saw only a jumble of white sheathed pipes, no security cameras. He walked past the room casually, as if he were going to another area.

The corridor ran in a square around the building and housed many of the building's housekeeping units. Some auxiliary units, such as the Order Section, Printing Unit, and the Distributing Room, which handled the department mail, were also quartered there. Three detectives lounged outside the Photographic Section, waiting for their "wet" mug shots to be developed. He was relieved when he did not recognize any of them, because if ever he had to say what he was doing in the Big Building at this time, he was going to say he'd come by to purchase extra magazines for his gun in the Equipment Bureau.

As he approached Room C-6 for the second time, he slid a credit card out of his wallet and stepped up to the door. He pressed his shoulder against it as he slid the card between the door and jamb. As he worked the card down, he smiled at the thought of how many times he'd seen cops in the movies do this and wondered if Hollywood would be surprised if they knew just how many times a day real cops gained access to places by using cards and thin metal strips. When the card reached a point above the lock, he pushed it down, disengaging the lock from the faceplate. Mildly disgusted by the cheap, slipshod security, he slipped into the room.

The fluorescent ceiling light shone down on a green metal desk that stood against the cinder-block wall to the right of the entrance. On the wall above it was a department clock with both civilian and military time marked on its face. To the right of the desk was a door. He opened it and peered inside at a small storage room that contained logs of the Big Building's security tapes. The dates the tapes were recorded were posted on their spines. Blank tapes were also stored in the closet. Closing the door, he looked around the room. Black veneer shelves spaced about eight inches apart lined the rest of the walls of the room. These held the building's security tapes. They were inside plastic protective sleeves, and the spines of each one had a paste-on label that listed the dates and times contained on the tape.

He quickly ran his finger across a row of them, searching for September 20 and 21. They were recorded on three tapes. He took down the sleeves, pulled out the big black cassettes, and put them inside the envelopes Suzanne had given him. He was about to return the sleeves when he realized their emptiness would stand out and might cause an investigation. He stepped over to the closet and opened it. Stepping inside, he took out three blanks and inserted them in the empty sleeves.

As he turned to leave, he heard a key being inserted into the door. The last thing he needed was to be discovered by building security. He darted into the storage room and pulled the door almost shut, leaving a crack that afforded him a view of the outer room.

A man and a woman dressed in civilian clothes entered. She quickly and quietly pulled up her skirt, slid on top of the desk, and whispered, "Push my panties aside."

Stuart rolled his eyes. He'd found himself in the middle of a lunchtime "quickie." He heard a fly being unzipped and for the next few minutes endured the muffled moans and groans of lovemaking.

When their romantic interlude was over, they left the room, gently pulling the door closed behind them.

Stuart emerged from his hiding place. The smell of fresh sex clung to the stuffy air. He wondered if anyone at John Jay had ever done a survey to discover how many cops got laid on city time.

When he slipped out into the corridor, he spied the lovers standing to the left of the door, trying to make their conversation look and sound like business. They weren't very convincing. They blanched and their mouths fell open when they saw him walk out. He went over to the shocked couple and confided, "I hope it was as good for you as it was for me."

Stuart opened the Squad's command log and signed himself present from IAD at 1440 hours. As he was making the entry he thought how some things in the Job never changed. The Internal Affairs Division had been upgraded to a bureau three years ago, yet it was still referred to as IAD. Just as well, he told himself as he ruled off his entry; in a few more years the Palace Guard will probably downgrade it back to a division.

He went into his office, locked Suzanne's envelopes in the bottom drawer of his desk, and went back outside. Jones was sweet-talking one of his girlfriends on the telephone. Stuart got his attention and mouthed, "Let's go for a ride."

"I'll catch you later, honey," Jones said and hung up.

As he was walking out of the squad room, Stuart noticed Barrelli leaning over the desk talking with Kahn. They reminded him of the couple outside of Room C-6.

Rapidly blinking green lights chased one another on and off as they seemed to race around Dreamland's plate glass window. "Want me to go inside with you, Lou?" Jones asked with a trace of concern.

"I want to speak to our ol' friend alone."

"Watch yourself in there. Rastafarians get kinda skittish around white cops."

Conversation came to a screeching halt when Stuart walked inside the bar. A wall of palpable hostility rose up to greet him, along with the pungent sweetness of ganja, while from the tape deck behind the bar Sparrow sang "Sa Sa Ay."

Almost to a man the Rastafarians sitting at the bar and the tables at the back defiantly dragged on their PCP-laced marijuana cigarettes and blew the smoke at Stuart. A faint trace of the crime scene unit's chalk outline of Hollyman's and Gee's bodies was still visible.

Stuart walked up to the bar. Glittering beads were woven into the bartender's dreadlocks; a bone was stuck through his right earlobe. "What you want inside dis place, white man?" the bartender growled.

"I'm here to see Isaac Ham. We're old friends."

"Don't know der man, no how."

"Go tell Isaac that Lieutenant Matthew is here to see him. But before you go, give me a bottle of Miller Lite." He tossed a five onto the bar.

The bartender put the bottle and a glass in front of him, looked down at the money, and said, "It be five more dollars."

Stuart took back the five and slapped down a ten.

A stocky man wearing unlaced high-top sneakers with their tongues protruding, baggy clothes, and a brown felt hat with a narrow brim and a tall cylindrical crown inched his way over to Stuart and said, "What you doin' here, motherfucker?"

Ignoring the angry man, Stuart drank his beer and poured more, listening to Sparrow singing "Who She Go Cry For."

"I said, motherfucker, what you doin' here?"

Stuart withered him with a look. "Since you're too dumb to figure it out, sonny, I'll tell you. I'm having a beer."

"I'm a black man! Don't you wash your white motherfuckin' mouth over me."

"You're not a black man. Black men are out busting their

humps to provide for their families. You're a black criminal. And you got a pretty good bark, sonny, but do you bite?"

The stare-down lasted several long moments before the man in the top hat spat on the floor and turned to leave. Stuart tensed for what he knew was coming. The man had half turned to walk away when he whirled back around, gripping a nine-millimeter automatic pistol.

Stuart rammed his cocked elbow into the man's face, at the same time clamping down on his wrist with his free hand and yanking it clockwise, spinning him around toward the bar. He hurled his body against him, pinioning him to the bar. He grabbed a handful of dreadlocks and slammed the man's face down on the bar, dislodging two front teeth. The man attempted to press the nine against Stuart's body, and again Stuart smashed the man's face on the bar.

"Help me!" the man cried.

Four Rastafarians leaped up from their chairs. The crack of an exploding round froze everyone in place. Stuart tensed for the bullet's impact, the pain. The man he was fighting looked with surprise at the gun in his hand. Only Sparrow's voice cut through the stench of cordite. Then, slowly, all eyes swiveled toward the entrance.

Jones filled the doorway, the black, green, and yellow colors of his African cap and scarf backlighted by the late afternoon sun rushing into the darkened bar. His nine hung from his right hand. "Calm down, my brothers," he said, sweeping his eyes over the crowd.

Stuart smashed the heel of his shoe into the man's foot. Bones cracked like kindling, and the man crumpled to the floor. Stuart grabbed the gun out of his hand, whipped out his handcuffs, and ratcheted the man's wrists to the bar's footrail. As he did that, he was reminded of an old-time black entertainer who had described the emblem of the NYPD as "crossed rubber hoses on a field of green shamrocks."

Jones walked through the bar and over to the whip.

Stuart examined his assailant's gun and said to Jones, "Made by China North Industrial Corporation. Mail-order direct from Beijing."

"It's good for the balance of trade," Jones said, casting a wary eye on the Rastafarians.

"Isaac, where are you?" Stuart called out.

The door to a small office to the left of the bar flew open; a tall, thin man in his sixties entered the room. Tiny blood vessels spiderwebbed his dark brown eyes. Isaac Ham's skin was so black that it resembled the purple in coal. His hair was white and woven into a complicated appliqué of cornrows. Brightly colored beads tipped his dreadlocks. As he walked toward the policemen, he motioned the Rastafarians to chill out.

"Lieutenant Matthew and his faithful gunbearer, Calvin Jones," Ham said.

"The last time you called me a white man's gunbearer I caused you some pain," Jones said. "You in the mood for some more pain, brother?"

Ham raised his hand with two fingers molded into a V and said, "Peace, brother." He led them over to an empty table in the corner. After they had sat down, Ham asked, "Have you come to tell me you arrested the men who murdered Hollyman and Gee?"

"The trigger man is dead, but the people who ordered the hit are alive and well and still doing business with you," Stuart said. "Not nice, Isaac."

"Business is business, Lieutenant Matthew. Unfortunately the followers of the great Haile Selassie do not have the same access to the banks and brokerage houses that the Eye-talians do, so we are forced to go to them with our laundry problems."

The bartender came over, set down a bottle of black rum and three glasses, and left. Ham poured the rum.

"How is Joshua?" Stuart asked as he picked up the glass.

Ham's eyes hooded and his face set. "My son is practicing law in California." He looked hard at Stuart and asked, "Why you ask 'bout my son?"

"Just curious," Stuart said, sipping rum.

"It's not cool you come here, Lieutenant Matthew. Tell me what you want and leave."

"I've come to collect a debt, Isaac," Stuart said.

Their silence deepened as each man's mind raced back to that August day ten years ago. The record heat wave that had been torturing the city gave no signs of abating. Stuart had been promoted to sergeant that July and was assigned to the Seventeenth Homicide District, which covered the One Oh Eight, One Ten, One Twelve, and One Fourteen Precincts. That evening he was the whip covering the district. The call came in shortly after five: a homicide in the Queensbridge housing project in the One Fourteen.

Death by auto-asphyxiation was not an unfamiliar sight for NYPD cops. The victims choked themselves as they masturbated in order to increase the pleasure of their orgasm. The sixteen-year-old boy lay naked on the bed, the rope noose around his neck fastened to the brass headboard, his flaccid penis in his hand, a porn flick in the VCR.

After examining the scene, Stuart walked into the kitchen. Another terrified sixteen-year-old boy sat at the table. Jones had caught the case. It was the first time Stuart had met him. When Jones saw the sergeant's shield pinned to Stuart's shirt, he motioned him out into the corridor that connected the apartment's six rooms.

"A couple of teenagers experimenting with life," Jones confided. "One got carried away."

"How you gonna classify it?"

"Can we step outside the apartment for a few minutes, Sarge?"

They walked out into the project's sterile sixth-floor hallway. Jones said, "The kid in the kitchen is Joshua Ham, Isaac Ham's son. His wife died five years ago and the kid is all he's got."

"Who's Isaac Ham?"

"A rising star in the Rastafarian Posses. I wanna hand the kid a collar for manslaughter two."

"It's an accidental homicide. How you gonna hit 'im with manslaughter?"

"This is his home. He got the rope. He helped tie it around the stiff's neck. He recklessly caused the death of another person."

"Com'*on,* that's a throwaway. The DA wouldn't even move to indict."

"He wouldn't have to," Jones said. "We collar the kid, then tell his father we're going to do him a solid and have the charges thrown out. We're good guys who don't wanna hand his son a rap sheet. That way Isaac is gonna owe us down the line. He'd have a heavy marker on his back."

Stuart shook off the memory, looked at Isaac Ham, and said, "Isaac, you just had a sit-down with Carmine Marino. I need for you to tell me what it was about."

Isaac picked up his glass and drank some straight rum. He put down the glass and looked at Stuart. His smile was contemptuous. "I've paid that debt many times over the years, Lieutenant Matthew."

"Some debts just don't go away," Stuart said, twisting around in his chair and looking over at the man cuffed to the bar rail. He looked back at Isaac. "I'm charging your friend with attempted murder of a police officer and aggravated assault on a police officer." He looked at Jones and asked, "Can you think of anything else?"

Jones leaned back in his seat, considering the ceiling. "Mopery in the second degree," he announced, snapping forward.

"What be that?" Isaac asked.

"Being a public asshole," Jones said.

"I got nothin' to tell you," Ham said.

"I'll also toss in criminal possession of a deadly weapon and possession of the narcotics I'm going to find in his pockets. Now, if your friend on the floor is a virgin, he'll only do twenty-five years, but if he be having a long rap sheet, he'll get life with no parole," Stuart said.

Isaac turned his head and glanced at his struggling friend on the floor. "He walks away this place a free man and you don't come this place no more."

"Done," Stuart said.

Isaac drained the rest of the rum from the glass and said, "All right. It's simply good business. The other Eye-talians charge us two points to do our laundry, Carmine charges us one."

"So he's gone into money laundering for himself," Stuart said, then added, "Frankie Bones Marino and him have the same surname. Are they related?"

"Frankie Bones be his uncle," Isaac said.

"They had Hollyman and Gee killed because one of them took out Beansy Rutolo. Why did they shoot Beansy?"

"Dey got into a fight," Isaac said. "Wasn't a planned killing, Lieutenant Matthew. Dey went to dat house to do business."

"What kind of business?" Stuart asked.

"Better you leave now, Lieutenant Matthew. There's no more to tell you."

"What kind of business?" Stuart persisted.

Isaac shrugged, said, "Why not?" and added, "We made the Eye-talians something to hold stuff. Made out of balsa wood— lots of 'em. Dey had to be perfect—round like a wheel and hollow. After all that work, dey wanted dem but didn't want to pay us our price. So dey fought with Rutolo."

"Talk to me, Isaac, tell me something, whisper into my ear and make me a happy man. What are they putting in those containers?"

Isaac clamped his mouth shut and folded his arms tightly across his chest. "You'd better go now, Lieutenant Matthew."

"Talk to me, Isaac, and I'll go away, and not come back no more, no more, no, I'll not come back no more."

Isaac's weary eyes swept over his face. "Dat's a big promise for a policeman to keep."

"You know I keep my promises."

Isaac's stared at him for a long time, deciding what to do. His eyes seemed to grow larger when he made his decision, and he moved close and whispered, "What you think, mon? Not sugar and spice but sumpin' very nice."

Stuart knew not to press his luck, so he got up off the chair, walked over to the bar, and asked for a glass and some paper towels. The bartender looked past him to Isaac, who nodded. Stuart stuck three fingers into the glass and bent down beside the handcuffed man. He told him to hold the glass in his right hand. The man glowered up at him.

Stuart said, "If you don't take this glass, now, I'm going to give your foot another boo-boo."

The man opened his right hand and held the glass.

Stuart stuck three fingers inside the glass, spreading them to create sufficient tension to lift the glass from the man's grasp. Using his other hand, he frisked the man for any more concealed weapons. Having found none, he unlocked the handcuffs and tucked them back into the pouch. He told the Rastafarian to stay where he was until they left, then walked back to the table with the glass held upward . "Isaac, your friend on the floor has twenty-four hours to get his ass back to Jamaica."

"You no can do that, Lieutenant Matthew."

"He tried to kill me. I can do it. And if he doesn't go back, I'm going to lift his prints off the glass and match them up with his prints on file. Then I'm going to pull up his rap sheet and his photo and send them to the IPPA in every city in this country."

Jones leaned close to Isaac to confide, "That's the International Policeman's Protective Association."

"And on his photo I'm going to stamp 'Code Six.'"

Jones confided to Isaac, "That means plant big gun and felony-weight narcotics on his black ass."

"Dat be unconstitutional, Lieutenant Matthew."

"Isaac, almost everything we do is unconstitutional," Stuart said.

16

It was the time between twilight and night, when the sky was a deep purple and the white luminance that dappled the horizon grew dimmer and dimmer. A flood of emergency calls had backlogged the Seven One's radio network. Occasional sharp cracks of gunfire were followed by the strident warbles of police sirens. The Seven One's detention cage was filling with the evening's catch. Jordon and Whitehouser were out in the squad room, processing prisoners. Jones was planted inside the anticrime surveillance van a block and a half away from Holiday's bar, with the Cellmate on the floor between his legs, waiting for Holiday to go cellular.

Stuart, closeted in his office with Kahn and Borrelli, inserted the stolen security tape into the Squad's VCR and pressed the play button on the remote.

Kahn leaned forward in the chair, her hands gripping her arms, her eyes fixed on the television. The faces of policemen scrolled across the screen with digital numbers showing times and dates flashing over the bottom part. Borrelli glanced at Kahn's grim face.

The first cassette played out; Stuart inserted the next one. It played for eleven minutes before Kahn said, "That's Ken," and got up and left the room.

Stuart stopped the tape. Kirby looked much younger than his

forty-seven years. He wore his blond hair short, and his weathered complexion showed few signs of wear. Large brown eyes shone clearly past the fold of skin that stretched over the corners of his eyes. His short nose was somewhat flattened and upturned.

Stuart ejected the tape and put it inside a large manila envelope, then went over to the form cabinet. He pulled a pair of latex gloves out of the dispenser box and snapped them on his hands. He then reached back inside the cabinet and took out two UF 95's—"Request for Photographs"—and rolled one of them into the typewriter.

He looked at Borrelli, smiled, and said, "Time for a little creative police work," and typed in a request for mug shots on Hollyman, dating it September 21, 1994, the day of Hollyman's and Gee's murders. In the signature box he typed in "Sergeant I. Brown, IAD," along with the shield number he had noted down from the computer tracking system at the Photographic Section. He then scribbled "I. Brown" across the typewritten one. He took the other form and typed out a request for Gee's mug shots.

Borrelli had laid out the latent prints he had lifted off Kirby's steering wheel on the desk with the friction ridges upward. Stuart took a tube of graphite and sprinkled it over the upended tape, adhering the black carbon crystals to the ridges. He laid the Request for Photographs form on the desk with the front part facing up and picked up one of the lifting tapes. He gently pressed the carbon-coated ridges against the front of the form, transferring the fingerprints Borrelli had lifted.

He went back into the cabinet and removed the Squad's Polaroid camera and took several photographs of the UF 95 request form. He then repeated the procedure on the request for mug shots of Gee. Leaning across his desk, he slid open the top drawer and took out a photographic copy of Kirby's fingerprint chart.

"How the hell did you get hold of that?" Borrelli asked.

"Earlier today I stopped at the Ident Section and told one of the clerks we were having a bachelor party for Kenny and were going to make up a phony rap sheet listing all his old girlfriends, and needed his prints for a Wanted poster we were making."

He tore the top sheet off a department scratch pad, rolled it into the typewriter, and paused a moment, thinking, before he typed, We got your prints on the mug shots and on the request forms. And we have you entering Headquarters the same date and time that the mug shots were ordered. And we have a tape of you discussing Andrea Russo's hit with Paddy. You're an accessory in two murders. You can kiss your pension bye-bye; you're going away for a long, long time.

He took out an unused multiuse envelope, typed Kirby's name and command in the first box, put it into a large manila folder along with the two Polaroid photographs of the UF 95 forms ordering mug shots on Hollyman and Gee and the note. He handed it to Borrelli along with the cassette.

"Joe, I want you to drive over the bridge and deliver the security tape cassette showing Kirby entering the Big Building to Elliot Goldman at Movie Gem Productions. It's on Eleventh Avenue and Fifty-seven. He's expecting you. He'll make up photographs of Kirby from the tape. Put those photographs into the multiuse envelope I made out, along with the rest of the stuff, and drop it into the department mail. Bring the cassette back to me."

"You think Kirby is gonna buy this con?"

"When he sees what's in that envelope he's not going to be rational. He'll be so terrified at getting caught that he's going to get real stupid, I hope."

"I hope so, too," Kahn said, leaning against the doorjamb.

Stuart sat at his desk with the contents of Suzanne's envelopes piled neatly before him. The IAD case folder on Paddy Holiday had been marked "Closed, no results possible due to subject's retirement." Stuart was not surprised to see that Kirby had been the investigating officer. Several nasty communications between the commanding officer IAD and the CO Pension blamed each other for Holiday's escape. IAD claimed never to have been notified of his pending retirement; Pension claimed the notification had been made. Stuart was positive Kirby had shit-canned the message, allowing the thirty-day clock to run out. He was mildly surprised to see that the current chief of detectives, Kevin Hartman, was boss at IAD at the time of the great escape.

As he flipped through the thin folder, he saw Kirby hadn't even bothered to do a preliminary investigation on the allegations against Holiday in order to protect himself against the accusation of not conducting a timely investigation. This told him Kirby had been sure his shenanigans would not backfire on him.

The information on Knight's Roundtable was contained in three blue folders. They included the rank, name, and assignments of the people who attended the meeting, all of it typed on dog-eared white paper.

This list has been looked over many times, he thought. Every borough commander was there, along with Chief Thomas Kirby, CO Narcotics, Ken Kirby's father; the CO Order Section; CO IAD; chief of detectives; and the holder of the now defunct rank of chief inspector, the highest-ranking member of the uniform force. The valiant protectors of "good money," Stuart mused, the same bastards who tried to shaft my father, who caused my mother countless sleepless nights and me to endure the endless taunts of so-called childhood friends. "Good money!" he muttered. "Phony fucks never did learn that dirty is dirty, and crooked is crooked."

He put a lid on his pointless anger.

Before Suzanne gave him the folders, she had written down the ranks and names of the people who held the current assignments of the old Roundtable crew. Many of the titles had been changed. The chief inspector was now the chief of the department; an assistant chief inspector was now an assistant chief; a deputy chief inspector was a deputy chief. But the same duties and responsibilities tagged along with the new titles, including the ability to control corruption within the Job.

Suzanne had also included the family pedigrees of the current people, with the names, dates of birth, and Social Security numbers of the wives and children. This told Stuart the avenue of investigation she thought would pay off; it was the same one he planned to walk down.

She had really offered up her head for sacrifice by slipping him this material. His concern for her gave way to missing her; he wished he had been able to give more of himself to her. He snatched up the phone and dialed his home number, hoping that she had left a message. She hadn't. Loneliness hit him hard.

He came to two pages torn from a spiral memo pad. "October 2, 1963" was scrawled in ink across the top one. The left-hand column contained the abbreviation *arv.,* which was old official NYPD short form for "arrived." Next to it was written "4:10p.," which was the old way of writing "4:10 P.M." in official records. After the time came the rank, assignment, and initials of the person.

He compared the initials on the steno pages with those on the white sheets; they matched. He leaned back, smiling. Someone had maintained an attendance log. Every damn conference ever held in the NYPD had an attendance log. A gathering of corrupt cops, and some idiot kept a record. Habits were hard to break. Or was corruption so pervasive that those involved thought what they were doing was somehow okay?

One entry in the log snagged his attention. "At 5:04p. DCI JMcM PBBS arv. w/ J.A." Stuart translated that as "At 5:04 P.M. Deputy Chief Inspector Joseph McMahon arrived with J.A."

Who the hell was JA? Whoever had maintained the log would not have listed a civilian. Which meant that JA was on the Job.

He gathered up the records and put them in his locker. He went into the bathroom and washed up. He signed out in the command log, "1920 end of tour," and left to keep his appointment.

Billy's, on Manhattan's First Avenue at Fifty-second Street, was an upscale saloon operated by the same family since 1870. The restaurant was a favorite watering hole for the high-rollers of the Seventh Avenue rag business and divorced Barney's businessman types who gathered at the bar each night to eat their dinners and tell the readily available high-maintenance divorcées how important they were. The bar was crowded when Stuart pushed through the door, but he spotted her immediately.

"It's not every night a cop offers to buy me dinner," Angela Albertoli said, toying with her cigarette lighter, watching him suspiciously as he sat in the bentwood Victorian scroll-back chair across the table from her. She wore a coral wool tweed and Lurex suit with brown fur trim.

Stuart looked up at the early-nineteenth-century photograph of the Sutton Place area hanging on the paneled wall and said, "It was good of you to see me on such short notice."

She lit a cigarette, blew the smoke upward, and said, "You said it was important. Besides, I was intrigued by your suggestion that I'm being used."

"I'm hungry. Shall we order?" He gestured for the waitress.

Angela selected broiled fillet of sole and steamed spinach. Stuart wanted pork chops and a baked potato with a side of applesauce. Both ordered a glass of the house Chardonnay. The waitress went over to the crowded bar to get them their wine. Angela's eyes followed. She leaned close to him and confided, "See that woman sitting alone at the end of the bar?"

"Yeah, I see her."

"She's a stockbroker who's gone to bed with every available man in this place and still can't get one of them to marry her."

"We all have our crosses to bear."

The waitress set down their wine and left. Stuart moved his chair closer and asked, "Have you received any odd business offers lately?"

"I get them all the time, Lieutenant."

"Wiseguys are not wise, or nice. They'll do whatever they have to do to make money. They'll murder, lie, cheat, destroy lives and reputations."

"Don't preach that stuff in my face. I know that better than you do. I'm an Italian American whose blood boils every time she reads about one of those hoodlums." She took a final drag of her cigarette, crushed it in the ashtray, and said, "I'm a Republican who hates Mario Cuomo, our lousy governor. But I vote for him every time he runs because he's Italian. Make sense to you?"

"Yes, Miss Albertoli, it makes sense."

"Will you stop with the 'Miss' routine? My name is Angela."

"I'm Matt."

She raised her glass to her mouth and sipped wine, peering at him. Her coral lips left a thick print on the rim of the glass.

"So what's this all about?"

"A certain Frankie Bones Marino, who you probably remember from your old neighborhood, just got a large number of hollow containers made up. From the way they were described to me, they sound very much like the shape of those cheese wheels I saw at your plant. So, I got to wonder what the wiseguys need these things for."

She looked at him with mild surprise and said, "What's that got to do with me?"

"That depends," Stuart shot back, "on what *you* have to do with Danny Lupo."

A slight frown of worry darkened her face. "First you, Lieutenant. What are these imaginary containers you've never seen going to be used for?"

"To conceal drugs, I think." He sipped a little wine. "Florida, California, and New York are the main ports of entry for drugs coming into the country. But New York is the main entry port for a new, powerful version of an old standby drug."

She lit another cigarette, her hands shaking slightly. "What drug is that?"

"China cat, heroin. It's grown and harvested in the Golden Triangle. It's then shipped to Italy, where it's processed and shipped to New York. The trade in this crap is almost exclusively among the wiseguys, Chinese gangs, and a smattering of ex-KGB thugs operating out of Brighton Beach, Brooklyn. Uncut it's almost pure and can be snorted, which causes it to be considered chic by all the schmucks among the rich and famous."

"How much money do you think is involved?"

"Depends on how much they can stuff into one of those wooden containers. Last I heard, the wholesale price for a kilo of China cat was one hundred sixty K."

"I bet they'd get thirty, forty pounds into one if it's the size of a cheese wheel, right?"

"Yeah, and then multiply that times the number of wheels."

She did some mental calculations. "That's a whole lot of money. What makes you so sure that I'm somehow involved in any of this?"

"Because if I were Danny L, I'd look for someplace to stash the stuff before I had to ship it. And what better place could I find than a cheese factory run by an ex-lover I was able to con?"

She looked away from him abruptly and said in a low voice, "I don't think I want this conversation to go any further."

He watched her, weighing his next words carefully. "Angela, don't let that bum destroy everything you and your family worked so hard to achieve. We're on to him now. If we find that crap inside your factory, we'd have no options. We'd have to take you down with him."

She turned and looked him in the eyes for a long moment. "I'm going to tell you a story about some liquid milk and about some cheese that's headed for Chicago."

The factories along Rangoon Street were completely dark when he stopped the car well away from any of the few street lights and killed the engine. The Albertoli plant was across the street; three freight cars stood on the siding next to it.

"When was Lupo's last shipment of cheese?" he asked, staring at the plant across the street.

"Yesterday. They don't keep them here long. More came in today, but they'll be gone by tomorrow."

"I don't see any security."

"They've only been around when the milk truck was parked in back."

"How many guarding it?"

"Four guys in two cars."

"What kind of alarm systems do you have?"

"Motion sensors and a silent alarm hooked up to the Jersey City police."

"How long to shut down the alarm system?"

"Thirty seconds after I enter the building."

"Give me the keys and the shut-off code, I'm going inside."

She put her hand on his arm. "I'm going with you."

"I want you to wait here."

"You're not going to be able to navigate around inside in the dark. You'll be stumbling all over the place, making one helluva racket. Those goons will be on you in a second."

"Okay." He reached across her lap and opened the glove compartment. The interior light did not go on. He took out a Mini Maglite and quietly opened the car door. The car stayed dark.

"What's with the inside lights?"

"Detectives unscrew the interior bulbs of department cars so they can sneak up on people in the dark."

They crept along the railroad siding until they reached the back of the first boxcar. They stood still, their eyes searching for any movement, their ears alert. They saw nothing to concern them; they heard only the normal sounds of the night: the hum of traffic in the distance, a plane descending to Newark Airport.

She took hold of his arm, balancing herself as she bent to take off her high-heeled shoes, whispering, "I can screw with them on, but I can't run."

They darted across the street to the plant's front entrance, where she handed him her shoes and took her key out of her pocketbook. She inserted the key and mouthed, "Ready?" He nodded. She unlocked the door and ran inside to the left, over to the keypad on the wall. He rushed in behind her. Standing to her right, with the Maglite cupped between his hands, he played the light over the keypad. She punched in the code.

Some faint light from the street revealed the dim outlines of desks and computers. They waited, allowing their eyes to grow accustomed to the dark. She slipped her hand in his and guided him through the front office toward the door leading inside the plant. As they passed the conference room, she glanced in at the silhouette of the oval table and thought of the things she and Daniel Lupo used to do on it. She cursed him under her breath. He wasn't going to mess her this time.

They slipped inside the plant and its sharp smell of cheese. Dark profiles of forklifts stood around the floor. She led him to a barred window that looked out over the rear parking field.

Two cars were parked next to each other with their rear bumpers up against the chain-link fence separating the plant from the sloping hills behind it. The driver of the car on the right tossed out a cigarette; it hit the concrete in a brief shower of sparks and died.

"No tanker truck, so what are they doing out there?" she whispered, and, bending low, guided him over to the refrigeration unit, where she pushed aside the thick vertical slats. They ducked inside. The sudden cold made him sneeze. He played the beam of the Maglite around.

"Daniel's cheese is under that tarpaulin."

He threw off the canvas cover, revealing six stacks of what looked like wax-coated cheese wheels. Each pile was ten wheels high. "If these things are stuffed with China cat, you're looking at over . . ." His face set as he did his mental calculations and said, "Jesus, it's gotta be over a hundred million dollars. How many loads did he ship so far?"

"One that I know of."

"I thought only soft cheese was stored under refrigeration."

"It is. Daniel suggested that we put his stuff here to avoid a mix-up with my cheese wheels. Now I see what he was really worried about. He didn't want anyone getting a close look at this stuff. That explains the guards, too."

Stuart rapped his knuckle on one of the top wheels. It did not ring hollow. "It even smells like the real thing. Do you have something that will cut into this wheel?"

She put her pocketbook and shoes on top of a box of soft cheese and walked to the back of the unit, where she rummaged through tools spread over a shelf bracketed to the wall. She picked up an instrument with a cylinder blade about ten inches long with a half-inch diameter. She placed the blade end against the side of one of Lupo's wheels and, using both hands, pushed it into the mold, slicing easily through the wax. The blade stopped when it reached the balsa wood, so she drew the blade back a little, tightened her grip on the handle, and pushed it in harder, cleaving the wheel's wall, penetrating a plastic bag of heroin.

She withdrew the instrument carefully. As she pulled the cylinder blade out of the mold, it caught on a jagged edge of the wax covering, causing the white powder inside the cylinder to spill onto the floor. She cursed and thrust the blade back into the wheel. This time she withdrew the blade and dumped the contents of the hollow cylinder into her palm. Shivering from the cold, she hissed, "I hope he gets cancer of the balls." Looking at the mound of white powder in her hand, she added, "He knew just how hard it had been for us to live with having Beansy Rutolo for an uncle, and he goes and stores drugs in my plant. I'd like to kill him."

"Why don't we fix it so he ships real cheese?"

She smiled. "I'm beginning to like you, Matt Stuart. Wait here," she said, and pushed her way out through the thick plastic curtain. She returned a short time later with a hand jack.

He lifted two wheels off the stack onto the hand jack, then three more. "Where is your loading platform?"

"Follow me."

They stole out into the plant, savoring its relative warmth after the chill of refrigeration. Bending low, she led him to the left, deep into the shadows and away from the window overlooking the parking field. She veered right, cutting across the floor and out onto the platform of the loading bays. "We'll stash them here between these two piles that are being shipped in the morning."

He lifted the phony cheese wheels off the hand jack and stacked them between crates awaiting loading. Then they made repeated trips back to the refrigeration unit until they had moved all of Lupo's treasure out to the loading dock.

After Stuart had stacked them carefully on the loading platform, he asked Angela where her cheese wheels were stored. She took his hand and led him through the cutting room, where wheels were grated and turned into wedges, and into the large storage area.

As he started to put the forty-pound wheels on the hand jack, he felt sweat coursing down his back and under his arms. He took off his suit jacket and placed it over a crate. A half hour passed before they had stacked the real cheese inside the refrigeration unit and placed the canvas cover back over the six stacks of cheese wheels.

"Tomorrow morning two of my detectives will show up here in a truck and pick up the phony wheels. They'll be invoiced as evidence with the police property clerk. Will you type up a phony invoice for the stuff on the platform so nobody working for you gets wise?"

"Absolutely."

They crept back into the front office, where she typed up the shipping order and invoice for the fake cheese by the light from Stuart's Maglite. They then went back inside the plant and out onto the loading bay, where she slapped the invoice and shipping order onto one of the wheels.

"Let's get out of here," he said.

"Aren't you forgetting something?" She smiled. "I left my shoes and pocketbook in the refrigeration unit, and you left your jacket in the back."

He grinned back at her and said, "Guess I wasn't cut out to be a burglar."

17

Holding Stuart by the hand, Angela guided him back through the darkened plant into the cutting room, where he snatched up his jacket and said, "Let's get your shoes."

She led him back inside and over to the refrigeration unit. As she pushed aside the plastic slats, she knocked over a stack of empty two-gallon wax solvent cans. The noise was like a bomb going off.

"Hey, somebody's movin' around inside," said the fat driver of the car parked on the left, sitting up and focusing his gaze inside the plant.

"I heard it, too," said the man next to him.

The fat driver grabbed the cellular phone lying on the seat. He punched in Frankie Bones's home phone number. When Frankie Bones answered, the fat man said, "This is Joe Bite. Somebody is poking around inside the fucking cheese factory."

"You sure?" Frankie asked, his voice thick with sleep.

"Yeah, I'm sure. Whaddaya want us to do?"

"Find out who's inside and what they're doing there."

"And when we do that, then what?"

"Call me back."

Joe Bite got out of the car. He motioned the others into a huddle on the driver's side of his car. "Me and the Mush are goin' around front," Bite said. "You two wait here and grab anyone who comes out the back door."

Angela balanced herself on a crate as she slipped on her shoes. "Let's get the hell out of here," she said, taking Stuart's hand and rushing toward the door to the front office. He opened the door and she slipped past him, dashing over to the key pad and frantically rearming the system. He opened the front door and sprinted into the darkness; she followed him, slamming the door.

They ran, hunched over, along the narrow sidewalk at the front of the plant until they passed the loading bays, and then they cut diagonally across the street toward the car.

"Hey, you!" shouted a harsh voice.

"Keep going," Stuart said.

Two shots rang out. Stuart and Angela froze. He tossed her the car keys and shouted, "Get outta here!" Then he whirled around to confront the threat.

Both of Lupo's men were leveling guns at him.

"I'm a police officer," Stuart said, holding up his open shield case. "Drop those guns."

"Fuck you," Joe Bite said, and fired once.

Stuart dropped to the ground and rolled to his left, ripping the knee of his trousers. He sprang up and ran toward the car, diving behind it just as two rounds plowed into the ground in front of him. He popped up and fired two rounds at them. One of the slugs tore into Joe Bite's leg, toppling him to the ground, where he writhed in agony, his screams filling the night.

The other pinky-ring turned and ran back toward the plant. The second car in the rear parking lot sped out, careened right, and raced toward the running man.

Stuart ran around the front of his category one car and slid in behind the wheel. He took the keys from Angela and turned on the engine. He drove the car out of the space, aligning the grille of his car with the grille of the other car. He switched on the high beams, slapped the light onto the roof of the car, and hit the siren.

The pinky-rings' car jerked to a stop alongside the running man. The rear door flew open, and the man dove into the car.

Stuart shoved the transmission into park and flung open the door. He slid out and, kneeling behind the door, stuck his nine into the space between the door and the doorpost and aimed the white tips of the truncated sights at the grille of the other car. He emptied the magazine. The sound of metal grinding on metal followed as the car slewed to a halt.

Stuart ejected the spent magazine and slammed home a full one.

The category one's roof light painted the scene in strobelike flashes of red, while its wailing siren smothered the sounds of night.

"Come out with your hands empty and over your head," Stuart called out.

Three men shakily emerged from the bullet-riddled car and stood with their hands high.

"I'm Salvatore Garibaldi, captain of detectives, Jersey City police." He was a big man with a big voice and bushy black eyebrows on a heavy, overhanging forehead.

Eighteen minutes had elapsed since Stuart made the 911 call on his cellular and Garibaldi's arrival on the scene. During that time, Stuart had phoned his old friend Jimmy Driscoll, the agent in charge of the Drug Enforcement Administration's New York office, and told him what had gone down. He also told him about the unusual shipments of cheese in empty milk-container trucks. Driscoll told him that he would come to Rangoon Street "forthwith."

Stuart, Garibaldi, and Angela were standing outside the cheese factory, watching police tow trucks hitch up the pinky-rings' two cars. Joe Bite had already been rushed by ambulance to the hospital; his friends had been handcuffed and taken to the local police precinct. Police cars filled the streets as crime scene detectives searched for spent rounds.

"Exactly what went down here, Lieutenant?" Garibaldi asked.

"Angela gave me a tour of her plant and explained how cheese was made. As we were walking back to my car, these guys appeared from nowhere and started shooting at us," Stuart said.

"Any idea why?" Garibaldi asked.

"No," Stuart said.

Garibaldi looked at Angela and asked, "Is that true?"

"Yes, Captain, it is," she said calmly.

"Did you notify your department what went down here, Lieutenant?"

"Not yet," Stuart said, watching the tow truck drive off with the cars.

Garibaldi's disbelieving eyes locked on Stuart's face. "You don't really expect me to believe that bullshit story, do you?"

"Sure I do," Stuart said cheerfully.

"Gimme a break. Four New York scumbags appear from out of nowhere and open up on a police lieutenant for no apparent reason? No fuckin' way, José. You listen good, Lieutenant, this is my turf, and I'm gonna find out exactly what happened here."

Stuart raised his hands in a gesture of surrender and said, "I'm working on a homicide, and I think I'm beginning to scare some people across the river."

"Wiseguys involved?"

"Yeah. Beansy Rutolo was the hit that set off all this shit," Stuart said.

Garibaldi jerked his thumb over his shoulder. "His family runs this plant."

Angela chimed in angrily, "He was my uncle, and he had nothing whatsoever to do with Albertoli's."

"That's not what I hear," Garibaldi said.

"Well, you hear wrong, Captain. My family and I loathe and detest Italian criminals. We don't find them glamorous or amusing."

Garibaldi softened and said, "It appears we do have something in common, Miss Albertoli."

"I'm glad," she said, relenting and smiling at the captain.

Garibaldi said to Stuart, "I need to look around inside the plant."

"Is that really necessary?" she said.

"Yeah, it's really necessary," Garibaldi said.

Openly showing her annoyance, she stalked over to the plant's entrance, unlocked the door, went inside, deactivated the alarm, and switched on all the lights.

"The lady is pissed," Garibaldi said, walking toward the door.

"It would appear so," Stuart said.

Once he was inside the plant, Garibaldi became a blood-hound. He was everywhere, looking in desks and behind crates, his eyes searching for evidence of crime. He walked out onto the loading platform. He looked behind the piles of fake cheese wheels containing the China cat. He moved slowly, looking every-where, missing nothing. He left the platform and walked back inside, with Stuart and Angela trailing behind him.

Garibaldi walked over to the refrigeration unit, pushed aside the slats, and stepped inside. He saw the tool Angela had used to break into the mold containing the heroin. It was lying on top of a crate next to the real cheese wheels that Stuart and Angela had substituted for the fake ones. He picked it up, idly tapping the cylindrical blade in his palm as his eyes crept over the inside of the refrigeration unit. He glanced down at the tool and saw some white residue in his palm. He sniffed and then tasted the powder. Then he saw the crystals sprinkled over the floor. His eyes bored in on Stuart's. "If it looks like heroin, smells like heroin, tastes like heroin, it most definitely ain't chopped liver." He grabbed Stuart by the arm. "Outside, both of you."

They pushed through the vertical plastic slats. Garibaldi looked at Stuart and Angela. "You two had better talk to me, and I mean right now, before I go and get a search warrant and tear this place apart."

Stuart noticed the small military decoration stuck into the lapel of Garibaldi's suit. A light blue field covered in white stars: the Congressional Medal of Honor. He suddenly recalled the saga of one Sergeant Salvatore Garibaldi, First Marine Division, who won the Medal of Honor on Guadalcanal and surrendered his life on another beachhead a year and a half later. Stuart had heard the story in a bar in Hoboken two years ago when he'd been part of an NYPD delegation that attended a funeral for a Jersey City detective killed in the line of duty. He ran his finger over the breast bar and said solemnly, "Your dad?"

"Yeah. Technically, I'm not entitled to wear it, but I do anyway. It's my way of honoring my dad. I never knew him, and this bar makes me feel . . . close."

"I'm sorry for jerking you around. But . . ."

"But you weren't sure you could trust an Italian cop from New Jersey?"

"I'm a suspicious guy, Captain."

"We all are. Now, what's happening?"

Stuart told him everything. When he finished, Garibaldi whistled softly and said, "You latched on to one helluva caper."

"It do appear that way, Captain."

"Why didn't you notify your bosses about this shootout?"

Stuart hesitated for a moment and then confided, "Maybe you heard the rumors about when the NYPD stopped taking 'good money.' They got rid of one evil and created seventeen devils. Captain, the God's honest truth is I don't know who I can trust in my job anymore."

Garibaldi nodded in understanding. "That can be a problem."

"How's the guy I shot?"

"He'll never tango again."

"And the others?"

"We're holding them for weapons possession and attempted murder of a police officer. But there's no way we can make a drug charge stick."

Stuart walked off by himself, his mind deep in thought. Garibaldi knew when to give a fellow cop some space.

Angela went over to the police captain and said, "I was so scared."

"You're a very brave woman."

She lowered her eyes.

Stuart came over and joined them. "I wish there was some way of convincing Lupo we don't know about the drugs. Then he might still come and pick them up."

"When did they pick up the last shipment?" Garibaldi asked Angela.

"Yesterday," she said.

"There's a good chance those loads he moved out are in a warehouse, probably in Chicago but maybe somewhere else, waiting for the final shipment. That crap is almost pure, but they still step on it once with lactose or powdered coffee creamer, and that takes time, and it takes more time to bag it for shipment," Stuart said.

"Once they hear what went down here, that stuff'll disappear," Garibaldi said glumly.

"Maybe not," Stuart said. "My guess is the goons sitting on this place don't have a clue where the other shipments are stashed. They might not even know what the hell they were guarding. What we gotta do is convince Lupo that we don't know about the phony cheese wheels."

"Which means," Garibaldi said, "that you gotta come up with some reason for you two being here, a reason that he's gonna believe. One of his guys probably called Lupo and his lawyers."

Angela gave Garibaldi a big smile and said, "I know how to convince Lupo we don't know about the drugs."

Both men listened, at first skeptically and then with mounting concentration. "It might work," Stuart said. "But she's putting her head in the jaws of the tiger."

Angela looked at both of them sternly. "It's my head to risk. And us Sicilians are big at payback!"

"It's certainly worth a shot," Garibaldi agreed, just as Jimmy Driscoll walked out onto the platform.

Driscoll had the look of a guy always late for an appointment. A heavyset man in his middle forties, his chin had no definition and appeared to have grown out of his neck. He was a chain smoker with a hair-trigger temper. Before he joined DEA, he'd been at the Police Academy with Stuart in 1974.

Stuart quickly filled Driscoll in on what had happened. The three policemen thoroughly examined Angela's plan. Stuart watched as Driscoll lit another cigarette. He said, "Jimmy, I'd like your agency to take the collars on this."

Driscoll dragged on his cigarette. "Why?"

"Because you have the resources, and because federal sentencing guidelines will guarantee that these humps spend the rest of their lives in a federal dungeon."

"You make it sound personal, Matt," Driscoll said, flicking his cigarette.

"It is," Stuart admitted. "I've lived through two major corruption scandals in the Job. And in every one, the guys at the bottom of the ladder take the fall while the guys on the top claim amnesia and walk off into the sunset with their pensions. Corruption can't happen without the tacit approval of the bosses. The bad cops in this case are all bosses in the Job. I want those bastards to go down hard, real hard."

Driscoll ticked off the problems, one by one, on his fingers. "One, you're talking about a major operation mounted on a few hours' notice. Two, you're talking about setting up communications and surveillance nets from here to Chicago, maybe beyond. Three, you're talking about getting the Chicago field boss up out of bed, not to mention my boss in D.C. Four, I sure don't look forward to telling them that we're setting up a green six operation to follow wheels of cheese to Chicago—maybe."

"You can tell your boss that chances are Danny Lupo is the top China cat importer here in the Rotten Apple. He's the prize, along with about five hundred keys of the shit he's already shipped." Stuart could sense Driscoll's hunger for the case. "Besides, those stacks of wheels sitting on the platform are crammed with China cat. *That* should get your boss's attention real quick."

Driscoll took a final drag and dropped the cigarette to the floor, where he crushed it under his heel. "Okay. We'll do it." He looked at Stuart and asked, "How do you see it going down?"

Stuart roughly outlined his plan. Driscoll suggested a few modifications, and they agreed. When they finished, Stuart said to Angela, "I'll drive you home."

"Salvatore has offered to take me," she said, and sliding her arm through the captain's, led him inside the plant, asking, "By the way, are you married?"

Stuart kept his eyes closed as he reached out and pulled the phone to his ear. "Yeah?"

"What the hell were you doing in New Jersey?" Patrick Sarsfield Casey blared over the line.

Stuart opened his eyes and sat up in bed, aware of the late-tour cotton in his mouth. "I went there with a lady friend. She showed me around her plant, and as we were walking back to the car these assholes started shooting at us."

"You'd better haul ass to the Big Building. The chief of detectives wants to see you, forthwith."

"I'll jump in the shower and be there in forty minutes." He hung up and swung his legs off the bed, glancing at the message light of his answering machine, hoping that Suzanne had called while he was asleep. But the light wasn't on. He looked at the clock: 9:10. "The chief of detectives," he groaned. "That guy couldn't find a prayer in a church." He pushed up off the bed and walked into the bathroom, saying, "It's show time."

Daniel Lupo stormed into his office and shouted at Frankie Bones, "Did they get our stuff?"

"As far as we can tell, it's still there," he replied nervously.

Lupo kicked his desk in rage. "That fucking Stuart is gonna steal my drugs."

"Stuart's not on the take."

"Bullshit! Everyone's on the take if the take is big enough. This is a score of a lifetime for a cop."

"A Jersey City police captain named Garibaldi questioned Joe Bite in the hospital. He also spoke to our other people in jail. He wanted to know what they were doing there. He couldn't understand why they started shooting."

"He didn't mention anything about drugs or the wheels?"

"Nothing. And they arrested our guys for attempted burglary, possession of firearms, and attempted murder of a police officer."

"But no drugs?"

"No."

Lupo walked out onto the terrace, took a halfhearted look through the telescope, came back inside, and asked, "Whaddaya think?"

Frankie Bones chose his words carefully. "Dunno. Maybe our guys overreacted."

"We gotta know for sure. We got a fortune stashed in that goddamn cheese factory, and we don't know if we can move it or not. What the hell were they doing there?"

"We'll know the answer to that in a little while. The brass have summoned Stuart to headquarters. As soon as they know, we'll know. If they did take our drugs, we'll steal it back from them."

Lupo snarled, "That shouldn't be a problem. Most of those bastards have been on our payroll for years."

They heard a commotion outside Lupo's office. The door flew open. Lupo's secretary attempted to block Angela, who shoved the woman aside and lunged at Lupo. "You rotten no-good son of a bitch! You almost had me killed last night!" She ran up to him, flailing at him with her hands and pocketbook, kicking him. Her bag struck him above his right eye, opening a small gash, sending a trickle of blood down his face.

Frankie Bones grabbed her in a bear hug, pulling her away from Lupo.

"What were you doing there with that cop?" Lupo demanded, dabbing at the blood on his face with a handkerchief.

"That's none of your goddamn business, you greasy slimebag."

"I'm bleeding, you fuckin' cunt!" Lupo shouted.

"Who are you calling a cunt, you limp-dick, motherless guinea bastard!"

Lupo rushed over and punched her in the face, knocking her to the floor.

Frankie Bones grabbed him, whispering, "Take it easy. Let's find out what happened."

She jackknifed herself off the floor, grabbed an Oriental blue-and-white vase, and hurled it at Lupo. He ducked as the vase barely missed him and shattered against the wall.

"That was an antique," Lupo shouted, outraged.

"It was a phony piece of shit just like you are," she said. She tried to go at him again.

Frankie Bones blocked and held her. Lupo came up to her and grabbed her by the chin. "What were you and the cop doing there?" he asked in a deceptively calm tone.

"That's none of your business," she said defiantly, her eyes glowing with hatred into Lupo's face. She suddenly stopped struggling and drew in a deep, calming breath. "Okay. Okay. I entered into a simple business arrangement with you that nearly cost me my life. I want fifty thousand dollars for the mental anguish your people caused me, and I want it in cash, today. If I don't get it, I'm going to grate your cheese and sell it. Then I'm going to sue you for the difference, but not before I personally report your cash milk deal to the IRS."

Frankie Bones was stunned by her audacity and let go of her.

"Let's try and work this thing out," Lupo said, blocking her exit and plastering an insincere, ghastly smile on his face.

"It's worked out," she said, brushing him aside. "And if you ever come near me again, Daniel Lupo, I'll get my grandfather's old shotgun and kill you."

She left the office without closing the door.

"Well?" Frankie Bones said.

Looking at his bloody handkerchief, Lupo said, "Maybe, just maybe, it's okay. But I wanna hear what Stuart tells his bosses before I do anything."

Police memorabilia covered the walls of the thirteenth-floor office of the chief of detectives at One Police Plaza. A collection of police hats from around the world covered the glass tops of four Parsons tables pushed together against one wall.

C of D Kevin Hartman stood at the window, staring morosely down at the morning traffic on Worth Street. Patrick Sarsfield Casey was squeezed onto the small sofa alongside Big Jim Gebheart, the detective divisions XO. Deputy Chief Aaron Flieger, the CO of IAD, a man in his early sixties with hair dyed raven-black—who had spent the last twenty of his twenty-eight years in the Job posing as a crusader against police corruption and who maintained his twenty-nine-year-old girlfriend in an East Side town house and his wife in Pelham—sat on a green Chesterfield armchair, nervously drumming his bony fingers on the arms.

All the men in the room looked distinctly unhappy.

Hartman turned from the window and asked, "Where's that 'Unusual'?"

"Here, Chief," Gebheart said, struggling up from the couch, picking up the Unusual Occurrence Report from the desk and handing it to him.

Hartman read the report aloud. "At time and place of occurrence, Lieutenant Matthew Stuart, CO Seventy-first Detective Squad, did discharge automatic service pistol under the following circumstances . . ." After finishing the report, he tossed it back onto the desk, saying, "This 'Unusual' doesn't tell us a goddamn thing." He asked Patrick Sarsfield Casey what he knew.

"I talked to a Captain Garibaldi from the Jersey City police. He said Stuart and Angela appeared to have walked in on a burglary."

"But what the hell were they doing there?" Hartman demanded.

Gebheart said, "What he was doing there isn't important. What's important is who he was with. Beansy's niece."

Hartman said, "Will you excuse us a moment, Inspector?"

After Casey had left the office, Hartman glared at Gebheart and said, "Are you losing it, talking like that in front of him?"

Gebheart tried to mollify him. "Patrick Sarsfield is okay."

"Oh, yeah? Are you willing to bet your life on that, Jimmy?" Hartman said, and got up and walked around the room, punching his palm with his fist. "All of us worked hard to guarantee our futures. I hope nothing's gonna screw us up."

Gebheart protested, "A cop was almost killed last night. Remember! A cop. That's what *we* used to be before we became realists."

"I resent that," Flieger said, jabbing a manicured index finger at Gebheart. "I'm still a cop."

"You're a hypocrite, Flieger. We all stopped being cops when we finessed the Job out of 'good money.' What would we have done if Stuart had been killed last night?" Gebheart asked.

Only silence answered his question. Then Flieger piped up, "We all knew what we were getting into, so let's not have any phony recriminations at this late stage. Yeah, sometimes we have to step on some hotshot cop to protect our friends, but we don't hurt them—at least, not real bad."

The intercom buzzed. "Stuart's here," Hartman said.

Patrick Sarsfield Casey walked into the chief of detectives' office with Stuart.

"You had a busy night, Lieutenant," Hartman said.

"Sure did, boss," Stuart agreed, sitting down on the chair in front of the desk without waiting for an invitation.

"I read the 'Unusual,' and I still can't figure out what you were doing there." Hartman stood over him, glaring.

"Hey, I was off duty. I didn't go there on police business," Stuart said.

"Just what kind of business took you there, Lieutenant?" Flieger asked nastily.

"Personal business, Chief," Stuart blandly told the boss of IAD.

A mirthless grin spread over Flieger's face. "I'm afraid 'personal' don't quite cut it, Lieutenant. You went armed into another state, not on official police business, with the niece of the subject of a homicide your squad is carrying. And while there you shoot some guy in the leg. You're in the deep stuff, Lou, the kinda shit that'll put you in jail or out of the Job."

"Why *were* you there, Matt?" Patrick Sarsfield Casey asked gently.

Stuart said, "I went there to get laid, and for the record, I didn't shoot until I, and the civilian I was with, were fired at."

"You went all the way to Jersey City to knock off a piece of ass?" Hartman asked incredulously.

Stuart shifted uncomfortably in his seat. "Yes. The lady is into game playing. She likes to make it on this big conference room table, and have you sit naked at the end in an executive chair, watching her play with her clit." He had their rapt attention. "She squirms her way down to you and spreads her legs, and—"

"We get the picture," Hartman interrupted.

"How long were you in that conference room?" Gebheart asked.

"About ninety minutes. When we finished we took a shower together in the bathroom in the back. Then, as we were leaving the plant, all hell broke loose."

"When you first entered the plant did you see any cars parked there?" Gebheart asked.

"No. The Jersey cops think we walked in on a burglary," Stuart said.

"You wouldn't be lying to us, would you, Lou?" asked the chief of IAD.

"I don't lie to my bosses, Chief," Stuart said.

Hartman motioned wearily for him to leave. Flieger followed him out, leaving the others to thrash it out. In the hallway the IAD chief grabbed Stuart's sleeve. "Maybe the others bought it, but I didn't!"

Danny Lupo hung up the phone, a smile riding his face. He leaned back in his chair, resurrecting the times he and Angela had screwed on top of that table. So she's still into that shit, he thought, visualizing her gyrating body. Suddenly the story Stuart told to the department boss made sense. It's just far out enough to be my old Angela, he thought. He looked at Frankie Bones.

"Hartman says it's okay. Take fifty K and give it to Hippo for Angela. Have him pick up the shipment. But just to be on the safe side, call Camacho and tell him we're flying the shit to Chicago, then get in touch with our friends at Newark Airport and arrange a charter flight."

"You sure about this, Danny?"

"Yeah, I'm sure," he said, extracting a cigar from the humidor. "But tell Hippo that if it don't look right or feel right when he goes to pick it up, he should haul ass outta there!"

18

A t six o'clock that Friday morning, Lieutenant Ken Kirby drove away from his Syosset home after telling his wife he had an early surveillance on a cop who was trading cocaine for sex. His wife had reached the point in her marriage where she didn't believe a word he said.

Traffic was light on the Northern State Parkway, and he arrived at his new girlfriend's Kew Gardens apartment at six-forty. His blond, twenty-five-year-old friend, with three years on the Job, was his best find to date. She loved to fuck; the only thing she wanted from him was help in getting off the street, preferably into one of the Big Building's "nothing to report" detective units.

She greeted him at the door wearing a skimpy batik-print shift and pulled him into the bedroom, where she helped him rip off his clothes. They spent the next forty minutes in bed, then showered together and had breakfast in her tiny kitchen, which had a window with an uninspiring view of Union Turnpike.

Kirby arrived at 315 Hudson Street at eight forty-five. The last person before him had signed in on the command log at 0805. He signed himself present for duty at 0806. As he walked toward the elevator, he looked scornfully at the group of cops waiting to enter the snakepit.

He got off on the fourth floor. The large space was filled with three rows of glass-partitioned offices. The walls were painted

pea green. Rows of fluorescent lights stretched across the ceiling. Half of the office cubicles were empty. Those spaces occupied by women had plants and other personal touches; the
cubicles occupied by men were sterile, save for an occasional
family picture.

Kirby's cubicle was in the middle of the last row, to the right of
the elevator. He walked in and looked with annoyance at the pile
of department mail on his desk. He pushed his chair back and
looked under the metal desk at the sign pasted to the side that
read BETTER TO BE ONE OF THE HUNTERS THAN ONE OF
THE HUNTED. He smiled and pushed closer to the desk.

A note from his captain was taped to his green desk blotter,
reminding him that he was four months behind in his monthly
activity reports. He grabbed the note, balled it up, and tossed it
into the wastebasket. He opened the envelope on top of the pile
and dumped out the contents. When he saw what came out, his
bored expression gave way to one of uncomprehending fear. He
read: "We got your prints on the mug shots and on the request
form. We have you entering Headquarters on the same date and
time the mug shots were ordered. And we have a tape of you discussing Andrea Russo's hit with Paddy."

When the words in Stuart's note sank in, he muttered, "Oh
Christ," as cold dread spread through him. He sat upright,
almost paralyzed by his fear. He looked up and saw his face
reflected in the glass. He recognized the terror. He'd seen it
many times in the faces of prey he'd stalked over the years.

His attention was drawn back to the pile and its terrible impli-
cations. He began separating the forms, trying to stay cool and
keep a lid on his mounting panic. He picked up the photograph
of his own fingerprint chart and placed it side by side with the
ninety-fives. Someone had gone to a lot of trouble to develop his
latent prints on the forms he had used to order mug shots of
Hollyman and Gee. It was a thorough job, nailing down thirteen
points of comparison on the match of his prints. He looked at
the photographs of him from the security tape; they had the date
and times across the bottom.

He could hear his heart pounding. He quickly shoved everything back into the envelope and sat staring at it with his mouth
open in shock. He had the uncomfortable feeling that everyone
in the office was staring at him, but when he glanced around all
he saw was people absorbed in their own private worlds.

He picked up the phone and dialed Holiday's. The barmaid
answered. When he asked to speak to Paddy Holiday, she told
him he wasn't around. He'd had some personal business to take
care of, she claimed, and would be back around noon.

"Tell 'im it's urgent that he call Ken."

When he put the phone down, it was slippery with his sweat.

Paddy Holiday sat naked in bed, waiting for his friend to come
out of the bathroom. His eyes roamed around the tastefully furnished room, stopping at the ornate French reproductions. The
Wilson, on Seventy-second Street between Park and Lexington
Avenues, was an apartment hotel with day rates. It was not open
to the public. Well-heeled men and women who could not afford
to be seen in less obscure hotels with their lovers, or have their
sexual peccadilloes exposed, came there to enjoy a sexual respite
with the partner or partners of their choice. The annual mem-
bership fee was five thousand dollars, cash.

No registration was necessary. A phone call reserved the room,
and the one hundred dollars for ninety minutes' fee was left on
the night table, in cash. The building was a five-story converted
town house with an underground garage with a self-service elevator that whisked clients and their friends directly to their
reserved rooms.

Holiday unfolded his cellular phone and called the bar. "Anything doin'?"

"Nothin', 'cept some guy named Ken called you, said it was
urgent that you call 'im."

As he punched in Kirby's number he became aware of the icy
fingers gripping the nape of his neck. In all the years he'd been
breaking bread with Kirby, this was the first time he'd ever used
the word *urgent*.

"Lieutenant Kirby."

"What's up?"

"Somethin's wrong. We gotta meet."

"Two o'clock, the Parade Grounds."

He slid the phone onto the teak nightstand just as the bathroom door opened. He smiled as the transvestite came out and approached him with the fluid grace of a ballerina.

"She" was in her late twenties. Her firm silicone breasts had large pink aureolas with erect, oversize nipples. Her real sex was tucked back between her legs, held in place by a "joy string," a thin, skin-colored plastic rope that fitted around the head of her penis so that nothing of her sex showed except a coiffed pubis sculptured into a woman's triangle. "She" smiled at him as she crawled up onto the bed and said, "Hi, handsome."

She knelt alongside him. "I love feeling you inside me, Paddy."

"I feel like I cheated you. You didn't come," he said, kneading her nipple.

"Would you like to make it up to me?"

His breath caught. "Yes."

She kissed him, drilling her tongue deep into his mouth. She sat up and fixed her blue eyes on his as she reached down and released the joy string. Her swollen sex sprang out from between her legs. She brushed her bright red nails through his hair, gently pushing his face toward her. "Make love to me, Paddy." She closed her eyes and moaned at the first brush of his lips.

Detective Jerry Jordon pressed the Cellmate's play button and listened to the tape of Holiday's conversation with Kirby. He was parked across the street from the Wilson in the department yellow cab he had signed out of Motor Transport last night. He pressed the button on the right side of the steering column, and a communications panel slid out from under the dashboard. It contained a single radio that received patrol, detective, and undercover bands. A black dial enabled detectives to switch back and forth among the different bands.

From the panel, Jordon picked up a cellular phone and was about to dial the Squad's phone number when he glanced down at the Cellmate and stopped. He returned the phone to the panel and pushed it back under the dashboard. He got out of the taxi and crossed Seventy-second Street, heading for the three-telephone kiosk on the corner of Lexington.

"Seven One Squad, Jones."

"Is the boss around?"

"He left the c of d's office a little while ago. He said he was stopping off at the Pension Bureau, making one more stop, and then coming back. Whaddaya got?"

"I got the retiree shacking up with a transvestite. He called Kirby on his cellular. It seems the lieutenant needs an urgent meet. They're getting together at two in the Parade Grounds."

"He musta got the boss's little present. I'll get on the horn to Electronic Intelligence and get a 'stage crew' ready."

"Calvin, we got a slight problem there," Jordon said, keeping a watchful eye on the department taxi. "In order to get a stage crew we need a court-approved order to wiretap, and in order to get that we gotta go before a judge and show reasonable cause. Where we gonna get our reasonable cause from?"

"I'll think of something. You stick with the retiree."

Jones hung up the phone, looked up at the Malcolm X poster on the wall by his desk, and said, "Whadda we gonna do, brother?"

Borrelli answered his phone, listened a while, and then, covering the mouthpiece with his hand, said to Jones, "Calvin, Plaintiff's on the line. She said her dog isn't eating right and wants to take him to a dog psychic to find out why. Wants you to pay for it."

Jones got up calmly and walked over to Borrelli. He took the phone out of his hand, hung it up, and went back to his desk. When he sat back down, he noticed Kahn standing by her desk, talking on the telephone. She was wearing a tailored black pants suit. Whitehouser was leaning back in his chair, watching her.

Borrelli had already picked up on Whitehouser's look and was glaring at him, ready to pounce if he made a move toward Kahn.

Whitehouser probably can't get it up, Jones thought. He looked over at Kahn and said, "Helen, let's you and me go for a ride and dig up some reasonable cause."

The old man in the wheelchair sat alone by the window, staring blankly out at the Atlantic Ocean. His skin hung loose around his neck and face, and his thin white hair reached down to his shoulders. Stuart was shocked at what the years had done to him. Every other old person in the fourth-floor dayroom of the Golden View Nursing Home on Shore Front Parkway in Rockaway Beach, Queens, sat in their wheelchairs, watching a game show on the big-screen television.

As a young detective, he had seen Arthur Knight at many retirement and promotions parties, long after the former chief inspector had retired. Even though Knight had been way into his sixties then, he'd still been a handsome, robust man with broad shoulders, a thick head of wavy hair, and a thunderous laugh. The man Stuart remembered was a man with dignity who commanded respect.

He picked up a heavy metal chair with a scrolled back and faded yellow leatherette seat and crossed the large room. He was surprised by the weight, then he remembered that all the aging Art Deco hotels along Rockaway's beachfront had been converted into more profitable nursing homes. He planted the chair beside the wheelchair and said simply, "Morning, Chief."

Upon hearing Stuart's words, Knight shook his head and blinked his eyes several times, as if trying to dust the cobwebs from his brain. He turned slowly to look at the stranger who had addressed him with the honorary title "Chief."

"It's been almost ten years since anyone called me 'Chief,'" he said in a creaky voice. "Who are you?"

Stuart snapped open his shield case and held it out in front of him. Knight stared at the round gold shield. The sight of it seemed to inject vitality into his frail body. His bony fingers reached out and touched it; his long, curved fingernails looked like white talons. "Where do you work, Lou?"

"I got the Seven One Squad, Chief."

"I hear they got even more women and even fags on the Job."

"'At's true."

"I've lived too fucking long." He leaned close, whispered, "You wouldn't happen to have a 'taste' with you, would you?"

"No, Chief, but I'll see that you get some."

"What squad did you say you had?"

"Seven One."

"When I came on the Job that was a good house."

"There are no good houses anymore, Chief, they're all shit-houses."

"How did you know I was still alive?"

"Pension Bureau. That's how I knew you were here."

"Do you have any children, Lou?"

"No."

"Do yourself a favor and don't. They'll break your heart. I worked all my life to put them through college and give them the things I never had, and what'd I get for it? They dumped me in this fucking dump."

As he listened to Knight's rantings, he tried to figure the best way to explain the purpose of his visit. He reasoned that any mention of Knight's Roundtable would send Knight into a protective shell of silence, something that most successful cops start developing at the academy and usually carry with them to their graves.

I'm going to have to do some fancy dancing here, he reasoned to himself. He let Knight fume on awhile longer about his children, then cut in, "Chief, the city's ordered a new captain's test, and I'm going to sit for it."

"Nothing like having those railroad tracks pinned on your shoulders, Lou. I can remember when I—"

"My problem, Chief," he interrupted, "is that the Job won't

promote anyone to captain who doesn't have a master's degree. I have all my course work done. The only thing I need is a thesis. And I'd like to do that on one of the legends of the Job, Chief Inspector Arthur Knight."

Knight looked out over the ocean, tears filling his eyes. "I'm considered a . . . legend?"

"Yes."

Knight wiped his eyes with the back of his hand. "Would your thesis be on file in the academy?"

"Yes, it would. Generations of recruits would be able to study and learn from your career."

"It'd be like being immortal in the Job." He waved him closer with his bony fingers. Stuart became aware of a faint musty aroma. Knight assumed the cop-to-cop talking position, hand cupped over his mouth. Stuart assumed the same position.

"You know, Lou, there are certain things that I can never talk about."

"I understand that, Chief." His eyes swept the room. "Things like the Roundtable will never be mentioned."

"Good. What's past is past and done and forgotten."

"Absolutely, Chief." He reached into his pocket and brought out a sheet of paper on which he'd written the names of four well-known bosses in the Job at the time of Knight's reign, none of whom had attended the Roundtable meeting. Below the four he'd written one other name. "It'd help me by knowing how you evaluated some of the people who worked for you."

"Who, for instance?"

Stuart read off the four names and was surprised at the clarity of the old man's response. The first man on the list could never bring himself to act like a boss, he wanted to be one of the boys. The second was a strong leader who never let his subordinates forget he was the boss. The third was a drunk but a skillful organizer. The fourth guy was one of those phony Holy Rollers who'd steal a hot stove. Then Stuart mentioned the name Thomas Kirby, CO Narcotics and Ken Kirby's father. The old man looked away and muttered, "Never really knew him too well. But he was important. Smart. Maybe too smart."

Stuart finally reached the name of the man who'd attended the Roundtable meeting with someone the log had referred to only by the initials *J.A.* and asked, "What about Joe McMahon, the borough commander of Brooklyn, South?"

"Joe was a competent, stand-up guy. His only deficiency was he couldn't keep his dick in his pants. He almost caused a lotta grief."

"What happened?"

"He was married, and he was dancing around with this police-woman. He used to bring her everywhere with him. One evening we're having that meeting that we mentioned before, and he shows up at the hotel with this dame. I reamed his ass and sent her on her way. I mean, this was an important meeting, know what I mean?"

"What was wrong with that guy?"

"He was pussy blind. Happened to a lotta guys back then."

Folding up the sheet of paper, Stuart asked casually, "What was that dame's name?"

When he heard her name, Stuart managed to keep his face from betraying his shock.

When Isaac Ham walked out of the numbers joint that was in the barbershop on Nostrand Avenue, four stores off Crown Street, and saw Detective Calvin Jones leaning up against the unmarked police car, both hands gripping his scarf, he cursed. Grimacing in irritation, he walked over to the detective and said, "How long you gonna be leaning on my black ass, man?"

"I've come to do you a favor."

"I get worried whenever a cop wants to do me a favor."

"This time there is no downside."

"I'm listening."

"Your young friend who tried to shoot my lieutenant, has he left for Jamaica?"

"Not yet."

"I can arrange it so that he can stay in the country. But he'd have to leave New York."

"And what I gotta do?" He looked at Kahn, who was in the passenger seat, and smiled.

She smiled back.

"You're a registered CI," said Jones, "a confidential informer. Which means that you've given us reliable information in the past."

Isaac Ham saw which way the wind was blowing. "And now I'm going to give you more, only this time, you're gonna tell me what it is, right?"

"Yeah, you're gonna give me some reasonable-cause information that's going to help us get the people who killed Hollyman and Gee."

Isaac Ham's face brightened; this was his kind of police work.

Stuart parked his category one car in the No Standing, No Parking, No Stopping, No Loading zone on Forty-first Street in front of the rear entrance of the Chanin Building. He had driven there directly from the Golden View Nursing Home. During the drive he had phoned the Squad. Jones had got on the line and told him that a CI had given up a meet at 1400 between Holiday and Ken Kirby, and that he was leaving to apply for a court order to wiretap.

"Where's the meet?" Stuart had asked.

"The Parade Grounds."

Stuart had looked at the dashboard clock, seen it was twelve-thirty, and said, "I'll try and get back in time. If I don't, run the show without me."

"Right, Lou."

As the car drew up in front of the Chanin Building, Stuart used his cellular phone to call the Franklin Investment Trust Corporation. When the operator answered, he asked to speak with Carmine Marino. He identified himself as Police Officer Tony Garvey from Midtown Precinct South.

When Marino came on the line, Stuart informed him that a van had been driven into the garage where his car was parked.

Something caused the driver to lose control and crash into the front of his car. They were going to give the driver a sobriety test. They would appreciate it if he could come to the garage and bring his license and registration with him. Marino cursed and said he'd be right there.

A few minutes later Marino strode purposefully out of the lobby, wearing a tense expression. He was dumbfounded when Stuart intercepted him on the sidewalk in front of the building. "C'mere," Stuart said, motioning him over.

"Who are you?" Marino asked him.

"I'm your worst nightmare, with a shield. Get in the car."

"Who the hell do you think you're talking to? I'm a legitimate businessman, a CPA, and you think you can—"

Before he could get out the rest of the sentence, Stuart spun him around and pushed his face up against the side of the car as he slapped the handcuffs around his wrists. He opened the door and pushed Marino into the passenger seat. He slammed the door, noticing that few of the lunchtime crowd stopped to look at the brief disturbance.

Stuart got into the car and, reaching across the seat, frisked the enraged man for weapons. "You got a right to a lawyer, and all the rest of that stuff. Now let's you and me go into the Squad and have a talk about your uncle and his boss." He picked up the magnetized roof light off the floor and slapped it onto the roof, switched on the siren, and sped off toward Park Avenue. Glancing at Marino as he swerved the car around a truck, he said, "Just like in the movies, huh."

Stuart kept the siren on all the way back to Brooklyn. He switched it off as soon as they drove inside the boundaries of the Seven One Precinct. He parked in front of the station house and pulled a still protesting Carmine Marino out of the car.

As Stuart led him across the squad room into his office, he mouthed to Borrelli, "Smasher."

Once inside his office, he took off the handcuffs and told Marino to sit in the chair beside his desk.

Massaging his wrists, Marino said, "I demand my right to call my lawyer."

"Of course, Carmine." He picked up the phone and set it down in front of the accountant. "Do your uncle and his boss know you're cutting into their money-laundering business?"

Dialing a number, Marino grinned at Stuart and said, "You say that to me and I'm supposed to cave in and tell you whatever you want to know. You've been watching too many movies."

"I like cop movies."

When Marino's lawyer heard where his client was, he wanted to speak to the arresting officer. Stuart took the phone and said, "Afternoon, Counselor."

"Is Mr. Marino under arrest?"

"Not at this time. We only want to talk to him."

"You are not to question him. If he's not under arrest, I demand that he be released immediately."

"Whatever you say, Counselor." Stuart hung up the phone. Smasher, his mouth a mass of white foam and bubbles, ambled in from the squad room and hunkered down in front of the accountant, baring his awesome fangs and emitting a low, bone-chilling growl.

"You can go," Stuart said.

When Marino made a move to get up, the hairs on Smasher's head and back stood up and his growl grew louder. "Get this animal away from me!" Marino shrieked.

"Smasher, tell the man his lawyer don't want me to talk to him," Stuart said as he dialed the phone. "Mr. Lupo, please," he said to the receptionist. "Tell him it's Lieutenant Stuart."

A few seconds passed before Lupo came on the line. "Yeah?"

"Danny, I figured it was time we talked," Stuart said, watching the frightened man in the chair staring at the growling rottweiler.

"Yeah? Whaddaya wanna talk about?"

"Danny, you're a murderer and a thief. That's a way of life, and I understand that. But you broke the rules when you tried to set me up with my own Job. And hurting the woman detective, that wasn't nice. You broke the rules again. And now you know what you got on your hands?"

"Why don't you tell me?"

"You got a major problem to deal with."

"What the hell is that?"

"That's an honest cop with a personal hard-on for you. I'm the guy who's gonna put you inside for a lotta years."

"Next time you wanna talk, call my lawyer first."

Stuart looked over at Marino cowering in his chair. Smasher was staring at him as if he were lunch. "Danny, just to show you I'm not a bad guy, I'm gonna do you a big one." He let the silence grow before saying, "I got your accountant, Carmine, with me in the Squad. The good news is, he's stand-up, won't tell us anything. The bad news is, he's gone into business for himself. He's only charging the Rastas one point to do their laundry."

Marino grabbed for the phone, shouting, "He's lying, Danny. I swear!"

Smasher leaped up on the accountant, toppling him back to the floor and planting his massive paws on his chest. He shook his head, showering frothy saliva over Carmine's terrified face.

Stuart hung up the phone, looked at the dog, and said, "Don't eat him, Smasher. He wouldn't taste good."

The dog gave Carmine one final shower and trotted back into the squad room. The accountant was shaking as he picked himself up off the ground.

"You can go now," Stuart said.

"Do you know what you just did to me?" Marino whined.

"There's always witness protection."

"Fuck you."

"See you in the morgue, Carmine."

19

The football spiraled through the air in a high arc toward the running receiver, who nestled it to his chest with splayed fingers. Two men were playing a game of catch on the Parade Grounds, a forty-acre plot of grass that, at the turn of the century, had been used as a marching field by the National Guard and the American Legion. Now the big field had five baseball diamonds on it. This wide-open space was sandwiched between Brooklyn's Parkside and Caton Avenues. Portable bleachers were set up behind the baseball diamonds and around the other playing fields.

Groups of women with baby carriages sat and stood around the bleachers, talking. A high school soccer team was practicing on the field. A bicycle rider raced down the sidewalk. He was wearing a black skintight Lycra bodysuit and a white racing helmet. He blew a warning whistle as he sped around two joggers.

The sky was blue, and the afternoon sun spread its warmth evenly. Gulls wheeled in a circle over the Parade Grounds.

Ken Kirby had arrived there at one-thirty. After scouring the field and bleachers for Holiday and not seeing him, he'd decided to sit by himself on the top row of the bleachers behind the baseball diamond off Parade Place. He kept looking over his shoulder at the street and scanning the wide-open field, ignoring the four women who had arrived there shortly after he had and sat on the first rung, talking and rocking baby carriages. "Kirby looks nervous," Borrelli said, adjusting the binoculars' focus wheel.

"I would, too," said Kahn. They had established a surveillance platform on the roof of a six-story prewar apartment building on Caton Avenue, across the street from the Parade Grounds. The bleachers Kirby was on were about eighty feet away, diagonally to their right. Kahn was sitting on the roof with her back to the wall, hugging her legs with her arms. On the roof, a breeze cut into the late autumn warmth.

Borrelli was kneeling beside her, watching Kirby through a hole in the bottom of the cardboard box they had planted on the ledge that ran around the flat. He made a slight wheel adjustment and said, "If we finish at a reasonable hour tonight, whaddaya say we go for some Peking duck?"

"That sounds nice, Joe."

"Good. And afterward we can stop by my place and get acquainted."

She rolled her eyes. "I've already been 'acquainted,' Joe. And I don't intend to walk down that road again."

"Whaddaya sayin' about tonight?"

"Thanks, but no thanks. I'll pass on the duck."

"Any sign of the retiree?" Stuart's voice broke in. He and Jones were inside the surveillance van parked at the curb on the opposite side of the Parade Grounds, on Parkside Avenue.

"Nothing yet, Lou," Kahn radioed back.

Borrelli shifted the binoculars to the women sitting below Kirby. All four "housewives" were part of the stage crew—detectives from Electronic Intelligence. The two baby carriages had parabolic microphones concealed inside their hoods. The dish antennae, which were the size of large dinner plates, had microphones in their centers. The antennae picked up conversations from as far away as one hundred and fifty feet and fed the words into the high-gain microphones, which had feed wires coming off ends that were connected to tape cassette recorders. The wires and recorders were concealed under the blankets. The lifelike dolls, when bundled in their blue and pink clothes under blankets, looked real from a distance.

All of the stage crew had transmitters strapped to their bodies with sleeve or chest microphones. Concealed under the women's hair were wires that ran up their sides and along their necks to the plastic receivers plugged into their ears.

Stage crew control was inside the Mr. Softee ice-cream truck parked four cars to the left of the surveillance van. The control lieutenant operated from inside a closed compartment four feet wide that ran the width of the truck and was directly behind the driver's seat. This compartment was crammed with electronic equipment. A videocamera with a telescopic lens peeked out the center of an ice-cream sandwich on the truck's side. The image of a jittery Ken Kirby showed clearly on the monitor.

Paddy Holiday spotted Kirby on the top rung but continued driving past him. He slowed the car to a crawl, his eyes sweeping the area, searching for a stare that refused to meet his, or something else out of place. He stopped the car and got out, standing by the open door, again carefully checking out the whole area. Satisfied, he got back into the car and drove away slowly. When he reached Coney Island Avenue he made a U-turn and drove back.

He drew the car into the bus stop on the corner of Argyle Road and parked, watching. Something wasn't right. Somethin's out of place here and I can't see it, he thought, watching Kirby cup his hands to shade his eyes from the sun. He was still looking around, searching, when he rounded the bleachers and went over to the baby carriages. He glanced in at the babies and hawkeyed the mothers for a moment before saying, "Afternoon, ladies." He climbed the four rows of benches up to the fifth, side-stepped down the narrow aisle between the rows, and sat on the bench next to Kirby. He could see that Kirby was badly shaken. "So? What's up?"

"Stuart made me as the finger on the two niggers your friends whacked."

"Whaddaya mean, made you? All you did was order the mug shots for the shooter."

Kirby was flexing his fingers nervously. "They got the ninety-fives I used to order those mug shots, and my fingerprints are all over them. They also got copies of the Big Building's security tapes showing me entering the building minutes before those ninety-fives were clocked in at the Photo Unit."

"Did you check to see if they even saved those forms?"

"You know the Job, they save everything."

"Not since they computerized all the department forms, they don't. How do you know it was Stuart?"

"The envelope came in department mail. Who else could it be?"

"How does he even know you exist?" His expression of puzzlement vanished as an idea hit him. "I'll tell you how, you hadda throw your old girlfriend into that phony GO Fifteen bullshit against Stuart."

"Kahn's a dumb bitch. She could never figure out this setup."

"She couldn't, huh? Well, she sure as shit figured *you* out."

"Whadda we goin'a do?" Kirby was desperate.

"What was in that envelope ain't the problem, Ken. The problem is that you did exactly what Stuart wanted you to do. You fucking panicked." He pulled a surly face and stood up, sweeping the area with new intensity.

Borrelli ducked down, leaving the box on the ledge.

"Holiday's getting skittish. He could be on to us," Kahn radioed.

"Come down off the roof," Stuart transmitted from inside the van. "Wait in the lobby. If there's a problem, I'll radio you." He peered back through the binoculars. Holiday and Kirby were both standing now, scrutinizing their surroundings.

Jones radioed the control compartment in the back of the ice-cream truck. Watching the video monitor, Control said, "Looks like they're on to something."

Holiday looked around, concentrating on the four house-wives chatting below. A vivid picture of the two women with a baby carriage bullshitting outside the bar the other day flashed into his mind. "If you were going to lay a wire on this meet, how'd you do it?"

"I'd probably plant RF transmitters under the bleachers."

"You could only do that if you knew for sure we'd be here."

"Yeah, you're right. I'd probably go with parabolic micro-phones."

"Where would you hide them?"

"Depends. I mean . . ." His stare fell to the baby carriages, and fear showed in his eyes.

"Yeah, that's what I think, too," Holiday said, stepping down onto the next rung. When he jumped to the ground, he walked toward the women, a menacing expression narrowing his eyes as he approached the carriage.

The mother pushed his hand away when he reached inside to touch the infant. "Don't you wake my baby!"

He shoved her hand away and yanked off the blanket, expos-ing the wires and cassette recorder. He grabbed the doll and threw it at the detectives. Before he had a chance to say any-thing, the women leaped on him, pushing him up against the fence. Two of the detectives pinned his hands behind his back while the third slapped handcuffs around his wrist.

Kirby stared down in disbelief. It was only when the detectives turned their attention up to him that he reacted by jumping off the bleachers and running across the Parade Grounds.

"Get him!" Stuart radioed to Kahn and Borrelli.

The surveillance van lurched up over the curb and sped across the grounds, heading for the fleeing man. Borrelli and Kahn burst out of the apartment house and gave chase over the Parade Grounds.

Kirby kept looking back as he ran. When he saw the van gain-ing on him, he cut sharply to the left, smashing into the soccer players, causing them to gape with astonishment at the gray, tat-tooed van speeding toward them. The van plowed across the field and sped ahead of Kirby, then careened left and stopped, blocking his flight. Stuart and Jones jumped down.

Kirby had just wheeled about to run back the way he'd come when he spotted Borrelli and Kahn. He waved his hands in a gesture of surrender and crumpled to his knees. Stuart rushed over to him.

"I'm a lieutenant on an IAD investigation," Kirby blurted.

"You're a scumbag and a thief," Stuart said, hauling him off the ground.

Kahn and Borrelli trotted over, panting from the chase. Kahn and Kirby exchanged grim glances.

"I love you," Kirby mocked.

"You son of a bitch," Kahn said, swinging her pocketbook at him.

Stuart blocked the blow with his hand. "He's not worth it, Helen."

Jones dug his hand inside Kirby's jacket and yanked his gun out of its holster.

The stage crew drove up in an unmarked van and dragged Holiday out of the backseat. Jones and Borrelli bundled Kirby and Holiday into the surveillance van. The older woman in the stage crew handed Stuart a tape cassette.

"Thanks for everything," Stuart said to the stage crew.

Smasher lapped up a large bowl of water in the squad room before he ambled into Stuart's office. The rottweiler stopped to scratch behind his right ear, then squeezed his bulk under the whip's desk, where he sprawled, his snout resting across his front paws.

Kirby and Holiday sat on chairs in front of the desk, watching Stuart pop the cassette into the tape deck. During the ride back from the Parade Grounds, Stuart had phoned Jordon and told him to take Whitehouser on patrol with him. Stuart didn't want the c of d's nephew telling his uncle about Kirby's predicament.

"I wanna call my lawyer," Holiday said, and then slumped into a hostile silence.

Stuart ignored him and pressed the play button. As their conversation flowed from the tape deck, Kirby kept glancing over his shoulder at Kahn, who was standing a little behind and to his right with her arms folded tightly across her chest. His pleading looks were met by her cold, expressionless eyes.

When the tape played out, a defiant Paddy Holiday said, "You went to a lot of trouble for nothing, Stuart. You don't have shit on us."

Kirby turned around and looked into the squad room. The sight of the empty room appeared to give him new courage. He turned to Stuart. "You haven't notified anybody in the Big Building that you're holding me here. If you had, this place would be jumping with brass. What the fuck kind of game you playing?" He made a move to get up.

Jones pushed him back down.

Stuart glowered at the pair, picked up the tape deck, and stood. Beckoning to Kirby and Holiday to follow him, he entered the squad room and perched on the edge of a desk. He motioned Kirby and Holiday to sit in a pair of rickety chairs fifteen feet away from where he himself sat. Jones, Kahn, and Borrelli trooped in and found seats.

After suctioning the tape deck's rubber recording plug onto the top of the earphone, Stuart put the phone to his ear. When he punched in the number for the Internal Affairs Bureau, his call was answered promptly by a woman detective. After identifying himself, he asked to speak with Deputy Chief Aaron Flieger.

"Lieutenant Stuart, Chief. I got something I think you might wanna hear." He placed the phone's mouthpiece over the silver screen on the front of the tape deck and pushed the play button.

When the taped conversation ended, there was dead silence on the other end of the line. Kirby and Holiday hadn't moved a muscle. Stuart pushed the record button. Finally Flieger said, "What does it mean, Lou?" The uncertainty in his voice was palpable.

"It means that one of your lieutenants is an accessory to a double homicide, and he's apparently been in bed with the pinky-rings for a real long time, is what it means," said Stuart. "Along with his friend, our former colleague Holiday."

"What about those things he said he got in the department mail?" Flieger asked. "Did you send them to him?"

"No, Chief, I didn't," Stuart lied. "A confidential informant gave up the meet, and on the basis of his information we applied for a court order to eavesdrop." There was a brief silence at the other end while Stuart watched Paddy Holiday gnaw at a fingernail.

"Are you sure about that, Stuart?" Flieger demanded.

"Hey, Chief, like I told you the other day, I'm from the ol' school. I don't lie to my bosses. I told you the truth the other day, and I'm tellin' it now."

"Good, good. About that GO Fifteen thing, I think I can take care of that problem for you and that detective, the female."

"I'd really appreciate that, boss." Stuart smiled over at Kahn and winked.

"About this thing with Kirby," Flieger went on, "I think it'd be better for the Job if we handled it as an internal matter."

Stuart shifted his glance to Kirby, escalating it into a significant glare. "Whatever you think is best, Chief, but I gotta tell ya that that might be a problem."

"What kind of problem?"

"The CI who gave us that meet is also a confidential informer for the FBI," Stuart said. "My vibes tell me they're on to Kirby. I expect they're the ones who sent him that shit in the mail." He shot Kirby an evil grin as he heard Jones emit a little giggle.

"I wonder why they'd go to all that trouble?" said Flieger.

"Who knows all that Kirby is into? Or who's into it with him? If anyone else is involved with him, they got a problem. That guy'll cave in the first time the feds question him."

"Why don't you cut 'im loose? I'll start my own investigation into his activities."

"You got it, Chief." Stuart hung up and pressed the stop button. He stood then, facing Kirby and Holiday. "You two can go now. But I wouldn't make any long-range plans. I'm making copies of this tape and sending them to Lupo. Whaddaya think he's gonna think after he hears it?"

Jones chimed in, "The man's gotta figure you sold your shield to him for money and that you sure as hell will spit him up to stay out of the joint."

Borrelli smacked his palms together.

Kirby looked as though he were ready to pass out.

Stuart held up a finger. "The first one of you to roll over will stay alive. The other's a dead man. My money's on you, Paddy. You're a survivor."

The two sullen men stood up and started to leave.

Kahn stepped forward, glared at Kirby, and slapped his face with her open palm. The force of her blow snapped his head back. They looked at each other for a few seconds, then he nodded, dazed by her rage. Looking away, he pushed past her. The mark of her blow had left a red blotch on his cheek.

20

A brown panel truck pulled up at the curb in front of Albertoli's. Hippo, Joey Hershey Bar, and a short, bald-headed pinky-ring climbed out. They stood around the truck with their hands stuck in the pockets of their multicolored warm-up suits, checking out the street. A locomotive was being coupled to the first of the three boxcars on the siding. Four unhitched trailers lined the curb back to back.

Hippo walked into the street, looking up at the rooftops. He walked back to his friends and said, "Youse guys wait here." He walked inside the plant. "I wanna see Angela," he told the book-keeper with the steel gray hair wrapped into a bun in back.

Angela came out of her office, looked at him, and thought, This goon looks right out of Central Casting. Smiling, she waved Hippo inside. As soon as he came in, he handed her an enve-lope, saying, "Dis is for you."

She grabbed it out of his hand, walked over to her desk, and fanned through the stack of one-hundred-dollar bills. She put the money back into the envelope and slid it into the top drawer of her desk. Walking past him, she said, "Follow me, handsome."

She led him through the plant and into the refrigerator unit that contained the real cheese wheels. "Here's Lupo's cheese. Get it out of here."

"How am I supposeta carry all that out to the truck?" Hippo said.

Angela called over two forklift drivers and told them to move the wheels outside to Hippo's truck. "It'd be easier if they drove their truck around to the parking lot," said Driscoll, driver number one.

"Yeah," said the second driver, one Salvatore Garibaldi.

Hippo walked outside and told his friends to drive around into the lot. Driscoll and Garibaldi drove into the refrigerator and began loading the cheese wheels onto their forklifts. They rolled through the plant and out the side door that led out into the parking field. The driver of the van opened the back door, and Driscoll and Garibaldi began unloading the cheese inside the truck. Hippo and the other pinky-rings stood alongside, watching the cheese being loaded into a rented van. They paid no attention to the unhitched semi parked in the back of the parking field.

During the early morning hours, Driscoll had stood by and watched DEA electronics wizards insert battery-operated transceivers into each wheel of cheese. Every vehicle on station inside the surveillance grid would be equipped with tracking devices that would receive the transceivers' broadcast. The signals, which consisted of a beeping noise and a signal strength indicator, broadcast a five-digit numerical code that allowed each vehicle in the grid to home in on the signal. In addition to the tailing vehicles that would leapfrog the suspects' vehicle, surveillance vans—equipped with videocameras with telescopic lenses and dish antennae on their roofs that bounced scrambled signals up to the CIA/DEA law enforcement satellite, where the signals were picked up and bounced back down to a transmitter that unscrambled each as it spilled across television monitors—were on station along the entire surveillance grid.

The unhitched trailer parked in the rear of Albertoli's back parking lot had the name SEABOURN painted on its sides. It was DEA's command and control vehicle. One wall of the long trailer was crammed with sophisticated communications equipment, which included fax machines and three computers, each with CD-ROM drive capabilities that projected photographs of streets in any city in the country onto a screen on the trailer's wall. The computers had the ability to enhance the image down to a single building. The trailer's underbelly was lined with powerful lithium batteries that served as the backup power source. The main source came from thick black electrical cables that snaked out the rear of the trailer and were tapped into overhead electrical cables that ran some thirty feet beyond the back fence.

Driscoll and Garibaldi drove their last load over to the truck. Driscoll tooled up close and drove the twin forks inside the truck's open door, where he lowered them and drove back in reverse, leaving the load planted safely inside. Garibaldi followed suit.

Hippo ambled over to the two drivers and handed them twenty bucks each. "Thanks, guys," he said, and climbed into the truck. As soon as the truck drove out of the parking lot, three dish antennae unfolded out of the trailer's roof and pointed skyward.

Hippo kept checking the rearview mirror as he punched a number into his cellular phone. Frankie Bones's gravel voice came on the line. "Yeah?"

"We got the stuff," Hippo said.

"No problem?

"No."

"You sure?"

"Yeah, I'm sure," Hippo said with a trace of annoyance.

"You know what to do," Frankie Bones said, and punched thehis cellular. He looked over at Lupo, who had both feet resting on his desk. "Hippo's got it. No problems."

"Good. Now what about your nephew?"

"I hadda talk with Isaac Ham. Stuart wasn't bullshittin' us. Carmine went into business for himself."

"Where is he now?"

"I sent people to his house. Him and his wife have disappeared."

"Find him, Frankie. He can hurt us, bad."

"And when we do?"

"Tell him that his uncle ain't gonna let anyone hurt him. Make sure you get all the records he has on our business, then do him and his wife."

"Done like a dinner," Frankie said, scratching his big nose.

"What did you do with Isaac Ham?"

"I sent him to Haile Selassie's heaven."

Lupo swung his feet off the desk and picked up the tape cassette. "Whaddaya think of this tape Stuart sent up?"

"I think we gotta problem we gotta get rid of. I never trusted a cop, it makes no difference if they work for us or not. They're still cops."

"You're right. Find out who this Ken guy is, and then get rid of him and Holiday."

"And Stuart?"

"No. At least, not yet." Lupo walked over and sat on the sofa next to his friend. "I'm getting bad feelings about what's happening, Frankie. I think we gotta start thinking about the people who could hurt us."

"Makes sense."

"What about that girlfriend of yours? Does she know anything that could hurt us?"

"She knows about Andrea, but not much more. Hey, we've been together a lotta years. She's good people, Danny."

"I was only askin'." He looked at Frankie and remarked casually, "If you figure she'd do time for you, that's good enough for me."

Driscoll and Garibaldi stood inside the command trailer with their arms folded and their eyes fixed on the wall, watching the panel truck drive across the New Jersey Turnpike Extension that spanned Newark Bay. "They're not heading for New York," Garibaldi said.

"I think they're making for the airport," Driscoll said. As they watched, the rented van passed under a large green sign reading NEWARK AIRPORT EXIT 14.

When the truck sped off Exit 14's ramp, Driscoll stepped across the aisle and picked up a thin headset with a pin-drop microphone at the tip. He slid it over his head and radioed, "All units, this is Mother Hen. Subjects appear to be heading for the airport. I want the identification number and description of any plane they use. Unit Two, when we have the plane IDed, check their flight plan with traffic control."

"Do you have the capability of following a plane to its destination?" Garibaldi asked.

Driscoll smiled and lighted a cigarette. "We have the ability to watch the bastards fly into hell."

High waves rose up out of the Atlantic Ocean and rolled toward the beach, gathering speed until the surf pounded the shoreline. The frothy mass of water was then swiftly recalled by the tides and formed up into another wall of water that came crashing back with relentless regularity.

An old beachcomber was sifting the sands for the summer's lost treasures.

Stuart walked up the Bay Sixteenth Street ramp leading onto Coney Island's boardwalk. He looked up and down the wooden promenade. The Cyclone ride loomed in the distance, its serpentine tracks rising and falling against the gray, overcast sky. Most of the concession stands along the boardwalk were boarded up for the winter.

Stuart crossed the boardwalk, heading for the young man standing at the end of Pat Auletta's Steeplechase Pier. It evoked old memories. The pier had been named for a local politician who had worked tirelessly for the community and whose son, Ken, was currently a prominent journalist. Stuart recalled the awe he had felt as a child when he first saw the intricate web of the long dismantled Wonder Wheel. Now, when he looked up and down the long stretch of wood, all he saw was urban decay, a few joggers, and aged people from nearby nursing homes. He went up to the railing and stood beside the man. Looking up at gulls wheeling over the shoreline, he said, "You wanted to see me, here I am."

"I didn't think cops were supposed to set people up to get killed," Carmine Marino said, staring out at the ocean.

"You thunk wrong, Carmine. We play by different rules today. It's like the old pirate days: no quarter given, none asked. Whaddaya want?"

"I want to walk away clean. No arrest, no testimony, no witness protection."

"What makes you think your uncle's people will let you walk away clean?"

"I knew this day was coming, and I'm ready for it. In case you don't know, wiseguys aren't wise, they're dumb. The only thing that makes them special is their willingness to kill anybody who gets in their way."

"I figured that out myself a long time ago."

Marino looked sideways at the lieutenant. "It's cops like you who worry me, Stuart. You're smart, and when you want someone real bad, you know how to use your department's resources to find them. You're the kind of a guy who doesn't know how to give up."

"I don't have the authority to make the kind of a deal you're looking for."

"I didn't come here empty-handed."

"Didn't think you did."

"I can give you the liquid milk hijack scam, the cheese futures scam, insider trading, gambling, drugs, money laundering, and the names of the brokerage firms that wash their money offshore."

"You want to be allowed to vanish. To retire to some exotic place and enjoy the fortune you stole from them. I need more, Carmine, a lot more."

"Let's walk."

They took off down the boardwalk, strolling toward the roller-coaster ride. A homeless man pushing his overflowing cart rushed by them with an air of desperation. Carmine leaned his head close to Stuart's and said, "You don't really know what you stumbled into, do you?"

"I think I've got a pretty good idea."

"I wonder. Lemme ask you something. When your police commissioner wants to know the effect of one of his policies on the department, say, ten, twenty years down the road, what does he do?"

"He gives the problem to Intelligence Division, where an analyst studies it and reports back to the PC."

"Did you know that soon after the Knight's Roundtable meet in 1963, the police commissioner asked the Intelligence Division to tell him what would happen if the department did away with 'good money'?"

"No."

"Would you like to know what the report said?"

"I can guess. Crooked cops would then turn to drugs."

"That's right."

"How do you know that?" Stuart asked.

"I read the report."

They walked in silence for a few minutes before Carmine said, "There were a lot of high-ranking people in the police *and* the Five Families who wanted to get into drugs. But before the drug cartels could establish secure networks in the city, they needed police protection. Which meant they had to do away with the 'good money, bad money' philosophy. Can you figure out how they did it?"

Stuart clamped his jaw, swallowing his rising anger. "Yeah. I can. The bastards took a cop who was known throughout the Job for his honesty and put him into the most corrupt division in the Bronx. That cop's name was Frank Serpico."

"They created a scandal as a diversion. It was brilliant."

"Serpico blew the whistle on corruption. And the Knapp Commission dealt the death blow to 'good money.' The Job stopped enforcing the antigambling laws, so no more payoffs. They closed down all the other things that brought in the clean money. And *then* the Palace Guard, pretending to stamp out corruption, prohibited uniform cops and precinct squad detectives from enforcing the narcotics laws. That opened the floodgates."

"And the cartels opened drug supermarkets throughout New York City." Carmine Marino took a deep breath of the crisp sea air. "I'm going to miss the beach." He looked sideways at Stuart. "Did you know that every drug network in this town is assessed a monthly protection fee that only goes to the top brass of the NYPD?"

"The Calis? the Medellín? the Lo Fungs?"

"All of them. Even the Russians in Brighton Beach. And if they don't cough it up every month, the police dismantle their operations. And they all pay because it's chicken feed compared to what they're raking in. Crooked cops come cheap."

"'Good money' used to flow up the chain of command. Drug money comes in at the top and stays there."

"Nothing lasts forever, Stuart, you know that."

"How does this arrangement work?"

"Holiday's one of the bagmen, I'm the paymaster. Every month I wire the money into accounts in the Cayman Islands. I have the names, account numbers, and amounts going back to 1969 of all retired, dead, and active members of Knight's Roundtable."

"You have all these records?"

"All on a nice floppy."

"Why did Lupo store drugs at the Albertoli plant instead of shipping them directly to Chicago?"

"Danny thought it was safer to use it. That way if the cops hit one stash house they wouldn't have cleaned him out. He's always switching his mode of transporting and storing drugs."

"Where is his regular warehouse?"

"I'm not sure. He moves around a lot. But last year one of our front companies bought a factory in Queens. I wouldn't be surprised if he uses it as his main stash house."

Stuart walked over to the wide steps leading to the beach. He climbed down and sat on the next-to-the-last rung, digging his heels into the cold sand.

Marino came and sat beside him. "Do we have a deal?"

"Yeah, Carmine, we got a deal."

Marino reached into the right side pocket of his tweed sports coat and brought out a computer disk. It had a yellow Post-it stuck to the top of it. He passed it to Stuart, saying, "The factory's address."

"What made you so sure I'd play?"

"You had to. You're an honest cop. And if you don't get them, you're a dead man, and you know it."

Stuart watched the waves hurling toward the shoreline. They hammered the shore in rapid succession. The roar of the collision pounded in his ears. He looked at the man next to him and asked, "Why was Beansy killed?"

"The Rastafarians didn't want to contribute to the fund. Beansy called a meet to try and talk some sense into them. They got into an argument, and Gee shot him."

Stuart sighed. "So that's what it was really all about. . . . Does Madeline Fine or Lupo's wife know about Franklin Investment's side business?"

"They don't have a clue."

They stood and climbed back up. "Have a good life, Lieutenant."

"You too, Carmine." He watched as the accountant walked across the boardwalk and disappeared down the ramp leading to the street. He realized that he was gripping the disk tightly in his hand. He looked down at it, hoping that when he ran it he would not find Patrick Sarsfield Casey's name listed. A rush of cold air ruffled his hair just as his beeper went off.

21

A black panel truck sped north along Lake Shore Drive. In the east, Lake Michigan glittered in the gathering twilight. On the slopes to the west, high-rise apartments rose like stately sentinels charged with guarding the great lake.

The truck sped past Soldier Field.

In the back of the Albertoli plant in Jersey City, Stuart slid the manila envelope off the seat and got out of his car. He walked over to the unhitched trailer. Bending low, he pressed the red button on the chassis. An aluminum stepladder dropped down from the underbelly. He climbed up into the DEA command and control trailer. He pressed the button on top of the steps, and the ladder folded up into a compartment. A sliding panel came out of the underbelly, covering the opening.

DEA agents manned the consoles. The CD-ROM drive projected Chicago streets up on the wall, while next to them simultaneous pictures of the black truck speeding along Lake Shore Drive were being beamed to the C&C trailer by surveillance vans in Chicago.

Driscoll and Garibaldi were standing on the far wall, watching the video. A halo of cigarette smoke surrounded Driscoll.

"What's happening?" Stuart asked.

"They had a chartered Gulfstream Four waiting at Newark. They flew into Midway Airport and offloaded the shit into that truck," Driscoll said.

"They're turning into Halstead Street, entering Greek Town," one of the console operators responded.

"What about the New York contingent?" Stuart asked.

"They're all inside the truck," Garibaldi said.

The black truck pulled into the curb across the street from a decrepit warehouse that appeared to be deserted. Its three stories had a flat roof and a peeling gray brick facade. A faded sign above the entrance read "Fenimore Brothers 1897." The curb cut led to a large wooden door with crossed support beams. To the right of it was a gray metal door that looked to be the employees' entrance.

The truck waited.

Traffic was light. An oil truck passed. A motorcycle sped into Morgan Street.

A telescopic lens zoomed in on the man in the truck's passenger seat.

"That's Ernesto Camacho," Driscoll said.

Stuart studied the man with the straight brown hair pulled back across his head and tied into a ponytail. He had a small gold loop in his right ear. His eyes were a frozen wasteland. "He looks like a mean bastard."

"He likes to kill people," Driscoll said.

"A sweetheart of a guy," Garibaldi said.

"And cautious," Driscoll said, watching the idling truck.

"You think that's the warehouse?" Stuart asked Driscoll.

"Probably. They'll plant there for a while to check out what drives by. Then they'll drive inside and unload," Driscoll said.

"I don't see any lookouts," Garibaldi said.

"Drug operations in the inner city have lookouts up the kazoo," Driscoll said, "but they don't like to use them on their warehouses. They figure they'd attract too much attention. Most of them don't even use video monitors for the same reason. But you can bet your paycheck that there're a couple of heavily armed guards inside."

"Those pictures are good," Stuart said. "How far away are your camera trucks?"

"I don't know," Driscoll said. "They could be parked two, three, five miles away and still get those pictures."

Stuart looked down the aisle at the computers. "Can your computers tap into offshore bank accounts in the Cayman Islands?"

"Yes. It's easy to get into their database, but to access accounts is another story. Ordinarily we don't have much luck. In order to violate an account, you need the account number and the password. Sometimes we can buy an account number from a bank official, but the password, that's a different story. The people we go up against are sophisticated *trafficantes* and money launderers; they don't use their kids' birth dates or their parents' wedding date as passwords."

"They're moving," Garibaldi called out.

The garage door opened and the black truck swerved away from the curb and sped across the street into the warehouse.

A male voice came over the DEA radio network. "Unit Five, give us a look inside that warehouse."

"Unit Five, ten-four."

Seven minutes passed before Stuart saw the homeless woman pushing her shopping cart along Chicago's West Randolph Street. Her long, matted hair stuck out from under a black-brimmed hat that had a large cloth sunflower sewn onto the front of the dome. She wore a dirty brown flare skirt over blue jeans and an olive-green army fatigue jacket. The shoelaces on her worn Timberland boots were knotted in several places. She pushed the cart up to the warehouse's smaller door and took out a cardboard lean-to. She opened it up and fitted it into the doorway. She crawled inside.

DEA Agent Rebecca Barton stretched out inside the lean-to, her back to the street. She opened her jacket and removed a viewing screen eight inches long and eight inches wide. She took a long cable out of her pocket and plugged it in on the side of the viewing screen. The cable's diameter was the size of a piece of string, with a fiber-optic lens at the tip. The handheld viewing machine was powered by an internal power pack. After switching on the machine, she began inserting the cable through the keyhole.

The cavernous warehouse interior dwarfed the men standing around inside. Pallets of cheese wheels stood in the center of the floor. Two of the pinky-rings from New York and two other men were busy unloading the cheese from the truck. Hippo and Camacho were standing by the pallets, talking. Three other men lounged near a wooden staircase without a banister.

Agent Barton whispered into her sleeve microphone, "I count nine altogether. Six are standing around the truck in the center of the warehouse, and three more are by a staircase in the left rear."

Her control, who was a block away inside the oil truck that had passed before, radioed to the receiver plugged into her ear, "Do you see any automatic weapons?"

"The guys at the staircase are toting M-16's. I don't see any weapons on the others."

"Get out of there."

Stuart watched as the bag lady climbed out of the cardboard shelter, folded it, stuck it back into her shopping cart, and pushed off down the street.

Inside the unhitched trailer, Stuart, Driscoll, and Garibaldi watched as the bag lady turned the corner. They could not see the DEA agents on the wall of their trailer as they cordoned off the streets around the warehouse. They stood looking at the picture of the box-shaped building, waiting for the next move.

The flow of traffic around the warehouse ceased.

Stuart checked the time.

Four vans drove up to the front of the warehouse. DEA agents, wearing flak jackets with the initials *DEA* emblazoned across the front and back, piled out. All of them were armed with M-16 automatic rifles with grenade launchers mounted under the barrel. Two agents moved swiftly to the doors and molded plastic explosive onto the hinges. When they finished, they ran back behind the vans. All the agents knelt and put on gas masks.

One agent held a square black box that fitted into the palm of his hand. A red light blinked above a black button in its center. He pressed the button. The doors flew off their hinges. The agents rose quickly to their feet and fired canisters inside the building.

Watching this happen, Stuart looked at Driscoll and asked, "Tear gas?"

"Tear gas with a vomit injector. They'll be heaving their guts up all over the place," Driscoll said, watching the gas billowing out of the doorway.

Joey Hershey Bar staggered out first, gasping and puking. The Hippo crawled out on all fours, retching. Camacho ran out of the warehouse, rubbing his burning eyes and throwing up streams of chunky yellow vomit. Agents wearing gas masks disarmed them quickly and handcuffed their hands behind their backs.

Stuart walked down the aisle and stopped in front of the first computer console. Driscoll came over to him.

Stuart said, "Can we keep what just happened in Chicago out of the press?"

"We can try. We'll take the prisoners to a federal building, have a doctor check them out, do the paper, lose the paper, do the paper again." Driscoll looked at his watch. "It's eight forty-five. I'll try and buy you twelve hours."

"Thanks, Jimmy." Stuart walked over to the console next to the staircase and picked up his folder. He reached in for the personnel papers that Suzanne had given him on the members of Knight's Roundtable and the disk Carmine Marino had given him earlier. "I need to see what's on this disk."

Driscoll took it from him and handed it to an agent working the console, saying, "Harry, see what's on this." The console operator took the disk and slid it into the slot.

As names, dates, amounts, and account numbers began to

scroll onto the screen, Stuart felt his heart pounding. The long list contained the names of dead and retired members. Only five were currently in the Job. The chief of detectives, Kevin Hartman, was the highest-ranking current member on the list. Gebheart, the detective divisions XO; Ken Kirby; Aaron Flieger; a captain in Personnel Orders. He shook his head in a mixture of disbelief and sorrow. He scanned the list quickly, looking for Patrick Sarsfield Casey. The name wasn't there. "Will you print that out for me, please?" he asked the operator.

"You got it," the operator said, and pressed a couple of buttons, activating the laser printer on the side of the console. He picked up the printouts and handed them to Stuart.

"Thanks," Stuart said. He looked around for Driscoll and saw him talking on the telephone. Video transmissions from Chicago had been discontinued, along with the CD-ROM drive's enhanced scale of Chicago's streets. The wall suddenly looked naked.

Driscoll hung up the phone and came over to Stuart and Garibaldi. "That was Chicago on the line. The cheese wheels stored inside the warehouse were filled with China cat. They figure we grabbed somewhere in the neighborhood of a hundred eighty mil street value."

"We need those guys to roll over on Lupo," Garibaldi said.

"They'll roll," Stuart said, handing Driscoll the printout with the names of crooked cops and their account numbers. "Can we check these account numbers with the Cayman Islands?"

"Mind a suggestion?" Driscoll asked Stuart.

"No," Stuart said.

"We could spend all night searching for passwords to break into those accounts and still not come up with anything. Why don't you give me everything you have, and I'll fax it all to our encryption unit in D.C. We have top code breakers and they use very fast computers. Let's let them come up with the passwords. It'll be a lot faster."

"Makes sense to me," Stuart agreed. He took the disk back

from the console operator, thanked him, and slipped it into his pocket. He looked at Driscoll and said, "I'm out of here."

"Where you going?"

"To dish out some payback."

22

Paddy Holiday paced the bar's kitchen, replaying the day in his mind. That thing in the Parade Grounds had really shaken him. After he and Kirby left the Seven One squad room, they went to Toomey's diner on Rogers Avenue. Holiday had to spend almost an hour convincing Kirby that the tape of their conversation was no big deal. If it was, Stuart would have arrested them.

Kirby told him he was going to throw in his papers and retire. Holiday suggested that he file for three-quarters. "Our friends will push it through for you."

After they left the diner, Holiday hastened back to the bar. When the barmaid told him he didn't have any messages, he phoned Frankie Bones to see if he knew about the tape and, if he did know, to explain to him that it was no big deal.

Frankie Bones did not answer his cellular phone. Holiday called back five times and still got no answer, thus increasing his apprehension. He wasn't going to be able to relax until after he spoke with Frankie Bones. He knew what they were capable of doing if they felt threatened.

His nervousness grew as the day wore on and he hadn't reached him. At five o'clock he got rid of a few stragglers at the bar and closed up. After switching off the barroom lights, he went into the kitchen to pay bills. He picked up his phone and dialed again: still no answer. His nervousness escalated to panic. Now was the time to disappear, at least until he could figure out what was going on.

He switched off the kitchen lights and pushed through the double doors. He froze. Frankie Bones was sitting on a bar stool, holding up a cassette. Two grinning goons stood by the entrance. Holiday became conscious of the weight of the .38-caliber Colt Detective Special under his sweater.

"We got a little problem, Paddy," Frankie Bones said, holding up the cassette.

"Frankie, no problem, everything's good, I swear." His voice cracked.

Frankie Bones slid off the stool. Approaching him, he said, "Whaddaya gonna tell me about this?"

"Frankie, it's all bullshit, I swear. Lemme explain, it's really no big deal. That fuckin' guy Stuart—"

Frankie Bones punched him in the face, plowing him backward into the kitchen, where he fell against the butcher block table and crumpled to the floor. Frankie Bones rushed in after him and kicked him several times in the stomach.

Writhing in pain and gasping for air, Holiday slid his hand under his sweater and clutched the Colt's checkered grips. He had the weapon halfway out before Frankie Bones kicked him in the face. One of the goons grabbed his gun arm by the wrist and elbow and broke the bone over his leg. Holiday screamed in agony. Frankie Bones picked up the Colt and stuck it into his waistband. Holiday was still screaming as the two goons pulled him roughly to his feet.

"I don't got a lotta time, Paddy. It's Friday, and Mary cooks for me on Friday, so I'm gonna ask the questions and you're gonna give the answers. Who is this Ken?"

"Lieutenant Ken Kirby, he's one of my sources. He works in IAD."

Frankie Bones's eyes fell to the meat cleaver on top of the

butcher block table. He picked it up and idly examined its gleaming, deadly steel. "This Kirby is the guy with the detective girlfriend?"

"Yeah," Holiday moaned. "My arm is broken."

"Don't worry about it. We'll get it fixed for you. Where does this Ken live?"

"Syosset."

"What does Stuart know about us?"

"Nothing, really. Somehow he hooked me and Ken into those mug shots of Gee and Hollyman."

"When he questioned you, what did he ask you about us?"

"Nothing, I swear."

"I love when guys swear. It makes me feel so, so trusting." He looked at the cleaver. "Now, I wanna know if you got any sources inside the NYPD that we don't already know about."

"No, I don't." Holiday was kneeling on the floor, as if in prayer.

Frankie Bones motioned to his friends to put Holiday's wrist on the butcher block table. Holiday tried to worm free. They pinned his broken arm to the top of the table. Holiday screamed.

Frankie Bones rested the cleaver's blade on his wrist. "If you're bullshitting me, I'm going to give you a new street name, Paddy the Claw." He raised the cleaver.

"I'm not!" Paddy shrieked.

"I believe you, Paddy. Now we're gonna take you to a hospital to get your arm fixed," he said, and buried the cleaver in Holiday's skull. He bent over the body and wiped the handle with his handkerchief. "I'm hungry. Let's get outta here."

Mary Terrella lit the candles on the kitchen table, set with her blue-and-white tablecloth with blue napkins. She had already showered and dressed. After twenty-two years, she still got deliciously nervous every Friday night waiting for Frankie to arrive. She was wearing her new black pants suit with white roses embroided up the sides of the sleeves and legs.

In the old days, they used to spend their Fridays bouncing

around discos and clubs. She liked it better now. It was more inti-mate, and she enjoyed pretending for one night a week that he was hers.

She opened a bottle of Valpolicella and was warming a fresh loaf of bread in the oven when she heard a car pull up outside and ran to the window. When she saw him sitting in the passen-ger seat, she crossed into the living room to put the latest *Carreras, Domingo, Pavarotti in Concert* CD on the player.

"You want us to wait?" the goon behind the wheel asked Frankie Bones.

"Drive up to the corner and park," he said, opening the door.

Walking up the pathway, Frankie Bones heard the music and began conducting with his right hand. Mary opened the door and greeted him with a big kiss, tilting her pelvis into him, say-ing, "Think I'll get lucky tonight?"

"You can bet on it." He mimed Carreras singing. "Beautiful. Beautiful."

"I made risotto and osso buco."

"I can smell it. I'm starvin'."

"Then let's go eat." She walked ahead of him toward the kitchen.

Pavarotti was singing *"Recondita armonia."* Still conducting with his left hand, Frankie Bones slid Holiday's .38 Colt from under his coat and shot her once in the back of the head. Her forehead exploded. She toppled forward onto her stomach, splaying awk-wardly across the kitchen threshold.

He stepped over her and walked to the stove. After bending down to smell the food, he went over and picked a plate off the table. Filling it with risotto, which he noticed was not quite beginning to dry out, and a big veal shank, he sat down and savored the food, the wine, and the music.

He was going to miss his Friday night dinners.

23

The darkened warehouse on the south side of Borden Avenue, just off Twenty-seventh Street, was squeezed between the Long Island Expressway's overpass and Hunters Point Avenue in Long Island City. It was a squat two-story building, attached on both sides to other warehouses. A ginkgo tree in a tiny plot of dirt decorated the curb in front of the building.

It was nine-forty Friday night, and this industrial area of Queens was deserted, save for the occasional car driving along Borden Avenue, heading for the entrance to the Midtown Tunnel. The detectives were parked a block away on the north side of Borden. Kahn sat behind the wheel, Stuart in the passenger seat, and Borrelli in the back. They were waiting for Jones to come back from night court with a signed search warrant with a provision for surreptitious entry. When Stuart had told Jones to apply for the warrant, Jones had asked him, "What about reasonable cause?"

"Tell the court that Joey Montie, AKA the Hippo, rolled over in Chicago and spit up Lupo's stash house."

"Has he?"

"Not yet, but he will."

"What do you want me to use for exigent circumstances?"

"The usual," Stuart had replied. "'Property sought may be

quickly and easily destroyed, and giving notice would endanger the lives of the executing officers.'"

"I'm on the way," Jones had said, reaching for the door handle.

After watching the warehouse for a few minutes, Borrelli said, "That place looks deserted to me."

"I checked with telephone security," Kahn added. "There's no phone listed at that address."

"Lupo doesn't believe in unnecessary expenses," Stuart said.

"I don't see any lookouts," Borrelli said.

"This area is DOA at night," Stuart said.

The car phone rang. Stuart snatched up the handset. "Yeah?"

"Bad news," Driscoll reported from the command and control trailer. "The media found out about the raid in Chicago. CNN already aired the story."

"Do they have names?"

"Camacho and his people. They don't know about the New York crew."

"Any word from D.C. on those bank accounts?"

"They've come up with the password on some of them and invaded the accounts. It's only a question of time until they break into the others."

"Where are Lupo and Frankie Bones?"

"They're at an engagement party for Lupo's daughter. I've got my people on them. What about the stash house?"

"We're sitting on it, waiting for one of my men to come back with a search warrant."

"Stay in touch."

Stuart had just returned the handset to its cradle when the phone rang again. "Yeah?"

"Lou, cleaning people found Paddy Holiday in the bar's kitchen with a meat cleaver in his head," Jerry Jordon said.

"'Round up the usual suspects,'" Stuart said.

"What?"

"I heard a cop use that line in a movie once. I always wanted to get to use it. Who's on the scene?"

"Me and Hector Colon. There's no physical evidence other than the cleaver, and no witnesses."

"Clean up the mess and do the paper. Where's Whitehouser?"

"He signed off duty at seven-thirty."

"If you should come up with anything, let me know." He punched "End" and rested the handset on his lap. He looked at Kahn and said, "I want you and Joe to do a walk-by. Pretend you're lovers."

"Okay," Borrelli said.

Stuart waited until they had gone before he pulled out Ken Kirby's phone number, which he'd copied off the papers Suzanne had given him. He punched in the number. When he heard Kirby's voice come on the line, he bit back his anger and said in a friendly tone, "How ya doin', Ken?"

"What d'ya want, Stuart?"

"The bad news is they whacked ol' Paddy with a meat cleaver. The good news is they didn't get you, yet."

"Paddy's dead?" Kirby was clearly shocked.

"As I see it, you got two options. You can get on the horn and ask the local gendarmes to protect you until I come to arrest you, or you can make a run for it. Of course, Lupo's hitmen are probably waiting outside for you now. And even if you did manage to escape them and me, you're going to be broke. We got into your Cayman Island bank account, which means that the IRS is also going to be hunting your ass. See ya 'round, Kenny." Stuart disconnected and then watched Kahn and Borrelli duck into the shadows across from the stash house.

Kirby stared at the phone. His face was calm except for the sudden uncontrollable tic in his right eye. He let the receiver fall from his hand and stood in the playroom, dimly conscious of the movie on television. He left the room and went into the second-floor bedroom. Except for muted sounds from the television, the house was quiet. His wife had gone to a movie with her girlfriends, and the children were asleep.

He closed and locked the bedroom door, walked over to the

dresser, and took his shield and .38-caliber S&W Chief out of the top drawer.

He sat on the bed, staring trancelike at his shield, remembering his first tour on the street: a one-arm post on Lexington Avenue, patrolling only the west side of the street. He recalled his first free meal, lamb chops with French fries and a salad. He stared at his shield for a long time before he stuck the gun barrel into his mouth and fired.

Kahn and Borrelli stood in the darkness, checking out the warehouse. Borrelli slid his arm around her waist. She pushed it away. "We're supposed to be lovers," he said.

"Just let's pretend, Joe."

"Helen, I'd like to take you out on a proper date."

Her eyes smiled at him. "Peking duck?"

"Yeah, but without any 'get acquainted' sauce over it."

"Sounds good to me, Joe." She touched the back of his hand with hers, smiled, and said, "We're supposed to look like we like each other."

He wrapped her hand in his.

The warehouse fronted Twenty-seventh Street. The detectives could not see any identifying company signs. A large double door in the front was padlocked. A high metal fence crowned with razor wire stretched behind the warehouse.

"I don't see any signs of life inside that place," Borrelli said, liking the feel of her hand in his.

"Because we don't see anything doesn't mean nobody's inside," she said.

He made a move to take her into his arms.

"We'd better get back, Joe."

"Yeah, you're right."

Jones was sitting in the back of the car, tapping the search warrant against the headrest, when they returned.

After they climbed back in the car, Stuart asked them if they'd seen any signs of movement inside the warehouse.

"Nothing," Kahn said.

290 WILLIAM J. CAUNITZ

"The question now is, how are we going to get inside that building?" Borrelli said.

Stuart grabbed the handset and phoned Driscoll in Command and Control. "Any changes?"

"Camacho and the Hippo turned. They're spilling their guts."

"Where are they questioning them?"

"In the Federal Building."

"Will you phone your people in Chicago and ask them to ask Camacho and the Hippo if they know the location of Lupo's drug warehouse?"

"Hold on."

Stuart could hear Driscoll talking to someone. A few minutes went by before the DEA agent came back on the line and said, "They don't know."

"Are Lupo and Frankie Bones still at the engagement party?" asked Stuart.

"Yeah. They just might not have gotten the word on Chicago."

"Maybe. But we gotta assume that they did. I'll call you later," Stuart said, and, holding the handset, looked at the warehouse. "I figure the Burglars are the way to go on this."

He scrolled through the telephone menu until he came to Electronic Intelligence, then pressed the send button. When the sergeant on EI's operations desk came on the line, Stuart identified himself and put in an urgent request for a surreptitious entry team, otherwise known in the Job as the Burglars.

The sergeant logged the search warrant's number, date and time of issuance, location to be searched, items authorized to be seized, and the name of the issuing magistrate. He gave Stuart a log number and told him a team was just finishing up a job in Forest Hills and would meet him in a little while.

Sixteen minutes later an unmarked station wagon pulled up alongside the category one car. A detective dressed in work clothes got out and walked around to the passenger side. Stuart whisked down the window.

It was tradition in the Job that the whip sit in the passenger seat, so the detective knew it was Stuart. "How ya doin', Lou? I'm Sergeant Joe Grossman. Whatcha we got?"

"That warehouse," he said, pointing.

"You wanna storm inside or sneak inside?"

"Sneak."

Grossman studied the problem. All the windows on the two-story building had grates over them. The buildings on either side of the warehouse were two stories also. Grossman said, "All of these warehouses have skylights on their roofs. Using ladders, we can get you up onto the adjoining roof and open the skylight for you. But that would mean climbing down two stories into a darkened warehouse. That's noisy and dangerous."

"What do you suggest?" Stuart asked.

"I think your best shot is to have us take out one of the first-floor windows."

"But they're set pretty high above the floor inside," Stuart said.

"That's right. You'd have about an eight-foot drop, maybe a little more," Grossman said.

"Let's do it." Stuart grabbed the car's phone and called the communications unit. He informed them that plainclothes units were effecting a court-ordered surreptitious entry at that location. He then notified the desk officer at the One Oh Eight, a precaution to avoid the possibility of uniform cops responding to a report of a ten-thirty, a burglary in progress.

The detectives quietly approached the warehouse. Grossman and one of his detectives raised two aluminum ladders padded with sound-suppressing rubber to a first-floor window fronting Twenty-seventh Street. The window was about ten feet above the sidewalk. The Electronic Intelligence detectives climbed up while the others waited below. Grossman hung a cloth overnight bag on a hook on the side of his ladder and checked the window out for alarms. When he saw none, he reached into the cloth bag and took out a butane-fueled miniblowtorch about four inches long. He lit it; a tongue of flame leaped out of the nozzle. Grossman directed the blue ribbon at the right-hand corner of the grille.

Stuart watched as the flame sliced through the steel. Within three minutes the grille was carefully and quietly removed and lowered to the detectives below.

Grossman took out two window holders that consisted of a foot-long aluminum bar with rubber plungers attached on both ends. He handed one to the detective on the other ladder. One Burglar suctioned his bar to the top of the windowpane; the other took the bottom. With the pane of glass secured, Grossman took out a glass cutter with a blade made of industrial diamonds and silently ran the blade around the edge of the glass. When the pane had been cut through, the detectives lifted it out of the window and, in sync, climbed back down, holding the pane between them.

Stuart and Jones climbed up the ladder. Stuart cast the beam of his Mini Maglite into the building. The large space was empty. He played the beam of light around the interior. The warehouse appeared to be abandoned. He turned off the light and climbed through the opening. Gripping the window ledge with both hands, he lowered himself down. He was about five feet off the floor. He dropped down and fell to his knees, sweeping the cavernous space with his nine.

Jones dropped down beside him. Had Carmine Marino been mistaken? he wondered, pricking his ears for any sounds.

Borrelli and Kahn jumped down.

The detectives remained still, trying to detect any sound or movement in the warehouse. "There's nothing here," Borrelli whispered.

"Maybe," Stuart said. "Let's fan out and check this place out. And be careful."

The four detectives spread out and walked across the floor. In the middle, Stuart stopped and raised his hand. The others halted, their ears and eyes straining. Stuart cocked his ear in the direction of the door on the warehouse's eastern wall. He thought he heard the faint sounds of cannon and explosions. He pointed toward the door. Stuart and Borrelli crept over and put their ears up against the door. Somebody on the other side was

watching a war movie on television. Stuart took hold of the doorknob and turned it slowly.

The door was unlocked. He opened it partially. The detectives
stepped back while Kahn took out her compact and opened it.
She placed her shoulder against the side of the doorjamb and
held the compact's mirror in front of her so that she could see
past the partially open door.

"A staircase leading down," she whispered.

The detectives crept down the staircase. Whenever they came
to a bend, Kahn would use her compact mirror to peer around
it. The television grew louder. The detectives stepped off the
staircase and found themselves in a tiny vestibule that led into a
closed door. The television was on the other side.

Stuart tried the door and cursed under his breath when he
found it locked. He put his ear to the door. All he heard was the
television. He motioned Borrelli and Kahn to get on the other
side of the door. He gestured for Jones to take out the door. "On
five," he whispered.

Jones moved back from the door. Stuart counted to five. Jones
rammed his foot against the door slightly above the lock, splin-
tering it open. Almost shoulder to shoulder, Stuart and Borrelli
leaped into the room. Two men sitting on a tattered sofa watching television swiveled their heads toward the two detectives,
then scrambled for a pair of Uzi machine guns on the table next
to the sofa.

Stuart and Borrelli fired rounds over their heads. "Freeze!
We're police officers," Jones said.

The men backed off and slowly raised their hands.

The basement was half the size of the upstairs. Six pallets holding clear plastic bags of white powder were stored against the
brick wall on the left. Halves of fake cheese wheels were stock-
piled to the right of the pallets, and an aluminum folding table
stood in front of them.

Across the room from the stash stood a refrigerator and a yellow Formica kitchen table with four chairs in front of it. The television sat on top of one of the kitchen chairs.

The detectives handcuffed the prisoners. "You got the right to tell us whatever you wanna tell us," Borrelli told the sullen men.

The detectives searched the place to see if anyone was hiding. They found no one.

Leaning against one of the pallets, Stuart unfolded the cellular phone they found on the sofa and punched in Command and Control's number. When Driscoll answered, Stuart filled him in on what had happened and what they had found.

"I'll send some people over," said Driscoll. "They'll start invoicing the drugs."

"Thanks, Jimmy. I think it's time for us to go and grab Lupo and Frankie Bones."

"I'll meet you at the engagement party."

Chez Pierre was one of the many wiseguy catering halls that dominated the wedding and Bar Mitzvah business in New York City and Long Island. It was located on Community Drive in Lake Success, across the road from the Fresh Meadow Country Club. Stone waterfalls flanked the entrance to the parking lot. Fieldstone sheathed the building's facade; slabs of black marble decorated the entrance. A black canopy trimmed in gold piping stretched out over the entrance's carpeted steps to the curb.

The dashboard clock read eleven-thirty when Kahn double-parked alongside Driscoll's car on Community Drive, across the street from Chez Pierre's parking lot. Stuart got out of the car and walked around to the other side of the federal car. Driscoll got out and said, "Lupo must have three hundred guests at the party. Drop a bomb in there and you'd wipe out the Mob as we know it."

"They gotta know what happened in Chicago," Stuart said, looking across at the valet parking attendants.

"Maybe not," Driscoll said. "They've been partying since seven."

"Where are they sitting?"

"Lupo and Frankie Bones and their families are at table one.

It's on the far side of the dance floor to the right as you walk in the hall."

"If we go in and drag them out, some of their people might try and be heroes, and some innocent people could get hurt. And if we wait until the party breaks, the same thing could happen."

"We could take them at home in the morning," Driscoll said, lighting a cigarette.

"I'd rather do it now. Where are their cars parked?"

"In the parking lot's VIP spots, right next to the side entrance."

"Bodyguards?"

"Not in the parking lot."

"How many men you got with you?" Stuart asked.

"There are five of us in this car and another five across the street."

"And there are four NYPD," Stuart said, casting another look at the loitering parking lot attendants. All of the young men and women wore black trousers and white shirts under black wool vests. Their function was to park guests' cars and then wait around until the party broke up to retrieve the cars. "Why don't I go to the party and try to lure Lupo and Frankie Bones outside into the parking lot? We'll replace the valet parking people with our people, and jump them when they come out after us."

"How you gonna get them to come out after you?"

"I'm going dancing." He called over the top of the car to Kahn, who was inside the department car with the others. "Hey, Helen, let's you and me go to a party."

Chez Pierre's lobby had a stone waterfall that cascaded into a blue-and-gold-tiled wishing pool. Coins covered the pool's bottom, and three grotesquely ornate crystal chandeliers illuminated the lobby.

Mambo music blared from inside the hall.

Gum-chewing young women dressed in tuxedo trouser suits directed guests. Clusters of pinky-rings stood around the lobby, talking. Some of them wore blue suits and ties; others were dressed in trousers and sports jackets with open-collared sportshirts. A line of women had formed outside the ladies' room. Many of the younger women wore brightly colored low-cut dresses and the older women wore muted shades.

Kahn walked inside and stood in the back, reconnoitering. The dance floor was crowded. Each table had a beautiful floral arrangement set into a tall glass vase. She turned and motioned Stuart inside.

Stuart slipped into the room and sat in an empty seat at the half-filled table to the right of the entrance. He could catch glimpses of the people sitting at Lupo's table across the dance floor. Lupo was talking to Madeline Fine, who was sitting on his left. Stuart assumed the woman on Lupo's right was his wife. Frankie Bones was not there. He did not know the other two couples at the table.

He got up and went over to Kahn. "Frankie Bones isn't there. Walk out into the lobby and see if you can find him."

Outside in the parking lot, DEA agents and NYPD detectives quietly rounded up the attendants. Borrelli, Jones, and two DEA agents became valets. They took off their jackets and stuck their nines in their waistbands under their borrowed vests. Driscoll had put in a call to the Nassau County Police Department, requesting backup and an ambulance. Patrol cars blocked off all traffic around Chez Pierre. The parking gofers were escorted out of the parking lot and kept safely inside the patrol cars blocking off traffic.

The detectives and the DEA agents waited, leaning casually on Lupo's and Frankie Bones's cars.

"Are you fucking sure?" Frankie Bones barked into one of the phones in the lobby. His beeper had gone off as he was dancing with his wife.

"Yeah, I'm fuckin' sure," the voice from Chicago reported. "They took the warehouse, the stash, and all our people."

"You sure it was the DEA?"

"Yeah."

Frankie Bones slammed down the receiver, ignoring the woman standing at the phone next to him. Detective Kahn gently hung up and walked back into the party. Lupo had just taken a sip of wine when a shaken Frankie Bones went over to him and, bending, whispered into his ear, "The DEA took out our Chicago operation. They got the drugs and our people."

The color drained from Lupo's face. "You sure?"

"I just got off the phone with Sally Boy. He said they gassed our guys."

"Stuart set this up. I want him dead."

"You got 'im dead, Danny. What are we gonna do?"

"We're gonna have a bad third quarter. But that's not the problem. The problem is how bad can our people hurt us?"

"Those guys aren't gonna turn."

A joyless smile crossed Lupo's face. "When you're facing three concurrent life sentences without parole in a federal joint in Marion or Florence, you turn. Where are they being held?"

"They're still in the Federal Building. They'll probably arraign them sometime today."

"You know what to do."

"It's gonna be hard, Danny," he said, his eyes wandering the dance floor.

"Hard ain't impossible."

"Done like a . . ." His mouth fell open. He squinted several times to make sure he was seeing right.

He was.

Stuart and Kahn were dancing the mambo, their bodies gyrating to the raucous rhythm. Madeline Fine saw them, and her brow wrinkled in puzzlement. Wearing big grins, they danced over to Lupo's table.

"Danny, you throw one helluva party," Stuart said. He looked at Fine and asked, "How ya doin', Madeline?"

Lupo leaped to his feet.

"We gotta go, Danny. Enjoy the rest of the party."

Lupo was crimson with rage. His breath came in deep, chest-heaving grunts. He stood with clenched fists, watching the detectives dancing away. He looked at Frankie Bones. When he spoke, his tone was as cold as steel. "We'll take 'em outside."

Lupo walked around to a few tables, gathering up five more wiseguys. Frankie Bones walked over to table two and tapped one of the pinky-rings on the shoulder, saying, "We got problems."

The pinky-ring reached under the table and picked up the gun bag, a straw-colored canvas tote holding nine unregistered revolvers and automatics.

Tramping purposefully into the lobby, ignoring the congratulations of friends, Lupo and his vengeful entourage stormed out into the parking lot with their guns drawn. Lupo was first out, followed by Frankie Bones and the others. They were greeted by an armory of shotguns and nine-millimeter automatics in the hands of detectives and federal agents. The partygoers froze.

Bewildered, Lupo and Frankie Bones looked around helplessly for an escape hatch. Slowly they lowered their weapons. Their soldiers followed suit.

The detectives and DEA agents swarmed over them, disarming and handcuffing them. One of the pinky-rings pushed Jones away. The detective rammed his nine against the side of the pinky-ring's head.

"That hurts," the thug protested.

"It's only the beginning, goombah," Jones said, tightening the cuffs.

Slipping a hand into his jacket pocket, Stuart removed the computer disk Carmine Marino had given him. Palming it, he slid his hand into Lupo's jacket pocket and then pulled it out. Turning his hand over to reveal the disk lying in his palm, Stuart said, "Look what he had in his pocket." He handed it to Jones. "Invoice this."

"You planted that on me, *you bastard,*" Lupo protested.

"Hey, Danny, *we're* the good guys, *you're* the bad guys," Stuart said.

After the prisoners were taken away, Stuart walked back inside. Madeline Fine was standing a few feet away from the door. "What happened?" she asked.

"Lupo and his friends have been arrested."

Lupo's wife and daughter ran screaming out into the lobby. Friends rushed to comfort them.

"Did you have to do this here, now? It's not very nice, Lieutenant," said Beansy Rutolo's girlfriend.

"Madeline, you don't know what not nice is," Stuart said, and proceeded to tell her how Lupo had turned the Franklin Investment Trust Corporation into one of organized crime's biggest moneymakers.

"I don't believe it," she said.

"Believe it."

"What's going to happen?"

Stuart looked at Lupo's hysterical family. "You and your niece will take over the business, bring in honest management, and get on with your lives. Lupo and Frankie Bones are going to spend the rest of their lives in a federal prison."

"Was my Anthony part of any of this?" she asked, avoiding his eyes.

"No," he lied. "Anthony was small-time. He wasn't a killer."

She sighed in relief. "I always knew he wasn't like the rest of them."

"How could you have allowed Lupo to run Franklin Trust?"

She shrugged. "He was smart and making good money on investments. Why would he do anything illegal? That never entered our minds."

Shaking his head at her faith in the man, Stuart turned to leave.

"Lieutenant." She grabbed his wrist. "Were you telling me the truth about Anthony's involvement with them?"

"Yes, Madeline, I was."

"One of your crosses in life has been that Anthony Rutolo helped out your father."

"I could never understand why he did that."

She hesitated, then looked at him pointedly. "If you want the answer, ask your aunt Elizabeth."

The telephone notifications directing the chief of detectives, his XO, and the other members of Knight's Roundtable to report forthwith in civilian clothes to the police headquarters auditorium were logged in the Big Building's command log at 0347 Saturday morning and signed by the police commissioner.

Chief of Detectives Kevin Hartman arrived first, followed by Deputy Chief Aaron Flieger, Jim Gebheart, and the CO of the Order Section.

They loitered outside the auditorium, talking in hushed tones, asking one another if they knew why they had been summoned by the police commissioner.

Hartman shrugged in bravado and said, "It probably has something to do with some bullshit press release." His strong tone belied the hollow feeling in his stomach.

Chief Flieger said, "You see the news reports of that DEA raid in Chicago?"

"What's that got to do with us?" Hartman said.

A uniform police officer came over to them and said, "The PC would like you to take seats up front."

The brass filed into the empty amphitheater and sat in the first row. The stage's lectern bore the emblem of the NYPD. An American flag stood on the left side of the stage, with the flag of the city of New York on the right.

Stuart and Driscoll accompanied the police commissioner onstage. They stood at the podium, staring with disgust at the uneasy men in the front row. DEA agents entered the room from both sides of the auditorium and took up positions in front of the seated men.

The PC ran his fingers through his white hair, gripped the lectern, and said, "You have disgraced this department, yourselves, your families, and the half a million honest policemen of this country." He looked offstage at the Seven One Squad detectives standing in the wings, then said to the seated men, "Thank God you were brought down by members of this department."

Driscoll stepped up to the podium. "You're under arrest for facilitating the importation, distribution, and sale of drugs, engaging in a criminal conspiracy, violating the civil rights of honest policemen, hindering prosecution, money laundering, and not paying income tax on your corrupt money." He looked at the other DEA agents and said, "Read 'em their rights and get 'em out of my sight."

Each one of the prisoners was disarmed and his shield taken. They were given their Miranda warnings as they were being handcuffed. Then they were led out of the auditorium.

Stuart walked over to the detectives and shook their hands. "Thanks."

"Any time, Lou," Jones said.

"The PC asked me to tell you that effective immediately you're all promoted to first grade," Stuart said.

"Lou, ask the PC not to put my name in orders," Jones said. "If Plaintiff ever knew I was making lieutenant's money, she'd haul my ass back into court, looking for more al-o-mony."

"I'll take care of it," Stuart said. Looking at Kahn, he added, "Whitehouser is getting a forthwith to the Fourteenth Floor in the morning. He's going to be told to put his papers in right away or he'll be brought up on charges and dismissed."

"Thanks, Lou," Kahn said. She looked at her partners and added, "Before we start on the paperwork, why don't you two spring for breakfast?"

"You got it, kiddo," Borrelli said, and the three detectives started for the exit. Stuart looked up and saw Patrick Sarsfield Casey sitting by himself in the last row, staring up at him. He sidestepped past the empty seats and sat down beside him.

Stuart looked at Casey for a long time before saying, "You were at the original Knight's Roundtable, yet it doesn't look like you participated in the corruption. Why?"

"I could never stoop to taking drug money, hurting cops."

"But when Knight's Roundtable started taking drug money, you became a team player. You knew about it and didn't do shit to stop it."

"I'm ol' school, Matt. I believe in the blue wall of silence. I could never bring myself to do what you just did."

"You would have saved a lot of people a lot of misery if you had, Patrick Sarsfield."

"That's something I'm going to have to live with."

"I told you about those mug shots, and you didn't warn Hart-man. And when I reached out to you, you got me the Cellmate that helped us break this case wide open. Why did you do that?"

He looked down at his hands. "I needed to feel like a cop again. And, I guess on some level I wanted to destroy Knight's Roundtable." He looked at Stuart. "The decision finally came down on my age discrimination suit. Everyone told me that I was going to lose, but I won. There is no more mandatory retirement age in the Job."

"I think it's probably wise to throw in your papers first thing Monday morning."

"I . . . I guess you're right, under the circumstances."

"Yeah, under the circumstances."

Stuart got up and walked up the aisle toward the entrance. He glanced back in time to see Patrick Sarsfield Casey wiping tears from his eyes.

24

Saturday morning broke clear and chilly.

Stuart had gotten home shortly after six o'clock. He needed to wash the smell of cordite and death from his body, so the first thing he did was undress and shower. He lifted his face and let the downpour wash over him. He felt the tension leaving his body; only the pain of losing Suzanne remained. After toweling himself dry, he shaved and splashed on some aftershave. He stepped into clean briefs and walked barefoot into the kitchen to make himself a cup of coffee. He should be dead tired, but he wasn't. He knew the exhaustion would come later.

He sat on the living room couch, watching CNN. The program featured a panel of experts, none of whom had ever been policemen, discussing the arrests of top members of the NYPD and giving their "expert" opinions on what should be done to stop police corruption.

Exasperated, Stuart got up and switched off the set. Back in the bedroom, he dressed: a blue cotton shirt, brown corduroy trousers, a crew-neck yellow sweater, brown tasseled loafers.

As he headed down the driveway, he slowed to watch a whirlpool of leaves, marveling at the beauty of their autumn hues: yellow, orange, rust, crimson. Their short life was over, and so was part of his. He drove on.

St. Joseph's Nursing Home was housed in a six-story apartment building on Manhattan's First Avenue, half a block north of Jefferson Park and one block west of Pleasant Avenue. The home was administered by Carmelite nuns.

Stuart drove into the parking lot in the rear of the building and pulled into one of the visitors' spaces. A statue of Our Lady of Mount Carmel stood inside the small lobby, and a painting of the pope adorned the wall. He walked over to the security desk. A big guy with the look of an Irish cop watched him from over the desk and said, "Can I help you?"

"I'd like to see Sister Elizabeth. I'm her nephew."

"You're the lieutenant who's on the Job?"

"Yeah."

"She's always talking about you. My name's Frank Kelly. I retired out of the Fifth Squad in eighty-two."

"Matt Stuart." They shook hands. Stuart looked around at the men and women in wheelchairs, thinking. It's amazing how many retired cops and their relatives you run across in the course of a set of tours. He looked back at Kelly. "You have any problems in the neighborhood?"

"Not really. The wiseguys from Pleasant Avenue look out for the nuns and people who live here. Six years ago a mutt from the Jefferson housing projects across First Avenue raped one of our nuns in the parking lot. The wiseguys grabbed him and tossed him off a nineteen-story roof. Since then, we don't have any problems."

Stuart smiled. "That's the best kind of crime prevention."

"You got that one right, Lou. Why don't you grab a seat in the chapel? I'll call Sister."

He genuflected and slid into the last pew. A wooden crucifix hung over the altar, and the air was heavy with incense. He said a silent prayer for his son, and Andrea, and Beansy.

"Matt, what a pleasant surprise." She wore the Carmelite habit; a black veil that covered her hair, a white guimpe under a dark brown habit, and a plain gold wedding band that signified her marriage to God. She genuflected and slid in beside him. An old black cardigan sweater that Matt's father had given her one Christmas covered her shoulders.

He leaned across and kissed her on the cheek. "How are you, Aunt Elizabeth?"

"This place keeps me hopping. I'm leaving next week for a week's retreat at our mother house in Maine. I'm trying to get a million things done before I go." Her deep blue eyes twinkled. "I see you're becoming a famous police lieutenant."

"Not really. I'm one of the anonymous players."

"You're all over the television."

"By tomorrow night I'll be gone and forgotten." He looked up at the crucifix, took his aunt's hand in his, and said, "My squad caught the Beansy Rutolo homicide. And his live-in girlfriend told me that you know why he testified for Dad."

"That was a very long time ago, Matt. Let it rest."

"I can't. The doubt won't go away. I could never understand why Dad went into that bar, especially at Christmastime. And the doubt is aggravated by the fact that a man who became an organized crime guy bailed him out of it."

She looked into her nephew's face. Brushing her thumb across her wedding band, she said, "Your father went into that bar to confront Anthony Rutolo about me."

"You and *Beansy?*"

"I wasn't always a nun, Matt." She looked down at her folded hands, then looked back at Stuart, a tinge of color suffusing her cheeks. "In those days, I had a reputation for being wild. I was young, foolish, and headstrong."

Matt Stuart shook his head in mute amazement. He was anxious for her to get where she was going, but he knew she had to get there at her own pace.

"My young rebellion was nothing compared to the kids of today, but it was a very big deal for the daughter of a cop, and from a good Catholic family, to boot." She looked at the flickering, ever-tended flame of the red vigil light.

"It may be hard to imagine, but Beansy, as you call him, was a real dreamboat, as we'd say, back in those days. Long eyelashes, handsome, a great dancer. And he had a kind of gentleness, a sweetness that was uncommon in boys. I used to sneak out of the house to meet him. One evening we . . . went too far, the only time it ever happened. And I got pregnant."

Stuart reached for her hand and gave it a squeeze.

"He said he'd marry me. I won't say he *wanted* to, we weren't twenty at the time, but he would have. I just couldn't face it. My family—your family—was prejudiced against Italians back then; they'd simply not have countenanced marriage. And truth to tell, it wasn't what I wanted, either."

"You do seem to have found what you wanted, Aunt Elizabeth."

She smiled and nodded. "I have. No question. But to go back, Anthony was so kind to me. He was working weekends and after school then, at the family cheese business, and he took on extra hours to pay for the operation. My family never did know. I visited a girlfriend in Schenectady, at their summer cabin, with no phone. Oh, it was all meticulously arranged for secrecy. But somehow your father found out what had happened, and he went to that saloon to have it out with Anthony. They talked, and when your father calmed down, he called me, and I confirmed that Anthony had been as supportive as he could be, and so far as I know, he never spoke a word about the matter afterward. He did feel guilt, I know that. And he did feel a measure of respect for your father, I know that, too. They got to know and understand each other during that conversation in the saloon. Each of them told me something like that, separately."

"Did you ask him to testify for Dad?"

"He did that on his own. It was his way of saying, 'I'm sorry'—and because he was there with him when the shooting happened, he knew your father was innocent of any wrongdoing."

Matt Stuart felt the weight of years removed from him; taking both his aunt's hands in his, he sat with her in the consoling silence of the chapel and prayed for his father—and perhaps for himself.

She wore a rust-colored turtleneck under a man's faded denim shirt with the tails hanging out over her jeans. A shaft of sunlight cut across her face as she struggled the bags of groceries out of the shopping cart and into the trunk of her car.

Before he left his house, he had telephoned her at home. When he got no answer, he remembered that she did her grocery shopping every Saturday at Waldbaum's.

She slammed the trunk closed and shoved the cart out of the way. As she was about to open the car door, he stepped up to her. "Hello, Suzanne."

Startled, she dropped the keys. He rushed to pick them up and handed them to her. She unlocked the door. "Matt, please don't make my life more complicated."

"Can we talk, please?"

She sighed in resignation. "Get in."

He walked around and slid into the passenger seat.

"I guess congratulations are in order," she said.

"I've missed you a lot."

"I've missed you, too."

"When you gave me the attendance sheet of Knight's Round-table, didn't you think I'd figure out that J.A. was Jennifer Albrecht, your mother?"

"Either way, it was a gamble. I couldn't stand by and do nothing while those bastards were trying to destroy you."

"Why did you lie to me about your mother?"

"I didn't. She met Chief McMahon later on, and fell in love with him. They were together until he died in eighty-one."

"Did he ever divorce his wife?"

"No. Mom accepted the fact that he would never leave his family."

"So you came on the Job and assumed your Ice Maiden persona as protection. . . ."

She inclined her chin, the slightest of nods.

"Protection against those people still in the Job who knew about your mother and McMahon. You were afraid they might use that knowledge as some sort of weapon against you. You were vulnerable."

"Something like that," she said, watching another woman pushing a shopping cart over to her car.

He took her hand. "I need you in my life, Suzanne."

"You just can't bring yourself to say that you love me, can you?"

"I'm afraid. I've been afraid." He averted his face.

Suzanne gave his hand an encouraging squeeze.

"Since the divorce, since the accident, I've walled myself off from any kind of real relationship. I feel like a part of me is dead. I know the Job, I function well inside the Job, but except when I'm with you the rest of my life is empty." He looked into her eyes. "You've come to mean more to me than I've dared admit to myself. Be patient with me, please. I can try to change. I *will* try to change."

As she listened to his halting words, she realized they were truly felt, that he was struggling with conflicting feelings. For a long moment they looked at each other, their defenses down.

She dropped her eyes. "There are things I can change, too."

Stuart smiled at her and asked softly, "Could we start by having dinner tonight?"

"Well . . . sure, I guess so. What have I got to lose?" Almost tentatively, she lifted her hand to touch his cheek.

"Somehow I'd like to think you've got something to gain, Suzanne. We both do."

Her hand moved caressingly from his cheek to the nape of his neck. With the slightest of pressure, she inclined his head toward hers. Quite chastely, they kissed and moved to embrace each other. As they came together, a sudden warm gust of wind swirled a few dry yellow and red leaves, the last dance of summer.